The Walk Down Main Street

Also from Ruth Moore

Spoonhandle

The Weir

Second Growth

Candlemas Bay

Speak to the Winds

Cold as a Dog

The Walk Down Main Street

RUTH MOORE

ISLANDPORT  PRESS

Islandport Press
P.O. Box 10
Yarmouth, Maine 04096
www.islandportpress.com
info@islandportpress.com

Originally published in 1960 by William Morrow & Co.
Reprinted July, 1988 by Blackberry Books
First Islandport Press Edition: March 2023

ISBN: 978-1-952143-65-6
Library of Congress Control Number: 2022946381

Dean L. Lunt | Editor-in-Chief, Publisher
Piper K. Wilber | Assistant Editor
Emily A. Lunt | Book Designer
Beth Leonard | Original Cover Art

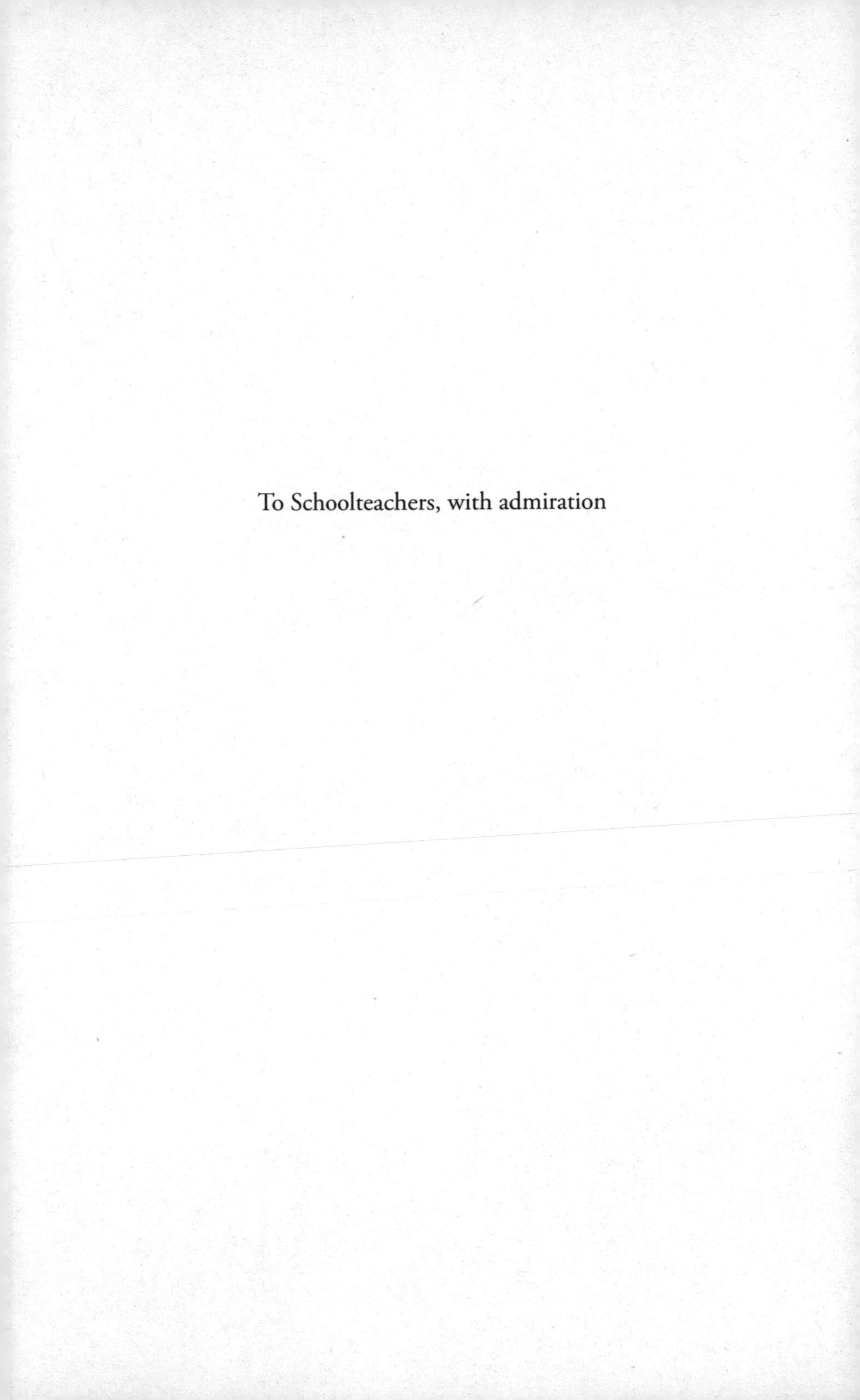

To Schoolteachers, with admiration

"The children of the world are one nation; the very old another; the blind a third."

—Jan Struther, *Mrs. Miniver*

Table of Contents

Part One

The day the basketball team came home from winning the State Championship, old Martin Hoodless was out in his cow pasture cutting down a tree. The tree was a big one, a horse chestnut nearly four feet through at the butt. It had stood for generations in back of the brook that watered the pasture—Martin had vaguely in mind that his great-grandfather had planted it, but it had been there longer than anybody living remembered.

It was old for a horse chestnut, and old age had gone wrong with it; for three years it had been dying. Last summer, its central section had put forth no leaves; a couple of limbs had been ripped off by this winter's wind. Martin had known for a long time that that tree had to come down. The stock sheltered under it in hot weather; his grandsons, Ralph and Carlisle, had a tree house in it. Horse chestnut was soft wood, anyway; when it started to rot, nothing could be more treacherous. Any time now those big limbs might let go without warning, kill either a cow or a kid, whichever happened to be around at the time.

Martin had no special reason for doing the job today. At least, he told himself he hadn't. It was a good day for cutting down a big tree—no wind; and he had the time; and a week's thaw had melted the snow so that a man could get around in the pasture without wading. Of course, yesterday was the first day he'd discovered the tree house.

What with the thaw, the brook had overflowed its banks, started to spill water down the slope toward Martin's barn and chicken houses. He had come up to clear the channel, a thing which he had to do later on in the spring, usually; and there was the tree house, built in a crotch halfway up the chestnut, on limbs that any damn fool would know might crack off irregardless, any minute.

Now, putting down his ax and saw, Martin took his pipe out of his mouth, so that he could tilt back his head and study the top of the tree. The two teeth he had left to hold his pipe stem were solid; they gripped, so long as he kept his head level; but at an angle, the pipe was likely to swivel, spill the charge of tobacco right out onto the ground.

This time of year, you might think that chestnut was a healthy living tree. Its tower of bare branches made a pleasant pattern against the watery February sky—no leaves, to show which limbs were alive. Unless you looked close at the bark, you couldn't tell.

The kids' tree house was a platform built out over four supporting branches, boarded in on three sides and with a tar-paper roof. It had a secret, private look; no matter how far you walked back and craned up, you couldn't see into it. Martin had tried, yesterday. He could have climbed the tree, if he'd wanted to or had had to; but a grown man would have the sense not to trust his weight up there. It was a wonder them kids hadn't broke their necks seven times over. That place on the trunk below the platform, there weren't even any handholds. They had a rope dangling down, so that the last six or eight feet, they must have had to go up hand over hand.

Now when, in deviltry's tarnation time, had they built this contraption? Must've been since last spring, when he was up here before. He'd always made it one of their chores to drive the stock to pasture, figuring that there wasn't anything up here that they could raise hell with; but, by tar, you had to keep an eye on everything. Waste half your time waging war. He hadn't missed any lumber from the pile, so they must've stolen a board-and-a-half to a time and sneaked the tar paper and nails out of the barn.

Well, he'd have a word to say about that waste of good materials. That lumber he had a use for, every stick of it, down around the chicken houses. And nails and tar paper, by tar, cost more than a cent.

That tree was coming down, and high time, too. Carlisle, when he got back from hassling around all over creation with the high-school basketball team, would find out there was plenty to do at home.

Give him something to use them muscles for, Martin thought, eyeing with some relish the thick bole of the tree. Saw a little wood. Do a little work for a change.

Let's see.

He'd have to make the undercut on the far side; wouldn't want to dump the whole works into the brook. But that meant he'd have to do the bulk of the sawing on this side, right under that cussid contraption up there. No knowing how much the extra weight of all that lumber—two-by-fours, some of it—would throw the tree out of true. If she started to come down whopper-jawed, he'd have to have some place to run to that wasn't into the brook.

It was a nice, technical problem, the kind Martin liked; he walked around the tree, figuring.

On the far side, out at the end of a live limb, was a bird's nest no bigger than a baby's fist. It looked built in, secure up there, and, somehow, permanent.

Martin observed it.

Well, that there, that was too bad. Nice old tree, been here since the start of time. All the shade there was in the pasture, too. And them birds—

"What to hell's the matter with you?" he said, aloud, to the tree. "Them birds'll be back, come spring, no place to go, and when I cut you down, this pasture'll be baldheaded as a Bible. Why can't you hang on? I'm seventy-seven years old, and I ain't even tired."

The tree didn't say that it was two hundred or so and damned tired, and didn't care one way or another what happened now. Up in the backcountry in the past five years, thousands of trees had been cut for pulpwood, watersheds stripped, so that the water level of the entire countryside had gone down. There was plenty of flow going down the brook now with the thaw, but going down fast. In summer, through the tree's growing season, the channel ran dry. That was what had finally done for the chestnut.

No one was aware of the battle that had gone on underground before the mighty, ancient root system had shriveled and stopped pumping. If the tree itself was aware, it had nothing to communicate. A small, wintry breeze stirred among its branches, that was all.

Martin wet his finger, felt the breeze.

"Going to blow, are you?" he asked the sky.

Better get a wiggle on. Had a lot to do, clearing up that mess of busted limbs on the ground, before he could even start his undercut. A tree that size was going to make considerable of a thump, coming down; no sense leaving anything around loose that could snap back and kill a man.

Establish your work-space; look ahead; hyper out from under when she goes.

That was the way he had been learnt to cut down a tree. Any one of the old-timers could drive a spike into the ground falling a tree, and so could he.

Who could do it now? Or cared a damn? Some squirt going through the second-growth saplings with a power saw?

Well, begin. He had her figured out now.

Down in the town center, a mile away, the fire whistle let go with a long blast. The sound, traveling up the scarcely moving air, shattered the quiet, seemed almost to be in the pasture beside him. Martin jumped and nearly dropped his ax.

Now, what? Always something.

Let a man get started on something he needed his head for, what happens?

A fire.

Wage a war, just to get your work done.

He glanced automatically at his own buildings below the slope of the pasture. He could see only the roofs and the upper half of them, but there they were, nudged securely into the land, the white paint of the long, low farmhouse gleaming in the sun, the red of barn and chicken houses, sleek, mellow, the color of old brick. All neat. All quiet. No smoke.

No smoke anywhere on the four points of the sky, so far as he could see.

Well, time was when he'd have had to drop everything and run. Not anymore, now. Let the young fellers on the Volunteer Fire Department handle it. They thought they knew how.

Down in the town, the siren on the fire truck let out a yowl, to which Martin listened, his jaw dropping as the familiar crescendo degenerated to a series of maniac yips.

That wasn't Win Parker on that sy-reen, by tar, that was someone fooling with it. When Win lit out from his garage and onto that pumper, taking it to a fire, he played that sy-reen like a cornet. No doubt about what was up, it stopped traffic all over town.

But this, by tar—Martin cocked his head—this was kids. Or some drunk, got into the firehouse, fooling around with expensive equipment that a man paid high taxes to maintain.

That was a pretty thing, that was. The Selectmen, them irresponsible cusses, were going to hear about this from Martin Hoodless.

At that moment, the whistle on the tannery blew and the Baptist Church bell began to ring. Almost at once, the Congregationalist Church bell started, dong-dong-dong, as if the ringer were turning it right over and over; from down the road the Pentecost Chapel joined in, bing-bing-bing, making a surprising discord. Then somebody, apparently, put a record on the mechanical carillon in the Methodist steeple—any record, grabbing one up at random—and turned it up to "Loud," for the chimes began to thunder out "Silent Night."

"What to hell is it?" Martin said, aloud. "The Second Coming?"

Every bell in town; every whistle.

The fog bell on Gannet Point Lighthouse, wasting electricity on a speckless clear day; and, yessir, by tar, that dignified, mellow bong was from the old Union Church.

Something had happened, all right. There'd been celebrations before, but the last time anyone had rung the old Union Church bell was on Armistice Day, 1918.

Cussid fools ought to know that steeple won't stand it, Martin told himself. Be a miracle, if they don't have bell and all right down on top of their heads.

He put down his ax and walked across the pasture to the fence. There he leaned out through the alders, so that he could look down the highway.

The main hardtop into town went by here, curving fairly close to the pasture fence, which stood on a ten-foot embankment where the builders of the road had leveled the grade.

Too close. Martin guessed he knew about that embankment. The Highway Commission had taken ten feet off his pasture, condemned part of his best land, and not paid him half what it was worth. All it was good for now, you could stand on it and look out, see down into town.

Everything seemed as usual. He could see the river that flowed down past the tannery—still frozen over, though the ice looked tacky from the thaw. Hoots of white steam were coming out of the tannery whistle. He could see all five church steeples, and in the Congo, the nearest one, which was also his church, sure enough, the bell was going right over and over.

Cussid fool would bust the rope, if he didn't the bell.

Always something.

Mostly foolishness, that decent people would have to pay for.

His eyes followed the line of the river, noting automatically the crumbly ice down by the harbor, which might mean an early break-up, an early spring. In the town, the rows of houses looked peaceful, their shingled roofs still gleaming wet from last night's rain. Heading down the harbor toward the sea was the Coast Guard's big buoy-tender from the Base at Fairport—a sight usual enough, except that her whistle, too, was blowing. There wasn't a thing he could see to account for all this touse. Whatever it was must be up in the Square, by the Town Hall.

Then he saw the parade. It was coming up the highway toward him, spearheaded by the fire trucks, pumper and hook-and-ladder, both covered from bumper to bumper with waving, yelling people. A lot of high-school kids, he saw; but plenty of others. And strung out behind as far as he could see were cars, trucks, jalopies, full of what looked to be every able-bodied man, woman, and child in town.

Winfield Parker was driving the pumper.

And what was he doing, fooling around like this with town property? On a weekday? Suppose there was a fire? What if a man had a breakdown with his farm machinery, needed garage work done bad, and the garage closed?

Leaning forward, Martin drew a sharp breath. Seated beside Win, working the pumper's siren, which was now giving forth a series of agonized blats, was Martin's own daughter, Susie.

Susie McIntosh, respectable mother of an eleven-year-old girl and two grown sons—if you could call them young squirts grown. At least, they were in body if not in mind, big boys for fifteen and seventeen. Susie, that he'd left, not two hours ago, washing dishes in his kitchen, here now, riding the fire truck, working the sy-reen!

She had her gall, too, riding on the same seat with Win Parker, him she could've married once, if she hadn't been so cussid baldheaded stubborn.

The pumper flashed by, giving him only a glimpse of Susie. Enough, though, so he could see she was all dressed up in that new blue dress that she'd fought a battle to finish, even sewed it on Sunday. And he'd had a word to say about that, too. Anybody who lived in his house could, by tar, respect the Sabbath. There were weekdays to work in.

Well, today might be a workday, but it didn't look as if anybody in town knew it. Considering who was here, every business on Main Street must be shut down tighter than a drum. He stared resentfully at the line of cars.

There was Jed Wallace, with his wife on the front seat and two–three of the bank people in the back; so that meant the bank was closed. So what about anybody who came in from out of town to do business today? Wasted his time and his trip.

That was a new Buick Jed had. Well, the town banker and President of the Chamber of Commerce. He could afford it. Why, Jed could pretty nigh have bought that Buick out of the interest Martin had paid in over the years, before he got his chicken farm started. Loans and mortgages to gag a man. Not anymore, though. Now, they could come to him. He had a darned good deal, now, with that down-state chicken firm. They supplied him with chicks, feed, and an assured market; he supplied the plant and labor. He also sold fertilized eggs for laboratories and for hatching, and eggs and broilers to markets and individuals down in the town. He was all paid up. Square with the world and putting money by. Didn't owe a soul a red cent.

There was Harry Troy and his clerks; must've closed up the supermarket. And Doc Wickham, so, by tar, nobody better be sick. And James Goss, the high-school principal, with the teachers, including that Jew, what was his name, Berg, that they'd hired last fall to teach science. That was a hell of a note, when the School Board couldn't find enough white men to teach school. Nothing like that had ever taken place when Martin Hoodless served on the Board. And there'd have been a flight of feathers, too, if any of the teachers in his time had shut down the school for some shindig, whatever it was.

That was a pretty good-looking car Goss was driving. A '57 Chevy. For a high-school principal, he was doing pretty well. Who did he think he was?

Head and whiskers thrust out through the alders, Martin stared testily at the next section of the parade, which was the grammar-school children, marching eight abreast and led by a dozen majorettes in costume, joyously twirling batons.

That was something, by tar, them little girls in short skirts no thicker than crepe paper, barelegged, and for all you could tell, half-bareassed, in the middle of February. Somebody ought to read their mothers the riot act. If any of his six girls had ever appeared like that, in public, there'd have been some tails tanned. That sign that said "Sixth Grade," that was Dot's grade. By tar, she better not be one of them dressed like that, or—

He leaned a little farther out, looking for his granddaughter, but she didn't seem to be there.

The movement in the bushes caught the eye of one of the little girls; she gave a shrill squeal of fright and pointed; for a moment, there was a swirl and disarrangement among the ranks, as if someone had thrown a rock into a flock of birds. Then they picked up the rhythm again; most began to laugh.

Well, he did have just his head stuck out of the bushes. S'posed he'd scared 'em. Let 'em cackle, for all he—

When did Charles Kendall get back from Florida? Come early, this year. And Hazel and George with him.

Humph!

You'd think a man's own daughter and son-in-law, after they'd been gone since December, the least they could do would be to come up and say hello. That was the way of it. Raise kids, once they got out on their own, not one of them ever gave a hoot.

George must be making out all right, working for Charles down at that motel: that looked like a new fur coat Hazel had on. Charles himself couldn't be doing too bad, either; that looked like another new car, and them cars cost more than a cent, the way he always had to have special machinery built in for a one-legged man, so he could drive. Maybe that motel was being worth its salt; looked like it might be; but whatever

Charles was making, Martin still maintained he'd been a fool to tear down The Emporium. Find it out, too, someday.

A woman riding in the back seat of Charles Kendall's car suddenly stuck her head and shoulders out the window and flapped a high-school pennant at Martin; and when he glared, affronted, she put a thumb to her nose and jubilantly wiggled her fingers at him.

By tar, that was a pretty thing to see. A respectable woman, so-called, right in front of everybody. Likely Bess Maitland wasn't any better than she should be. Living all winter long alone, caretaking that motel, while Charles and George and Hazel tarryhooted off to Florida. How could they know what kind of a rig she ran down there? Martin guessed he could put two and two together. A woman alone, and all them empty beds.

He was suddenly aware that a last, belated vehicle had stopped in the road below, and that someone was yelling up at him. It was his next-door neighbor, Hezzie Mooney, in his Ford pickup; only both Hezzie and the truck were so camouflaged that for a moment Martin couldn't see who it was.

Hezzie had stuck his head out of the pickup window and had craned upward, the better to see Martin. He wore a black high-school beanie, on which had been stitched a red hawk in flight; it sat high on his head, being too small. He was in his Sunday clothes, which was what had puzzled Martin. You usually saw him in work-frock and cap, with a three-day growth of whiskers.

"What you doing up there, Mart?" he was yelling. "Why ain't you up front of the parade with the families of the team?"

His pickup was covered with pennants, streamers of crepe paper and a white sheet painted with red and black letters. The paint was fresh and the letters had started to run, but their message was still clear.

WELCOME HOME, RED HAWKS, they said; and in other letters, slightly cramped, STATE CHAMPINS, 19. Hezzie had started to put in the date, but he had run out of sheet.

"Chrissake, Hez," Martin said. "Is that one of your wife's good sheets?"

"Sure is," Hezzie grinned. "I never swiped it either. Mattie give it to me. Nothing's too good for them boys. Come on down, load aboard here with me. I got room, Mattie's up on the pumper. She wouldn't wait. I'd be up there in the front rank myself, only I see this paint had started to run and I tried to fix it. How's it look? Pretty good, eh?" He craned backward to see.

"Thought it might be your old Klew Klux sheet," Martin said.

"Oh, hell, no, we give all them away years ago to the kids," Hezzie said. "Once they was having a Halloween pageant up to the school."

"What'd you do—kill a pig on it? You must be drunk."

"Well, you know, I might be." Hezzie carefully turned his head from side to side, testing. "I just might be, just a little. When my boy Jerome fired that foul shot that tied the game, and then old Shirttail whanged one in and won it, why, when Mattie and me got home around one this morning, we broke out that whiskey she'd had in the house ever since the doctor give her a pint for the asthma, back during Prohibition."

This was not entirely true, since Hezzie had bought the pint at the liquor store on the previous afternoon, just in case the team won the game. He did not, however, want it said around town that he had bought liquor just to get drunk on.

"Well, all I can say, it would be a fine time this morning for the Russians to land," Martin said. "What, has the town gone crazy?"

"Why, shoot," Hezzie said. "Last night would've been the time, Martin. Wasn't nobody left in town but the sick and the aged. Oh-oh!"

He hadn't, Hezzie realized, been able to stop himself in time. It was never a good idea to twit Mart Hoodless about anything, let alone his age. Hezzie had stayed, if not good neighbors, at least on speaking terms with him, for half a lifetime by keeping that in mind. "How come you never went?" he went on, cordially implying, he hoped, that Martin must have had other good reasons. "If you didn't want to drive your car, Mattie and me'd been glad to shove the kids together, made room for you. Ralph and Dot could've doubled up—"

"Ralph?" Martin interrupted silkily. "Dot?"

For all he had known, his two younger grandchildren had gone to bed at the usual time. At least, he had told them to. Going out of town to games, on a school night or any other night, had been settled early in the season for the kids. He himself of course always went to bed at eight o'clock. If them kids had sneaked out, afterwards, they'd get told. He continued to stare down at Hezzie, his face like a block of wood.

"Why, sure, the whole high school went," Hezzie went on happily, unaware that now he had put his foot in too far to pull it out, "and most of the grammar school. Them that couldn't crowd onto the school buses, why, the rest of us hauled 'em. I and Mattie, we had six kids altogether, including our own, in my old Pontiac. Some of them hills between here and the capital, I didn't know but we was all going to get out and push, but the old gal made it. And what a rooting section we had! Why, we had the edge on Boone Academy within forty miles of their own hometown! Had the edge on them, by gorry, more ways'n one. Fifty-six to fifty-four, by the god, and the State Championship!"

Martin's voice cut in over his, stopped him in full babble.

"A carful of kids, and you likkered up, hey?"

"Oh, my gorry, no!" Hezzie said, shaken. "Why, certainly not, Martin! I never drunk a drop till I got home, and then all we had was, I and Mattie and Sue, we just had a little touch-up to celebrate."

"Susie?" Martin said.

Hezzie stopped, fuzzily remembering that Susie had said that basketball, to her father, was like a red rag to a bull. The reason she hadn't driven to the state capital with the rest of the town was, that if she had, life wouldn't be worth living. But Hezzie was committed now; besides, this morning, painting his sheet, he had finished up the pint.

"What to hell's the matter with you, Mart?" he demanded. "For chrissake, your own grandson! Why, he and my boy Jerome was on the TV last night, and they're in headlines this morning all over the state. You won't have a TV in the house, so Susie was over home last night to watch it on ours, and she waited for us to get back, so's to come home with the kids. 'Course she wanted to see that game—her own boy, she's proud of him. Mattie and me's so proud of Jerome that if I knew what the Rebel Yell was, I'd give it. I d'no b't I will anyhow!"

He put back his head and gave out a hoarse roar, which, shortly, died to a wheeze. "Nope," he said, shaking his head. "I hollered too loud last night. Nope, that ain't the Rebel Yell."

"Sounds to me more like a sick bull."

"Oh, now, Mart, you've hurt my feelings." Hezzie waved his hand. "Well, I got to go—see you later. Fairport was to call up when they sighted the bus come through. I guess they did quite a while ago, it's pretty nigh time."

The new State Champions had been put up at a hotel in the capital last night, instead of being made to take the long drive home before they were rested. The townspeople, however, had hustled back to prepare a welcoming celebration, a parade and a banquet in the Town Hall. The only reason they weren't having a twenty-one-gun salute was that the old Civil War cannon on the Square couldn't be made to shoot.

And that was too bad, too, Hezzie thought. Wouldn't have been any trouble at all to fire that old cannon off twenty-one times—they had the powder—only it was too rusty.

"Stark, raving crazy!" Martin said. "The whole town. Over a bunch of kids throwing a ball around!" He pursed his lips and spat disgustedly into the air; the gob sailed in an arc down to the hardtop, where it landed with an audible sound.

"By thunder!" Hezzie said. That reached him, that did. That got him right where he lived. It was unthinkable that even an old sourball like Mart Hoodless couldn't appreciate what those kids had done. "Look, we got the best team in the whole damn state!" he began. "We won the Champ—"

"That put down the cost of living, does it?"

"Well, a man's got to have something to think about, besides high cost and atom bombs!"

"I get along, thinking the way I think. I don't buy me no TVs, but I keep my barn painted."

Hezzie reddened. "I kind of like that faded-out color mine is," he said. "Wouldn't want nobody making the mistake it wasn't my barn."

"No danger, is there?"

"No, there ain't! And what's more, the fifty bucks I won on that game last night, I ain't using that to buy paint, either. Mattie and me, we're driving down to Boston in two weeks' time to see our team win the All-New England Champinship against them big-city teams when the play-offs come. Get a load of this!" He fumbled in his hip pocket, pulled out a sheaf of bills, which he waved. "Fifty green old, pretty old smackers! I betcha there was two–three thousand dollars changed hands, bet on that game last night! That ain't hay, that ain't, brought cold into this town this time of year. That buys aigs, if nothing else!"

"And you stood to lose fifty dollars on a game of ball!" There was no expression on Martin's bony face. His voice, merely, indicated icy disgust.

"Hell, no! Feller bet me two-to-one. They was that sure, blast 'em! But that old Shirttail, seventeen baskets, and that's a record. Way behind, couldn't seem to get started, them Boone fellers playing dirty ball, and all of a sudden old Shirttail, he got the combination. I see him start to ramble, I begun to holler, and I hollered loud. There was this guy from Boone, over in their section, he turned around, slit-eye, and he hollers to me and he says, 'I bet you twenty-five, two-to-one, that Boone clobbers 'em.' So I took him up on it, and when he paid me, damned if he wasn't crying tears. I would've, in his place. Boy, oh, boy! That Shirttail!"

"Whose shirttail?" Martin snapped. "Somebody going around there undressed, was he?"

Hezzie stared.

"You are the only man in the whole, entire, complete screaming state," he said impressively, "don't know who Shirttail McIntosh is, and him your own blood grandson! Why, if you was to go out in the woods this morning and holler, 'Shirttail,' the squirrels and the birds would set up and wave wings and tails. Look, Mart, honest, you don't get it. We ain't had a State Champinship since the year of nineteen forty-seven, when Art Grindle was on the team. We never beat the New England that year, but we got a good chance now, a mighty good chance. We ain't never had nothing in this area to come up to Carlisle. He's a damn sight better than Art Grindle ever was, and so's my boy, Jerome."

"Art Grindle," Martin said. "Now, whatever become of him, I wonder? Hmmm! Ain't he the one started out robbing filling stations when he got too old to play ball?"

Hezzie straightened up, breathing hard. His face turned dark purple. "Why, you dirty-minded old son of a coot!" he bawled. "If you think that Jerome or any of them nice, clean-living young athaletes—"

"I don't know nothing about Jerome," Martin said. "But I've got a say in Carlisle, by tar! From now on, he's going to settle down at home and do some work. I've had enough of this cussid foolishness!"

Hezzie's jaw dropped; he grunted slightly, as if someone had punched him in the wind. "Why—why—" he began. Then the implication of this struck him, full. "If you was to do one thing, one thing to bollix up that ballteam now—if you was to keep Carlisle home from Boston . . . why, you'd never sell another aig nor do business of any kind with any man in this town!"

Martin said nothing.

"Why, you black-frosted old snapper-jaw, the way this town feels about that ballteam, they'd blister them nice-painted buildings of yours, and I wouldn't lift a finger, not one finger, to stop it!"

"There'll be some backsides shot full of birdshot," Martin said succinctly, "if anybody comes frigging around me for any reason whatsoever."

He pulled his head in out of the alders and was gone as if someone had yanked him backward.

Hezzie recoiled. He was, ordinarily, a peaceable man. Up to a while ago, most of his argument had come out of his pint. Now he thought, sobered, he means it. The old futz would shoot somebody. Nobody in the world could feel the way he did, after last night; but here he is, on the off-end of the stick, just the way he always is about everything; goes his own way, irregardless of whose toes he steps on.

Oh, gorry, what did I ever stop to yak with him for? If he sticks to it—and nobody in the time of man ever knew him to change his mind once he got his feet braced—if he sticks to it, and the rest of the town finds out I was the one poked him up—

Why, that kid had got to go to Boston! He couldn't be made to get off the team now!

Brought up that old Klew Klux thing, too, when he was trying to rip me up about my sheet. Hell, he was into that a lot more than I was, I wasn't nothing but a boy then, that was a long time ago, 1924 or '25. It was him and his crowd scairt that horse, it wasn't me.

Hezzie remembered it, though, the time the Klew Klux got started in the town; somebody got everybody all fired up about protecting homes from Catholics and Jews, and they all went parading around in sheets at night; even burned a fiery cross in a farmer's pasture, scared his horse; so that the horse ran away down through town and ended up slap in the window, glass and all, of the fish market on Main Street.

That kind of made everyone think, because after all, if you were going to destroy property, and Alec Greene, owned the fish market, was some old ory-eyed mad; and then the Baptist minister pointed out that there wasn't any Jews or Catholics living in town anyway, so the thing kind of died a natural death. Until years later, around '32, oh, sometime during the Depression, when the school kids needed Halloween costumes and nobody could afford to buy cloth, why, here were all these old sheets stashed away in a carton up to the Lodge Hall . . . Old Mart, by gorry, he never let anything die. Them useless old sheets, he figured they'd ought to be kept, God knows why or what for; he wouldn't lose an opportunity to twit about it, come hell or high water, make out somebody was to blame for something, when all they were doing was good and well right.

Well, he'd get Klew Klux or something, if he tried to futz up that ballteam . . .

From up the highway, the tumult of auto horns and yelling increased in volume, and Hezzie, glancing up from his slightly fuddled meditations, saw that the parade was coming back. Out in front, he could see the bulky sides of the big orange school bus.

Oh, blastit and dammit, he'd planned to be right up in the front of that parade with his truck, yelling and hollering when the bus went by. Might have got a glimpse of Jerome. Instead, here he was, on the tail-end. Slap in the middle of the road, too, and the parade coming. No, wait a minute. Turn around here, and he could lead the whole shebang right down into town.

Everyone had seen last night's game, either on the TV or at the capital, driving a hundred miles there and back. Their own Red Hawks had beaten Boone Academy, won the trophy, got the State Championship. The best damn team in the whole damn state.

The town, dreaming along in monotony, year after year, was on the map at last—its name in headlines all over the state; pictures of the ballteam not only in sports sections but on front pages. Familiar faces, sons and neighbors' sons, names they knew. Jerry (Dead-Eye) Mooney. Bill Parker. Jacky Wallace. Dick Wickham. Joel Troy. And now everywhere, raves and photographs of Carlisle (Shirttail) McIntosh, he who had all at once started to ramble, seventeen baskets, and that sweet shot that swished through in the last seconds to win the game.

It was no individual triumph, last night, at the Capitol Auditorium; it was a town triumph. All winter long the town had watched its team, packing the gym at home games, driving miles through snowstorms when the games were out of town; excitement growing to frenzy as the toll of victories mounted. Last night the lid had blown off; and when, at the game's end, the television cameras had begun to sweep across the packed rows of clapping, screaming townspeople, they, too, had felt the brief, sweet breath of fame. They, too, had been on TV.

And those few who had stayed at home because of illness, or some other irrevocable reason, had seen on the screen of the magic box, where hitherto had appeared only the wild sunbursts of the stars, Cheyenne and Sugarfoot and Lucy, and the wrestlers and the prizefighters, the faces of their own neighbors; and this glamorous time was not yet over. When the team went to Boston, to play—to win—in the All-New England Tournament, the whole thing would happen again.

Only, this time, even bigger headlines, more pictures; the town's name truly known. Mooney and McIntosh, Parker and Wickham, Wallace and Troy, bywords all over New England.

And what could be better for a tourist town, Jed Wallace was thinking, than thousands of dollars' worth of free publicity? Of course he was proud of his boy; he was some old proud of Jack, and the main thing was the game, the fun, the excitement. Why, as Jed said to Win Parker out of the corner of his mouth, it brought people out into the streets who hadn't seen the light of day for years.

But the publicity was there, all right; no banker worth his salt was going to turn up his nose at that. Why, if the team won the All-New England, people would drive out of their way by the hundred, next summer, just to see this town. It was fantastic, the interest there was in ball; not just around here, but all over the country. Nationwide. Millions of people going to games, watching them on TV. A good healthy thing. It got people to town, made them spend money, bet some, on the ballgames—why, in the old days, come the end of February, the old folks used to die; now they picked up stick and went, by gorry, to the basketball tournament, bet a packet and won themselves a bundle.

Jed had won a little something, on this one, himself; most people would be surprised to know how many nice pieces of change had been deposited today, before the bank had had to close early, because of the banquet.

As a matter of fact, business had been so good this morning that he'd considered not closing at all, but, on second thought, he'd realized that everybody'd be up here at the banquet. After all, the Chamber of Commerce had done a darned good job on the tournament, making sure that local businessmen got their proper amount of credit for helping to sponsor the telecast, arranging the banquet, one thing and another. People would expect to see all the members there at the speakers' table—look funny if his chair was empty, and he'd be expected to say a word or two, old Jed always was. Besides, no sense letting the other members hog the spotlight.

Though there were times, and this was one of them, when if Jed never saw another banquet, made another speech, it would be too soon. The boys were always after him to talk at meetings; they knew who to get for a good laugh, what to expect from old Jed. Fireworks, loud and funny; but not too loud and never too funny. A man could get sick of it after a while; Jed had been sick of it for years. Now he'd rather huddle up in his office and be cozy with a nice monthly financial report; but no sooner did he, than what happened? Some women's club. Or the Lions.

Besides, last night he'd met some old college chums at the game. He had quite a lot of acquaintances up around the state capital; made a point of keeping up old ties and establishing new ones. Never forgot a face. For, while he'd inherited his father's bank and got stuck in a small town, he wasn't quite dead yet above the ears, and a man needed his own kind, the hep boys up topside; somebody you could talk to without having to edit the grammar out of your English, just in case the clients thought you were putting on the dog. So it had been Old Home Week, last night, for Jed. He'd got home late and his mouth still tasted like the sole of a turkey's foot. Jed shuddered slightly, remembering—yes, he'd arranged it—that this particular banquet was going to be turkey.

He moved decorously through the crowd toward his seat at the speakers' table. Goodwill beamed from him upon all. It gleamed conservatively from the old-fashioned watch chain bowed across the expanse of his stomach, glowed on his round, smooth cheeks; spread, warm and moist, from the little drops of sweat that ran down his neck under his collar; for he mopped with his handkerchief as he went, aware that there were those whose approving grins meant they saw old Jed sweating like a pig and not too proud to let folks know it.

"Chet, my boy!" he said, flopping down, at last, at the appointed spot. "Let me shake your hand. I shook it last night, let me shake it again today."

Chet Alison, the basketball coach, grinned nervously, and stuck out his hand, wincing as Jed shut to on it. Doc Wickham and Win Parker, already at the table, burst out laughing.

"They say the President of the United States keeps a special sawbones to shoot in a charge of novocaine, after every five thousand handshakes," the doctor said.

"Well, where's your needle?" Win said. "Nothing that the President's got this boy ain't entitled to, is there?"

Chet flapped the hand in the air, regarded it ruefully, turning it back to front, playing up, as he knew they expected him to. His muscles ached right back into his spinal cord and his hand was as sore as a boil from the fervent handshakes of hundreds of fans, who, in the emotional time after the game, had wrung and pumped up and down and pounded him on the shoulder. Jed's crowd had discovered this last night; they were still finding it funny to come along deadpan, shake hands good and hard, and then, when Chet humped up, die laughing, slapping each other on the back.

Big joke, he thought. Men and brothers, all up there in the big time together.

Last night, when everybody in the world had jammed down onto the auditorium floor around Chet and his team, Jed and the Doc, Win and Harry had been Johnny-on-thespot all over the place—the smart damn citizens who had hired the best damn coach of the best damn ballteam in the whole damn state; they'd had their pictures taken with all the bigwigs, the President of the Ball Association, the President of

WQRS-TV, and the Governor; they were in all the newspapers this morning. Right in there, at last, punching.

Well, where was his squawk? What he was having right now ought to be what any sports coach needed to get where he was going—to a big university somewhere, on the way to coaching pro ball. The big time, the big money, a known name; so that when people saw it on the sports page, they wouldn't need to ask who Chet Alison was. And once you were there, you had it made. After all, the guys in the catbird seat in any country were the athletes, and always had been since the start of time. Yon didn't need to go to history to know who the real heroes were. Look at Knute Rockne—dead since the '30s, even this year they had a memorial program for him on the TV.

Not that Chet Alison was any Knute Rockne, not by a long shot; and after last night, what happened, he told himself, it looked as though it might be some time before he would be. True, his kids had won some games; they had a Championship. And a Championship could get a guy chosen Coach of the Year, take him a ways on the long crawl up to the top. Only this one—holy cow!

The experts—other coaches, sportswriters, anyone in the know—could tell you now what Chet Alison's three years of work had turned out. Five prima donnas. Every man his own TV show.

Earlier in the season, it had been a beautiful team. The five boys who were its nucleus were all seniors. Chet had worked with them for two years; they had functioned like the five fingers of his hand. He'd had plenty of reason to be proud; and why not? The book boys could yell their heads off about athletics programs, the kids weren't learning anything but basketball, all that; all you had to do was look at the facts.

What you did, you took a batch of pigeon-toed kids with their balls falling down, muscles and emotions all futzed up; no use to anyone in the world. You trained the muscles and channeled the emotions into something that was like nothing else on earth. Because if there was any emotion cleaner, purer—distilled, maybe you could call it—than the one you got from winning a game with an auditorium full of fans yelling and falling on their faces, Chet had yet to know what it was. He had played plenty of ball himself—four years high school, four years college, two years with one of the big pro teams; had never wanted to do anything else. He would still have been with the pros if he hadn't injured an ankle; and that, of course, was where he wanted to be. But you couldn't play ball with a foot that gave under you at odd, unexpected times, if you didn't watch it. So here he was, starting at the bottom, coaching high-school kids. Being beat on by the women's organizations, the Department of Education, the School Board, and the smart damn citizens. And, this morning, it looked as though his next job would be right here, too, or in some other hick-water town; because what Chet Alison had built up, three years' patient work, it had taken the smart damn citizens just two months to tear down.

Two months ago, he would have backed his kids against any high-school team he ever saw. They were that good.

With kids, you had it made to order, not like with older guys who might be in it for kicks, yes, but mostly for money. With kids, you had all that wad of backed-up emotion wandering around, no place to go. They hadn't had a chance to prove themselves yet, or found out whether they were any good. They were all ready to die for something; so far as Chet was concerned, it might as well be for a school. So you took the school spirit and you wound the emotion around it good and tight, like a thread; then you made with the discipline and the commando-training; and then you sat back and watched the thread unwind, all by itself.

They had hearts like lions, those kids; they had been a coach's dream.

And then they took the walk down Main Street.

If only he could have kept them away from the hangouts—the drugstore, the restaurants, the poolroom. But he could yell his head off. Stay off the streets. Go home to bed. What to hell, get rested, or whatever. Don't run around listening to the crap.

But who was going to stay home, when everybody in town was gathered in one place or another, talking ball? A kid would happen by, if only to say no, he couldn't have a Coke, he was in training, and there would be a kind of holy silence for a minute; and then Jed or Win or Harry or the Doc, or Giles Wood who drove truck, or Melly Hitchcock who wasn't doing anything right now, whoever was there, would gather round for a good old session, shutting up every so often to hear what the ballplayer had to say. Before a game, in the town, the pressure was terrific.

Wherever a player went, someone would slap him on the shoulder. Someone would say, "Boy! You better win tonight, I've got fifty bucks right where it'll hurt, if you lose!" or "Kid, if you lose tonight, you better not stick your face in here. There's a lot of dough riding on the way you heave that old bullet!"

Brother!

When they won, they had it made. There wasn't anything in town they couldn't have; the businessmen stood treat, free-loading all over the place. If they lost, they were bums; they'd better not show their faces in here.

Well, they hadn't lost. They'd come into the stretch headed right, sure-god, for the Championship. And along Main Street, it had got so that if the truck delivering newspapers was late, if the sports pages didn't get in on time, God help the truck driver.

In a way, this was good. If the fans didn't build up a head of steam, whang went your ballgame. The thing was, you couldn't put that much heat on kids who had all they could take anyway, without something having to give.

In the Tournament, they did fine, breezed along, till for the first time, they hit something like real competition. Chet had kept telling them. The team to watch is Feathers Ryan's. Boone Academy. They're who'll hit you in the finals, and Ryan is one hell of a coach, so watch it.

So on that night, what happened?

Oh, they already had it made, they were top-seeded team for the Championship, all crammed full of crap about names in the papers and making basketball records, every man for himself in front of the TV cameras. If McIntosh hadn't all at once got hotter than a pistol, it would have been slaughter.

One of the sports write-ups, this morning, had called Chet Alison a smart cookie to have held McIntosh back in the opening games, not letting him look as good as he was, so that Ryan's boys would concentrate on Dead-Eye Mooney. When someone had suggested that to Chet, after the game, he had shrugged and grinned.

Nice idea, if the sports boys would buy it.

Generally, they weren't buying it, for the simple reason that Shirttail McIntosh wasn't that good. He had, merely, exploded; gone off like a skyrocket; everyone knew that kids sometimes did that, but it wasn't anything you could depend on. And a coach's reputation was built on his strategy, his ability to develop teamwork. It wasn't a matter of luck, or prima donnas.

Chet cast a speculative look at the bright heads and faces of the Champions, who were seated by themselves around a raised table in the center of the room, on which the big trophy gleamed like a silver moon.

The pretty shine on those faces was going to get rubbed off and some other things rubbed in damn soon, or the first slick big-city team they ran into in the All-New England was going to make hashmeat. Like a bulldozer.

Chet was aware that Win Parker had nudged him and was saying something in his ear, and he turned, on his face his habitual, boyish, amiable grin.

"Look at old Goss," Win was saying. "You'd think he was at a wake. Boy, somebody ought to goose him a couple times, get him into the spirit."

James Goss, the high-school principal, sat at the head of the third raised table, where he and the rest of the teachers had been seated by themselves. This table was somewhat quieter than the others, although some of the younger teachers were conversing quite gaily. A slight atmosphere of isolation hung over it, as if the occupants felt a little out of place and would have been happier if moved elsewhere. James Goss, a stout, stocky man of around forty, in a well-worn dark tweed suit, sat carrying on a sober conversation with Alfred Berg, the science teacher. James was bald, with a few straggles of sandy hair growing at his temples, and a neat, clipped sandy mustache. As he talked, his fingers twiddled with various objects on the table—a spoon, a saltcellar, a water glass—whatever they encountered in a detached exploration of the tabletop.

"That music teacher Berg's sweet on, she's quite a dish. What's her name—Callahan?" Win was saying.

"Callander," Chet said briefly.

"What nationality's that, ya know? It's a new one on me."

"No idea."

"Born over acrost somewhere, they tell me."

"So I hear."

"I see on her record when we hired her, though, she was brought up out West somewhere—Illinois, Indiana, some such place. It never said nothing about her being part Jew. She sure don't look it, but going out with Berg, I guess she must be; they don't intermarry, do they?"

"I wouldn't know," Chet said.

He had not missed the sidelong glance, the glint in Win's eye. Town gossip passed through Win's garage like sand through a screen; and the whole town knew that both Chet Alison and Alfred Berg had been going out with Ellen Callander. Win, actually, was making book on which one would win out with her, or so Chet had heard through the grapevine of his ballplayers. You could hear a lot around a locker room, if you had the kids' confidence.

Chet was well-informed. It was a good idea to be, to know how the winds were blowing in the town, and kids were always having over stuff they heard at home.

Chet knew, for example, that of all the smart damn citizens, Win Parker was the one to keep on the right side of. Win was not noticeably active in town affairs; he was not even Chairman of the School Board, though he had been for many years a member of it. He always said he didn't want to be Chairman, he had too many other fish to fry; let Harry do it. Since Harry Troy was Win's brother-in-law, most people in town figured it was all the same thing. At times they mentioned this, or grumbled about it, privately; but nobody wanted to be on the School Board badly enough to do anything about it. Nobody wanted to be on the School Board anyway; it was a lousy job, paid only fifty dollars a year, and you laid yourself open to being beat on by any knothead in town who had a gripe; so let Win handle it; anyone, usually, thought twice before they started to beat on him.

So every three years, regularly, when Win's term expired, he ran for the School Board and was re-elected, and nobody ever opposed him. The Moderator at Town Meeting just asked four or five voters to come down and drop their ballots into the box, to make things legal, and that was that. Win never ran for any other office; he was not appointed to other committees, except, of course, he was a perennial member of the Chamber of Commerce; his name appeared only twice in the Town Report—once as a Member of the Board, once as a supplier of gas, oil, and service for the school buses and fuel oil for the school furnace. Yet if any man wanted to carry weight in town politics or swing a project, he had better not waste time or money on it until he found out what Win Parker thought, first.

You wouldn't think he could swing a convocation of guinea pigs to look at him, Chet thought. Unless you watched his mouth a while, he added, listening to Win, nodding, occasionally grinning, to show he heard, that he went along.

In his youth with that build, Win had probably been a good-looking guy; tall, rangy, with a lot of red hair; Chet had seen the type. You heard, around town, that he'd been quite a boy for the girls, and still was. But he had let himself go. Fat around the middle and a fat neck. And steatopygia, as the pro-team's doc used to call such developments, Chet thought, from the vantage point of the highly trained college athlete, from the pinnacle of twenty-six looking at forty.

Win was as bald as a platter, except for a red fringe over his ears. Fat had spread his face, thickened it, so that his nose was a button, his eyes sunk deep above lardy cheeks. But the lips above the big, round, dimpled chin were two red marks, like a parenthesis, one-half reversed. The mouth was generally open, grinning or laughing—in any gathering you could always tell Win's hoarse roar; but when the lips closed, they vanished, folded neat as a magician's trick over the big, square regular white teeth.

Around town, Win was known and appreciated as a card. He was very good at nicknames; the ones he applied to people were apt and comical. Based on something ridiculous, or off-beat, or ugly, Win's nicknames usually stuck to people like burrs. He had a whole collection of absent-minded-professor, Jewish, Scottish, mother-in-law, darky, and Roosevelt stories, with which he regaled gatherings on any occasion. He believed that what he stood for, his way of life, was the best in the world, and so was the place he lived in. Oh, there might be other places; other people might live in them; something was the matter with them all. They were inhabited by coloreds and Jews, wops and Polocks, hunkies, and summer people. Nobody could be more affable than he to the tourists who used his garage in summer; nobody could be funnier about them after they had left in the fall.

He dearly loved the idea of education for children, because he had been brought up in the tradition of good schooling for everybody; he stood solid as a rock in his determination that both of his own children should go to college. His boy, his girl, were going to have the best there was. Yet Win was deeply suspicious of any man or woman who had more education than he did. Hell, he had a high-school diploma; hadn't gone any further, but he guessed he was as good as anybody. A college man, a professor, a schoolteacher of any kind, to Win, was funny.

"Look at the damned eggheads," he would say.

Now, he nudged Chet with his elbow. "Berg ain't a bad-looking guy, for a greaseball," he said. He paused, eyeing Alfred Berg with a level look, and Chet grinned inwardly. The story was that the Board had hired Berg only because, with the shortage of teachers, they couldn't find anyone else for what they were willing to pay; and Berg, because he was a beginner, just out of college, had signed a contract for a small salary.

So far as Chet himself was concerned, he thought impatiently, who cared a hoot what the guy was? I sure don't, so long as he keeps out of my hair.

This guy, Parker, ought to play pro ball for a while, get some of the crap shaken off. A player could be a pink-striped negro, for all anybody gave a damn, just so he played a good game of ball. Jewish, Italian—who cared a curse? And colored guys. You'd get a long ways in pro ball, looking snotty at some of the finest athletes in the world.

"I hear around that you and Berg have had a few chews," Win said. He paused, one eyebrow raised, and when Chet said nothing, went on. "Over the ballplayers keeping their ranks up, I heard."

Chet said, "Oh, not much. I hold my own."

And wouldn't you like it a lot, he thought, if I dropped something about the pretty music-teacher situation that you could peddle to the boys? Well, bud, you can go fry.

So far as Ellen Callander was concerned, she was pretty. She was nice. A woman. One woman out of ten you might remember; the rest, you forgot tomorrow, along with other necessary and temporary physical satisfactions, like a dinner you ate last week. Unless you fell in love, of course, which was another matter, and one with which Chet, at present, was not overly concerned.

He had been married once and was now divorced; he supposed he had been in love. In the beginning, at least, his feelings had given him a convincing performance. He would willingly have gone back to that time, when certain spiritual satisfactions combined with physical ones to make the whole experience memorable; but the time that followed, after the first six months or so, was nothing any man would care to have repeated.

His wife seemed to have got the idea, maybe from their honeymoon, that sex was a man's life, that nothing else meant anything in particular. He agreed, but with reservations. He had never been able to make clear to her that while sex was a core and center around which you moved, there were, nevertheless, times when a man's job meant something. It was a matter, only, of keeping things in proportion, first things first, separate things, apart. She could never understand it when he was absorbed, concentrated—when, actually, he didn't want anything to do with her or anything else that would distract him. He was, at the time, playing forward on one of the big pro teams. The competition was fierce. To stay where you were, you couldn't just go in, happily, and play a game once a week; you had to work at it, like at anything else. To her, it was just a game. When she wanted to play footsie, she wanted to play footsie.

Well, that was all very complimentary; but a fool would see that it couldn't work, and it hadn't worked; in the end, it had busted them up. The final rock they split on was her little habit of wanting to yak after intercourse, have it over a play-by-play description, while what he wanted, when he was through he was finished, he wanted to sleep. So they'd called it a day. Now, he didn't even know where she was.

"Well, pass along word, if Berg bothers you," Win said. "Passing in school, that's one thing we don't have any trouble keeping fixed up for the boys."

Chet nodded. "No real trouble," he said.

"We can always have a little chat with him," Win said. "Harry's an expert, you know. It always turns out they want their contract back." He grinned, sitting back hard in his chair, which creaked. "Damn these damn picnic-chairs! There's a print of me on every one of them that's unmistakable. Well, don't let Berg bother you. I guess he'd give a nice piece of change, if he ever parted with any for any reason whatsoever, to be sitting up on top like you and on your pay."

"Could be," Chet said.

There it was again—rubbing it in who ought to have the credit. The smart damn citizens who saw to it that the town paid the money for the best damn coach. Alison was, he knew, a high-priced coach for a town of this size. He was paid more than any one of the teachers in the school, including the Principal; the town, being interested in ball, saw to that, and no one grudged Chet a penny. It was worthwhile to hire the best—a man who not only looked like an athlete, but was, for Chet had not only played college and pro basketball, he was also a trained boxer.

Maybe Berg would, Chet thought, giving Win his polite attention, but don't think I'd be caught dead here, bud, if it wasn't for my damn ankle. I'd be up in bigger time than you'll ever see.

But Win had just caught something that Dr. Wickham had said, across the table.

"What was that, Doc? What were you just saying about Shirttail's knee?"

Dr. Wickham pursed his lips. "Nothing much," he said. "Kid's got a slight sprain. Skin scrubbed up some. Be all right after he rests it a day or so. Be all right, anyway, in two weeks, by the time we go to Boston."

For it had been one of the wonders of Shirttail McIntosh that he had got knocked cold in the third quarter of play, and had pluckily finished the game with a bandaged knee.

"By judas!" Win said. "You know, it was a wonder them Boone fellas hadn't killed him. I counted four on top of him, and I see that tall fella, that Jones, give him the elbow. By the god, they was dirty players! Damn referees must've been asleep on their feet."

"Harry said he saw that, too," Doc Wickham said. "I had to hold Harry back, he'd have gone right down there on the floor, socked somebody on the nose."

"Where is Harry?" Jed Wallace asked. "Thunder, we ought to get going, don't want to be here all day."

"Harry's over by the door. Or was, when I come in," Win said. He craned up and looked. "Yeah, he's still there. What gives over there? Seems to be quite a touse."

What gave was a tumult which stemmed directly from Hezzie Mooney, who on sober second thought, had figured that maybe a few of the more responsible citizens of the town ought to know about his conversation with Mart Hoodless; only a few, of course, and confidentially, because, cracky, if the old man really meant it, meant to keep Shirttail home from Boston, maybe some of them ought to go out there on the q.t. and do a little reasoning. Hezzie had gone around the hall, picking out this one and that one, taking each man aside and whispering feverishly into his ear. The effect, almost at once, had been electric. A roar of talk started, punctuated here and there by a high, shrill commentary, as people passed word along; and Harry Troy broke out of the crowd and came hustling up to the speakers' table.

"That goddam fool of a Hez," he said breathlessly, in a carrying voice. "He's got old Mart Hoodless all stirred up. Says Mart says he won't let Shirttail go to Boston."

"Oh, by god!" Doc Wickham said. "Why didn't somebody muzzle that bastard?"

"Okay, Harry," Win said. "No use hollering stuff all over the hall." He eyed Harry, across the table, and Harry sat down.

"Well, it'll be up there in a high sling," Harry said in a lower voice, "if the old man gets his feet set, you know that. And he will, because if we don't stop it, there'll be twenty-five fools out there arguing with him."

"So how do you think you can stop it?" Doc Wickham said.

Jed Wallace smiled. He lifted a hand. "Now, pipe down," he said. "Harry, cool off. I'll stop them. And if anybody has reason to argue with old Mart Hoodless, I will."

Harry mopped his face with his handkerchief. He and the others glanced at each other with understanding grins. Sure. Sure enough. If Mart Hoodless would listen to anybody, it would be to a banker.

"So keep your hand on your number," Jed said.

He got to his feet, picked up a table knife, closed his fist around it, and banged resoundingly on the table. His voice boomed out over the hall.

"Hey, there! All you jokers sit down!"

He waited. Reassurance stuck out all over him, pleasure, enjoyment, good clean fun.

In the close-packed crowd by the door, people glanced around, hesitated, then grinned at each other and started to move to their seats. Old Jed. He never hollered like that unless he had something pretty good to say.

Hezzie Mooney, as the crowd melted around him, found himself standing alone, and made for the nearest vacant chair, his mouth still open.

"Time we got down to the eats," Jed said.

There was still some bustle in the room, it wasn't quiet enough to suit him, so he rapped with the knife on a water glass and waited again.

"The ladies missed the parade so they could get dinner for us—they're a-getting sore," Jed went on. "They've got turkey and the fixings all ready, so leave off the chawing and buckle to."

Jed pulled back a chair, still clowning, watching grins begin to widen on worried faces. His accent, tailored to match the most countrified speech of any client who ever came into his bank, broadened out, as he leaned forward to deliver his punch-line.

"Them rumors you been hearin', they ain't nothin' but gossip. Nothin' to worry about, folks, nothin' in the world. So eat, drink, and be merry."

He grabbed a paper napkin from the table in front of him, tucked it into the front of his vest, grabbed a fork to go with his knife, holding the implements upright in his fists.

"By gorry, I'm ready. Girls! Let 'er go!"

His last words were lost in a clamor of cheering and clapping. Old Jed. He always fixed it. They ought to have known.

But at the central table, the one with the streamers and the decorations and the big silver trophy with STATE CHAMPIONS 19—engraved on it, but not yet the rest of the date nor the names of the team, because there hadn't been time—at the central table, Carlisle (Shirttail) McIntosh, six-foot-three, seventeen years old, a hundred and sixty pounds, light on his feet as a cat, sat listening to the tumult, his face slowly reddening to the roots of his wavy, honey-colored hair.

By dinnertime, Martin Hoodless had the rubbish cleaned up under his tree, the dead limbs chunked into firewood, the waste piled for burning. Everything had worked out just as he'd planned—after dinner, he could start sawing down the tree, but now he was hungry.

And there'd better be somebody home and dinner ready, he told himself as he walked down the slope toward the house. If dinner's late, I'll make the fur fly.

He was all cocked to let go, and he was almost disappointed coming into the shed, to smell dinner cooking. He hadn't figured Susie would be back; and so she wasn't. But a fine fire was crackling in the range, kettles were bubbling, and Dorothy, his eleven-year-old granddaughter, was slicing bread at the counter. Dot's face was pink and the light hair at the back of her neck was curled into tendrils damp with perspiration.

Been hustling, Martin thought. Well, it's about time someone done a little hustling around here.

Dot was slim and graceful on her feet, like Susie; in fact, they looked alike, the same clear-cut, chiseled features, pink cheeks, and light curly hair. You wouldn't think that Brant McIntosh had had anything to do with Dot, or with Carlisle, either. Ralph, the fifteen-year-old, looked like Brant, the spit-and-image, but Carlisle and Dot were all Susie, in the same way that Susie herself had none of Martin's looks, but took after her mother.

Helga Larsen, Martin's wife, had been pure Swedish; she had been a maid at one of the summer cottages where Martin, as a young man, had been a gardener, so new from Sweden that she could barely speak English. "Talking in tongues" was the way Martin said he had carried on his courtship of her.

She had been a big woman and a healthy one; she and Martin had had six girls, of whom Susie was the youngest and the only one left at home. The Swedish genes were strong; it had always been a touchy point with Martin that not one of his kids took after him. "Damn bunch of hunkies!" he would say, looking down the length of the dinner table at the row of towheads.

Helga and one of the children had died in 1922, the year Susie was born; the others were married. One, Hazel Whitney, lived here in town; the rest were scattered in cities and towns all over the country.

Some of them Martin hadn't seen for years. He heard from them at Christmastime, usually, but long ago he had given up trying to keep track of them. Even their children, his grandchildren, mostly looked like Helga. Susie, at thirty-five, was so much like her mother at that age that sometimes she gave Martin a start.

"Hi, Grampa," Dot said, as he came through the door. "Dinner'll be on the table, just as soon 's you get washed up."

Huh, Martin thought. Pretty anxious to let me know dinner's right on time, ain't you, and everything just as usual.

In silence, he washed at the sink, combed his hair at the mirror over the telephone, plumped himself down at the table.

"Where's your mother?" he demanded.

None of them ever told him anything; all right, he wasn't going to let on he knew anything.

"Oh, she's just stepped out," Dot said. "I guess she'll be back pretty soon."

Stepped out? Well, that was a lie. It was going some, when a mother got a little kid to lie to cover up for her. Give him time, he'd catch the both of them on that.

He stared at Dot, as she began bringing dishes to the table. "Stew again, eh?"

Dot set the platter in front of him. "Why, you always say a stew or a chowder's better on the second day, Grampa," she said composedly. "This one ought to be just right."

The fragrance of the stew hit him full in the face. It was; exactly as he liked it, and he'd made an issue of stew too many times to be able to find fault with it now. Well, there must be something else.

He cast a critical glance over the table. There wasn't a thing out of line that he could see. Fresh, clean tablecloth, everything necessary in its place. Salt-and-pepper shakers. Vinegar cruet. Sugar and cream. Butter. Ketchup. Couldn't find a thing. One thing about Susie, she was sure teaching that little kid how to housekeep. Not that that made him feel any better, after that baldfaced lie.

Seated across from him, watching his eyes go over the table, Dot knew quite well what he was doing.

Go on, she challenged him silently. Find just one thing. Just one, yah, yah!

She had set Martin's table too many times not to know the list by heart; she could have said it backwards. Breadbuttermilksugar-saltandpeppernapkinsvinegarwater. And ketchup, for petesake! Nobody on earth would put ketchup on stew, but if it wasn't there Grampa would flip.

She kept her face polite and pleasant. She hoped. Inside, she was boiling. Times, she liked Grampa all right, he was fun to be with, but when he was put out he could make you mad just by looking. It didn't mean anything to him that she'd stayed home today to get his dinner, when home was the last place she wanted to be. The whole town was down at the parade-and-banquet, and the sixth grade was marching. They'd practiced drilling for weeks, just in case the team won. Dot had been one of the drum majorettes, too; now they'd have to re-shuffle the whole diagram, because she couldn't be there.

But this morning, Ralph had come into her bedroom before she was even awake. She had come to with a jump, to find him standing there, sort of poking at her shoulder.

"You go on out of here," she said, only half awake.

"Somebody's got to stay home today, Dot."

"What? What?"

"Look, wake up, will you? Listen," Ralph said. He looked awful, his hair on end, his eyes bloodshot, with sleep seeds in the corners. He hadn't been in bed more than three hours. "Somebody'll have to stay, get Grampa's dinner, or he'll tear the house down."

"So what? So Ma'll be here."

"Ma will have to go, or it wouldn't look right. She's Carlisle's mother," Ralph said.

"Let him get his own dinner. For once. It wouldn't kill him. For once."

"Look, Dot, you know we've got to keep him smoothed down till Carl gets gone to Boston. You know we have."

"Well, you don't help do it," Dot said. "What if he caught you, sliding down the piazza post, nights? I guess you know who'd ever get to go anywhere, then."

"Yeah," Ralph said. His jaw hung down a little. He looked anguished. "Yeah, I know all that. I'd stay home myself, if I knew how to get the darn dinner."

"No, you wouldn't," Dot said.

Boys! They always slid out from under. Ralph good and well knew nobody'd expect him to stay home today.

"Well, I will see him dead and starved to death and buried, before I'll stay home," she said.

But she knew how it would be. All winter, Grampa had made the house a running battleground, because the boys wanted to play ball. He thought school was just a place where you sat down and learned things out of books. He hated ball. The very mention of it was enough to start him raving. Two or three times, it had been nip and tuck whether he would let Carlisle go on playing. If he got mad, real mad, just now—

"Oh, all right," Dot said disgustedly.

Susie, at first, had said no, of course she wouldn't go, leave Dot home to get dinner, with Grampa probably as cross as a bear. It wouldn't fool him, he always knew more than they thought he did, she reminded them.

But it was the way it looked, Ralph said. Grampa shoot off around town about the ballteam, if some of Carl's family weren't at the banquet, everybody would think it was funny, not backing him up or something, after what he'd done. It was the way it looked, couldn't she for petesake see? And Dot didn't care, did you, Dot?

"Of course she cares," Susie said. "Besides, they need Dot for the marching."

"They can make out," Ralph said. He glanced at Dot and she nodded glumly, without comment.

Susie noticed the glance and Dot's response to it. They really felt she ought to go. Well, so did she. If a whole town was giving a banquet for a boy, his family certainly should be there, and that included Grampa. It's ridiculous, she thought, that we can't all four just go down quietly and enjoy ourselves, without all this touse.

"I think I'll just put the stew on the back of the stove for Grampa," she said, and was startled at the shock on the faces of her two youngest.

"Look, Ma," Ralph said, with an air of weary patience. "Will ya try to get it straight? Just try? There's only the Boston games left, but they're the big ones. If Grampa really shut to—if Carlisle—if Shirttail McIntosh couldn't play—"

"Of course he'll play," Susie said briskly. She was about to go on and say that if the worst came to the worst, she would handle Grampa, but she decided against it. Living in his house, and with him paying the big-half of the expenses, Susie had always felt it only fair that Martin should have the say; if there were times when she couldn't back him up because she felt he was wrong, she knew she could do battle; but the resulting argument she kept between Martin and herself, whenever she could, and away from the children.

"Aw, you know Grampa always gets his damn old own way," Dot said.

"Now, that'll do," Susie said. "We'll have no more of that kind of talk, Miss Dot!"

The kids were tired to death, she could see, and no wonder. They had both gone to the game, all those miles, and home in the small hours, and the strain still showed. Ralph was pale, with shadows under his eyes, and his voice, normally a pleasant baritone, was now something between a creak and a croak. Dot looked much as usual, but she was quiet. It took something more than ordinary tiredness to quiet down Dot.

"Well, the last ballgame!" Susie said. "That is certainly the one I've been looking for. Maybe this house can simmer down again and we can all get a little work done. I don't know as I blame your grandfather. You boys haven't pulled your weight in the boat since the season started, and you know he's got an awful lot of work to do, taking care of all those hens."

"Oh, Ma!" Ralph said. "Not today." He put both hands on his stomach and gave forth a realistic retching sound.

"Stop that," Susie said. Her fingers itched to give him a good cuff, but she caught back the impulse in time. With the kids all to pieces this way, perhaps right now wasn't the moment. "All right," she went on. "First things first. We've all had ourselves quite a fling, and things are out flapping and rough around the edges. After today, we settle down. Or else."

"Okeydoke," Ralph said. "But will you go to the banquet, Ma?"

"Yes, I'll go, if Dot thinks she can manage. Or maybe I'll just go to the parade, show myself, if that's what you kids want. Then I'll scoot back here early, and you can run down to the banquet, Dot."

Well, the promise of that had helped some, but the parade, the marching, was what had been important to Dot. She sat now opposite Martin, praying that Susie would hurry. Get back soon. Get back now. Not so that Dot could get down to the banquet before it was over, at least not entirely, but before she lost her temper with Grampa sitting over there and looking like that.

That kid, Martin was thinking, looks just like a cat with its whiskers covered with cream. By tar! If that wasn't just exactly the way Helga always had looked when she had got ahead of him! And Susie, too! He felt the back of his neck start to bristle. There weren't no womenfolks, no eleven-year-old kid going to get ahead of him. Dammit, there must be something. His glance, coursing the table, fell on the plate of freshly sliced bread and bored into it like a gimlet.

That wasn't homemade bread, by tar! That was store bread.

He reached for a slice, buttered it, took a big bite, and began to chew. Then he stopped in mid-chew and stared at the slice in his hand as if it had bitten him back.

Dot was eating, hadn't looked up, apparently hadn't noticed. So he got up, strode to the stove, yanked off a front cover, and spat the mouthful into the fire.

He turned to find her staring at him, wide-eyed with shock.

"Are you puking in the stove, Grampa?"

"No, and you needn't be so nicey-nicey, either! I ain't puking in the stove. I'm a-spitting out that cussid bread."

"Oh," Dot said.

The bread. Now what could he have found wrong with that? It looked all right. Just a plateful of sliced bread.

"I buy flour," Martin began. "I supply fresh milk and butter right off the cow. If your mother had time to run to the store for bread, she had time to make some."

Dot blinked.

Oh, that wasn't fair! Up to now, it had been a good fair fight, almost fun to see who'd win it. And she had, hands down. Well, grown-ups had the say, they could play that way if they wanted to. What could you do?

"Dirty pool," she said, under her breath.

"What? What's that I heard you say?"

No, sir. He wasn't going to fool her into sassing him, have a real excuse for flipping his old lid.

"That's Pepperidge Farm bread," she said, with niceness still in her voice. "It's the very best there is. It tastes good."

"I don't care what kind it is or how it tastes. It's store bread, and for all I know it's full of dog's toenails. Where's the biscuits?"

"There aren't any."

"Any pilot bread?"

"I guess so, if you want some."

She set a plate of pilot crackers at his elbow.

"These came from the store, too," she said, unable, at last, to hold back everything. "No knowing what dirty old man has had his hands on these."

Martin glared up at her. He recognized the direct quotation from himself. He smashed his fist down on the plate of crackers, sending crumbs flying in all directions. Dot burst into tears, and at that moment Susie walked in through the door.

"For heaven's sake, Pa!" she said. "What on earth do you think you're doing? I just got this kitchen floor washed and swept."

"When? When did you? You ain't been home since yesterday!"

"All right," Susie said. Her eyes took in the situation. "Now, get into your coat, Dot, and scoot. There's lots of time, they're not near through yet. Simmer down, Pa, and eat your dinner. I've brought us home a fresh pumpkin pie for dessert."

"Which you bought at the store, too, I'll bet a diamond!" Martin said. "You ain't had time to make one, by tar!"

"No, I haven't. That's one of Bessie Maitland's pies," Susie said serenely. "Hazel gave it to me to bring home to you. Oh, she and George got back last night. She said to give you her love, she'd be up as soon as she gets settled in."

"Well, I should think she might. Been gone all winter," Martin said.

He had resumed eating his dinner, and since stew, to his way of thinking, was no good without bread to go with it, he had buttered another slice of the store bread and was putting that down, too. "And don't let on to me that where you been's down to see Hazel," he grumbled, between mouthfuls. "For I know better."

"I know you do. I know what's the matter, don't bother to go into it."

"Learning your kids to lie, by tar!"

"Oh, shoot, Pa! I just didn't tell you, I wanted to avoid the touse. I had to go down to the parade, I promised the kids. Hazel said when she gave me that pie she hoped it would pacify you. We knew what was likely to happen, when Bessie told us about you peeking out of the alders at me on the fire truck."

Martin's eyes reddened.

"Well, it's a poor bird that'll befoul its own nest!" he bawled. "When a man's own daughters get together and run him down to the neighbors—"

"Oh, Pa, don't be so foolish!"

"—let alone telling him a passel of lies. When all your life I've supported you and them sprouts of yours—"

"All right," Susie said. "I thought we'd get around to that sooner or later."

"Something ought to remind you, once in a while."

"Something does."

"When all I ask in return for it is my house kept decent and maybe a batch of bread once in a while."

"You can have homemade bread any time you bring home a yeast cake. You didn't buy any, remember?"

"No, and I never will. If your mind was on your work instead of on a lot of crazy kids throwing a ball around, you'd have a jar of potato yeast on hand, like you ought to."

"We've been all over that," Susie said. "As long as yeast cakes are as simple to use and only cost a few cents, I will not have a stinking old pot of potato yeast sitting around the cupboard."

"It don't stink, so long's a woman ain't a nasty housekeeper and washes out the jar once in a while. It never kilt anybody when I was a boy and it makes twice as good bread."

"I hope you think you can tell the difference. If you want to know, there hasn't been anything but yeast cakes or dry yeast used in this house for years. I lay in some every time I go down-street. And if you'd let me shop for the groceries instead of insisting on spending every penny yourself, I could save us a good many times the cost of a few yeast cakes, let me tell you!"

"That'll do. Any money that's spent around here, I'll spend."

"All right, it's your money. But don't you dare to kick to me about my housekeeping. You know you don't mean a word of it, anyway, you're just trying to make me mad. Look, I went to a lot of trouble to get home in time to get dinner. I'd have made it, too, except I was so glad to see Hazel and we got talking. Poor Dotty, she gave up marching in the parade, and we all wanted to go to that banquet. That was Carlisle's banquet, and I wanted awful bad to stay. We even tried to have things you like—stew, and all—and I made off with Bessie's pie she brought to the banquet, so you could have a nice dessert. So why don't you just cool down? Nobody's wronged you, as I can see."

"Things I like, hanh? Store bread? I like that, do I?"

"Well, you seem to have eaten it all," Susie said.

Martin stared at the bread plate. So he had. Got to talking and never noticed. Cleaned her right up.

"A man's got to have something to go with his stew," he blustered feebly. "Any port in a storm—"

But he seemed to have lost that round. Susie wasn't even flustered. She cut a big wedge out of the pie and set it in front of him.

"Eat it," she said. "And for heaven's sake, enjoy it, it's lovely pie."

"I'll enjoy it, don't worry. It's the first thing brought into this house in years that hasn't cost me money."

Susie said nothing to that. She was eating her own pie with relish, and presently Martin tried again.

"It ain't right on an old man," he said. "The work there is to do around this place and them great lazy sods of kids, and you with all that insurance money put by."

Susie sighed. "Yes," she said patiently. "In the bank. Till the kids get ready for college. And you'd be the first one to set up a squawk if I took it out and used it for anything else." He would, too, Susie knew, because the matter had come up before. Martin might be economical about everyday expenses, but he did believe the kids ought to be educated, and he'd agreed, long ago, that that was what Brant's insurance money ought to be kept for. What he was doing now, merely, was working around an ultimatum, and Susie thought, I'd better watch it, or he'll brace his feet and no knowing what will be to pay.

Martin snorted. "College!" he said. "If that's where they're headed, then they better do some schoolwork. Learn to read a book, hadn't they?"

"Yes," Susie said. "And don't think I'm not having that out with them, as soon as this ball craze dies down. Right now, they're passing. They're scraping by, but—"

"Well, they wouldn't if—Carlisle wouldn't, if them teachers down there wasn't scared to flunk him. That's a pretty thing, that is. Teachers, supposed to be learning a boy his education, afraid to put him down a low rank, because they know good and damn well that every last man on the School Board has bet their shirts on the ballteam, and if he don't pass, it ain't the boy gets bounced out of school, it's the teacher."

"I know that's been said. I don't know if I believe it."

"Well, you better believe it. I tell you right now, it's no use to put by money to send kids to college that don't know how to read and write, ain't trying to learn. They don't help me, I'll have to use that money for their board. I can't support 'em free and clear; I'm a poor man."

"I do a lot of work around here, remember. The kids do, too, when they're not driven out of their minds. I'll see to it they do again." Better make this strong, she thought, get him off the track if I can. "Most of the time, if we worked some other place as hard as we do here, it would pay our way."

"Hanh! Well, let me tell you, right here and now, I'm sick of it. Either them kids start working or—Where to hell do you think you're going?"

Susie had gone to the entry and was putting on her hat and coat. "I give up," she said. "I'm going down to the banquet. I wish I'd never come away from it, tried to butter you up. If you've cooled off enough by suppertime to let me in the house, I'll be home to get supper."

"Well, go then! Go! And you better none of you show up here again!" Martin yelled.

"That's all right. We'll be welcome down to Hazel's anytime. We can all have jobs in Charles's motel. For pay."

She shut the door firmly behind her.

Martin, his ultimatum forgotten, sat stunned. Even Helga, mad as she used to get with him every once in a while, had never walked out on him. He was scrabbling to his feet in a flurry, when Susie put her head back in the door.

She grinned at him. "I forgot to tell you," she said. "Hazel brought me back a present. Know what it is? A vacuum cleaner. It'll be the first new thing brought into this house since eighteen eighty-eight."

"By tar!" he began. He stared at the closing door, then got up and yanked it open, just in time to see her starting off in the car.

"Dammit!" he bawled. "Don't you touch that automobile, dammit!"

But Susie only waved to him and rolled on out of the yard.

Well, she'd pay for every cent of the electricity, or he'd throw the damn newfangled gadget right out of the house. He'd stood out against most of it—washing-machines, them; or oil or gas in the kitchen, or an oil furnace in the cellar, when there was nothing on most of the farm but good wood to burn. The only reason he'd had electricity put in, anyway, was because he'd needed it in the hen houses.

Martin started back for the pasture, feeling quite soothed and calm. He'd a good rousing row, a hot dinner under his belt, and now there was a nice, hard job of work to do. It was no more in his mind than in Susie's that she wouldn't be back by suppertime.

Out in the pasture, he went to work. Back and forth, back and forth, with the cross-cut saw. Every once in a while, he would think how much easier the saw would have worked if there'd been a hefty boy on the other end of it, but he'd used it before alone and he could again; and then, back and forth, and he would forget everything but the pleasant rhythm and the deepening slit following the blade into the chestnut's ancient bole.

It was a pleasure to work with that old cross-cut. That was good steel in that blade. You couldn't find steel like that in any blade nowadays. It was tempered so's you had to have a special file to sharpen it. Setting it took about all a man's strength. There wasn't another man besides him in town able to file and set that cross-cut, now that John Norton was dead.

Martin grinned, remembering the fellow down in town—who was it?—oh, yes, February Jones; his pa called him February because he was born in a leap year on February 29th—Feb Jones, who had brought up to Martin a cross-cut he'd sharpened and set himself. Wouldn't cut, he said. Couldn't make it cut. Couldn't figure out what ailed the thing. And Martin like to died laughing when he saw what was wrong—Feb had set the raker teeth on that saw just the same as he had the cutting teeth, and no wonder it wouldn't cut.

This one would, though. If a man knew how, he could tune a saw like a fiddle. Martin ought to know—he could do both. Years gone by, people depended on Mart Hoodless for a number of things. He'd been First Selectman of the town a lot of times, and Chairman of the School Board, and always on the Volunteer Fire Department; and in those days, there hadn't been a square dance in the country that he hadn't played the fiddle for, called off the numbers:

"Chicken in the hen house, turn on your toes,
Rooster hop in, and out she goes!"

Lord, that old fiddle music was some old far off and gone. People didn't care for it now. Music, if you could call it that, had to come off a phonograph record, or squawking out of a radio or a TV, and wasn't nothing a man would want to listen to, at that. When he was a kid, you picked up a fiddle and fooled with it for fun in what little spare time you had; you got good enough so you could play for a dance, or evenings over the cider when neighbors dropped in. Helga. How she could dance! She could spin till she was red in the face and dizzy and all that pug of blond hair dropped down, and still be ready for more.

Martin straightened up for a breather, mopping his face and neck. He looked around at the quiet pasture, at the farmstand down below. Funny how people could be gone out of a place and it stay the same, as if it said, Nothing is changed. When everything was changed forever.

Helga. Dead thirty-five years now. Going on for thirty-six. A mighty big lot of a man's life he spent learning how to be alone. Gone a long time, all that hair, all that fun and laughing. All those rousing old cat-and-dog fights, which she'd enjoyed as much as he had. Bring home tamarinds and scallops for supper, to celebrate the mortgage being paid off, both expensive, but the two things he liked best in the world to eat, and his idea of a holiday meal; and Helga would fix them and eat them, too, though she hated the sight of both of them, just wanted to help him celebrate. Whoever saw tamons nowadays? Wonder where they went? And half the scallops you bought now were nothing but whacked-up skates'-fins.

Not one of them girls was half the woman their mother was, ever understood him the way she had. Susie came the closest, or she had, once; but Susie hadn't been the same since that damn worthless son-of-a-gun of a Brant McIntosh, her husband, had gone off and got himself killed in the War. Well, Susie wasn't old. Time hadn't even begun to move for her yet.

The way those little girls used to bounce around the kitchen to his fiddle-playing. He could see them now. Darn little hunkies, tow heads and flying skirts. None of the kids, nowadays, had any real fun.

Martin bent back to his sawing.

Nowadays, if a kid learnt to play a fiddle, it wasn't for fun; what he had in mind was playing it someday on the TV, being on one of them programs. Why, Saturday mornings, bright sun, when a kid ought to be learning to do things, sharpen a saw, be an able man, pull his weight in the boat, where was he? In some dark room with the windowshades pulled down, watching TV, or up at the school gym throwing a ball around.

By mid-afternoon, Martin was three-quarters of the way through the tree, already watchful just in case that last section of trunk should be rotten, and the chestnut, out of balance from the weight of the tree house, should give before he was ready. He stood up to uncramp his muscles and to look again at the summit of the tree, trying to estimate just how much out of balance it might be; and he saw that two people had come into the pasture without his noticing—his grandson, Carlisle, and Hezzie's boy, Jerry Mooney, still in their Sunday suits from the banquet. Apparently, they hadn't seen him, the way he'd been hunkered down behind the tree.

They came footing it, one behind the other, across the pasture, must've come up on the highway side, from town. Carlisle, he saw, was limping.

Lame, hanh? That'll help out, wrastling around bags of hen-feed. And I suppose he thinks if he sneaks home the back way, I won't see him. Well, I see him.

He stood where he was, waiting for his presence to become known. Something about them, a head-down, dogged intentness in the way they came, made him keep silent out of curiosity. He stood peering out through the lowest crotch of limbs, saw them come to a stop, facing each other. Martin made sure they were not in the way of the tree, in case it came down, and still said nothing.

"All right," Jerry said. "Take your damn coat off."

Carlisle said, "Gladly."

Before Martin's astonished eyes, they proceeded to take off not only their coats but their Sunday pants as well, folding the clothes neatly to one side. Then they squared off and silently laced into each other.

Well, if kids nowadays didn't beat the old toko. Mad enough to fight, but took time to strip down to undershirts and shorts. On a February day, too, what kind of a way was that? It was all right with him if Carlisle took care of his clothes, them Sunday suits cost more than a cent apiece, and this was the only one the boy had. But stop long enough before a fight to take your pants off? Your coat, so's you could swing; but your pants?

And the way they talked. "Gladly." What kind of talk was that?

That damn TV, Martin muttered to himself, is going to make cussid fools out of the whole of them kids.

Holy old hornets, you got mad at a feller, you jumped him, you didn't wait till you had time to go out in the pasture and take your pants off. Why, the poor little slobs, probably it wouldn't seem like a fight to them if they didn't strip down to the hide like them athaletes on the TV.

At that, it didn't seem to be much of a fight. A lot of waving arms and clinching. Both their noses were bleeding, but neither one seemed to have the steam to put behind a good punch. Carlisle, Martin saw, craning his long, skinny neck, with the disgusted Adam's apple, higher over the crotch of the tree, Carlisle had a banged-up knee. It had been bandaged with some kind of an elastic strap which had come loose and slid down. The kneecap was raw; he was black and blue up and down the thigh. Jerry, too, had some bruises. A big one on his arm and shoulder, apparently a day or so old, had turned greenish-yellow.

Well, at least they'd done something hard enough to get marked up. But, by tar, they didn't know how to fight. Wide open, both of them. Why, if Martin had ever had the chances in a fight that either one of them had over and again, he could have knocked his man galley-west. That Mooney boy didn't even have his fists doubled up. He was flapping his arms up and down, hands open, like a girl.

Right now, they were clinched, rocking around, no one making a mite of headway. As he looked, they collapsed to the ground, rolled a little way from each other, and lay there.

What in hell? Nobody's punched anybody. Out, and they hadn't been fighting five minutes.

Then he realized that they were both crying.

Martin stared. He snuffled disgustedly, pulled his handkerchief out of his hip pocket and blew into it, a prolonged toot. Nobody heard it, apparently. So he leaned down to his saw and began to work again. Back and forth. Back and forth.

It took only a few more strokes; that last section of trunk was rotten; it was going to give, just as he'd thought it might.

The tree seemed to gather itself, not with any perceptible movement or tremor, but as if, before anything happened at all, it was getting ready. Martin whipped his saw from the crack and leaped nimbly back out of the way. For a moment the tree stood upright, as solid it seemed as it had ever been; then the saw-track in its bole began slowly to widen. The chestnut shuddered; its summit leaned against the sky. Two hundred years came down with a scattering smash that shook the pasture, the tree's passing more spectacular than any show it had ever made through all its years of serenely white-candled springs.

The tree house was split, its roof flattened to its floor; splintered boards, broken two-by-fours crushed out of it on all sides. The birds' nest had survived; it was still plastered firmly into the woven twigs of the branch it had been built on.

Even a bird learns how to do a job, Martin told himself. He gathered up his ax and saw and left the pasture. From his upright, lanky back in the worn denim work-frock, to his knotted hands clutching the tools and his brown, whiskery, hatchet face, he was as if chiseled out of a block of disgust.

He walked in silence past the fallen warriors, who, sitting up now, were staring at the tree in appalled amazement, their tears not dry on their cheeks.

Well, it hadn't fallen very far from where they were. It had, as a matter of fact, fallen tick-on-the-nose, on the spot Martin had meant it to. They hadn't been in any danger; if they had, he'd have hollered to them to get to hell out of the way. They wouldn't, either one of them, have any notion of the amount of thought and planning that had gone into doing the job right; one of them cut down a tree, it fell where it fell, and God help all under it.

But it scared 'em, by tar. It jiddled up their pendulums. They don't know nothing, probably think I'm crazy.

Let 'em. By tar, let 'em. I give up.

He walked away, not looking back.

Part Two

"B-brother!" Jerry said. He stared, horrified, after Martin's back. "Is that old coot crazy? Looks like he tried to kill us!"

He started to get up, thought better of it, and flopped back onto the ground, where he lay flat with his arms over his face.

It's the old chestnut tree, Carlisle thought. Grampa's cut it down. So all right, so Grampa's cut it down.

It didn't seem to mean much, one way or the other. Later on it might. He had a lot of stuff stashed away in that tree house. His whole Indian collection was there, among other things.

He thought, dully, Have to go dig around sometime, see if I can salvage some of it. Not now, though.

Now, he was too tired. He and Jerry both had been too pooped even to fight.

He sat on the ground, beginning to sense odds and ends of discomfort that still seemed too far away to matter much. The chill of the frozen February earth crept through his thin cotton shorts; his bottom was soaked and numb. His nose stung. The whole middle of his face felt stiff, where one of Jerry's wild haymakers had landed. Worst of all, his knee was beginning to feel as if someone had stuck a hot stick up through it into his thigh.

If he'd sprained that some more, the coach would really tear his head off.

Say Alison could think of anything to add to that creaming after the banquet. Old Alison. Didn't even wait to let anybody get rested up. Hauled the whole team over to the gym and bled all over them.

This was supposed to be a ballgame, not a chance for some movie star to mug the cameras. What did we think we were doing, mousing around like The Pelvis, making a film? Sure, oh, sure. We had a Championship. But if we wanted to know how good we were, read it and weep.

And Alison had yanked a newspaper out of his hip pocket, slammed it down.

They all knew which one it was. They all knew the write-up by heart. It was Flits Anderson's story on the game.

> Chet Alison's Red Hawks showed pretty ragged teamwork . . . They stood to get clobbered but good, and would have, if Shirttail McIntosh hadn't got hotter than a pistol . . . That's a fabulous fellow . . .

And so on. It was Shirttail McIntosh who was fabulous. Not Jerry Mooney. It was not Chet Alison, nor his team.

So haul-ass home, said Alison. Get rested. No hanging around the drugstore to get slapped on the back, told how great you are. You and I know how great you are. So on Monday morning, I'm going to start working the hell out of you.

He'd hauled back his foot, kicked the rumpled newspaper under the lockers, started for the door.

Three years, beating on you creeps. Three years and what have I got? Five lovelies. Every man his own ballteam. Every man his own TV show. You know what'll happen when some ballplayers meet up with you in the All-New England? There'll be chunks scattered from hell to Connecticut.

Well, another creaming, so what? You'd had plenty; took it in your stride. Only this one, coming right now in the middle of the let-down, was hard to take. Oh, you had a let-down after any game, the day after was always terrible, when you couldn't keep your eyes open in class, and the teachers played along, tipped a wink to the rest of the kids and let you sleep through the period. All except Mr. Berg; Buggsy was likely to start yakking.

"Look," he would say. "Are we running a school here? Or a ball club?"

So the poop was, make some kind of a showing in science, because Buggsy wouldn't play along. Well, he was new here. He'd learn.

For about a week before any game, you built up to that let-down. Practicing every minute of spare time, study periods, after school, evenings; feeling yourself get smoother and smoother; as if time itself as it grew shorter were some kind of fizz poured into your muscles, while the pressure built up, inside and out—inside of you, outside in the school and town—until on the night of the game you walked on electricity, feet off the ground, everything you touched seeming to crackle and spark.

There was nothing like it; nothing like it anywhere in the world.

Then, the day after, the let-down. Only this let-down, this one after the Tournament, this was fierce. All you could think about was, last night was the greatest. The end. You'd given it all there was. And now you had to start over again, and this time it would be tougher. Geez-Louise, how could it be? That Boone team was the toughest I ever saw; somebody said they all spent their summers up in the North Woods with the lumberjacks.

So we took 'em.

But the whole team had marks—banged elbows, sprained muscles, pulled tendons. When you moved, you felt as if somebody had pounded you with a plank.

It didn't do any good to say, knock it off, when you get rested the old fizz'll start pouring all over again.

It seemed to Carlisle, sitting on the ground in his shoes and shorts, even thinking, I'll get a cold and I won't be able to play; and, my knee'll stiffen up and I won't be able to play, that it was not worthwhile ever to try to move again. It would be better to lie back and let the cold strike in, until you got numb enough not to ache all over.

A red-hot twinge shot through his leg, and he glanced down at it. The bandage was off, slipped down around his ankle. He'd scrubbed off some more skin. It had bled a little; had grains of mud and dried grass smooched into it.

He reached down, finding his arms and shoulders stiff as ramrods, yanked the bandage into place, gritting his teeth as the heavy elastic rasped over the raw, scrubbed flesh.

Wow! Well, it hurt now. It would be all right by Monday. It would be healed by the time the team went to Boston. It had better be!

Old Jerry looked out colder than a pickle. No wonder, the cluck. After the beating he took last night, today he has to organize a battle with me. Both of us so pooped that all we could do was lean chins on each other and fall down.

Jerry'd catch a cold.

Heck, they both would.

They wouldn't be able to play.

What if Alison found out about the fight, found out I took a chance on hurting this knee some more. Baby doll!

He said, tentatively, "Jerry?"

Jerry didn't move. He lay there on his back, his arms over his eyes. After a moment, he muttered, "Oh, crise, shut up!"

Carlisle got up. It was like unfolding a chunk of cardboard. He could bend his knee, he found; he limped over to the neat pile of his clothes and began to dress.

So all right. So old Dead-Eye was still sore.

Up to last night, he had been the hotshot. Fabulous. The One. School record for baskets in a season, record for rebounds; record for baskets in a single game. So every time he uncoiled that loose frame of his, let go one of his beautiful, incredible shots from some impossible position, the fans went wild, the sports boys blew up headlines. Jerry. Jerry Mooney. Old Dead-Eye Mooney. The colleges were watching him, it was a cinch he'd be able to go about anywhere he wanted to on an athletic scholarship. Heck, the colleges would be fighting each other, when the time came, to see which one got Dead-Eye Mooney.

The rest of us work just as hard—we work harder, feeding him. Some of are just as good. If we had his chances to show it. Last night, the way the cookie crumbled, one of us got just that little old chance.

You'd tried. You knew better than not to go along with Alison's diagrammed plays. Pass, pass, pass. Smooth as butter up the floor. Plunk into the basket. Nine times out of ten, who plunked it? Dead-Eye Mooney. In like Flynn.

But at the end of the half, the score was twenty to six. The poop was that Feathers Ryan, the Boone Academy coach, was outfoxing Alison all over the place; the Hawks were taking a shellacking, Mooney having an off-night. Might as well shut up shop, go home, stop the slaughter.

The thing was, Jerry wasn't having an off-night; he was hot. But Ryan's boys had been told what to do; they were over him like a blanket, sometimes as many as four men on him at once, so that he either couldn't shoot at all or his shots went wild.

That was the way things stood, when Shirttail McIntosh, instead of passing as expected, had looped a long one. A hell of a long one that went through swishing. A beaut.

The old roar went up from the stands. It made the lights flicker. The sound seemed as if it must have started inside himself; and all at once something happened to him that had never happened before, at least, not to that degree. Before, sometimes, he had felt as if it were about to happen; he had got up to the edge of it but never quite over. This time he got over. It oiled up and happened. That was when, he supposed, he had started to ramble.

He kept seeing the basket—not a plain, webbed circle, far up the floor, but like a single point of fiery concentration, isolated, as if he and it were alone up there. Time and again he would see someone's hands come up to receive the ball, or Jerry's hands, and the Boone men start for Jerry; it was like seeing through glass. The only real thing was the basket; there it was. For him. And so he would pivot and shoot and the ball would go through.

At third-quarter interval, they were only one point behind, and Boone hadn't been standing still, either.

The stands had gone crazy. You couldn't hear yourself think. Someone nearby kept bawling, "Oh, you Shirttail!" and some others took it up, until a lot of people were chanting it. The team, clustered around Alison, their heads bent close together, had a hard time to hear what he was saying.

"Look, you've fooled the hell out of them, but they're on to you now. So, dammit, you pass that ball!"

So he had meant to. But the moment he had stepped out on the floor, he saw the basket again. The same way. Hit it, nothing to it. And hauled back to shoot and found himself at the bottom of a pile-up of Boone players—accidental, of course, only you knew better—with his breath gone from somebody's elbow in the breadbasket, and a skinned and twisted knee. For a moment, he'd thought he was dying. Then he was back on his feet, time out for a bandage, and dizzy; but back on the floor again.

Jerry said, as they trotted out to positions, "Now you know how it feels, damn you!" He was white around the mouth, and that was when Carlisle first realized that he was sore. The rest of the game hadn't helped that any.

All they could seem to do, now, was hold Boone to that one point ahead; toward the end, it was still that way. Boone, with only minutes to go, got the ball and slowed down with it. So it was nip and tuck to a certain end, when Jerry managed to get himself fouled. He was good at that; it was a personal foul, two shots. Jerry could have won the game right there, but he did something he hadn't done in a tight spot all season—he missed a foul shot. He got one but he lost the second, so the game was only tied. And then Boone, bringing the ball down the floor, got jerky and lost it. Shirttail McIntosh intercepted; he let fly the long, cleanly arching shot that won the game.

Only this time he could not have said how he had done it, because through the sweat and exhaustion and the red film in front of his eyes, he had barely been able to see, much less aim.

Buttoning his jacket, fumbling with numb fingers at his tie, he wondered, now, what had happened to him.

Maybe it was like that conditioned rat Buggsy yats about in class. When the bell rings, it doesn't think; it just starts drooling.

And then the TV cameras and the sportswriters and the presentation of the trophy; and his picture and Jerry's and the team's for the papers. Only it was him now, in like Flynn, with Alison standing just behind, his hand on Carlisle's shoulder; and the still shrieking, crazy fans; and the families of the team brought down to say a word for the television; Win Parker and Doc Wickham and Jed Wallace and Harry Troy. Hezzie Mooney.

"Yes, by gorry, I'm Dead-Eye Mooney's father, and I'm only a one-by-two dirt farmer, but I guess I raised up a pretty good kid"; and Jed, squared up to the camera, grinning: "Yup, I am, I'm the President of the Chamber of Commerce down there; yes, sir, we've got a pretty up-and-coming little town."

And the team all standing around the big trophy, the sweat coming in black stains through the backs of their basketball pants, so tired it was hard even to breathe—the TV man had to speak twice before Carlisle could get his breath behind his voice, and then, when he did, the words came out squeaky, the way they had sometimes years ago, when his voice was changing. So he took to nodding his head yes and shaking it no; and the man said, "You're a pretty modest boy for anyone who played the brand of ball you did tonight; any of your folks here in the hall?"

Well, Ralph and Dot somewhere, but skip them, you wouldn't be able to get Ralph within forty yards of a camera, and God help all here if you got Dot. Carlisle wheezed out that his mother was watching on TV, and the man said, "Well, say hello to her. Say hello to Ma." So Carlisle grinned and said, "Hi, Ma."

Jerry suddenly rolled over onto his hands and knees, pushed with the palms of his hands on the ground, and got to his feet, stiff-legged, like a baby learning to walk. He stalked over to his clothes and began to dress. His teeth were chattering and the white around his mouth had turned bluish.

"You better wash your face in the brook before you put your shirt on," Carlisle said, watching him. "We can't let it get around that we've been fighting."

"Your damned old grampop knows. He saw us," Jerry said. He slid down the sloping bank, dipped his fingers gingerly in the icy water, and began, with great tenderness, to wash the mud and blood off his face. He was going to have an old snorter of a black eye, Carlisle saw. At least I nailed him once, he thought, with satisfaction.

"I don't think he saw us fighting. If he had, he'd have yelled to us to get out of the way before he let that tree go."

"Yeah? Well, the way he acted, he was damn sorry it didn't clobber us. Probably been glad if it had, the way he seems to feel about the ballteam."

"Oh, shut up!" Carlisle said.

His knee hurt, and he was sick of Jerry. He'd put up with Jerry's dirty cracks after the game, at the hotel, coming home on the bus—seemed any player if he wanted to make himself look good could louse up plays; make the rest of the team look like flatfeet; seemed if you wanted to, you could set out deliberately to make some other player mad so he'd miss his shots; and who were we playing, Boone or each other?

Well, everybody knew Jerry. He'd get mad and say anything, yak it out of his system, so let him, it didn't mean much except Jerry was mad. The team had put up with a lot of that from him, for a reason; probably the way Hitler's men didn't haul off with a boot in the tail, but let him chew the carpet, so long as he took them where they wanted to go.

So why get sore? You felt too good about winning the trophy; you didn't even point out what would've happened to it if somebody hadn't started to ramble.

And then Hez Mooney had started the whole town to yakking about Grampa; maybe Grampa was an old red-neck, but you knew it; and who wanted to listen to his folks being talked over in public? And on top of that, Alison's creaming; and finally, on the way out of the gym, Jerry let go with a couple of cracks about Debby Parker. So the only thing to do was take him somewhere and wipe it off him.

Only a fight right now, within the team, it had better be kept quiet. Alison would flip. And as for the townspeople, the drugstore gang—they'd be likely to lynch us, or something, with the Boston games still to play, the big ones coming up.

And how'll he explain that black eye? Everybody saw him at the banquet. Alison would know he hadn't got it in the game.

Carlisle reached for his jacket, took an unwary step, and just managed to keep himself from going down. Jerry stared, his wildly smeared, exhausted face lengthened with horror.

"Oh, geez, your knee! Is it worse? Can't you bend it? Geez, if we've clobbered that knee, with the All-New England coming up—Look, don't step on it! I'll go get Doc Wickham right now, see if it's all right to step on it."

"Take it easy," Carlisle said. "I just slipped on a patch of ice. Doc Wickham, that old blabbermouth! He'd run right to Alison."

"Yeah, he would. That's right, he would." Jerry came up out of the brook, mopping, carefully, with his bloody handkerchief. "Oh, god," he said hollowly. "You've got a black eye."

"I have?" What with other discomforts, Carlisle had forgotten about the stiff feeling in his face. He fingered it cautiously, feeling the lump on his cheekbone, the eye already partially swollen shut. "Geez, I have, haven't I? So've you."

They stared at each other lopsidedly, each trying to assess the damage, what was going to show, on the other's face.

"We can say we had an accident with a car," Carlisle said.

"We haven't had anyone's car. It's got to be better than that. We can say old Mart Hoodless dropped a tree on us."

"Nobody'd believe that either. Lay off Gramp, will you? He's an old crab, but nobody'd believe he's crazy."

"Ah-h, everybody knows he's a woolball. He's low-Joe around town now, too, the way he's trying to futz up the team. I guess people'd be more likely to believe me than they would him."

"Oh, go on home," Carlisle said. "We had a fight, so we had a fight. You started it, remember, it's your baby. Go on!" he went on, as Jerry opened his mouth to answer. "Get home, take a shower or something. You know what happens if you get chilled after you been sweating."

The echo of Alison. Don't sit there on your—Get into the shower room. Don't stiffen up. Stay limber. So on and so on.

He thought, If he tackles me again, I won't be able to shut my hands, I'll just fall flat on my face; but Jerry apparently was thinking along the same lines, for he backed up, cautiously, a few feet, then turned and set off across the field toward home, setting one foot stiffly in front of the other.

Conditioned rat, Carlisle thought, turning away, himself setting out across the pasture. Couple of conditioned rats.

The fallen chestnut blocked his way, and as he walked around it, he saw that the tree house was flattened. To get at any of the stuff that was in there, he'd have to rip the roof apart with a crowbar; his aching muscles winced at the thought. The Indian collection was probably kaput, anyway. Oh, the flints would be okay, but the bone tools were frail; they'd be broken.

Grampa, he thought. He sure goes to a lot of trouble to get his damned old way.

It had been a pretty good collection. Over a period of years, off and on, when he'd had time, he'd dug it out of the Indian shell mounds scattered in places where there were clamflats along the coast. A young summer guy, passing through with a pack on his back, one year, had got him interested—showed him how you could dig darned nice things out of those old clamshells—harpoon points, arrowheads, stone axes, different kinds of tools the old tribesmen used. The young guy had said how those old braves would take a piece of felsite or some other kind of hard stone and chip little pieces off, one here, one there, to make an arrowhead. With no metal tools at all, maybe just a bone chisel. He said that according to the Carbon 14 test, some of those old shell heaps were six thousand years old. That long ago you'd think they'd be about three bounces ahead of the monkeys, but they were still that good with their hands. Even with an electric stone-polisher, you couldn't do half the job making an arrowhead that those old boys had done with their bone chisels.

Carlisle had hung around for a few afternoons down on Tanner's Island watching the fellow dig in the shell heap there and asking questions. Apparently, the man had liked him, or something, for he'd showed him how to dig, how careful you had to be; and then, when he'd been packing up to leave, he'd handed over a book. "Here, if you're interested. This'll tell you better than I can."

For a couple of years that book had been Carlisle's Bible; he'd read it practically out of the covers. It was now somewhere in that mashed-up mess of the tree house. He supposed he could dig it out if he had the energy. Or the time.

But, oh, lord, he was bushed!

Two years ago, this would have killed me, he thought. Anything happen to that Indian stuff . . .

But, heck, you got older, you outgrew the kid stuff, like tree houses and Indian collections. Let Ralph have it. That eager beaver. He'd dig it out, be glad to. Oh, he'd futz it up, old ham-hands, busted everything he touched, but he was the one who was crazy about Indian stuff now. A guy got older, he had something better to do with his time.

Carlisle set his weight on his sore leg, found it was bad, but not so bad as it might be, and limped off across the pasture toward home.

His grandfather met him at the door.

"Come home, did you? No place else to go?"

"Yeah."

"That was some fight. Don't them great battlers on the TV ever double up their fists? Who beat, finally?"

"Nobody. We were too pooped to fight, if you want to know."

"Well, you better get your overalls on and come out to the barn. Or are you too pooped to milk a cow?"

I'm too pooped right now to tell him to keep his trap shut, Carlisle thought. He pushed past Martin and limped wearily up the stairs. But the time'll come when I won't be.

He heard water running in the bathroom and saw that Susie was in there filling the tub. She grinned at him and pointed to the tub.

"Ralph'll help Grampa," she said. "Your clean pajamas are there on the hook. When you get washed, you hop into bed Are you hungry?"

Carlisle shook his head. Later, he knew, he would be, he'd want to eat the house down; now all he could think about was sleep.

Susie clucked at the sight of his knee. She didn't say anything, though—didn't even ask if it hurt when she cleansed it, dressed it in soft gauze that felt a lot better than Doc Wickham's tight bandage. She hung his good suit neatly in the closet, picked up the soiled bandage from the floor.

"Don't throw that away. I'll have to put it on again," Carlisle said, from the bed.

"I'll have to scrub it, if you're going to wear it," she said. "What is it, anyway? It's a filthy mess. Now you sleep."

She went out and shut the bedroom door. He heard the key click in the lock and be softly withdrawn, and thought, with a grin, Good old Ma, he won't kick the door down; then he rolled his aching face into the clean, sweet-smelling pillow and went to sleep as if someone had slammed him over the head.

Susie carried the bandage along to the laundry, where she dunked it distastefully into a bucket of suds and left it to soak.

Horrible tight thing. It must have hurt something fierce.

Whoever put it there, on that raw knee, must have been out of his mind. It would certainly give support to a sprain, but it would also slow down circulation; it was airtight, too, and the whole kneecap was scrubbed nearly to the bone.

With three kids, Susie had tended to plenty of scrubbed knees in her time; she'd always thought that the sensible thing for a bad bang like that was to rest it.

Of course, Carlisle hadn't had time to rest; he'd had to get right up and keep running. So probably those professional he-men down there, Dr. Wickham and the coach, had used whatever they figured would keep him going longest.

Well, he certainly looks as if he'd kept going as long as he could. He's lost pounds, and he's so worn out he can't talk, and he's black-and-blue all over. That lump on his cheek, that's come up since last night. It doesn't make sense for a boy to be slammed around so, just playing a game.

She had been putting together a casserole dish to bake for supper, and she went back to the kitchen now to finish it and fix the fire in the range. Slow fire for an hour, then a good hot one for the biscuits with which she planned to soothe Martin's hurt feelings about the store bread. A wood fire took handling to get the exact results you wanted, but Susie was an expert. A few heavy sticks of locust, dampered down, would burn slowly, leave a nice bed of coals; then pop in some beech or maple to heat up the oven for the biscuits. . . . She stared at the empty wood-box.

All right for you, Mr. Ralph.

Goodness knew where *he* was. She had caught a glimpse of him after the banquet, hardly more than a pair of heels vanishing out the door of the hall, so probably he was still running round town fattening on leftover excitement. Thank goodness, she'd caught up with Dot in time, made her come home and go upstairs for a rest. For once Dot hadn't peeped, she was all ready to light down.

Susie carried in an armful of wood from the shed, congratulating herself that Martin hadn't spotted her; because if he had, he'd have come and carried the wood himself, sounding off all the time about the kids being no good; and then, of course, he'd have had to be told that she'd put Carlisle to bed; *that* row she hoped to put off until suppertime.

This is a madhouse, she thought, waiting by the range until the locust wood caught, so that she could close the drafts. Everybody with different plans, and me in between trying to fill up the jags. Sometimes I could fly.

Well, fly or not, things had to be thought about. Supper would have to be put back, if Ralph didn't get home in time to help his grandfather with the night chores. There were a lot of chores, too many for one old man alone, they'd take Martin a long time. She herself could go out and help; it wouldn't be the first time. The casserole would keep; when it came time to bake the biscuits, she'd get Dot up to tend them. Even if you did want to fly, where was there a place to fly to?

Earlier on, she had been mending the week's quota of socks in the sewing room off the kitchen, and there was still some time left while the casserole got under way. She hadn't stayed very long down at the banquet, only long enough for Martin to get good and well out of the house; there'd been too many things to do at home. Sitting down again, she picked up the mending where she had left off with one of Ralph's socks which was more hole than it was sock—a cavern in the heel so huge that the darning egg flopped right out through. She was an expert at this kind of hole, seeing that this was the kind there was usually most of, and it had to be mended carefully so that ridges in the darn wouldn't raise blisters on an active boy's heel. She had always had to make do, even when Brant, her husband, had been alive; and while Martin, now, saw that everybody had enough, he wasn't generous with money; nor did she expect him to be. She paid her expenses, and the children's, in whatever way she could.

What she had was Brant's service pension, which, used up monthly, didn't go very far; and for a backlog, she had his insurance safely banked, to be kept, she hoped, for the children's education. This insurance had always been a sore point with Martin; today was not the first time he had pointed out that since he was bearing the heft of the expenses, he should handle all the money. But on this, Susie sat as solid as a rock.

Martin, of course, didn't want to use the money—he had plenty of his own laid by; she had no way of knowing how much—actually, what he wanted was to have the say about her money. How it was to be spent, and for whom; and it would not be spent on anyone whom Martin happened to be put out with at the time.

So Susie was taking no chances. When the time came, the kids were going to college. They were going to get what there was to learn; they were going to have equipment that Brant hadn't had; what would surely have helped him if he could have got it. Maybe, as Martin pointed out, if the kids were worth anything they'd get their educations for themselves. But if Brant had had some help, ever; if he hadn't been slammed around so—in spite of his War Medal, most people, including Martin, always figured that Brant hadn't been worth the powder; they'd made up their minds about him when they'd first known him, and the medal hadn't changed anything. But Susie remembered him as the best man she had ever known. True, he'd never been much in a practical way, but there were other things that kept you going. Important things; Susie knew that when Brant had gone overboard off the Coast Guard picket-boat, something irreplaceable had gone with him. Times now, even after so many years, she would find herself brought up short, remembering Brant's slow endearing grin, the way his silky black hair grew, clipped and soft on the back of his neck, other things that had faded some with time, but not much.

"Let other folks quar'l and fight, Susie. I got something better to do with my time."

No, she wouldn't in a thousand years accept Martin's estimate of Brant.

I was practical enough for both of us; and a lot of men don't seem to realize it—Pa doesn't—but a woman needs something in the house besides a good provider.

She sat now, frowning over the devastated sock, thinking not of Brant, but of Brant's sons.

I'm just going to have a ripping old fight with both of them. I know Pa's hard on them, but he wouldn't be, if only they didn't make him so mad all the time, running out on chores. And their schoolwork . . . they used to get all A's and B's, and now they're just sliding by. Of course, Carlisle, all he has to do is look at a book and he's got it, but when can he look? He doesn't do any homework, and every minute of his spare time at school, he's practicing ball. And he's changed so. He used to be quite interesting to have around the house, fun to talk to. And now he's old high cockalorum, till I could shake him. He used to care about his grades, too.

She recalled how, weeks ago, when Carlisle had brought home his half-term grades, along with a note from Mr. Berg, she'd hauled him over the coals.

"What's the matter with you, anyway?" she'd said. "Mr. Berg says you've got too good a brain to waste it like this."

Carlisle had sat there, elbows on the table, listening. She'd delivered quite a lecture, ending up with Martin's side of it about the chores on the farm.

"He never lets on he's tired, but I know, times, he is. He's old. Lifting those heavy bags of feed and all those crates of hens, it tells on him. He figures we all ought to work our board, and so do I."

Carlisle still didn't say a word.

So she thought, I've put this as reasonably as I can, now I guess I've got to crack down. When they're little, you can keep in touch, no trouble at all; but from thirteen on, they go somewhere, they live in a place of their own.

"Now, you listen to me," she began, raising her voice; and Carlisle, suddenly, put his head down on his folded arms on the table. For a moment, she thought he was crying, and she was appalled. He hadn't cried since she could remember; but he looked up almost at once.

"Look, Ma, will you for petesake go to some games and *see?* I can't stop. I *gotta* play."

Susie liked a good ballgame as much as anyone; she hadn't been going to any because of Martin; it never seemed worthwhile to put up with the fuss.

Well, maybe I'd better, she thought, completely puzzled. But it's only a game; what's he so upset about?

After what she'd seen, watching the games, she'd realized what Carlisle had meant. No boy who wasn't crippled or sick could take the responsibility of wrecking that team—face up to a whole school, a whole town, yelling "chicken" and "yellow" and "bum."

You could see Martin's side and Mr. Berg's side; but you could see Carlisle's side only too well. From the time last fall when the team began to win and chances for the Championship to look good, the pressure on him had been terrific. Everywhere you went, you heard nothing but basketball. In stores, restaurants, drugstore, poolroom—any place with room for a gathering of fans—you'd see people talking over the games. Someone standing out in the middle of the floor, showing how *he'd* have done it, if he'd had a-holt of that ball, like Dead-Eye had it, or Dick, or old Shirttail; or maybe how *he* used to pivot, years ago, when he played ball.

And last night, sitting in the Mooneys' living room, watching the Tournament finals on Hezzie's TV, what she'd seen had sobered her. You saw more detail on TV than you did at a game; the cameras played across the crowd, picking out faces, pointing up in brilliant black and white the wide-open cavities of mouths, the frantic, beating hands; the soundtrack brought in raving, animal-like yells. People you knew, like Bessie Maitland, of all people, with her pug fallen down on her neck sideways, pounding with both fists on the shoulders of the stranger in front of her. All screaming at a boy unconscious on the floor to for godsake get up, get up, play, finish the game. So the boy got up.

For goodness' sake, it's only rooting, she'd told herself, or tried to. People just getting excited, having a good time. What could be wrong with that?

All the same, there was something about it out of reason for grown people.

Plain rivalry, wanting to win, you could understand; but this was more. Mixed with it was a queer kind of senseless emotionalism; for one thing, a lot of ill-feeling. You could see, last night, how the two sets of fans had felt. The TV cameras pointed out fistfights here and there, as a part of the good clean fun. People from two towns, neighbors, snarling, all ready to beat each other up. Times, at the home games, on the rare occasions when the team had lost, you saw some of that, too. Among the fans leaving the gym, the language she'd heard had sickened her. Griping—cursing, some of them—all of them furious.

The team lost the game. They were so-and-sos. Bums. A bunch of no-good little bastards.

Talk like that about kids! she'd thought. And about kids who'd worked their hearts out trying to win!

School spirit, well, you had that when you were fifteen. You outgrew it, didn't you, for goodness' sake, by the time you were fifty?

It was certainly strange. People needed something to show loyalty to, that was understandable, if it were only loyalty. But there seemed to be in almost everybody a whole area of unpredictable emotion, tamped down, ready to break free. When there wasn't a war, or the Communists, or a town row, they had to have something to prove that their side, their town, their team, whatever was theirs, was better than anything anybody else had.

Mine, mine, mine is better than yours, yours, yours. Without qualification, all black or all white.

You've got nothing to offer me, I've got nothing to offer you.

Oh, Brant, she thought. And, suddenly, found herself crying.

Part Three

The first time Susie ever saw Brant McIntosh was at a dance in Fairport. She had gone to the dance with Win Parker, not because she especially liked Win, he was only one of several possibilities, but because he was a good dancer. At eighteen, Susie was mainly interested in getting out and around, having a good time while she looked over the field; she had little trouble in doing this, because she was a pretty girl and popular.

She was put out with Win because he insisted on dancing too close; he would grab a handful of her dress behind and twist it so that it came up in the back, uncomfortably high across her calves and stretched tight across her front; then Win would move in, plastering himself to her until it seemed she could feel every inch of his hard, perspiring anatomy. Sweating, he had a slightly goaty smell; dancing with her back arched and her feet hardly touching the floor was uncomfortable, and a waste of time, when you liked to dance.

"Look, Win," she said. "Let loose. You're hurting my back." Win grinned and clutched tighter. He had his own ideas of what a girl ought to like.

"Win," Susie said. "Cut it out, will you? You're getting me laughed at."

She had already caught some wise looks, a couple of winks, from men dancing by, and no wonder, with her dress pulled up to the bends of her knees.

Win, it seemed, liked that. The way you handled a girl at a dance or anywhere else proved in the eyes of others, or in your own eyes, that you were male. It was something, apparently, that you had to keep proving, or you weren't.

He said, "Be yourself, kiddo, who cares who laughs?"

Susie wasn't one to take too much too long; she had Helga Larsen's reasonable temper, but she also had a fair slice of Martin Hoodless's hot one. She put both palms against Win's bulged-out chest and gave it a husky shove, so that he staggered away from her, barely saved himself from doing a fine pratfall right in the middle of the dance floor. Nearby couples began to roar with laughter.

Susie turned around, leaving the astonished Win standing there, and walked off the floor. She walked straight into the arms of a tall, slim fellow in the Coast Guard uniform, who had been standing by the door.

"For heaven's sake, dance with me," she said; and the young man grinned and said, "Yes, ma'am. It'd pleasure me."

Dancing with him was wonderful; he was light-footed himself, and he held her as if she were a feather.

"I'm Brant McIntosh," he said. "From Arkansas."

Susie nodded. The boys stationed at the Coast Guard Base over in Fairport were from all over the country. Some were Southerners; there was even one from Oregon. Susie knew quite a lot of them—they came to all the dances; nice fellows, most of them, and all a little lonely, because it took a while, always, for strangers to get acquainted in the town. She hadn't seen this one before; he must be new.

"I'm Susie," she said. "Susie Hoodless."

"I know who you are," Brant said. "I asked a fellow. I never reckoned my luck'd hold out long enough to get you to dance with me."

A hand fell on his shoulder, spun him around. It was Win Parker, with his jaw stuck right out into the world. He said, "I'm cutting in."

Susie said, "No, you are not, Win. I won't dance with you again."

"By god, you will! Or nobody else will."

"Oh, cool off," Susie said. "Go soak your head in a bucket. I came to a dance, not a wrestling match."

She didn't bother to lower her voice, and around them the laughter started again, which didn't help Win's temper. Being laughed at in public had never been a part of his plan. He said to Brant, "Beat it! Take your hands off my girl!"

Susie said, "I'm not your girl. So, you beat it."

"Lady wants to dance, fella," Brant said. His voice was soft, his smooth, darkly tanned face, pleasant. "Where I come from, we do what the lady likes."

"Where you come from!" Win's jaw muscles stood out in lumps; under each of his eyes was a bright red splotch. "Where in hell's that? You talk like some kind of a goddam negro."

"Down Arkansas," Brant said, "white people, colored people, they all sound the same."

He said this with an air of, politely, giving wanted information, and started to turn back to Susie. Win's fist flashed out, smacked into Brant's face; Brant sat down, hard, on the floor.

He sat there fingering his jaw, meditatively gazing up at Win. He said, "What's the use of that? It's a nice dance, folks having a good time. What you want to break it up for?"

Win was teetering now on the balls of his feet, his fists doubled and cocked, the fighter's stance.

"Come on! Up!" he howled. "Outside!" He stuck out his jaw some more. "I'll learn you fellers come up here, fool around with our clean, white American girls—"

The band stopped playing with a long roll on the drum, the signal to Fonce Hallock and Barty Jones, the town cops, that a fight had started. From nearby, Charles Kendall left his partner, came over, and laid a hand on Win's shoulder. "Knock it off, Win. You'll only start a free for all."

But Charles was too late. Fights between the local boys and the Coast Guard, the "foreigners," were fairly common. Four of the Coast Guard boys had been grouped by the door, five or six others dancing in various parts of the hall. They descended on Win, joyously, and the local boys joined in, defending local honor. Out of the melee, presently, crawling between someone's legs, came Brant McIntosh. He stood up, brushed dust off of his uniform.

"You like to go home?" he said to Susie. "Don't look like there'll be any more dancing."

"Did you get hurt?" Susie asked breathlessly.

"Stings some," Brant said. "What a wallop!" He rubbed tentatively at his jaw, turned his head to look at the fight.

By now, Fonce and Barty had arrived, wading in, breaking it up.

"It was an awful wallop," Susie said indignantly. "If I were you, I'd want to kill him."

"Why, no," Brant said. "I don't hold it against him. Wasn't me he hit. He had to hit someone, account of he couldn't hit you."

He grinned at her lopsidedly, wincing as the muscles stretched in his sore face.

"You think I ought to flail in there, pound him in the face with my fist," he said. He shook his head. "I'm sorry, fights and quar'ls don't make sense to me. I'll walk you along home, if you'd like to go."

Martin Hoodless had his own ideas about the man his daughter ought to marry. He had, as a matter of fact, made all of his daughters' lives miserable on that score; no wonder they had taken their husbands and left town. Susie was the last, because Hazel, the next youngest, was already promised to George Whitney.

Martin created. What in hell was the matter with Susie? Win Parker's father owned the biggest garage in town; the Parkers had money. And how about Charles Kendall? The Kendalls owned The Emporium, that big store catered to the rich summer-people. Charles, by tar, was sure-god willing.

As for Brant McIntosh, who was he? Nobody around here had ever heard of him or his folks; he might as well have been somebody from the moon. He talked just like a negro. And the state of Arkansas, where to hell was that? Who ever heard of it? Anyway, it was too far away to amount to anything.

"I've heard of it," Susie said. "It's a part of the United States to anyone who lives in the United States and not just in his own hometown. And the way he talks, he talks like a Southerner. Southerners do."

"Dammit, don't you sarse me—!" Martin began, but she was out and away from the house before he could say any more, calling back something as she went.

As well try to lay your fingers on quicksilver, as try to hold Susie at eighteen. She was the best-looking of all Helga's good-looking daughters and the gayest of that spirited lot. She was also the hardest to handle. For where Helga had kept the others in line, Susie had had only a series of older sisters to mother her—Pauline and Georgianna and Mary and Hazel: all hand-in-glove, all standing foursquare together against any kind of trouble; sometimes, a little too much for Martin.

They would, he told himself, lie the legs off of a brass teakettle for each other, and then stand up together and swear there were never any legs on there in the first place. No wonder Susie had grown up spoiled.

What she had called back to him as she'd left the house was, "Sweden's farther away than Arkansas!"

So Susie married Brant and brought him home with her to live. Since he was stationed in Fairport and often had duty at night, it didn't seem worthwhile for them to get a place of their own, even if they could have afforded it on a coastguardsman's pay. Besides, Martin needed a housekeeper. It didn't seem right to go off, leave him alone. George Whitney, of course, had his own place down at Kendalls', where he worked at The Emporium; he and Hazel were only waiting for Susie and Brant to get set up at the farm, before they moved down there.

Brant got leave, and he and Susie went for their honeymoon to his home. He wanted her, he said, to meet his great-grandmother. She was the only one of his folks that he'd ever talked much about. His mother was dead; his father married again.

"I been away from them," he said. "I got half-brothers, sisters, I ain't never seen." He spoke distantly, as if, Susie thought, he didn't want to see them. But his great grandmother, she'd brought him up after his mother died. He liked to tell about her.

Brant's home turned out to be a shack, set down in the middle of Arkansas. The whole middle of Arkansas looked to Susie to be a plowed field, and a muddy one at that. The time was spring—late March; the big rivers were in flood. In some little towns that the train passed through, she could see water the color of coffee with milk in it flowing through the streets; in others, Brant pointed out rows of freight cars sitting on the sidings, ready, he said, to take away the people, in case the rivers went too high.

"These people here really got it bad," he said, shaking his head, looking out the window as the train pushed deeper into the flooded land.

And Susie, peering past his shoulder, would see mile upon mile of muddy, flat, plowed land, crawled over by the sullen, milk-tan water, with here and there a tree—brown bark, no leaves, but covered with bright pink blossoms.

"Them's redbud trees," Brant said. "They in bloom now. It's their time to blossom."

Far away, across the mud and the water which sent back a sluggish gleam from the woolly sky, would be a small, gray-weathered shack, sometimes with the windows stuffed with rags, or with no windows at all, or maybe a front porch sagged in. It didn't occur to Susie that anyone would live in them; they looked more like shelters for stock, deserted, and as if they leaked.

But then, she puzzled to herself, I wonder where, outside the towns, the people do live?

Once they passed a shack quite close to the railroad; it stood on a rise and the water had come into its dooryard on the three sides that they could see. There was nothing on the rise but the shack, some odds-and-ends of clutter, a little redbud tree in violent bloom, and an enormous dead, pink pig, lying right by the door.

Oh, they must be pigpens, Susie thought, but Brant said again, shaking his head, "These folks sure got it hard. Look, that fella, there, he even lost his pig."

"You mean people live in these—houses?" Susie asked.

Brant glanced at her. "This's backcountry, honey," he said. "Most places, all over, when it's backcountry, you don't find palaces, I reckon."

He looked harassed, uncomfortable, and she wondered why. When they got to his father's house, she saw why.

They got off the train at a medium-sized city, not too far from the river. Here, too, were lines of freight cars on sidings, ready in case of flood; here, too, the water had come up into the streets. The Mississippi, Brant said, had backed up two other big rivers. "And it looks like it's going to get worse," he said, as they crossed the street from the station platform on a plank walk built up over muddy, creeping water.

"Won't get to Pappy's place, though," he went on, reassuringly. "He lives a smart piece back from the river."

"Well, I'm certainly glad to hear it," Susie said. She had been about to say that she didn't like the way things looked, all that water right in the street; but he hadn't made it sound like any emergency, and besides, she found, she needed her breath. March was hot in this part of the country, it seemed. You couldn't get a good gulp of air down; if you did, it felt soft and muggy, like breathing steam. She thought of a March day at home—the crisp, cold, snapping New England weather.

She didn't like, either, the taxi Brant hired—a battered Model T that looked as if it might fall apart at any moment; nor the look of its driver, a whiskery old individual in a floppy, big woolly-looking black hat. But taxis were hard to find, Brant said; he was lucky to get anything. People were on the move, especially the ones whose houses were flooded out down by the river.

They set out from town in early afternoon, she and Brant in the back seat of the Ford, with their suitcases, the driver up front sitting hunched down so far that the brim of his hat touched his shoulders on either side. A few miles out, they turned off the main drag into a side road, which went along fairly smoothly for a while, and then, suddenly, degenerated into a gravel track with what seemed to be the Mississippi River flowing over it in places, and full of great, gowelled-out holes. The Ford started to lurch and slam down, and one shock knocked the driver right out from under his hat, which seemed to hang motionless in the air for an instant before it dropped back onto his head. He patted it carefully into place and looked around with a toothless grin.

"These chugholes," he said, "they bad."

Bad! Susie thought. Why, you wouldn't drive to the gravel pit, at home, on this!

But she didn't say anything. She'd already made one mistake, she thought, asking Brant if people lived in those shacks; ever since, once in a while she'd noticed him giving her a silent, sidelong glance, as if he wondered how she felt about this place where his home was. So, now, she smiled at him and clasped his hand, winding her fingers with his. Maybe this was different from New England; so what? Places far apart from each other were likely to be.

They went for a long way. Suddenly the driver stopped the car, for no reason that Susie could see; they were out in the middle of the wild somewhere, no houses—only plowed fields on either side of the road that stretched for miles.

"That cart-road in there's mighty muddy," the driver said. "I don't reckon this old car go through it."

Brant was silent. He swallowed; Susie could see his Adam's apple move in a nervous gulp. On his face was the look that, in time, she was to know well—a kind of bewilderment that always came at a crisis, or whenever he knew he had to make up his mind about something. Then, to her surprise, he began taking off his shoes and stockings, rolling up his trouser legs.

"Come on, honey," he said. "Better take off yours, too. That mud'll ruin 'em. The rest of the way, we got to walk."

"But, Brant!" She stared around, a little wildly. These were the same forsaken, waterlogged fields she had seen from the train. "Where is there to walk to?"

"Pappy's place," Brant said. "It ain't but about half a mile."

He pointed, and now she saw the shack. One of these same gray, weatherbeaten ones. The cart-track to it was merely two deep, water-filled ruts, splitting the cotton fields, which seemed to lead away forever on either side.

"Never mind," Brant said. "I reckon it would be too muddy. You stay here in the car, honey. If Pappy's there, ain't gone with the mule, I'll come back and fetch you in the wagon. Fetch the suitcases, then, too."

He turned and splashed off into the mud and Susie sat staring after him. As early as this, she had found out that whatever you wanted was all right with Brant; he would go along. She didn't know if she liked it, altogether; sometimes it was like pushing a pillow. Kind of strange, after Pa, to have a man around who was so easygoing and soft-spoken. Nice, in a way; but Susie wished, sometimes, that Brant would speak up to her, she'd like that better. Now, something about the droop of his shoulders, the loneliness of his receding figure across the tremendous, watery landscape, caught at her heart.

She thought, He thinks I don't like it because his folks live in one of those shacks, and I don't wonder. But how was I to know? I've got another pair of shoes. I will not appear to his people in muddy bare feet.

She called out, "Brant, wait for me!," opened the car door, and stepped out.

The road was narrow with very little shoulder, the car parked close to the edge. Brant had got out on the other side; but what Susie had stepped down into was the gutter. It felt awful. Not cold, but gooey and squashy, and she kept on going down. For a horrified moment, she thought, I'm going to sink out of sight. But she found bottom with the mud to her knees, the water soaking her skirt.

The driver turned and looked at her, his mouth slightly open. He said, "You down off the hard, Missy."

"Well, whatever I am," Susie said, "Help me quick. I'm stuck," and as he started to scrabble himself together, she let out a good loud yell. "Brant, come back!"

Brant looked around. He came, tearing. He pulled Susie out of the mud minus her shoes, which he delved down and found; and Susie, watching him, thought furiously, What a country! I wouldn't live here if—if—

And then she saw him standing there, still with that helpless, bewildered look, holding in either hand one of her shoes, which weren't like any shoes on earth but only great, raggedy chunks of mud; and she began to laugh, the same rich shouts with which Helga and Helga's children had filled Martin Hoodless's house for years on end; so that the neighbors had come to say, "Them Hoodless kids, that Helga, they laugh at the darnedest things!"

She said, "Don't look so sunk, darling. If I'd had the sense of a dead hen, I'd have taken my shoes off, the way you said. It's no worse than clamflats, and I've waded plenty of those. Come on, now, let's go see your folks."

Brant grinned, a little sickly. He chucked the muddy shoes in the car. "I guess you better wait a while," he said to the driver. "I'll get back for the suitcases with the wagon."

Susie held out her hand to him and they set off down the muddy cart-track together. But he was still sunk. Or something. As they went, he grew more and more silent. Susie talked; she tried to kid him out of it.

"They'll think you married a mud-hen, honey. I did want to look nice for them to see, but look at me! Well, I guess they'll realize I couldn't help it, this road in here. Brant, honey, what is it? What's the matter?"

"I wish I hadn't come," Brant said. "I wish I hadn't brought you. I reckon I never thought how it would be. But Grama, she's mighty old. I've used up my leave, I might not get another chance to see her—"

"Hush, honey," Susie said. "You know everything's all right with me."

They were nearing the house now. Suddenly, he twisted his hand out of hers. "You let me go first," he said, and stepped into the track a few paces ahead. "And don't talk, now. You let me do the talking."

"Why?" Susie stopped in her tracks.

"Pappy's funny," Brant said. "I don't know—well, women, around him, they got to have manners."

"For heaven's sake! It's not manners in this part of the country for women to talk?"

"Not around Pappy," Brant said, briefly.

Not manners to talk, she thought resentfully; and lost all her good intentions. This time, she said it aloud. "Well, what a country!"

They came around a corner of the house and up to the door. The weather-rotted structure looked as if it had been dropped from a height, splattered and spread, the ridgepole sagged like a swaybacked horse, the windowpanes rag-stuffed; lonesome, unlived-in, fungus-grown.

Oh, poor Brant! she thought. Poor darling. If he's sunk, no wonder.

Then the door swung open and there stood a big old man.

He was Brant's father, no doubt of that. He was Brant at sixty, at seventy, however old he was; only he was a different kettle of fish; oh, different from Brant! No hesitation, no doubt, no bewilderment in his face. Brown, hard cheeks; big, sharp, straight nose; mouth, taut-lipped and thin, shut-to like a trap. Brown, rough-looking pants tucked into high boots brown to their tops with dried mud; brown shirt, with sleeves rolled up over leathery, hard-corded forearms, so that it was hard to tell, except by texture, where the shirt stopped and the arms began. Only the rifle, held loosely in the big, knotted hands was lighter in color than the skin of the arms.

Far from being unlived in, the house, Susie saw, was stuffed with people. Behind the old man, you could see nothing of the room, only faces, peering silently and curiously out past his shoulders and the crook of his arm; lower down, there were at least five children looking out between and around his legs.

Brant said, "Howdy."

The old man said nothing at all. He stood there, looking at Brant; his hands on the rifle might have been carved out of wood.

Brant said, "I got married. This here's my wife."

The old man didn't move his head, but the slits of his eyes flicked a little, flicked over Susie, flicked back to Brant.

"Whar she come from?" he said.

"She come from up where my Base is," Brant said.

"What to hell kind of a foreign country is that to come from?" said Brant's father. "She white?"

Susie couldn't help it. It was so exactly like Martin Hoodless; here she and Brant had crossed practically the whole United States to listen to the exact same thing. Susie laughed.

She said, choking, "When Brant and I got married, Mr. McIntosh, my father said, 'Where's Arkansas? Who ever heard tell of it? What to hell kind of a foreign country is that to come from?' "

The old man didn't even look at her; he was looking at Brant, and Brant's face was wooden.

"You ma'ied a Yankee," the old man said.

Susie said, "What if he did?"

She had laughed, but nobody else had; the laughter had trickled away to silence, somehow lonesome and forlorn. And what kind of a way was this for Brant's own father to treat him, when he hadn't been home for three years? And those people inside there, they must be his folks, what did they think they were doing, just peeking out, staring, nobody even saying hello?

"So what if he did?" she said again. "It's all one United States, isn't it? Up there, we like Brant. We made him welcome."

"Shut yore woman up, Brant," the old man said. "Or I'll do it for you."

Let him lay a finger on me, Susie thought. One finger. I'll scratch his eyes out, the old—

She was about to say so, but he turned; his massive, slow-moving body slid back inside the door, upsetting a couple of his children; he swung the door nearly closed and said, through the slit left open, "You better take your damn-Yankee woman back where she come from," and closed the door.

"Well!" Susie said. "Of all the—Brant! Oh, honey! Let's get away from here."

"I've got to see Grama," Brant said somberly. "Come this far, I can't go away without seeing her. You go on back to the taxi, honey. I'll catch you up."

"Brant," Susie said. "Oh, honey, come on. Don't fool with them. They aren't even glad to see you!"

But seeing his face, reddening under the tan, the helpless, hopeless, I-can't-do-anything-about-this-no-use-to-try look, she turned and went stumbling back along the rutted cart-track. Her stocking-feet felt cold now, all the clammier because the muggy, woolly weather made her sweat; her skirt flapped wetly around her knees. She cried nearly all the way back, but before she got close to the car, she fished her compact out of her bag and fixed her face, so that the taxi-driver wouldn't know she'd been crying.

He apparently was asleep, hunched down in the front seat. His big old hat looked as if it were empty, resting on his shoulders without a head in it.

And he'd better stay asleep, she thought, setting her jaw. Because I'm going to get some dry clothes on.

She was almost too uncomfortable to care whether he was or not. Even though she was still sweating in a soggy kind of way, her teeth were beginning to chatter. She opened her suitcase, got out clean stockings, dry shoes, and a skirt. At once she felt better; but in a moment she was too warm.

What a dreadful country! You couldn't even stand the weather.

There was no sign of Brant coming. The two ruts across the cotton fields reflected the white sky; at the end of them, the shack stood, closed, blank-windowed, not a sign of life about it.

Apparently, without her, they'd let Brant in.

Well, if he wanted to see his great-grandmother, that was natural; he was fond of her.

Susie waited. The taxi-driver slept on. The sun, if there was a sun behind that sheep's-wool sky, began to drop in the west. The light changed on the cotton fields. Susie thought of the road back to town, of what it might be like in darkness. The Model T didn't look like the kind of a car that would have very bright headlights. Brant must realize. Unless he was trying to find a place for them to stay.

And, she thought, with a little twist of panic, I don't think I want to be here, even with Brant, after it gets dark. Not anywhere near that awful old man.

For a while, she went over in her mind the things she wished she had told him, and hadn't. No, sir. She'd see the day she'd be scared of him.

But Brant didn't come.

Maybe, she thought wrathfully, at last beginning to be mad at Brant, maybe he plans to spend the night with his "kin" and leave me sitting out here in the car.

"Driver," she burst out. "Do your lights work?"

The hat slowly moved as the taxi-driver reared a little. He didn't turn around; he said, "What you say, Missy?"

"I said do your headlights work."

"No, ma'am. They ain't skurcely no good. No."

"Then I want you to turn around, take me back to town. Here, here's my husband's suitcase. Set it out there, alongside the road. And look, just twist this note around the handle for me, will you, please?"

The note, hastily scribbled, read, "I'll be at the hotel in town, when you're ready."

The taxi-driver was relieved, she could see that. He didn't want to make the drive back to town in the dark any more than she did. He did as he was told, silently.

The return to town didn't seem long, partly because Susie's rage, far from cooling, grew. One thing about Helga, or Helga's children, it took a lot, but once they got mad, they stayed mad for a good long time.

The car came over a slight rise in the long flat road, and she saw, in the twilight, the dark roofs of the town; but suddenly, the driver stopped and got out. He stood up on the running-board, looking.

Susie craned to see past him.

"What is it? What's the matter? Why are we stopping?"

"Them lights off," he said. "Power must have gone. Makes me wonder. Them rivers coming up all the time."

And she was suddenly aware of, beyond the town to the east, the great waste of dark coffee-colored water. The big rivers in flood.

For a moment, Susie felt real panic. Suppose the flood came in the night and she had to be taken away with the people in one of those freight cars? Where would she be taken? Off somewhere into this awful countryside, and how would she ever find Brant or get home again?

Oh, Brant, darling. Why didn't I wait for you?

In the town, the driver stopped at a corner. In the darkness, Susie made out the dim outlines of a street, sloping down.

"This here," he said, "this go straight down to the hotel. I don't much like to drive down there, right now. You stick to that plank walk, you be safe."

He pulled out her suitcase, stood for a moment looking uneasily down into the dark town.

"You find out from them hotel folks how to go, case you have to move in the night," he said.

"Is—is the flood much worse?" In spite of herself, Susie's voice quavered.

"That water come up plenty, since noon. See, Missy, there's a train due around now, if we ain't missed it, if they send her through. She comes, better get on her, go through to Memphis."

But I can't, she thought. If I go, Brant'll think I've walked out on him because I'm sore over what happened. Well, I am. Only I've got to see him, make sure he knows it isn't over the way his folks live . . .

The driver got into the Model T and drove away. Well, he hadn't been much, but he had been a link with somebody human, somebody to talk to. And this town, now, looked as if there weren't anybody human left in it.

But I'm not going. I'm' waiting for Brant, at the hotel.

And then, groping her way down the dark, sloping street, balancing her suitcase along the rickety wooden walks built up above the water, she heard the train-whistle. Presently, the train itself came into sight, sweeping around a curve, pulling up at the station. It was a long train, lighted the full length of it—except for a few flickers that might be lamps or candles, the only lights she could see anywhere in the town. They looked wonderful. But they were reflected in broken yellow stabs and daggers in the water that swirled black and scary down the street between the hotel and the station. The hotel was dark; the town looked deserted, lost, on a plain of darkness.

Susie crossed the wooden bridge over the street to the station platform. Under her high heels, the planks echoed hollowly. They quivered under her and swayed. They were only a few feet above the water now. The train was jammed, and it was in a hurry; she tumbled up the steps of a day coach just as it started to move.

She hadn't any ticket, of course; when the conductor came around, she had to buy one. She dug in her purse, silently thanking God that when Brant had taken charge of their money, something had told her to hang on to part of it, just in case.

Mad money, she thought shakily; and then, Oh, Brant, darling, I guess I always knew you aren't very sensible, and maybe in a crisis you can't think what to do in time; and you let me walk into something that was awful and could've been worse, without saying a word; but what you did, most people wouldn't see it, but it took courage to do; and this isn't mad money, honey, you hurry back as soon as you can.

It seemed to take forever to get home. She was deathly tired; she slept sitting up all the first night. When she woke, the train was still somewhere in the South; the first thing she saw when she looked out of the day-coach window was one of those shacks, all by itself in a muddy field.

"That's the way they live," she told herself stonily, staring out at it through sticky eyelids. "Well, I hate the South. I hate it all. And the people, too, just as much as they hate me. Dirty, busted-down, horrible . . ."

At Philadelphia, the train crossed through city slums before it got to the station. There were rows of old tenements, shabby, racked out.

Take them apart, set them out in a muddy field, she thought suddenly. They'd be shacks.

It was the same across New Jersey. Shacks here and there in the Jersey meadows; shacks speckled over the Massachusetts countryside. They were the same; and people lived in them.

And on the bus from Fairport home, in the familiar country, covered now with snow—for it was snowing, a late March storm, and snapping cold, so that she got out her topcoat and huddled into it, shivering—peering out of the bus window through the swirling flakes, she saw Hank Tiverton, the junkman's shack, where he lived with his wife and six children.

Really saw it, noticed it as it was for the first time.

Right here at home, just as bad, just as dirty, just as cluttered. Worse, because Hank Tiverton collected junk for a living and he had old cars, old sinks, stoves and refrigerators, and a lot of rusty chunks of iron dumped in his front yard. The other difference was, Hank Tiverton had a car; a Buick, which sat shiny and beautiful, in the refuse-scattered yard, outside his rag-stuffed front windows. That was what you'd always noticed before—the car; because people sniggered at it and asked each other how come Hank to have a car like that, and wouldn't you think he'd fix up his house first, but of course when the roof leaked him and his wife and kids could go out and keep dry in the Buick, and wonder if it's paid for . . . and wouldn't you know?

Tiverton's wasn't the only one, when you came to think of it. Around over the countryside, in woods, on the banks of streams, on the outskirts of town, there were lots of tumbledown places; they were all people could afford after they'd made the payments on the car, or all they bothered to fix up for themselves to live in. Because almost all of them had some kind of a car—the one nice thing, that they'd really gone overboard, put in everything they had, to get.

Well, was it a thing to be sniggered at, to be criticized for? Maybe it was; you know you wouldn't do it yourself.

Or did you know any such thing?

When the time came when people had been so banged around and beaten on, when their lives got so awful that they just sat there not caring whether they had one nice thing or not, that was the time for the country to start worrying, or if it didn't, it ought to. As it was, the new cars, or the new secondhand cars, sitting hub-deep in muck in the shabby front yards, were like a flag flying on a last outpost. A thumb-to-the-nose at things the way they were. We may be down, blast you, but we're a long way from being out. When we're out, we won't fly any flag.

My kids, she thought. Our kids, Brant's and mine, they're going to have a chance. They're going to be educated, so they can see things.

She got off the bus on the highway leading down into the town, to save herself the long walk back up to the farm, carrying the suitcases. She climbed the embankment by the road, pushed through the snow-covered alders, crossed the pasture under great-great-grandfather's horse-chestnut tree, and appeared to Martin just as he was sitting down to his solitary supper.

"Well, for godsake," he greeted her. "Where's your white nigger?"

Susie stared at him. "Don't you dare!" she blazed. "Don't you ever dare to say such a thing to me as long as you live!"

For ten days the newspapers continued to be full of headlines about the great Mississippi flood; a whole countryside was underwater; thousands of people driven away from their homes. Susie could see that water every time she closed her eyes; the sullen milk-tan creeping over the muddy land. It came up fast in the night; some people lost their lives. . . . She had bad dreams about the water, nights when she could sleep. There was no word from Brant.

She called the Coast Guard Base each day, knowing he would have to come back there; he wouldn't overstay his leave unless something had happened to him. To the curious, she explained that she and Brant had got separated by the flood; he had left her in town, she said, while he went down to see his family, not sure whether it would be safe to take her down into that wild country; the river came up in the night; I was lucky to get a train east. . . . She met Charles Kendall on the street and he said, "Susie, let me know, if there's anything I can do." He felt awful, she knew, because she'd married somebody else. It was nice of him to say that. Hazel and George Whitney got back from their honeymoon; Hazel listened, horrified, to the flood story; but not even to Hazel, who, except for Brant, was the closest person to her on earth, did Susie explain what had really happened. That was Brant's; it belonged to him.

Then, one morning, she called the Base; and Brant was there.

"Honey, for heaven's sake!" Susie said. "Why aren't you over here?"

"Well, they got me working," Brant said. "I just made it in time, before my leave give out."

"Well, thank the Lord you're back. I've been worried out of my mind. I suppose you couldn't have let me know, but—"

"I kind of put it off, calling on the telephone," Brant said, "knowin' I be here today; and then it was today, so I can come see you myself."

Put it off! Susie thought. You might as well throw up your hands—but that was Brant, he was like that. And nothing mattered anyway, but the dear knowledge that he was back. She felt dizzy with relief at knowing he was all right, with joy at hearing his voice.

"Well, you hurry over here, as soon as you can. As soon as they'll let you go. Oh, darling, did you find your great-grandmother? Is she all right?"

"Gone, Susie. She died on me," Brant said.

"Oh-h, Brant, honey!"

"I be over this afternoon, soon as I get off duty," Brant said.

He came strolling in at four-thirty, carrying a big bundle wrapped in dirty, tattered newspaper. Susie screamed and made a run at him, and he put the bundle carefully on a chair and took her in his arms.

He was so glad to see her; and he seemed proud of her because she'd had the good sense to get while the getting was good. The train she'd taken was the last train out; he himself had got caught by the flood.

"No knowing where you'd landed, you'd waited for me," he said.

That night, they'd hauled everyone in the town away off to hellangone into the backcountry.

"Taken me a year to catch up with you," he said, smiling at her, that same slow, endearing smile.

"I was afraid you'd worry, not knowing where I'd gone," Susie said.

Brant nodded. "Worried, all right," he said. "I was up and around all over town in a dugout. Nobody was left there, so I reckoned you'd gone with the others. Then I ran across that taxi-man, he said you'd taken the train east."

"Oh, darling," Susie began. And stopped. Because that look was back on Brant's face again. That look!

"Well, I think three years ago, that's the last time I see my old Grama," Brant said. "She mighty puny, even then. Well, ninety-five years old, that's a old person. She left you her 'Gyptian Cherry Tree quilt. Left it for my wife." He turned and began unwrapping the newspaper bundle he had brought.

In the middle of Susie's chest, something that felt like a round, cold, curdled spot began to grow. That awful old man, his father—you could see that Brant wasn't going to say a word about him. Or the way Brant thought Susie must feel about his people.

Well, if he won't, then I'll have to, she thought. Or it'll always be something hanging between us . . .

"Honey," she said. "I meant to wait at the hotel. But I couldn't."

"I don't blame you none for that," Brant said. "You done right to go."

"I did go off mad," Susie said. "I may as well say. It always makes me mad as hops to get scared, and I was good and scared. I just wasn't acquainted at all, and the country was so new and strange to me, and the people so—"

Brant's fingers, busy with the wrappings on his bundle, became still. He stood up.

"Lots of good people around there, Susie, honey," he said. "You wouldn't want to think they're all like my old man. He's still fighting the War between the States. He hates Yankees; but he hates colored people, too, and any man with a necktie on, and any man ever read a book. Don't you judge by him. There's always some mean-spirited people, any place, make a big noise, make trouble, give the place a bad name. Like anywhere. Like up North. I been around a lot up North, here. Give or take ten cents, I never could see much difference. Those ones, they're around all over. They keep putting ever'thing back a hundred years; seems like they want to. But those ones, they're not all of it. Don't you go around thinking so."

"No," Susie said. "And none of them, either my relatives or your kin, are going to drive any wedges between us, honey, split us apart. Just so you know how I feel."

Brant grinned. "That's right," he said, and shook his great-grandmother's quilt out for her to see.

"That pictures a song," he said. "A old, old Christmas song, about Joseph and Mary and the Child. When they start down to Egypt, Joseph, he's mad about her having a baby don't belong to him. Mary's thirsty, and then they come to some cherry trees, cherries just ripe, and Mary ask Joseph to pick her some. So he rant around, says her to let the father of her baby pick cherries, he ain't going to. So then the voice of the Child was heard, spoke right out of Mary, said, 'Bow down, Cherry Tree. So's Maw can reach her some cherries.' And all them cherry trees bowed low. Scared poor old Joseph," Brant said, the slow smile starting in his eyes, spreading to the corners of his mouth. "I always feel sorry for Joseph, seem like he had a mighty lot to contend with, couldn't blame him, nohow."

It was a pretty quilt—brown trees, with round red cherries and bright green leaves, painstakingly cut out and appliqued with tiny stitches, hand-sewn and hand-quilted. But it was filthy. It looked as if it had been hauled through seven cities.

Brant's eyes left hers, went back to the quilt.

"Grama, she used to tell the story," he said. "Those ones, there, trailing on the ground, like, they the ones bowed down. These ones here, these ain't bowed yet, but they going to. Grama, she washed it, time over time, and her grama, too. Only she was sick and puny. She got to be buried in her second-best quilt, Susie, she wanted for you to have this."

Before Susie could say that it was beautiful, that of course she could wash it, that she understood, the door opened and her father came in from the barn. Martin stopped dead in his tracks. He hadn't expected to see Brant; and the look on his face was exactly like the look on Brant's father's face, when he'd seen Susie.

"Well, hang Jeff Davis to a sour apple tree!" Martin said. "If here ain't Old Hookworm!"

Give or take ten cents, Susie thought, you can't see a difference.

She took a deep breath.

"Look, Pa," she said. "Brant's great-grandmother's left me her quilt. It's over a hundred years old."

"Jesus, it looks it," Martin said.

"Brant got that dirt on there, bringing it up out of the flood," Susie said. She slipped her arm through Brant's, twining her fingers with his. "It's a wonder he could bring himself, let alone carry a quilt. That's only Mississippi mud on there, it'll wash off, be as good as new."

"Sure will," Brant said. "That old-time cloth, it don't never wear out." He spoke with pride, his eyes on her, smiling.

"I wish I'd seen his great-grandmother," Susie said. "She must've been an awful nice old lady."

She stared at Martin, and Martin swallowed. He didn't often back down, but he did this time.

"Yeh," he grunted. He looked morosely at them, standing there together. Then he turned around and started for the door. "Well," he said, just before he slammed it. "I figgered the Mississippi River had come up over you."

Brant was drowned toward the end of the war, when his son, Carlisle, was six years old and the other two children babies. He fell overboard from a Coast Guard boat, returning to a Florida base, one evening in early darkness.

There was no reason that anyone could see for his falling overboard; the sea wasn't rough, outside of a light chop. The boat was merely coming quietly home, off patrol-duty. Most of the crew, which was a small one, were in the pilot shelter; and Brant had been roosting on the rail, near the stern, just sitting there, waiting to get back to the base. No one aboard heard any splash or outcry. The men in the shelter might not have heard a splash above the sound of the boat's engine and the rush of the water, but they certainly could have heard a yell, if there had been one.

They felt the propeller thud briefly against something, hesitate, and then rev up again; the engineer slowed down, but there seemed to have been no harm done. They figured, at first, that they'd run into a mass of weed in the water; someone called out to Brant to look astern, see if he could see anything. And then they discovered that he was gone. They circled the spot for hours, but his body was not found.

Susie was shattered. She felt as if she had been torn in two, one-half of her irrevocably gone, the other a stump, mutilated and aching. Weeks went by before the thing made any sense to her; but later, when she could think again, she couldn't help but know what had happened. You couldn't have lived with Brant as long as she had without knowing that anything he could put off, he did put off, as long as he could. He hadn't wanted to die; Susie knew that was the last thing he wanted. But by the time he got ready to do something about it, like open his mouth and yell, it was too late. He had, finally, succeeded in putting something off for good.

Susie wrote to his father, but never got any answer. No word, either of hate or love, came up out of Arkansas. The forces that had shaped Brant, banged him around, knocked the fight out of him, yet left him with a curious, indestructible gentleness, had no comment on his destruction.

And should have had none. They had no right to him. He belonged to me.

All these years after, times she was alone—like lying in bed at night before she went to sleep, thinking as she did, nowadays, not mostly of Brant, but of his children—Susie would find herself back there; back there in the days before she lost Brant. Lying in a certain way, on her left side, she could hear the beat of her heart. The steady, sturdy sound, in the place where, once, Brant would put his head down, listening.

"That go on, Susie. That don't change. That the sound of love."

Part Four

Carlisle slept the clock around. He might even have slept longer, if, in the late afternoon, Dr. Wickham hadn't dropped in to look at his knee.

Susie had been cleaning house, running the new vacuum around the living room. It was her day to clean and usually she was all finished by this time in the afternoon, but she had been dying to use the new vac, and she had had to leave that till last, so that the sound wouldn't wake Carlisle. If it waked him now, it wouldn't matter—he must surely have had his sleep out, by now.

"He's still sleeping," she said, regarding the doctor with surprise. "Did Pa call you, Dr. Wickham?"

She didn't think it likely that Martin had; though he might have, as a sarcasm, to point out to her that if anyone stayed in bed all day, he must be sick. She knew she hadn't called Dr. Wickham, and he wasn't known around town for gratuitous visits.

"Oh, just thought I'd drop around," he said. "Have a look at old Shirttail's leg." His voice was still a little hoarse from rooting, at the game.

"Why, what's the matter? It just looked like a badly skinned knee to me," she said, startled.

"Oh, you know the coach, he's like a broody hen. So I told him I'd come by. Besides, this town can't take any chances, right now, with that ballteam." The doctor wagged his head, grinning, to point up that no matter how jittery Alison might be, he, the doctor, wasn't, of course. "A pin scratch, we've got to make sure it's healed before they go to Boston. Where is this hero? He hasn't been walking on it, has he? I told him not to."

"No, he's been asleep since yesterday. But if it's a pin scratch, why shouldn't he walk on it?" Susie asked, puzzled. "He did seem awful tired, Doctor."

The doctor nodded. "They all were. My boy, Dick, was out on his feet and all hyped up. Fell into bed as if he'd been shot. Well, no wonder. That was some game, you know it? So-ome game. I hollered my head off, I'm still hoarse, you notice. But then, I haven't talked to anyone downtown who didn't sound like a frog. What's he do, walk in his sleep or something?" he added, watching her, his head humorously on one side, as she unlocked Carlisle's door.

Susie made no comment. What she'd locked the door for was her business. Though Doc Wickham probably guessed perfectly well why she'd done it. He just wanted to hear what she had to say about Martin, so he could repeat it to a couple of cronies down at the club. She had, she reflected, known Doc Wickham a long time.

At some time or other, Carlisle had been awake enough to yank off the top of his pajamas, which were tossed over the foot of the bed. He hadn't bothered to unbutton them, he'd just ripped; she could see a ragged strip of cloth hanging down with the buttons on it. Maybe he did it in his sleep, she thought, doubtfully looking at him.

His face was rolled into the pillow; his hair was damp with sweat. He had thrown back the covers, so that the upper half of his body was bare. Susie could see the bruises on his arms and chest; they seemed to have come out since last night, or maybe she hadn't caught sight of enough of him to notice. There was one, a spectacular greenish-purple, that covered the whole cap of his shoulder.

"Sweet Almira!" Doc Wickham said. "He sure had one peach of a workout! That damn Boone team, nothing but a bunch of thugs." He nudged Carlisle's shoulder. "Hi, fella. Come up out of it. Can't sleep forever."

Carlisle rolled over. His nose, also, was black-and-blue and slightly swollen; he had a magnificent black eye.

"Holy cow!" The doctor bent down for a closer look. "What hit you? That didn't show up, night before last. What have you been doing?"

"Whassa matter?" Carlisle mumbled. He stared upward glassily. "Oh. Whassa matter, am I sick?"

"Sick? A root'n-toot'n ring-tailed heller like you, sick? Poopsie!" said the doctor. "Yank that leg out of the pajamas and let me have a look at your knee. Hey, what's the idea, taking off the dressing? I told ya, keep it on there, didn't I?"

"It was filthy," Susie said. "I think he fell down in a mud puddle. I had to re-dress it, wash out that elastic thing you put on there. It didn't seem to me that was doing much good."

"Oh, sure. Take off the elastic bandage, sure. But I told him not to touch that dressing." The doctor was poking at Carlisle's knee, which was swollen, but didn't look so bad to her as it had last night.

"Okay," he barked. "What'd you do to it? And how'd you get that eye?"

"I fell down, like she said," Carlisle said, sullenly.

"Why in hell didn't you bring it down to me, then? Or let me know? All that pounding-around Alison's given you about keeping fit, hasn't any of it sunk in? Holy cow, the whole town's depending on you!"

Susie said crisply, "What's the matter with the knee?"

Dr. Wickham stopped short. He grunted, peering down at the knee. "Why, nothing. A little skinning here and there, a slight sprain. Some bruising of the tissues. Nothing serious. Nothing to worry about."

"Then why are you taking on so? I expect I'm able to take care of a skinned knee. It wouldn't be the first one I've done up. If there's something more than that, I want to know."

"There isn't."

The doctor began painting the knee with some kind of disinfectant which apparently stung, for Carlisle winced.

"Now, he's got to stay off this all he can for a couple days. Walk to the bathroom and around the house, if he wants to. But no traipsing, understand? No running around town to get your back slapped. In a couple of days, Alison's going to start to work the hell out of you. You've still got some more games to play. So you stay put."

"Okay," Carlisle said. He stared down at his knee. "That's all that's the matter with it, is it? That's for sure?"

"That's for sure. Couple days, you'll be as good as new."

He snapped his bag shut, got to his feet. "Want to see the living, uh, tar knocked out of those West-New England boys," he said. "That was a pretty handsome brand of ball you played the other night. Seen the papers, have you? The whole town's gone nuts. You go down Main Street, you'll probably get ridden around on somebody's shoulders. Wouldn't help that knee."

If Carlisle hadn't been lying down, Susie thought, Doc Wickham would without doubt have slapped him on the back.

"And no more foolishness." At the door, the doctor turned. "Like falling down in a puddle. Dead-Eye Mooney's got a shiner just like yours.

Fell down in the same puddle, I guess. Alison's no fool. Any more of that, you'll know what to expect from him."

Susie followed him to the front door.

"I don't think I like this," she said, eyeing him. "And it seems funny to me, your coming way up here for a skinned knee, when we didn't send for you, unless that knee is worse than it looks."

"I told you. Alison sent me. Just checking. Just in case. If it's the money that's worrying you, this is for free. You won't get any bill from me. Glad to do it. We're taking doggone good care of those boys until after the Boston play-offs, you know."

"Oh," Susie said. "And what happens then?"

"What happens—what d'you mean?" He glared at her. "Why, after that, if they're sick anytime, they come to me, get a bill, like anybody else. This—why, this is a town service, doing it for the town. All in this together, aren't we?"

He got into his car and drove off down the hill.

Susie stared after him resentfully.

I ought not to let him rub me the wrong way, she thought. But he does. He always has.

It was a good thing Martin hadn't been home. If he had run into Doc Wickham, come up here all on his own to tend to a skinned knee—Martin had his own ideas about what a doctor should be called for. And right now, he was building up like a thunder-squall. He had been, last night and this morning, suspiciously silent, even when she'd gone out in Carlisle's place and helped with the chores. Ralph hadn't got home until after supper. He'd made the mistake of saying brashly, in front of his grandfather, that he'd been celebrating; and Martin, instead of flying up in the air, as he usually did, had merely said, well, he was planning a celebration, too. This morning, he had climbed into his truck and gone off to make his town chicken-and-egg deliveries, without saying a word.

Susie sighed. She went back into the kitchen to get Carlisle's breakfast.

She got a magnificent one to take up to him on a tray, and was rewarded by seeing his eyes glisten at the sight of the grapefruit, toast and bacon, scrambled eggs and milk.

"Gee," he said. "I'm starved. I could eat a cow."

"Could you eat a steak, if I fixed it?"

"I sure could."

"On top of all that?"

"Uh-huh, I could."

Susie nodded. He was always too excited to eat much before a game; yesterday, at the banquet, he'd been too tired. It was a situation which had always concerned her; she couldn't see how a boy could do what Carlisle was called upon to do on a near-empty stomach.

"I'll bring it up," she said.

"No, I'll come down. I'm all right. The doc's an old hen. He's just a basketball fan, anyway."

"You do what he says. You ought to see yourself. You're a living sight."

"I am?"

"Yes, you are. Wait . . ."

She stepped across the hall into her own room and fetched her hand-mirror. "Just look at yourself," she said.

He studied with a kind of fascinated horror his black eye, his swollen, empurpled nose.

"Geez-Louise!" he breathed. "Looks like an old eggplant." He glanced sideways, caught Susie's eye, and they began to shout with laughter.

"Maybe I'd better bring up the steak raw, put it on that eye," Susie said, mopping her own eyes with her handkerchief.

"Not on your life! You bring it up raw, I'll eat it that way." He pulled down the corner of his mouth, made a tremendous face in the mirror. "Geez-Louise! Isn't that horrible!"

By the time Susie got back upstairs with the steak, the first breakfast was as if it had never been. Coming through the door, she was struck anew by the awesome face, beaming at her from the pillow.

"How on earth do you do it?" she asked. "How could anyone, possibly?"

"Huh? Do what, Ma?"

"Why, same old routine, day after day, night after night, doing nothing but play ball. I should think you'd be bored to death. And you come out of it all pounded to pulp."

"Hah, honorable wounds," Carlisle said. "Come home with your shield or on it. Quote. The Greeks."

"The Greeks!" Susie said. With a bump, she set the tray down on the night table, so she could straighten out the bedclothes rumpled up across his middle. "If any ancient history had ever stuck to you at all, except in splotches, you'd know it wasn't a Greek said that. It was a Roman."

"Who cares? Somebody was going into the arena—"

"Stadium, if you mean the Greeks. 'Arena's' Roman, too."

"Oh, arena, stadium, Sportpalast, Madison Square Garden. It's been going on a long time, Ma, and more people like it than don't."

"Okay, Shirttail," Susie said.

"How come history's so important, all of a sudden? You seem to be up on it, or something."

"Well, I read a book now and then, strange as it may seem. And if you remember, we used to talk about it once in a while. You used to be real interesting to have around the house."

Carlisle stared at her, a slice of steak arrested halfway to his mouth. "What's that mean, for petesake?"

"Why, I enjoy hearing about different things, the Carbon Fourteen test and Indian relics, things you used to like. Now there seems to be only one. My soul, honey, ball, ball, ball! Surely there's something else in the world."

"Well, sorry I bore you," he said. He looked quite put out, and Susie grinned at him.

"I don't suppose you do, really," she said. "But it isn't as if you didn't have a brain. You do."

"So they tell me, down at the school. I'm smart. I could do anything, be anything, with the brains I've got. Quote. Old Buggsy."

"Who?"

"Buggsy. Mr. Berg."

"Well, for heaven's sake, if that's his name, call him by it."

"Yeah. So it does me good to hear a lot of old has-beens and never-wases gobbling around fixing up my life. Be a lawyer, be a chemist, be a doctor. Let 'em learn how to do their own jobs before they go futzing around with me. Heck, I know what I'm going to be, and that's the only thing the school does teach, lucky me. I'm going to be a pro ballplayer."

"What?" Susie said, flabbergasted.

"Sure. You heard me."

"I thought we—I thought you were going to college."

"I am. That's where I'll get my experience. Most of the pro teams, they're college men. The poop is, even a good high-school player don't get much of a break with the pros till he's had four years on a college team."

"I see. But what puzzles me, how are you going to get into a college, if you don't keep your high-school grades up?"

"Oh, they pass you," Carlisle said, bored. He glanced at her face and his voice rose a little. "Look, Ma, let's face it. You ever know a good ballplayer not to pass, down at the school? And I'm Shirttail McIntosh. In like Flynn."

"That isn't right. And you know it."

"So what do I do, Ma? Is it up to me that the only teacher down there who absolutely knows his job cold is the coach? Look, the whole town, they don't give a crawdad whether it's a school or not, what they want is a Championship team. So they see to it that the coach is a darned good one, and he's who they pay the money to, and the rest of the teachers are oddballs, whoever they can get to come for what money they got left."

Don't give a crawdad, Susie thought. It was Brant used to say that. Well, Carlisle couldn't remember Brant that well. He must have got it from me.

"That's how you feel," she said.

"That's how the cookie crumbles. Shoot, Ma, who would you rather learn from? A man who's been right up there at the top, name on the sports page all over the country? Or old Ma Beasley?"

"There's Mr. Berg," Susie said. "He's a competent man, with a science degree."

"Oh, Buggsy!" Carlisle said. "That Jew!"

"That does it!" Susie said. "Don't you dare spout that ignorant foolishness to me! Don't you bring it into this house!"

"Huh? What did I say?"

"Why, in one breath you sneered at Ma Beasley because she's old and in the next at Mr. Berg because he's Jewish. Makes me wonder who you think you are!"

Carlisle did not look up. He muttered, "Oh, for petesake, another creaming." The expression of mild surprise on his face changed to one of tolerant patience and boredom.

"Don't you lie there and look at me like that!" Susie said. "You realize you might just as well say it out loud, 'Poor old Ma, she doesn't know anything, so what she says doesn't mean anything'? Well, you listen to me. I've known plenty of he-men who go around sticking out hairy chests, belittling people who aren't just exactly like themselves. They don't really know what anybody else has to say, because if it doesn't jibe with what they think, they don't listen. That's ignorant, sweetie-pie. It's bad manners. It bores me out of my life."

"Uh-huh," Carlisle said. "Okay, Ma."

"And it's all very well for you to say you don't need to know anything, you can play ball so the athletic people at the colleges will take care of you, but it seems like a poor idea to me."

"Ma, you worry too much."

"Maybe I've got cause to. There's been a big change in you in the last year. It sticks out some. The way you talk about the school being no good, and the teachers, as if you were fifty miles up in the air, looking down! Why, I've talked to Mr. Berg, he's a nice young man, and a smart one, and Ma Beasley I know about firsthand—she taught me, too, remember? And one thing I learned from her was not to look down on anyone different from me, with a different religion, that is. That's why I wonder sometimes who Shirttail McIntosh is. S-Shirttail!" she sputtered, found herself sputtering, and pulled up short. "Just in case the man you're studying with now, the one who's right up there at the top, hasn't let on anything about things like that. Are you listening at all? Have you heard a word I've said?"

"Sure. I read you loud and clear." He did not look up from what appeared to be a deep study of his fingernails.

"Doesn't it mean anything, then?"

"I'm a bore around the house, and I don't like Mr. Berg; you don't like Mr. Alison, I guess."

"I don't know Mr. Alison. I just wonder where you're getting all these notions. If it's from him, then I certainly don't like the way he thinks."

"You don't know how he thinks! He don't care what a man is, for petesake! Why, on that pro team, the one he was on, they even had two-three jigs."

"Jigs?"

"Sure. Jigaboos. Negros. He played ball on the same team, didn't make an atom of difference to him."

"Oh," Susie said. "It was certainly nice of Mr. Alison not to mind. Wasn't it?"

She turned her back on him and walked to the window.

"Talk about listening! You don't listen!" Carlisle stormed at her. "He says you got any of that snob in you, forget it, you better stay out of pro ball. Because jigs are some of the best ballplayers in the world, that's all! Why, a man could be a monkey for all he cares, long as he can play ball, win games, I've heard him say so!"

Susie spun around. "All I can say is, that before a man's entitled to patronize anybody, he'd better be pretty sure who his own folks were a few generations back," she said. "He could be anything, for all he knows, and so could you and so could I. And let me tell you, Mr. Shirttail McIntosh, in like Flynn, it's knowing about it that makes any difference, and not one other single solitary thing!"

She brought up short, aware of her flaming anger, and of Carlisle's, too. The discussion had got out of hand, slanted off in the last direction she'd ever expected it to take. She started to pick up his tray, saw that her hands were shaking, and set it down again. Carlisle hadn't noticed; he was staring sullenly past her, as if she weren't there at all. She couldn't trust herself to say any more, and since it was clear that he wasn't going to, she picked up the tray again and carried it down to the kitchen.

She stood for a moment by the kitchen sink, looking out the window at the gray sky.

Gray and watery, like that sky in Arkansas, that day; only the countryside under it was rolling spruce-clad hills, spotty with melting snow; not flat, limitless, mud-clogged cotton fields. The air outside was damp and cold, not damp and muggy. But it was all the same sky and all the same country, if you thought so. You couldn't see ten cents' difference.

Oh, Brant. Brant, darling.

I've tried to bring him up to respect something besides his own. You couldn't help me if you were here, you couldn't even help yourself. You said it wasn't any use to try.

He's got something you didn't have. He's got fight. But the thing you did have, the precious thing I valued, that made me love you and not forget, I'm afraid for. Maybe he's growing up too fast for me to keep up with. Maybe everybody gets it pounded out of him as he grows. But you didn't let it get pounded out of you, and you could have.

Oh, Brant.

It takes more than being slammed around to make a man. A man lives in the world, not just in one town, or in one house in that town . . .

After his mother had gone, Carlisle lay staring moodily out the window.

Well, one more creaming. What did one more amount to?

What does she think I am—Superman?

Three jobs to do, any one of which would take all the time there is, if I did it the way it ought to be done.

Grampa and Ma, the teachers and the coach, all raving at me at once. No matter how you hacked away at it, nobody was ever satisfied. The creaming you got depended on which one of them caught up with you first.

Ma was sure on the warpath. Better make a gesture.

He yanked a pile of textbooks over onto the coverlet beside him, opened *Hamlet.*

Picture of William Shakespeare, bald-headed guy with whiskers. World-famous man. TV star of his day, or whatever they had instead of TV. Had one thing he could do better than any other guy, so the world remembered him, studied him in the schools.

Funny-looking.

Almost all great men, if you believed the pictures in the books, stuck around on the walls in classrooms, looked funny. Anyway, old. Bust of Julius Caesar in the assembly room, crappy wreath of leaves around his bald head. Looked like Joe Crow the Indian. William McKinley. Woodrow Wilson. Pinch-glasses. This guy Shakespeare.

How far would they get today? Stack him up alongside of Elvis or Jimmie Rodgers? Even old Jack Benny looked better than this guy Shakespeare. One thing about great men nowadays, they were at least halfway good-looking.

Wonder how I looked on TV?

Wonder if they keep the film somewhere? Maybe you could get hold of it, have it run off like a movie. Be nice to see how you looked to other people. How you looked to Debby Parker. Pretty good, maybe. At least, she said you did.

Seventeen baskets. In one game. That was a state record. So hang it up. It hadn't been done before, not in this state, in a Tournament game. The world would remember that, all right. Until somebody else did better.

"The world will little know nor long remember—"

Now, what the heck was that?

Oh, sure. Speech he'd made in assembly, last Memorial Day. Did pretty well with it. He had a good voice.

Thought once he might learn to be an MC, an announcer, if he could get the training.

But how?

Miss Bates, the English teacher. Read everything pop-eyed and reverent, in a voice like a dying calf; as if it were the Bible; skipping the dirty parts, of course.

This stuff. This *Hamlet*.

> SCENE I.
> *Elsinore. A platform before the castle.*
> *Francisco (at his post). Enter to him, Bernardo.*
> *Ber.* Who's there?
> *Fran.* Nay, answer me. Stand and unfold yourself.

Yeah, unfold yourself. Oh, crap!

From somewhere an automobile horn sounded, three short, three long, three short, and Carlisle rose up in bed, galvanized.

That was Debby. She was parked out in the highway beyond the back pasture, blowing for him, their private signal. He got out of bed, testing his knee. Not bad. Stiff. A little exercise would limber it up. Doc Wickham—anything he said was for the birds. He was just a basketball fan; what he told you was best for the fans, not best for you.

Carlisle dressed, taking care not to make any noise that Susie could hear. He opened the door to the back stairs, listened, and tiptoed down.

His knee bothered him on the rough ground up through the pasture, but it was feeling better with every stride. He crossed the brook, noting as he passed that Grampa hadn't been back to do any more work on the chestnut.

No, and he won't be. He'll leave the dirty for Ralph and me. Gwan out and cut wood. Gwan out and cut wood. Till we go nuts.

He glanced at the tree's butt with distaste, feeling the beginning of a massive boredom, cut into the alders, and slid down the embankment, coming out into the highway a few yards from Debby Parker's parked car.

Debby saw him and began to laugh. "Oh-oh," she said. "You ran into a tree."

"Nope."

"Jerry?"

"Uh-huh."

'That goofball. He's telling his side around town. Your grandfather cut a tree down on you."

"Thereby fixing the ballteam, because he doesn't want me to go to Boston. Tell Jerry to be my guest."

Debby glanced at him. "People are all ready to fight," she said. "My father was ranting around the house this noon."

"Tell 'em all to go fry. Where'll we go?"

"Fairport? Want to eat?"

"Nope. Just ate. Anyway, no money."

"I've got some."

"Nope."

Debby always had plenty of money, a lot more than he did. Her father was Win Parker, the garageman; he was loaded. His son Bill might be the boy and one honey of a ballplayer, but Debby was the apple of Win's eye. She was a pretty girl, smart in school; Bill was a year older, but she had long ago caught up with him and would graduate this year in the same class. Win saw to it that she had nice clothes, money to spend; after some argument, he had even given her a car, and exactly what she wanted, too—a small, English-made car, which she loved and talked to as if it had been a person named Katy.

"Look at that little old doll," Debby would say, patting the steering-wheel. "Little old Katy, that living doll. She goes through while the others have to go around."

Debby and Carlisle knew each other so well that most of the time they had no need to talk. They had been going steady since grammar school, for five years now; going steady was the custom. You had to have a solid front, they would have said, if it had ever been necessary, or possible, to put the reason for it into words. It went without saying; you had to have somebody you could be sure of. Besides, if you weren't set by the time you were a freshman in high school, you were out of luck; everybody except the schmoos was paired off by then. Out of luck like old Ralph, who hadn't bothered in grammar school and now didn't have anyone; not that he let on to care a hang.

Debby did not even need to glance at Carlisle now to know that he was nerve-jangled, stiff with tension. Worried, too, about his knee. The limp was what she'd noticed first, when he came down the embankment and got into the car.

"Okay, let's just ride," she said, letting in the gears. "Look at that little old doll! Look at old Katy! She'll pick up like that right in the middle of a hill."

"Little but mean," Carlisle said. He grinned, lopsidedly, settled back, relaxing, on the seat.

They went a long way. Beyond Fairport, the highway angled off northwest toward the new turnpike, in the western part of the state. Katy's speedometer crept up past sixty; to sixty-five. The red Danger light let into the dashboard blinked on. Debby, eyes on the road, didn't look down. The British, in her opinion, were a conservative and contradictory people; they built a beautiful little car that would do ninety—maybe more, but ninety was the best she'd done on the turnpike before the cop stopped her—and then they stuck in a red blinker that flashed red if you went over sixty. It didn't make sense.

She was sensible, Win Parker's daughter, and a realist. Growing up in Win's household, where what was true, what was honest, had to have Win's approval before it was either; where things done, actions taken ostensibly for her good, were not for anyone's good except Win's, or for the indulgence of one of his whims, Debby had learned realism young.

Win was boss in his household; his womenfolk did as he said, thought as he thought. Or else.

Years ago, his wife, overwhelmed by commands, ideas, daily opinions, delivered usually in a blast at her, had given up. Evelyn Troy had been a gay, pretty youngster; she had walked into marriage blindly, not even seeing the trap snap shut until it was too late. She had been crazy about Win; big, bluff, masterful Win. At first, when he ironed her out, she either didn't mind, or she argued back in a reasonable and affectionate way, which she found out, in short order, didn't do. You didn't argue with Win; it was like arguing with a bulldozer. Through the years, her reasonableness and affection had changed, first to bewilderment, then to anger, finally, to apathy. At forty, Evelyn Parker again did not mind. Mostly silent, she remained wrapped up in six or seven minor ailments, in her son Bill, and in Heaven, where the weary go to rest.

Debby loved her parents; she regarded them, also, with a cool, unbiased eye. She had had to learn, early, that neither of them believed facts; facts, to them, were what they believed. Her mother lived in Never-Never Land, in which God the Father and Bill the son mingled in a rosy haze. If ugliness, or reality in the shape of Win Parker, invaded, Evelyn drowned it all in streams of gentle tears, which turned off gently when the trouble had passed by.

Win, however, was something else again. His daughter Debby read him loud and clear. She knew he loved her—oh, Bill was the one who was going to amount to something, Bill must have the best, Bill must go to Harvard; he was the boy, he would have his way to make in the world. Debby could go to college if she wanted to—any college, let her pick it out, play around with that, it didn't matter. All she would ever do would be get married. Not that Win ever skimped her; he spoiled her in everything. But there was to be a difference between her and Bill, a difference in the end product, which she contemplated thoughtfully.

I'm going to get married, raise children, so my education doesn't matter? I'm going to be somebody's wife, so I might as well stay ignorant?

Looking around her at some mothers' sons, Debby concluded early that anything she could learn would help.

At seventeen, Debby Parker was two people. She was the dutiful daughter, just disobedient enough to keep Win's ego satisfied, so that he could blow her up into the air, haul her back into line, get a kick out of it; the pretty, clear-eyed daughter who heard with no comment the hypocritical, full-of-humbug, set-as-a-rock notions, based on no logic, open to no change; who listened, while deep down, out of sight, inside, lay buried a hard, secret knot of personal integrity.

He's your father, you love him, said one of the two people in Debby. You owe him everything.

And the other said, Watch him, he's your enemy, he'll make you like himself if he can; don't let him know about anything you believe or value, because he'll do his best to clobber you, the way he clobbered Ma.

She learned this, in sorrow and bewilderment, when she was quite small.

On occasion, the way Win functioned paid off for Debby. It had paid off in the matter of Katy, that doll.

Down at his garage, Win had a lot of fun with those little foreign cars, whenever one was brought in for service, a road check or a lube job. It always tickled him, the way the owner would tiptoe around, scared to death the work wouldn't be done right, bothering the mechanics and shoving under their noses the service manual put out by some British, French, Italian, or whatever this-and-that foreign company made the car.

"Look," the owner might say, his finger on the place on the diagram. "That. Right there. That's an oil cup. It takes motor oil, not grease. See. It's plainly marked."

And it always was, the manufacturer's instructions nine times out of ten supplemented by the owner's check-mark and the words, underlined, DO NOT PUT GREASE IN THIS CUP.

Win's mechanics would nod, always polite, always deadpan.

"Oh, sure, sure, Mister. Don't worry. We service a lot of these foreign jobs in here."

But unless the man was himself a mechanic and stayed around to watch what was done, he drove his car out of Win's garage with a good, sound American lube job done on it, grease where grease should be, like in a Plymouth or a Chevy or a Ford. Later on, when the weather got a little colder, maybe, and his steering-wheel stiffened up, because its lubrication system, designed for oil, was jam-packed with Grade A grease, shot in with a good, efficient compressed-air grease gun, the man, if he wasn't a tourist and a thousand miles away at the time, might go back to Win.

Win was always sympathetic.

"I dunno, Mister," he would say, his hand, gentle as a mother's, turning the wheel, which, by now, might be making an odd grating sound. "These foreign cars, I dunno. You got a worn part in there, that's for sure. Probably means the steering-gear'll have to be rebuilt, but where, I dunno. I can't do it, my wrenches are all too big, and I don't stock the parts. Take me three months to get 'em, I dunno but more. They tell me there's an agency for these jobs in Boston. I don't know how good their mechanics are, that's the sixty-four-thousand-dollar question. But they'd have the parts and the tools to fit her. You drive careful, you can get her as far as Boston."

Watching the car drive away, he would grin. "Wowie!" he would say. "There's a guy going to do twenty miles per, for the next five hundred miles. Geez, if they're going to send them damn sardine-cans over here for the snob trade, why don't they build 'em so's an ordinary garage can service 'em? Oil in the steering-column, for godsake!"

Last Christmas, Win had given Bill a convertible. Debby didn't even bother to find out what he'd planned to give to her; she'd put in for a car, too. It wasn't fair that Bill should be the only one to get a convertible, when she could drive just as well, and wanted one just as much, and Win could afford it. So she had asked Win, and had got a flat "No, dammit!" for an answer. Bill was getting a car for the same reason that he didn't have to do housework or pick up the mess in his own room. He was a boy.

But when Win found out that Debby didn't want a car like Bill's—what she wanted was one of those finicky little English cars—he said yes. He liked to give her things. Things . . . they were what she had no lack of. And he could give her an English car without relaxing any of his principles. A good, clean-built, powerful, American-made car, that was for a male—that was for Bill. Any car made outside the United States, of course, wasn't a car at all. It was a toy, good enough for a girl to play around in. If that was all she wanted, it was all right with Win.

He found, too, when he bought Katy for Debby, that he got quite a charge out of having an English car in the family. Seemed to show that he knew what was what, could afford something imported if he felt like it. When Katy was down at the garage for service, people stopped to look.

"Yeah, that's my kid's car, belongs to Deb," Win would say. "English-made. British steel. She gets thirty-five, thirty-eight miles to the gallon."

Sixty miles or so up the river highway, Carlisle came out of his silence. He stretched and yawned, loudly, flexing his arm muscles. Debby felt his elbow brush her cap.

"Phew, I feel better," he said, blowing out his breath. "I was all ready to flip."

"I thought you might be. Are you just tired, or has everybody been bleeding all over you?"

"Oh, little bit of both, I guess. Has Jerry been mousing around the gym, you know?"

"Mm-hm. Bill said he was."

"He's got to Alison then, with that yarn about Grampa."

"I expect so. It's all over town."

"Well, Grampa's used to trouble. He'll be tickled to death to take on the whole town."

Debby said nothing.

"What am I supposed to do? Run around town, tell people Jerry's a liar? He gets any sorer at me, we won't even be able to play ball on the same team. Run and tell Alison we had a fight? The way I feel, one more creaming, I bust right out through my crust. You've got to remember, we've got some more games to play."

Debby was watching the road ahead and, presently, saw what she was looking for, a side road off the main highway. She turned the car into it.

"Hey," Carlisle said. "We'll get stuck down here, maybe?"

They knew the road well, having come here often, but not in February. Last summer, in the days before Katy, Debby had driven her father's car down here. It was a secret place, far away from home, where they could find privacy; it was also a discontinued river road that led down to an old lumber yard on the bank. As with any gravel road, the bottom was likely to go out of it after a winter thaw.

"Ho!" Debby said. "Katy can go places the big old bathtubs can't. Watch this little old doll!"

He watched while she put the car down the road. The steep ruts ran with water, mud sloshed under the tires; now and then, the transmission scraped along the high crown of the road, and Debby eased off, careful, avoiding rocks, searching for traction with the wheels. They stopped on the riverbank at the road's end, and Carlisle grinned.

"Pretty cool dolls," he said. "Both of you."

He kissed her, letting his lips linger, feeling the tiredness and the tension drain away. This was always the way it was with him and Debby. After he'd been with her a while, whatever had been stewing around, clobbering him up, was gone. After a while, there was just Debby; and then his own daydreams.

This far north of the river mouth, the ice was still solid, sullen, grainy white from bank to bank; but it had a look of thaw about it, and in the quiet you could hear a sound of water moving under it, far off, secret, sleepy. The grass in the little clearing by the rotting wharf was a shabby-moth-eaten tan. It was hard to believe, now, how this place looked when it was green, full of violets, walled in like a room, with alder leaves. When that time came, the last game would be over; they would have the All-New England. The Championship. The big one.

He leaned his chin against the top of Debby's cap, feeling her, warm and secure, against him, looking off over the river.

And I'll have my athletic scholarship to college. And go. Away from this town. Away from Grampa's damn hen farm. Away from being split in seven pieces at once, because there's too much to do, stuff to be done. Away learning to play pro ball. That one thing and nothing else.

Reminded suddenly of something, he lifted his face from Debby's cap. "Did you get the chem paper done, honey?" he asked.

Against him, Debby stirred. She leaned back and sat up. "Yes. It's in the glove compartment."

"Good, don't let me forget it, will you? I'll have to copy it tonight, so the fellas can hand it around tomorrow. Hey, what's the matter? You look all shook up."

He reached for her, but she caught both his hands in hers. "No, wait. Let's talk. You aren't thinking about me anyway. I can tell."

"The heck I'm not!"

Debby grinned at him. "Phooey," she said. "After a game, you always have to cool for about three days. I'm used to it, the lord knows. But look, there's something. You know I don't mind doing your science papers, because you've got more to do than you possibly can, but—"

Carlisle drew back. "Why yak about it now? The ball season's almost over."

"Mr. Berg knows about the phony papers. He's known all along."

"So what if he does? What's his gripe?"

"Well, I expect it's his job, for one thing."

"Oh, Deb, pack it up, honey. I'll pass. They slide you through, and you get a scholarship if you play good ball."

"I know all that. But Mr. Berg says, a scholarship, if it's on phony grades, you can't keep it. If you don't know your math or science, you'd be lucky if you lasted a semester."

"What is this?" Carlisle said angrily. "Some more of Buggsy's crap! That greaseball doesn't know anything about athletics. The colleges do what the high schools do. They don't flunk out a ballplayer."

Debby gave him a long look. "My father," she said thoughtfully, "he says 'kike.' Or 'egghead.' It's all one to him."

"So what if it is?"

"I like Mr. Berg."

"Okay, I'm sorry I called him a greaseball. Except, he is, you know. And we're all pretty sick of him trying to futz up the ballteam."

"He's only doing what he's paid to do, isn't he?"

"Well, he won't be paid to do it much longer, if he doesn't change some. And I don't think much of his throwing off to you behind my back—"

"Oh, Carl, stop it! Just the sound of it makes me tired. Or it would, if I weren't so scared."

"Scared? What about?"

"We always said we'd go to college together, it was the only chance we had to get away—"

"I still want to. So what gives?"

"I've got to get away. My father climbs all over me, he can't stand the way I think. And I hate to say it, he's my father, but I can't stand the way he—I can't stand people who see somebody with something they haven't got, maybe it's only good grammar, so they don't try to make themselves better, they cut the other fellow down to size. Call names. Greaseball. Kike."

Carlisle leaned back in the seat, put both hands behind his head. He said, "Uh-huh."

"I don't mind if you have things of your own you don't want to talk about," Debby said slowly. "People do. I do. But you could say so. You don't need to say, 'Knock it off, you don't know what you're talking about.' Because that's what 'Uh-huh' means."

"Okay. Everybody else has been bleeding all over me, you might as well. Only, why do you have to pick now? You've got to remember, I've got some more games to play."

"Oh, the game," Debby said. 'The game, the game, the great game!" She beat her hands softly, impatiently, against Katy's steering-wheel, and Carlisle stared at her, astonished.

"What's the matter with you? That's a heck of a way to talk!"

"I'm as bad as anybody," Debby said. "I know. I fall down and screech and yell whenever there's a game and we win it, and I bawl when we lose, and when I see you playing, I—but it's—it's—"

"Look, Deb, we were top-seeded team—we got the Championship. You don't get up there by spreading yourself all over the map."

"I know. I know you don't have time to do other things. But do they have to get lost?"

"Ah, forget it. C'm here. Be my girl."

There was a long silence in Katy, at the end of which, Carlisle moved impatiently to his own side of the seat.

"Okay," he said. "Have it your way."

"I'm sorry," Debby said. "I tried to tell you. I'm just scared. I can't help thinking—"

"You can tell old Buggsy from me that it isn't his kind of crap will get me to college now. Playing ball will."

"What if you lose, down in Boston? What if your knee bothers you, or—"

"You worry too much. My knee's okay. If it bothers, a shot of novocaine'll fix it."

Debby said nothing for a moment. Then, she leaned down and started Katy's engine.

"What am I?" Carlisle said. "How much do people think I can do, for petesake?"

"I know you can't do any work now," Debby said. Her voice came, clear, over the slow throb of Katy's engine. "The way things are. I've helped. I want to help. I only tried to tell you—"

"So what's to be scared about?"

"What scares me is, you don't care. What you want to depend on now, it—you could lose it. I mean, a lot of ballgames that people have got excited about, until nobody thinks about anything but championships and write-ups in the paper, and pictures of this and that, stuff in the town, stuff that means a darn lot more to our parents than it ever could to us—"

"Well, what if it does? They got to have something. They get old, stunk off with their lives, they've got to have something to go nuts over."

"So nobody gives a hoot about you, not really, whether you graduate, or what happens. All they want is for you to win their crazy bets for them."

"So maybe that's so, I'm riding it on in. I'll make college. If I don't, I can always go out for pro ball."

"And just be a big, beautiful hunk of ballplayer for always and always," Debby said.

"So you don't like a big, beautiful hunk of ballplayer?"

"That's the trouble," Debby said. "I do."

She slipped Katy into gear, set her to climbing the steep, muddy slope to the highway.

"Look at that living doll!" she said. "Look at that little old girl climb!"

Part Five

Out behind Martin Hoodless's third broiler-house, the farthest one from the barn, was a grove of young spruces. Twenty years ago, this had been a stand of mature hardwoods, which Martin had logged off and sold for saw-logs at a fine profit. Softwood seedlings had replaced the grove; these were now nearly big enough to be cut again, this time for pulpwood. Underbrush grew thick around the edges of the grove. Inside it, the boles of the spruces were close together, tall and clean, except for tufts of healthy growth at the tops. Martin had not thinned the grove much, knowing he would get longer, cleaner sticks that way, which he would cut as soon as they were thick enough to meet requirements at the paper mills.

In the middle of this grove, cunningly hidden in an underbrush-surrounded clearing, to which he had been careful to make no beaten path, Ralph McIntosh had made a place to practice basketball.

He had nailed up a wooden backboard to a tree and had fastened to it an iron barrel-hoop of the right size and an exact measurement from the ground. The basketball he was using belonged to the high-school gym. The gym had a lot of basketballs; so far, the team managers hadn't missed this one.

On a day early in the ball season, just before Christmas, at practice, when the air in the gym was full of basketballs, Ralph had tried a long shot from the side, a wild one, which had struck the floor in a far corner and bounced straight out the open window. He'd thought someone besides himself must have noticed it, of course; but nobody had, and he was about to leave the floor to go after it, when the coach stopped shooting-practice, and laid out a game. Ralph, being the center of the second-string team, couldn't leave just then.

Ralph had been made center only because he was tall. He had been slow at first in starting to grow; for a long time, Carlisle had been taller than he; but during the past year he had shot up, his mother said, out of all reason. He was now, at fifteen, six-foot-four, taller than Carlisle by an inch or two.

Ralph was at once the hope and the despair of Alison—the hope, because of his towering height; there was no boy in school any taller—and the despair, because he could not learn to handle his hands and feet. Gangly and awkward, he flapped around the ball court as gaily and irresponsibly as a puppy, having a wonderful time, usually; but except that he could always get a tip-off, not a great deal of use to his team. A ball passed to him might end up anywhere; he could heave it the length of the floor, but where it landed would be anybody's guess.

At times, Alison made his team practice in weighted jackets and galoshes—weight, especially on the feet, developed leg muscles and limber footwork; take off the weight and the contrast a boy felt made him really able to travel. Alison made them wear sunglasses with the lenses cut out and tape stuck over the lower half of the lens-frames, so that they could not see the ball they were dribbling, and thus could learn to control it without looking at it, eyes free to watch opposition. Ralph, at such times, togged out in bulky jacket, glasses, and galoshes, was a sight to break any coach's heart.

He would start down the floor, dribbling madly, the oversize galoshes slap-slapping, head swiveling, eyes determinedly not on the ball, but not on anything else, either; he had been known to dribble the entire length of the gym without realizing that he didn't have the ball at all—someone else had it.

So that Alison, seeing, would cover his eyes; he would let out the squawking, breath-lost croak that meant no man such as he should be called upon to watch this sight; that he had no words. Or, rather, that he had many words, had he not lost his voice, out of disgust and exasperation. He was very good at that. His voice could take skin off; but more skin went, sometimes, when he didn't say anything.

After one of these times, Ralph would grin; head down, sheepish, he would go back to try again. Nothing Alison said seemed to make an impression on him. He never got mad. Other players, when the coach chewed them, would throw the ball up into the air, yell, "Oh, shove your damn team, to hell with it, I'm through!" and walk off the court, which was what Alison liked to see. It was his job to make fighters out of his boys—fighters who could get mad; and those boys would be back.

But he couldn't make Ralph mad.

"Get sore!" Alison would bawl. "Get in there! Fight! What are you scared of? Afraid you'll touch somebody? Gwan, murder him! Dammit, you'll never make a ballplayer, if you can't get mad. Look at your brother! He gets mad, doesn't he? Or aren't you any relation to him?"

The real trouble with Ralph was that he was a kindly boy.

He took a lot of kidding about this and that—about not getting mad, about not having a regular girl when nearly everybody else had been all set for years, about his gawkiness. Around school, occasionally, he was known as the Witless Wonder. He seemed not to mind kidding.

But one reason he didn't at once mention the basketball outside in the bushes was because he didn't want to hear what Alison would have to say when he found out that a shot of Ralph's, aimed at the basket, had gone out the window.

After that particular practice session, Ralph had had to hurry home to help with chores; he'd found he could hitch a ride, and he'd piled into a friend's car, forgetting all about the ball. Then, that night, just as he was going to bed, he remembered it. It might get lost. Anybody passing the gym might find it, carry it away. Gone forever.

A basketball, to Ralph, was a treasure beyond price. Grampa refused to have one on the place, wouldn't let either of the boys spend money to buy one. All the other fellows had them, with backboards set up in their yards. They practiced whenever they had a moment, nights after school, Saturdays without end, sometimes by moonlight.

Ralph put his clothes back on, listened at his bedroom door to make sure nobody was around to stop him, and slid down a post of the porch outside his window. It was a moonlit night in December, crisp and cold; snow on the ground was frozen stiff, so that it crunched under his leather-tops like good frosting on cake.

Wonder if Ma's got any cake? Wonder if she's got any cold potatoes in the cupboard?

One thing Ralph dearly loved was cold boiled potatoes dunked in the cream on a pan of milk. They tasted best if the cream was just on the turn, not really sour yet; but to get that, you had to swipe one of the pans out of the buttery that Ma had set to raise cream on for butter; and that always made her pretty mad.

Before she'd found out what made a pan of milk look like that, she'd thought the mice had got into it, and she'd set traps all over the buttery shelves that never caught anything; and then, one night, she'd surprised him in the act, so she'd said not one word, but three or four.

Well, anyway, better not loot the cupboard, tonight; she was still edgy with him over that dish of rhubarb; but geez, she didn't need to get so mad—I was only trying to keep the Strontium 90 out of it.

In school, Ralph was the only sophomore taking physics; he was doing it on Mr. Berg's recommendation. Mr. Berg had persuaded James Goss to let Ralph try; Ralph had an extra period, and modern schools were doing that sometimes, nowadays, Mr. Berg said, with talented youngsters.

Ralph was charmed at the idea of being thought talented; he'd never thought he was, particularly compared to Carlisle, who just looked at the stuff once and got it cold. Ralph had to work at it; but he liked the crazy tripe, particularly the way Buggsy explained it.

Strontium 90. Geez, after Buggsy got through yesterday, you could all but see it, floating around in the air. Why, hundreds of miles from where the atom bombs went off, that stuff might come down out of the stratosphere, start Geiger counters to clicking. Even here, if the wind was right, blowing from Nevada or New Mexico. And just a few days ago, according to Buggsy, they'd fired test shots out there. It sounded serious to Ralph.

And then, when he got home, there on the outdoor bench by the kitchen door, was this darn great pot full of rhubarb, sitting cooling. Susie had cooked some and set it out to cool for supper. Poor old Ma, she wouldn't have any idea about such a thing as Strontium 90. At her age, she just thought things were going to go on, just the way they always had, couldn't convince her different. Geez, leave stuff like that out here open to the sky!

So Ralph picked up the dish and carried it inside. He was going to set it on the kitchen table, but as he went in, he all at once remembered that he was in a hurry—ball practice started in about fifteen minutes at the gym—and what he'd come home for was his clean gym-suit he'd forgotten to take to school this morning. If he wasn't on time, Alison would flip; and, thinking what Alison would say, Ralph shot up the backstairs, still carrying the bowl of rhubarb. Without even thinking, only that he needed to have his hands free and one of them was full, he set the bowl down in the middle of his bureau. He didn't remember it again until the next night, tonight after school, when Susie tackled him about it.

She had ransacked the kitchen, bewildered, wondering what kind of a lapse of mind she'd had, where on earth she'd put down that dish of rhubarb. She had been flying around working hard, a lot of things to do; her memory said she'd set the bowl on the outdoors bench to cool. It wasn't there. It had vanished without a trace. Couldn't have been dogs, they'd have left the bowl. So where? The conclusion she came to was that some tramp must have stolen it; and at supper, Martin created loud and long because she'd promised him rhubarb to go with hot biscuits, and all she'd come up with was canned peaches.

The boys had ball practice that night; they didn't get home to supper. As they sometimes did, they caught a sandwich at Joe's Lunch downtown, and then went back to the gym. Susie went to bed early and didn't see them that night; at breakfast, everybody was in too much of a hurry to talk. She didn't think about the rhubarb again until she went upstairs, around ten, to make the beds. There sat the bowl, smack in the middle of Ralph's bureau.

Well, she'd had time to cool off a little by the time he got home from school; but the thing now was, starve, man, you have many times before.

Ralph went loping down the hill, tall and gangly in his wool windbreaker and cap with the earflaps pulled down, his knitted mittens flopping on his hands as his elbows jerked with every stride. Over on Palmer's Hill, he could see the light of a big bonfire against the sky, hear kids hollering. Half the school, the ones who weren't down practicing ball, were over there skiing. He'd thought of asking, earlier, if he could go, but that was a sure way, on a school night, to get Grampa's feet braced, and Carlisle, of course, had had to go down to the gym. The first team was rounding off for one of the big games, practicing secret diagram plays, which they'd try out against the second team tomorrow night; and knock us cold with them, too; but that's okay, we've been knocked cold plenty of times before. So get Grampa sore, he'd say nobody could go out, and Ralph had given up and gone to bed early.

Main Street was deserted. Cheyenne was on tonight; everybody would be at home, glued to the TV. The moon shone on ice-rutted asphalt; cold white light mingled with red-and-green flecks from the strings of colored bulbs put up across the street intersection by the Chamber of Commerce, to remind everyone that it would soon be Christmas. The north wind sucking between the buildings had set the strings of bulbs to jiggling up and down against the sky. Moonlight speckled with red-and-green poured glassily through the blank frosty plateglass of the A and P and IGA stores, cheek by jowl in the Wallace block, gentling to pastel the bright henna of dyed oranges. A set of stainless-steel tableware in the hardware store window sent out an icy glitter. In the bank, the night floodlights focused on the vault, dark gunmetal and chromium, levers and combination dials outlined in shadows of black.

The drugstore went dark, as old Mr. Warren shut up shop for the night; two men came out, one of them the chemist, the other, Ralph could tell by the cane, Charles Kendall.

Charles, seeing Ralph, lifted a hand. "Hi, Ralph."

"Hi, Charles."

"Going somewhere in a hurry, I guess."

"Not specially," Ralph said, grinning. "Got to go over to the gym a minute. Just running to keep warm."

"Ain't you boys practicing tonight?" Mr. Warren said. "I thought the Fairport game was coming up. Ought to be over practicing, hadn't you?"

"Oh, they don't need the second team tonight," Ralph said. "Mr. Alison's bringing out his secret plays."

Mr. Warren grunted, approvingly. "He's a dabster, that coach is," he said. "That team this year's a corker. The way they're shaping up, looks like we might get a try at the Championship, eh, Charles?"

"So I hear," Charles said. "You too cold to eat some ice cream, Ralph?"

"I sure am not," Ralph said.

"George sent me over after some," Charles said. "And Hazel's got a marble cake she said wouldn't keep till morning. I tried to get George to come himself, but somebody just shot Cheyenne off his horse, and George had to stay to see whether he was dead."

"Cheyenne?" Mr. Warren said. "Why, old Cheyenne's never dead, what's the matter with you?"

"No, doesn't seem to be, does he? George ought to know better, but he never seems to. Grover, would it be too much trouble to open up again, let me have another quart of ice cream?"

Grover Warren, who had been locking the door, snapped his key in the opposite direction. "Gawd, no trouble, Charles," he said. "But a whole quart? You want to kill the kid?"

He opened the door and went in, fumbling around the jamb for the light switch. A warm, pleasant smell drifted out of the darkness—the composite, mouth-watering smell of a good drugstore, made up of medicines, leather goods, face powder, fried hamburgers.

"Got to allow for contingencies," Charles called after him.

"Okay. It's his gut-ache. What kind, Ralph?"

"I've got vanilla, here," Charles said. "George likes vanilla."

One thing about Charles, when speaking of relatives, he never used that possessive so annoying, so condescending, to kids—"Your Uncle George," "Your Aunt Hazel," "Your mother," "Your this-or-that," which generally meant, in Ralph's book, when spoken by an older person, that so-and-so was related to you, you owed them something, there was this or that you ought to do. It was one of the things Ralph had to be patient about, but not with Charles Kendall.

"Strawberry," he said, blissfully. "Maple walnut. A pint of each, if he's got 'em."

Deep within he felt the beginnings of a prolonged and contented rumble. Ice cream and cake. And Uncle George's TV would be on.

Heck, he could pick up the basketball on the way back.

He followed around into the side street where Charles had parked his car so that it would be headed in the right direction. Charles never had any trouble with driving, and he had special gears built into his cars; but he didn't go through the process of turning around when it wasn't necessary. Ralph always marveled at the way Charles handled himself on his one leg—at least, his one good leg and what he sometimes referred to as his "prosthesis."

"My prosthesis is giving me hell," Charles would say.

He had had plenty of chance to learn medical terms with regard to his disability, in the military hospital where he had spent a year getting replacements for the various parts of himself left at Anzio.

"Itches the whole length of it," he would say. "Damn thing is wiggling all over, all the way from me to the South Pacific, so I can't even scratch what itches."

Charles had been in the Marines; he had left two fingers of his left hand, as well as his leg below the knee joint, at Anzio.

"Why, they scooped me up like a jigsaw puzzle in a shovel," he would say. "I wouldn't be surprised if I was two or three people. Whatever they needed, they grabbed it up and sewed it on. Had a big pile of stuff lying around—"

Hazel Whitney—wife of George, and Susie's next-older sister—would put her fingers into her ears. "Stop it, Charles, you're giving me the horrors."

"It gives me the horrors," Charles would say. Grinning, he would wink at Ralph. "All I had left was my head and two ribs. The rest of it's shopped around for from all over."

Hazel, with Bessie Maitland's help, ran the kitchen and housekeeping at Charles's motel. George did the heavy outdoor work, while Charles himself handled the business end. At first, when he had come back, he had done only that, or, as he said, wryly, after the accounts were made up he could sit and shell the peas, if the kitchen department had any peas to shell.

Now, unless he happened to be tired, his disability was not apparent to anyone. He held his wide shoulders straight and walked without a limp; he carried a cane only when he had done too much and his stump got tender, or when the ground was icy. He had to be careful not to slip off balance or he was likely to go down, he said, like a sack of potatoes. The cane he carried in winter had a sharpened steel point.

That was the one he had tonight, Ralph saw. He had leaned it between the seats; its clean point sparkled, catching moonlight through the windshield as the car turned into Main Street and headed toward the side road leading down to the shore and to the motel.

To Ralph, there was something wholly admirable about Charles Kendall's steel-shod cane. Not because it showed Charles to be a cripple;

of course not that. But it was admirable in the way that the man himself was admirable; it was self-contained, made for a purpose; it did what it was built to do. Ralph, often, had to give up trying to find words for what he wanted to express; at this point he always had to give up with regard to Charles and his cane. The way he expressed it to himself was that he sure liked good tools.

The motel, of course, was closed in wintertime.

"Closed, thank God," Charles would say, in early October, when the last of the late-stayers had gone, the final loaded car pulled out, headed for the city. Then he and George would really start in to have fun. They might shove a string of lobster traps into the water—do that, for a while, if they felt like it; or go handlining until the bad weather set in. During the season, they went up-state on hunting or fishing trips; last fall, they'd invited Ralph to go with them, and they had all, as Charles put it, had a pious good time. Usually, during the winter months, they took Hazel to Florida, which was the way both of them referred to their winter vacation. Hazel loved Florida; but both Charles and George had reservations.

"When I'm cold, I like to build a fire and get warm," Charles said. "And in Florida, by gum, if you're cold, you're frozen."

And George: "Thunderation, I like snow! I like to see the weather twenty below, and that old bay out there smoking, and me in the house with a fire going, knowing I ain't got to go out in it."

This year, they had been late in going, mostly because of Charles's and George's agility in thinking up reasons for putting it off; but they were now planning to leave just after Christmas.

Ralph had hoped against hope that maybe this year they wouldn't go. Of course, he could always come down and visit with Bessie Maitland, who stayed on as caretaker through the winter, watch her TV; Bessie was his good friend. But with the others gone, it was never the same. Of course, they'd all be back by March or maybe February, so that the men could get traps ready for spring fishing and the motel cleaned for June opening.

The motel was generally jammed throughout the summer, though Charles contended that it wouldn't keep on being, if people kept on wanting so much for their money.

"Rotten spoilt, the tourists are," he would snort. "Swimming pools, they want now, and a TV in every unit. And curb service, including booze and a crack at the waitress."

George would rear up slightly from his TV program.

"Well, if you count the Atlantic Ocean, you can supply all but the last two. We ain't licensed according to state law, and God help all who try to get funny with Bessie."

Seasonally, Charles hired a good deal of help, but Bessie Maitland, head waitress, caretaker, and a good deal more, was permanent. Bessie was tall, rawboned and tough. Because of certain prejudices acquired in her youth, she had long ago declared war upon tourists. One and all, she said, they gave her fur on her tongue. She had been known to stand in the window of the crowded dining room, watching with unconcealed joy a party depart, while she muttered, for all to hear, "Go! Go! And don't come back!" She had a fine, full vocabulary which she did not scruple to use; she had, also, been known to use her fists, in one of which was a full water pitcher, on a male guest, who, sensing in her rich conversation an invitation of sorts, had made a pass at her.

How much of an asset she was, she, as well as everybody else, knew quite well. Charles, certainly, knew it, and considered her a pearl of price. She was a natural, deadpan clown; the guests loved it. In a country in which the old salts of the earth had become, for obvious reasons, professional, the tourists sensed in Bessie a certain sincerity. Most of them came back as much to see her as to see the countryside and seashore. And somehow, the notion got around that it was not they whom Bessie hated—not the nice, regular people sitting at the tables now—it was them tourists.

Bessie had been born on one of the off-shore islands, and had grown up there until she was thirteen, never coming to the mainland or seeing a motion picture or an automobile. So she said. Or owning a pair of shoes, or—she would add, in a decorous half-whisper—a pair of underpants. Such things, in those places, in those days, she would say delicately, were not known. A rugged life; one of a family of eleven, she, her mother, and all the little ones had been turned out-of-doors in a snowstorm by her father, who had brought home from the mainland, on that cold winter night, a whore known as Poison Bet. It was her or us, and she beat. The whole family had waded, barefooted, over rocks and snow and frozen saltmarshes to the other side of the island, to an uncle's house. Left bloody track-marks all the way; and no underpants, not one of us, the whole night long.

Bessie's stories of her childhood, her youth, her hard-won survival, were known, it might be said, nation-wide; they were taken home to far-off places, California, Michigan, New Mexico, told, re-told, and believed, thereby maintaining a tradition.

Whenever someone made a complaint about Bessie, as some of the tourists did, five or six times a summer, Charles did not hesitate. He fired her, in the presence of the complainer.

In wintertime, Bessie lived in one of the motel units, which Charles had had winterized for her use. She would have been more than welcome to use his house, he said, when he and George and Hazel were away, but she did not wish to. She saw enough of it, she said, during the summer, when she had to sleep in the cook's room, off of the kitchen, in that old Kendall house.

"Why, that great ark of a thing," she said, "all them empty upstairs rooms, come a thunder-and-lightnin'-storm, or the northern lights, and them old Kendalls walking, I'd be so scairt I'd run outdoors in my shape."

It was Bessie's unalterable opinion that all unusual natural phenomena were caused by the walking of ghosts; both of her old grandmothers had believed that, and nothing had ever proved to her that it wasn't so.

So Charles had one of the motel units insulated and a floor-furnace put in. He said Bessie was worth more to him than any amount of heating and electric bills. Also, she care-took the motel, and woe betide trespassers, two- or four-legged, who crossed the premises when Charles was away.

Now, as Charles drove abreast her motel unit, with Ralph in the seat beside him, they saw Bessie through the window, sitting in comfort in one of the upholstered chairs, watching TV. Her feet in knitted bedroom-slippers were thrust out across a coffee table moved up in front of the chair. Her hair was in tightly twisted metal curlers, giving an Oriental headdress effect; she had on an old white turtleneck sweater with a large red-and-black letter "H" affixed to the front, where it rounded fulsomely over her bosom. For the rest, she had on a bright pink flannelette petticoat.

"Whew-we!" Charles whistled, stopping the car. "Bessie must be chilly tonight." He chuckled. "I wondered where that old high-school sweater of mine went to."

He rolled down the car window, bawled in his high, pleasant tenor, "Bessie! Want some ice cream?"

Bessie did not move nor take her eyes off the TV, but she waved a hand.

"Want to come over with us, or shall I bring it in?"

Bessie waved the hand again; she got up and proceeded to dress, craning her neck at the TV program while she pulled on a heavy pair of wool slacks over the petticoat, thrust her feet, slippers and all, into an enormous pair of flyer's boots. She paused for a moment before the TV before she snapped it off, and then emerged, tying a shawl over her curlers.

"Damnedest thing," she said. "Gun goes off and the man falls down dead, and then they all just walk away and leave the body in the middle of the street. Them sheriffs always make that little speech about law and order and cleaning out the evil characters, but, my lord, I should think they'd have to clean up the streets every once in a while. I'm getting real edgy waiting for some one of them to pick up that body."

She got into the back seat of the car, cheerfully banging the door. "Well, hi, if it ain't old Ralph," she said. "I'm sorry you had to wait, Charley, but I was in my daycollaytay."

"If you mean that pink petticoat," Charles said, "you didn't need to cover that up. Everybody in town's seen it, if they happen to drive in to my house after dark. Why don't you ever haul down the Venetian blinds?"

"Well, I don't like to be shut in," Bessie said. "Curtains all down in a room, gives me a funny all-over feeling. I did have to let 'em down on the side toward the woods. They was a damn deer come out every night, stood there looking in the window at the Tee-Vee. Cussid thing. Anything I can't stand, it's a nosy wild animal."

Charles grinned a little; without comment he started up the car, let it roll on down the road toward his house on the headland overlooking the water.

The big old Kendall house was all that was left of the original stand of buildings, put up by Charles's grandfather, which had been famous all over the county as The Emporium. When Charles, via military hospital, had come home from the War, his neighbors had expected he would run The Emporium, as his father and grandfather had done before him. That the old store was losing money and had been for years made no difference. It was The Emporium; it was a landmark; within memory, it had always been there. Who could ask for anything more?

It appeared that Charles could. The store, built in the 1880s, had been vastly successful in those far-off, leisurely days when millionaires from the cities were buying up shore property and building the mansions with twenty, thirty, or forty rooms, called "cottages." Charles's grandfather, a shrewd and canny man with an eye for a business opportunity, had owned two hundred acres of land with a magnificent sea-view; he had sold half of it for cottages at rousing prices and had used the money to put up The Emporium.

In those days, The Emporium had really been something to see. Old Man Kendall had not built it in or near the business block of the town, as a lesser man might have done. It stood on his own property, near enough to the ocean to command a view, but not so far from the highway as to be inconvenient. Its separateness from the town and its beautiful surroundings indicated that here was something special—for those who were discriminating, who had plenty of time. Its three stories of rambling wooden structure were encompassed by a wide porch, on which, in time, great masses of pink rambler roses grew. Many a porch in town copied Old Man Kendall's Dorothy Perkins roses.

Another man having gone so far might have kept on and created something modern and up-to-date, like a town or a city store. Not Old Man Kendall. People vacationing in the country, he figured, while they would be pleased to buy the same quality of goods they could get at home, liked to see things countrified. He crammed his three floors with a collection of merchandise really magnificent in scope; all kinds, from everywhere. Almost overnight The Emporium took on an atmosphere of age and quaintness. A nice, old, general store, where the customers could wander among cracker-barrels and bung-starters and find, of all things, a Chinese incense-burner.

Actually, most of the cracker-barrel material was front; in summer, was when it moved. Old Man Kendall's in-season prices were too high for the local people; they were not interested, anyway, in the two departments out of which he made most of his money. One of these consisted of old articles rummaged out of his neighbors' attics and scattered around the store in spots where the customers could come on them without too much trouble—old punkin-pine chests, what-nots, odd pieces of glass and china, hand-made dry sinks, commodes, and water-benches. A picker-up of unconsidered trifles, Old Man Kendall got most of these items for nothing, or for chicken-feed. The Chinese incense-burner, which he found in the ruins of the old Troy house barn, and sold to a lady from Baltimore for seventy-five dollars, was exactly what the lady thought it was—a bronze, carved-and inlaid Oriental work of art, brought home from China by some old clipper-ship captain, in this case, Abijah Troy, who had bought it in Shanghai for what he thought was chickenfeed. So the lady was satisfied; Old Man Kendall was satisfied; and on happy customer relations such as this he built his business.

His other line was fancy groceries and specialties, which he imported in quantity, often on order. You could buy a Persian melon at The Emporium, if you wanted or could afford to pay two dollars for it; or Stilton cheese aged in brandy for four dollars a pound. Ladies in leghorn hats could rest on the rose-embowered porch in Boston rockers while they made up their minds about the delicacies of S. S. Pierce and Company, or put in an order for homemade fresh strawberry ice cream. Anything you could get at home in the city you could get at The Emporium if you put in an order with Mr. Kendall a day or so ahead of time; of course you paid more for the extra service and for quality. One thing about Old Man Kendall, he went to trouble.

In 1945, The Emporium, Charles found, was still as handsomely valued and taxed by the town fathers as if its entire three floors were still filled with exotica and overflowed by wealthy summer-people spending thousands. Taxes, according to custom, went up, not down; the word around town was that The Emporium was a gold mine. It always had been so; it must be now. Charles's father and grandfather, people said, could have bought and sold, not all, but most, of their customers without feeling a dent; they had run that business like a steel trap; if Charles couldn't do it now, then something was wrong with the modern generation.

Without a doubt, times had come to a sad change. Something—bears in the bears' woods, perhaps—had eaten up the millionaires. Modern tourists took one look at The Emporium's sunburnt height and rose-covered porch, and with visions of twenty to fifty percent tacked on to prices, made tracks for the A and P.

So Charles tore down The Emporium. He kept his grandfather's big house to live in; but along the shore he strung twenty units of modern, well-equipped motel, thereby causing regret, a fluttering of dovecots and shock. It was felt by some that motel-style would not attract the better class of tourist; certain people, among them the hotel men, felt, also, that the project might well be viewed with alarm. Who could say what shady carryings-on might take place in those unsupervised units?

Charles was advised of this municipal concern; and old Sidney Widgett, self-appointed custodian of the past, as well as of town morals, really gave him a blast.

Sidney was in his late eighties. For nearly three generations he had stood, a mighty fortress, against progress, which he called "change." Time out of mind he had bedeviled public meetings, his portly figure, dignified now by weight of years, clad in decent black suit, white shirt with stiff collar, and black string tie; always in the front row, generally rising to a point of order. His oratory was not the less spell-binding because it was old-fashioned. It oozed sentiment, which seemed to be what people liked best; and at one Town Meeting which Charles remembered, when an article in the Warrant wished to see if the town would raise the money for a new grammar school, Sidney had brought the entire meeting to the verge of nostalgic tears with a dissertation on the old remembered privy of the little red schoolhouse, based on the premise that what had been good enough for people's great-grandfathers was good enough for their kids. Abraham Lincoln hadn't had a flush toilet, had he?

On this day, he faced Charles portentously, in his hand an ancient, faded pennant. Charles recognized the pennant; his grandfather had had some of these made up for the opening of the store in the eighties. In Charles's boyhood, one or two of them, faded even then, had been pinned diagonally in wall-spaces between the store windows. He could not remember when they had been taken down, burned, or thrown away; Sidney, it seemed, had salvaged and kept one. He held it under

Charles's nose long enough for the legend, the emporium, 1880, blue on dingy white felt, to be read, then waved it, his white chinwhisker pointing furiously at the half-dismantled building.

"I bring you a memento mori," he sounded off in his fruity, old-politician's voice. "A remembrance of two good men, your father and your grandfather, who, to their eternal good fortune, have not lived to see this day, when their son and grandson lays the hard-earned savings of their lifetime on the altar of Sodom and Gomorrah!"

Nonetheless, Charles went ahead; he built a big motel and a good one. He made money; and as soon as this became known, the criticism died a natural death.

Since, in those days, he was still shaky from illness, he needed help; George and Hazel Whitney helped him, and, after an interval, Charles offered them a partnership. George had kept the failing Emporium open during the four years of the War; he had been kept out of the service by recurrent attacks of asthma, of which it was said around town, marriage to Hazel had cured him. George himself believed this. He had been known to remark, proudly, that marriage to Hazel would have cured a man of anything.

Charles had grown up, gone to school, with George and Hazel; there had been a time when two couples, George and Hazel, Charles and Susie, had gone everywhere together. But Susie, out of a clear sky, had married Brant McIntosh; and Charles found necessary a rearrangement of his plans. In time, like most young men of the district, he had gone quietly off to the War; on his return, he had been busy, learning to live with his disability, getting himself set up in his new business. George and Hazel made him comfortable; the three lived amiably, now, as one family, in the old Kendall house, set on the headland a few hundred yards from the motel.

Bessie got out as the car came to a stop by Charles's back door. Her voice did not diminish as she went through the kitchen toward the living room. Ralph and Charles, following, heard her going on, without hesitation.

"I was just telling Charley about that damn deer, Hazel. Now, Hazel, I've made up my mind. We ain't going to use one atom more of that Ocean Bloom soap powder around this motel."

"Oh, dear," Hazel said. "I thought we'd finally found one we liked."

"Well, I draw the line. Three commercials in fifteen minutes is more than human flesh can stand. And they not only flash 'em on, but that young man, the one that looks like a dahlia, has to read every word of the printed matter out loud. Don't they think I can read, for godsake? So no more Ocean Bloom, they have lost a customer. I was just telling Hazel, Charley, if them soap-powder people keeps on, I don't know what I will be able to bring myself to wash anything with, let alone listen to their programs."

Hazel, coming out to the kitchen, grinned widely at Charles, and, seeing Ralph, pounced on him with a little yip of welcome.

"Oh, Ralphie! Isn't this nice! How's Susie? Grampa as touchy as ever? How'd you get let outdoors, this time of night?"

"Slid down the piazza post," Ralph said.

"Good for you! Go right in and sit down, while I dish. Charles, do you want some coffee?"

A bright fire was burning in the fireplace, and Ralph made a beeline for it, settling his long frame into a big wing-chair, feeling at once, as he always felt in this house, relaxed, happy, approved of.

George Whitney, slumped in an easy-chair in front of the TV screen, on which a gang of yelling Indians on horseback pursued a hard-riding cowboy toward a wavering horizon, lifted a hand to Ralph, but, otherwise, did not move or speak. Nothing ever interrupted George listening to one of his programs. The house could catch fire and burn down, Hazel said, and there he would be sitting in the ashes, his feet out on that hassock; there would be George.

"—to say nothing of the way they slosh perfume into the scouring powder," Bessie went on, not having stopped.

"Why, I thought all you ladies liked stink-pretty soap," Charles observed. He too sat down in front of the fire. He gave a slight moan of relief, as the weight came off his stump.

"So I do like it," Bessie said. "In my bathtub. And I've got some pine-scented bath salts that's mm-mm, sweeter than wine. But such things got no place in a decent woman's kitchen."·

"That's gratitude!" Charles said. "Here's some poor devil of a soap company paid half a million, hired mental experts and social scientists and what-all to find out what you ladies like, and you—"

"I could have told 'em for three cents postage," Bessie said. "Hell, four cents, now, ain't it? 'Dear Sir, since I know that the last thing you want is an unsatisfied customer, I take my pen in hand to inform you that I am now scouring my pans and pots with river sand from the bar below the tannery. This does not make my coffeepot smell like the toilet in the Boston and Maine railroad station, or my kitchen sink remind me of a man that's spent all night down to Miss Sadie Brewer's—' "

"Good," Charles said, hastily. "That's fine. Send it."

"I ain't put it strong enough. Have I?"

"Mm. Tell 'em to send you a couple of thousand for the idea."

Bessie sniffed. "My ideas is free as the air they come from," she said. "Not that I think they'll have any effect on a mess of men, don't know what it's like to wash greasy dishes in French cologne. If they did, you'd see some puking. My, Hazel, that's a swell-looking cake. Is it a mix?"

Hazel, guiding a laden tea-wagon in through the living-room door, smiled and shook her head. "That's Ma's recipe," she said.

Bessie leaned over and began to cut the cake while Hazel poured coffee. As the knife slid through the towering, frosted structure, Bessie began to cluck with approval.

"That's lovely, that's just lovely," she said. "Just look at that, will you? Them mixes, they're wonderful, I do agree, if you're in a hurry, but the cake they make's a little too fluffy for my taste. Me, now, I like a nice chewy cake. They's some kinds that's even better if they fall a teentsy bit."

Ralph sat listening, digging into his big mound of ice cream, stopping now and then for a mouthful of cake. Good old Bessie, the piece she'd cut for him looked to be a full quarter of the cake. He could hear the clock ticking in the hall, the quiet falling of the fire, the occasional clink of a spoon on a dish, against the muted background, the yo-hoing, of George's TV Indians.

"How's basketball this year, Ralph?" Charles asked.

"Pretty good."

"That Mooney boy's quite a star," Bessie said.

"Yuh. Carlisle's good, too."

Most people would have said, "How about you?" and then, of course, you'd have to say oh, you weren't much, only center on the second-string team; but Charles didn't, and Bessie said, "They do say, around town, that our team's got a chance for the State Championship, the way they look this year. My, that'd be something I'd certainly like to see. Why, this town never had but one. When was that, George? That Grindle boy, the one they put in jail, he was on the team."

Over by the TV, George stirred slightly. "Must've been nine-ten years ago," he said. "That boy's getting out, next spring."

"You know, that was one living shame," Bessie said. "I don't know what on earth could've come over that boy, I swear I don't. There he was, a lovely tall boy, good-looking, played a handsome game of ball, he could've had anything in the wide world he wanted. And then, the way he turned out, no good for nothing, even the Army wouldn't put up with him."

"Hold on," Charles said. "That wasn't the way I heard it, Bessie. He hadn't been in the Army, remember? He'd just enlisted, a while before they arrested him."

"Oh, yes, I guess that's right. Well, it all come as a terrible surprise. Why, that boy, one time, he was the starspangled hero around this town."

"He was a nice kid, too," Hazel said. "I recall that summer he odd-jobbed for George, down at The Emporium. He could eat almost as much cake as you could, Ralphie."

Ralph grinned peacefully. For once, he was full. He'd finished his last mouthful and it had come out just right, just enough ice cream, just enough cake.

"I see they've still got pictures of him up there at the high-school gym," Bessie said. "In that glass cage, along with that Championship cup he won for 'em. I noticed them the last time I was in there to a game. My land of lights, remember what a touse there was that year, when the Women's Club and everybody wanted to throw them pictures out of the cage, and old Mr. Goss wouldn't let 'em? Put his foot right down and sat on it."

George grinned. "More power to him," he said, and subsided again.

Reluctantly, Ralph got up. It was getting late; everybody would be going home from the gym, and somehow he had to sneak that basketball back in before the janitor locked up for the night.

"I guess I better be on my way," he said. "That was swell cake and ice cream, Aunt Hazel."

"Have some more, there is some."

"Couldn't. I'd bust."

Charles said, "Want some of us to ride you up the hill?" He cocked a humorous eye at George, who had slumped down in his chair, until all that was visible was the top of his slightly balding head.

"No, thanks," Ralph said. He grinned at Charles, both of them knowing that George couldn't be pried away from the TV. "If I get over to the gym in time, I can hitch a ride."

"Well, take it easy. And come again," Charles said.

Hazel went with him to the door. "Tell your mother I'll be up sometime soon to say good-bye," she said. "I expect we'll be taking off for Florida next week."

Ralph pelted along the moonlit street.

Gee, that guy, Grindle. Whatever would make a guy do a thing like that? The story was old, kind of vague, happened when you were a kid, long time ago; but once in a while people talked about it. Young kid, eighteen, robbed a gas station, slugged the attendant and killed him. Gee, what would you have to be to do that?

Charles and Uncle George and Aunt Hazel and Bessie, gee, they were swell. Ralph wished they wouldn't go to Florida. That was a nice, quiet house; a nice tick to the clock. With dismay, he saw as he turned the corner, that he'd stayed too long. The gym was dark; the door locked; the windows of the long, low high-school building glittered blank and deserted under the moon. Everybody had gone home.

He found the basketball under a bush. Its smooth skin sparkled with frost crystals in the moonlight; it was icy cold, as he snuggled it into the crook of his arm.

Now what to do? He'd have to take it home; and not back through town, either. Sure, it was late, but somebody might see him; word might get around that he'd stolen a basketball.

He went through the bushes back of the high school, cut across to the highway, and set out up the macadam at a long lope.

The moon was high in the sky, with a few big stars and a white wisp of cloud blowing along fast. The frozen fields looked wide and empty; the broad expanse of the river was black, with ice making out from its edges. The town was mostly asleep; there was a single, lonesome light in the tannery office, the one the night watchman kept going all night; there were a few yellow squares of windows here and there; and a colored, reddish-greenish glow over the business block.

Ralph climbed the embankment into Martin's back pasture. He waded the snow to the foot of the horse-chestnut tree, shoved the ball into the front of his windbreaker, and managed to get the zipper closed partway, enough to hold it; then he went up like a squirrel.

The trunk of the tree was icy and the bulk of the ball at his front bothered; for a moment, he wasn't quite sure he could make the last few feet where he had to go hand-overhand up the rope—the rope was stiff and slippery with frost. But after a couple of tries, he got one foot on a crosspiece nailed into the trunk, and the rest of the way was easy.

Geez, it was cold and lonesome up there in the tree house this time of night. Kind of nice, though; nobody here. The moon shone in through the open side onto all those Indians things of Carl's—arrowheads, stone axes, bone harpoons.

Those things were sure nice. Ralph reached up to finger a flint blade, feeling the chipped stone, rough and icy cold to his touch. Geez, he sure liked that stuff!

Maybe next summer Carl would let him go along, help dig in some of the shell heaps, show him where some of them were. Of course, there was the one on Tanner's Island, but you couldn't touch that, that was Carl's best place. He had it all laid out with stakes and string. If you touched it, he'd take your arm off.

But by next summer, I'll be a year older then. Maybe he won't think I'm so ham-handed.

There wasn't any place up here out-of-sight to stash the basketball. But nobody ever came here but Carl; and Carl didn't come anymore. Last spring, when they'd built the tree house, he'd spent a lot of time here, and all summer. Of course, now, he was too busy, but he seemed to have lost interest, too. So he wouldn't be up here; you could just park the ball anywhere, in a corner; nobody'd find it.

Ralph noticed as he stepped across the floor that the tree house seemed a little shaky; one corner had sagged down a little, seemed like. Have to tell Carl; maybe they could come up together and fix it. Geez, if this ever fell down, with all this good stuff in here . . .

No, it wasn't any use to tell Carl. Even if he listened, he wouldn't have the time. Maybe, by the time the ball season got over, he'd go back to being human again; maybe by then you could reach him with the end of a pole. You sure couldn't now.

Since that night in December, there hadn't seemed a safe time, to Ralph, when he could get that ball back to the gym without being seen. Someone was always around; someone's eye was always on him. He couldn't, of course, take it down mornings on the school bus; even if he sneaked out in the late evening before the gym was shut for the night, he was still taking an awful chance, lugging a ball down through the town.

After a while, he brought it down from the tree house; he kept it, now, in the hayloft, dug deep down into the hay, so that it would be handy to get at, whenever he had a minute to practice. Now, in February, it had come to seem like his own ball. Secretly, he had set up the backboard out here in the spruces; and whenever he could sneak away, he was out here practicing set shots.

Sometimes, it seemed to him, he might be getting good. Some days, he could stand here on his carefully measured foul line and whang in the swishers, one after another. Whenever he missed, the ball would like as not bend down the barrel-hoop, so that he'd have to poke it back straight with a pole. Some days, he'd have to do that often. Other days, he didn't have to do it at all.

So far, Alison hadn't said that he was getting any better. So far, Alison hadn't taken him, even as a sub, to any of the out-of-town games. Now, of course, with the season nearly over, there was only one more chance; but so far, the list of subs, the ones who'd be going to Boston with the team, hadn't been posted.

Of course, it made a difference when there were people around, all that noise and rumpus and yelling and joggling. But here, in the still of the woods, times Ralph could stand here and whang them in, one after another.

This morning, a few days after the Championship game, he stood on his foul line, listening to applause. Every spruce tree around the clearing was jammed with fans; the crowded stands went up to the roof of the sky, where bright electric lights shone down on the Witless Wonder. The fans were on their feet, yelling, "McIntosh, McIntosh, McIntosh!" Chanting, "Oh, you Witless Wonder!" And he stood there, toeing the line.

Ralph McIntosh, the Witless Wonder. He did not turn a hair. The stern expression on his face did not alter. He bounced the ball. Once. Twice. He took aim, while the din arose to a roar; and he whanged in a swisher.

He retrieved the ball. This, after all, had been a personal foul; he had another shot coming. The first shot had tied the game; now to win.

Bounce, bounce the ball.

Pay no attention to the yelling; it does not affect you.

Noise is for the birds.

Calm, collected, passionless, Ralph McIntosh tried again. He missed by a foot; the ball bent the barrel-hoop down and sideways, knocking it loose from the backboard. Ball and basket fell together to the foot of the trees.

The Witless Wonder stood for a moment regarding the disaster. Couldn't fix that without a ladder. The ball had rolled back to within a few feet of him. He stooped and picked it up.

Old Ralph. Beat himself all winter, worked like a dog, even stole a ball. Didn't even get on the team as a sub. Spent his time hoping and praying that somebody'd get sick, break a leg, get lost—nobody on the team, just one of the subs, of course—so he'd get a chance to go to Boston.

He eyed the ball malevolently. On one side of it, a long scratch in the leather seemed to grin back at him with equal malevolence.

"Oh, poop!" Ralph said. "To hell with it. To the lowdown-low, eat-mud, last-dirtiest, double-hell with it!"

Part Six

When ten boys out of Senior Chemistry did not show up for class, Alfred Berg started for the principal's office.

This is it, he told himself, between set teeth.

Evenings and nights after school, those weren't his business; at least, he hadn't made it so, even though nobody on the basketball squad had completed a homework assignment since November. But when it came to practicing on actual classroom time . . .

As he went by the entrance to the gym, two of his class, Carlisle McIntosh and Dick Wickham, flashed past the door, passing a ball down the floor. Alfred turned abruptly and went in.

After all, he'd received no notice that anyone had permission to cut class to play ball.

He stepped in through the door and narrowly escaped being trampled on, as the team raced back from the far end of the gym. As it was, Jerry Mooney had to pivot fast to avoid running into him. The ball rolled out of his hands into the sidelines, and Alison let out a strangled blat. "What to hell—watch it, Berg, will you?"

"Sorry," Alfred said. "But my chemistry class began fifteen minutes ago. I came in to remind these fellows of the time."

"Well, go and see Goss," Alison said. "Goss has got it taped—he'll tell you."

"He hasn't, so far," Alfred said. "Until he notifies me about class cuts for ball, this period's still chemistry."

He turned to go. As he was about to pass through the door, somebody—whoever had the ball—threw it, not at him, but at the wall above the door. It bounced back, hard, into his face, would have hit him dead center between the eyes, if he had not fielded it neatly. Still holding it, he turned around.

The boys had moved into a tight little knot, backed by Alison; all faces deadpan, they stared at Alfred in silence.

To his astonishment, Alfred felt the skin tighten on the back of his neck. His first impulse was to back away.

Good Lord, Alfred thought.

He walked across to the group, handed the ball to Alison.

"Everybody seems to be a little hyped up, here," he said.

For a moment, Alison stared him in the eye. Then he snapped, "Okay! Whoever did that, apologize!"

Jerry Mooney said, "But gee, Mr. Alison, I never threw it at him; it missed the backboard, that's all."

"I expect you'll do better than that down in Boston," Alfred said quietly.

As a matter of fact, there had been nothing the matter with the shot; it had been a beauty, the ricochet nicely calculated.

"Dammit, he'd better," Alison said. "Okay, now let's take that last play over again. If you'll just get off the floor, Berg."

"It still goes," Alfred said. "I'm expecting these guys upstairs in five minutes."

He went along the corridor toward the principal's office.

Stuck my neck out that time, good and proper, he thought. Maybe I need a vacation. Along with everyone else, it could be.

He was still a little astonished, a little shaken. Granted that he and Chet Alison had never been particularly friendly, because they had little in common; still, he'd never disliked Chet. True, relations between them had slipped a little since they had both begun to go out, off and on, with Ellen Callander, but so far Ellen hadn't expressed a preference. It had seemed like good, honest competition to Alfred, best man win; he thought very likely Chet felt the same way. As a matter of fact, Alfred admired Chet for a good, sound professional job of work; Chet was paid to train a ballteam and he was doing it. Alfred, himself, had been a ballplayer, a fairly good one, at the University of Colorado. It had been a lot of fun, spare time.

But this—this business in the gym, this was wacky. Of course, with all the excitement and super-charged emotion around, perhaps something of the kind was to be expected. Boy, that was concentration in there, that was dedication; what could you expect if you interrupted it with a thing like chemistry? About what you got. But for a moment, there, when the youngsters had gathered up around Alison, Alfred, to his shocked amazement and concern, had been reminded of something else—an incident which had taken place last winter. The incident was similar to this one in no way except for the one thing which recalled it to him; at least, he told himself it wasn't.

Brought up in the West, and new to this Eastern country of sea, lakes, and streams, Alfred had been fascinated by it. He had hunted and fished—that is, he had hunted and fished until the ball season started, when he found he was expected, along with other teachers, to take tickets at ballgames, chaperone bus trips to out-of-town games, such things; so that nobody had much spare time. He had, in early fall, got acquainted with two of the state game wardens, who had become his good friends; they had invited him to go along on a weekend, to hunt for a pack of dogs which were ranging in the woods, chasing deer. They were not wild dogs; they were domestic pets, accustomed to firesides and the affection of children. They could, however, and did, tear running deer to pieces, a slow, revolting killing that sometimes took a day to two to accomplish; and their owners, ignorant of the state law or unwilling to be bothered, let them roam the woods.

The wardens, both dog-lovers, were heartsick at what they had to do. They chased the pack into a cave, finally; one of them shone a flashlight into the mouth of the cave, and Alfred had caught a glimpse of the dogs, all big, sleek fellows, one of them a beautiful collie. He had never forgotten the five pairs of eyes in the split-second before the other warden began to shoot—the stone-silent, gem-glittering, you-go-to-hell stare.

Kids! Alfred snorted, disgusted at himself. You lunk, you do need a vacation. Your mind's going.

After all, I like kids.

In fact, Alfred Berg liked kids so well that he had turned down a medical career, to teach science. He liked teaching, too; he had equipped himself for it, and so far as he could tell, he was capable; he needed experience, of course; but, he told himself, that would come. He did not consider teaching, as some did, a thankless job, or a stop-gap on the way to something else. The possibilities within it seemed to him to be endless, entertaining, and vastly rewarding.

His uncle, a surgeon in a Western city, had done his best to talk Alfred out of it.

"Look, Al, why waste yourself? With your record at Colorado, there isn't a lab in the country wouldn't be tickled to death to have you, and with this breakthrough in science—"

"With this breakthrough in science," Alfred said, grinning at him, "I figure I'm going to work right where it's most useful."

"Ah-h, a teacher doesn't cut any ice in a town—he's considered a kind of transient freak, a necessary evil—"

"So you say. If he's a good one, he doesn't need to be."

"Well, it's a profession that's more or less under a cloud. Be realistic, Al. The pay's bad. You'll find a lot of freeloaders doing it because they can't do anything else."

"So that's one reason for the cloud. I don't think you're right, Uncle Ed. And if you are, all the more reason for me to be the best there is. If I can."

"Oh, hell! I was going to blow you to a medical school—your choice. But if you don't want that, take what money you need and tour the country. God, you'll need to know something about small towns. Maybe it'll change your mind."

"Good!" Alfred said. "And thanks, I will."

For a full summer, he toured the country in his battered, secondhand car. He saw all he could of it, East and West. Among other things, he found himself a job in this Eastern seaside town.

It was not a very good job; the pay was poor, even for a beginner. He had realized, from the first, that there was some feeling in the town because of his name, which was Jewish. He did not think too much about this, having encountered it before, though less often, of late years, in many sections of the country. It seemed to him that race and religious prejudices were, after all, simple matters of ignorance, which better education might cure.

His Uncle Ed said, "If you think that, God help you."

Now, Alfred walked thoughtfully along the corridor toward the principal's office.

Stuck my simple-minded neck out, he told himself again. Well, let's see what James has to say.

James Goss, the principal, was behind his desk dictating a letter to his secretary, Sally Adams, who wasn't a professional stenographer—at least, not yet; she was a senior in the Commercial Department whose shorthand and typing were only fair. She and another senior, Josephine Conway, worked spare time for Mr. Goss. It was good experience and gave them some pin money; and the system was one which had the full approval of the School Board, who felt strongly that any tax money paid out at the school ought to be pumped right back into the town, not wasted on an outsider, which was what would probably happen if they hired for James Goss a full-time secretary.

Mr. Goss had long ago given up pointing out the inefficiency of the system. The yearly change of girls caused chaos in his files; throughout the basketball season, particularly, nobody had much energy left over for office work. But the School Board felt that Goss and his office cost too much anyway; if his files got mixed up, he had three months' vacation to straighten them out in, didn't he?

Sally and Josephine were very busy girls. In addition to their office job and their schoolwork, they were cheerleaders, belonging to the squad which went everywhere with the ballteam. At all of the games—home and out-of-town—dressed in brilliant costumes, carrying majorettes' batons, drilled and disciplined, they produced a bright, frenetic ballet. Cheerleading was fiercely competitive; places on the squad were battled for as keenly as the boys battled for places on the team, though it was a foregone conclusion that the prettiest, peppiest girls would always be chosen. You had to be good to make a showing against other schools, who also chose their prettiest and peppiest.

It was a lovely thing to watch, this ballet of the cheerleaders at the ballgames.

Wonderful! Al Berg would think, watching them swarm out on the floor, like a passage of bright butterflies.

They wore white Hungarian blouses embroidered in the school colors, red and black; knee-length red ballet skirts deeply gored with white; low, soft, black ballet slippers. The skirts billowed and swirled as they followed their ballerina, the captain of the squad, through intricate figures and patterns, marching up and down the shining floor, marked off in white paint zones for the game to come. Now and then, the ballerina would raise her megaphone and cry something into it; and then would come the crash of voices, yelling together in rhythm—the school cheers, the booms, the thumps, the locomotives.

And, Oh, beautiful! Al would say to himself, meaning not the sound, which was a saw-toothed cacophony of shrill young voices, harsh, dissonant, as if the sound over a cliff-full of seabirds had been amplified a thousand times. Not the noise, which was dreadful. What was beautiful was the enthusiasm, the energy, the grace. At the ends of the hall, under the baskets, the home team and the visiting team, in their own bright colors, would be warming up; Al could see the set, earnest faces, the clean-muscled arms and legs, the flash of light on the gleaming young heads.

Oh, it was pageantry, it was Mardi Gras. No wonder, after the winter streets of the drab town, the hamburgers and canned music, the Westerns, the dull jobs, the screaming necessities, that people turned, as one person, to this real show. For real it was; it had everything. Color, movement, rivalry; the loyalty to one's own, the beautiful children.

Sometimes, when a boy would break out of scrimmage and come flashing down the hall, dribbling the ball—a boy who in his everyday clothes looked blank-faced, awkward; whose voice, inarticulate nine-tenths of the time, said nothing because it had been taught nothing to say—when this boy came down the floor, legs pumping, lungs bursting, and on his face a light, Al Berg's heart would turn over within him, and he would find himself close to tears.

Let them split their atoms, he would say to himself, or to the bright, dusty air, electric with the animate form of the flying, dark ball. Let them split their atoms, drag energy enough out of a glass of water to power a city. Those are miracles; but the real miracle is this power here, locked up, capable of release; and without it, the others might as well never be. Because this is the beginning; this is where it starts. Without this, the other miracles are nothing, not so much as a cry against the universe's desperate dark.

Don't curb it, he would think, watching the fierce ebb and flow up and down the floor. Point it, aim it, and let it rip! Then what a power you would have that could not be set down, if you could ever be taught to use this outside a ballgame!

He knew how it would be tomorrow, the glory departed, the apotheosis done. In class, the slumped shoulders, the dull eyes, the faces as if they had died of something sluggish and chronic which had taken a long time to kill.

And who to blame? Because this is treasure; this is valuable. If you do not match valuable things with things of equal value, they will, blindly, seek their own.

Al said now, to James Goss, "Jim, there's a mix-up. Most of my chem class is in practicing ball."

James turned in his swivel chair. His hand, palm flat on the desk, began a nervous finger-patting, a little rhythm, tum-tiddy-um-tum. Tum-tum.

"Sally, didn't that note go up to Mr. Berg's room?"

"Oh, yes, Mr. Goss! I typed it, and Jo took it up right after." Her round blue eyes with their heavy fringe of dark lashes swept a wide, innocent, cool glance over Mr. Berg, returned to James Goss, full of quick, helpful concern.

"You didn't get it," James said.

"Well, no," Al said. "Jo forget it, maybe?" he asked Sally.

"Oh, no, Mr. Berg! I'm sure she didn't. She went right out of here with it, headed your way. Could it have got slipped under some papers, on your desk, maybe?"

"No," Al said. "Well, just so you know, Jim."

James cleared his throat, a prolonged, uncomfortable harrumph. "I know it's—har—unorthodox," he began. "But Alison feels the team needs extra practice time, before Boston. Especially now that we're having some difficulty with Carlisle McIntosh's grandfather."

"Old Mr. Hoodless?" Al asked. "Is he objecting?"

"He says Carl can't practice nights after school," Sally burst out. "He's crazy! Everyone says so!"

"Crazy?" Al said. "I hear around that McIntosh is playing ball with his knee shot full of novocaine. Am I right, Jim?"

James nodded "Dr. Wickham—har—doesn't think it will hurt him," he said.

"I'm sure he must know," Al said. "But even so, how would you feel, if it were your boy, Jim? Maybe old Mr. Hoodless has got something there."

James harrumphed again. "I understand it's more a question of keeping the boy home to help on the farm," he said.

"Maybe he's still got something. He's an old man and that's a big farm. Needing help wouldn't make him crazy, Sally."

"He cut down a big tree on top of Carl and Jerry," Sally said fiercely. "Didn't even holler to them to get out of the way. He tried to fix them so they couldn't play ball. If that isn't crazy, what is?"

James said, "Har—Sally. That'll do. That's enough."

Al grinned. "Who told you that, Sally?" he asked.

"All you've got to do is look at them. They've both got black eyes. Carl's knee is hurt worse than it was in the game." Sally's eyes snapped. She turned back to the typewriter and began to type, very fast.

"Now, wait, Sally," James said. "Take that—har—slowly. I don't want mistakes in that particular letter."

"That's an odd story, Jim," Al said. "Where did that start? I don't believe old Mr. Hoodless would—"

Sally stood straight up. "If you're calling Jerry a liar, Mr. Berg," she said, "all you've got to do is go up in old Mart's back pasture and look at the tree."

She stalked out of the room, temper flaming. Ordinarily, she was a quiet girl, demure in Mr. Goss's office, but just now loyalty was insulted. She was Jerry's girl; she had been going steady with him ever since grade school.

"The ball season," Al said, looking after her, "is rugged, Jim."

James nodded. "I'll speak to her. She'll apologize."

"Don't bother. I can't be apologized to all over the school. Besides, it's only nerves. The poor little devils are so hyped up they don't know what they're doing. Let it go. They'll jiggle down, after it's all over. If they don't distill away in smoke and steam before. What am I going to do, Jim? I can't possibly grind enough chemistry into these kids before June, so that they can pass a decent examination."

"Har," James said. "Do what you can, Alfred."

"Is that all?"

James shrugged his plump, stooped shoulders. "What else," he asked, "is there?"

"When? They don't do homework assignments. All the time I have to get at them is this class period."

"Har," said James. "It's an old problem. I find it gets solved, each year. Unsatisfactorily." He looked at Al, thoughtfully. "Where's the rest of your class, Alfred?"

Alfred grinned. "Okay," he said. "I'll head back. They're in the lab, though, and Debby Parker's monitoring for me. The ones she'd have to restrain from playing pitch-catch with the microscopes are all in the gym."

"I should be glad of it," James said. "If I were you."

His vague eyes suddenly sharpened and focused.

"If you have even a part of your class you can work with—most of us—har—are not so fortunate."

"No?" Alfred said, surprised, not at what James had said, but because James had said it.

"Two of my classes consist entirely of free-loaders," James said. "They are—har—not interested in anything I can teach them. Alison, however, is teaching them something. I suppose it is all a part of education. Alfred, you will have to stop bucking Alison, if you want your contract renewed."

Alfred stared at him.

"After twelve years here," James said, "and I may say I have worked hard, I have had to conclude that the town wants a school, yes; they have gone to considerable trouble and expense to build a fine one, and any citizen, if I asked him that question, would consider me crazy. Of course his children must be educated, it goes without saying. If you should suggest to him that this is not a school, but a ball club—as it has come back to me you have suggested in front of some of your classes, Alfred—he would think at once that something was wrong with you. He would try to see you fired."

"Well, isn't it?" Al said, angrily.

"Isn't it a ball club?" James hesitated. "No. It isn't. It remains a school, because of the, say, five out of twenty whom you and I are able to teach. We have turned out a few doctors, lawyers, teachers, to balance"—he paused with a wry smile—"to balance Arthur Grindle. Not so many as we should have turned out, however. Look. Chet Alison is paid more than you are. He is paid more than I am. Because the town wants to insure the prestige it gets from having a good ballteam. It is not hard to see why, psychologically. We are still primitive in our American towns with regard to education. What it amounts to is a—har—a kind of schizophrenia. This magazine article"—he indicated a publication on his desk—"the author says, here," he went on, "that nowhere in the world are there such beautiful school buildings, such precision equipment, so many millions spent on the education of the young. Yet nowhere in the world is the educated man so distrusted. The eggheads," said James Goss, "the crackpots. You and I. Any schoolteacher in any town. It is possible, in America, to defeat a man for the presidency by calling him an egghead; in other words, an intellectual; an educated man, whom common, ordinary, decent people would do well not to trust."

He paused, staring down thoughtfully at the blotter on his neat desk. "This is why," he continued, in his precise, schoolmaster's voice, "why, actually our beautiful school buildings consist of gymnasiums costing hundreds of thousands, around which classrooms and labs hang like the appendages they are. Oh, necessary appendages, I grant you, but the real reason for a school is its gym, presided over by its high priest, the expensive athlete. So that we with our learning shall not make the children into strangers to their parents. You know?"

"I've heard," Alfred said. "I think you're putting it too strongly, Jim. It's a generalization. I don't think you can—"

"Harold Savile," James said. "You've heard of him?"

"Sure. Who hasn't? My uncle's a doctor, he's worked with him in St. Louis."

"Harold Savile. The head of a great clinic," James said. "He invented a gadget which helps dying people to get back their breath to their lungs. He has carried on some of the most exciting research in modern medicine. His work has saved thousands of lives. In New York City, when he goes there, there are circles which turn out hundreds of people to do him honor. He was born in this town, was graduated from this high school. He visited here last summer, but outside of a few who said, 'Oh, yeah, big doctor somewhere, ain't he?' nobody flipped so much as a button. No. What they get out the fire engines for, ring the bells, is the basketball team. You think you can buck that, Alfred? You can't. Work with your few. Slide Alison's boys by."

"Is that an order?" Alfred asked. He felt dazed; as if someone had whacked him hard on the head. He had always supposed that something went on inside James's plump, balding, enigmatic head; in talking with him, one sensed intelligence, but closed and guarded.

"No," James said. "I can't order you. But you're starting your career, and a black mark, in our field, is—har—a black mark. It's not worth it to you. Besides, the boys you're most concerned over will probably go to college on athletic scholarships, anyway."

"That's good?" Al said.

"Har—" James said. "I'm a little tired, Alfred, and, I expect, discouraged. I don't often indulge myself in letting go. I expect this conversation had—har—better not go further than this room, Alfred."

"Oh," Alfred said. "Surely. Of course, Jim."

"Then I can say that athletic scholarships are far from good." James fumbled nearsightedly with the papers on his desk. "I tell myself, at times, that we are not fighting a losing battle," he said. 'That we have help in high places. The President of Yale, for example, an article of his—har, where is it? I had it here. I suppose Sally's got it—har—under something. But never mind." James stopped his aimless fumbling. His eyes, behind his conservative lenses, glinted. "I can quote you chapter and verse. What the President of Yale wrote about the national traffic in athletic scholarships is burned on my brain in letters of fire. It is, he says, 'one of the greatest educational swindles ever perpetrated on American youth.' "

"Yes," Alfred said. "I read that, too. About the aim being not education, but entertainment—"

" 'Not the education of that youth, but the entertainment of its elders; not the welfare of the athlete, but the pleasure of the spectator.' "

"Yes," Alfred said. "I wonder how many people read it. Outside of school dopes, like you and me?"

"Well, I collect these things," James said. "To keep myself from feeling like a voice crying in the wilderness. There are more of them than there used to be. Times are changing. I tell myself. The Russians will either kill us or they will educate us. After twelve years—" The fire suddenly went out of James. He took off his glasses, rubbed his eyes, hard, with his thumb and forefinger. "After twelve years of teaching,

I'm inclined to wonder which, har, fate we would object to most." He put the glasses back on. "Some of us, that is. I will say, Alfred, you are a useful and a valuable man here. Don't make it possible for our Triumvirate, Mr. Parker, Mr. Troy, and Dr. Wickham, to humiliate—perhaps discredit you."

"No," Alfred said. "Thanks, James."

"Are you seeing Miss Callander tonight, by the way?"

"Why, yes. Yes, I am. I'm having dinner with her."

"Ask her to call my wife about the Heart Drive, will you?"

"Why, sure, uh, Jim."

He had almost done it, Al thought, as he went down the corridor toward his lab. He had almost said "har" in the middle of a sentence in a conversation with James Goss. It was a thing you had to watch. That it had come out "uh" was more luck than anything else.

He was passing his own empty classroom and he turned in at the door. Better sit down at the desk, cool off, build back the good old deadpan. James Goss had gone the long way around to tell him that he wasn't going to back Al Berg against Chet Alison. Rationalized it pretty well, too. Under the circumstances, I suppose you can't blame him. He needs his job; he's got a family. Still, it was a mouthful to swallow.

Everybody in the school would know by now that Old Buggsy had had another run-in with the coach, and Alison had come out on top again.

So I had better not appear all rumpled up. Put on the front. Imperturbable, that's me. Still, why? I'm good and sore. It would only be honest if some of it showed.

James's note had turned up, he saw, as he got up to go along to the lab. It was there, a white oblong, conspicuous in the middle of his blotting-pad. Sally must have located Josephine.

He tore open the note, reading James's precise, apologetic phrases about Chemistry IV being excused this afternoon from class, and was about to toss it into his wastebasket, when he saw that someone had been playing a paper-and-pencil game with his name on the envelope—the ancient game, known to any school child, in which the names of a boy and girl are written down, one under the other, and identical letters canceled, then the rest counted according to traditional formula.

Only Al's name hadn't been paired off with a girl's—with Ellen Callander's—as he'd thought, at first glance.

> ~~A~~LFR~~ED~~ BER~~G~~
> ~~DA~~MN KIK~~E~~

it read.

Lord, he thought. The things they think of!

Well, of course, something like this might have been expected to happen sooner or later. Kids picked up stuff from their parents, and he'd known there was some feeling against Jews in the town.

He stood looking at it for a moment, and then, quietly tucking the envelope in his pocket, he went on to his chemistry lab.

Alfred stayed late at his desk, finishing up his daily chore of paperwork. Usually, he didn't mind it, but tonight it seemed endless, something that would have to be done all over again, tomorrow. Tonight, he felt tired, with an inner, bone-grinding weariness.

Being tired was nothing new. He often was, and he generally enjoyed the feeling. It only meant you'd done a good day's work, you were ready to eat, rest, and do another. He sometimes thought of the big Greek with whom he had worked on a road gang one summer, when he was in college: Pappidopolous, known as Pappy, who would break out his enormous lunch carried in a ten-quart pail, saying happily, "When I can smell sweat, then I am hungry." To Pappy, eating, resting after a tough job, was one of the most rewarding experiences in life; and after that summer, the youngster, Al Berg, not yet dry behind the ears, had come to see how that could be so.

This feeling, now, was mixed with discouragement, dispiritedness. It hit him as he was going over the last of a batch of chemistry papers. Debby Parker's paper was faultless; that, of course, went without saying. Alfred could have marked it A-plus without reading it and have saved himself time; but he went carefully through it, for fun, admiring its organization, the neat, logical reasoning. That was a nice mind—in the traditional sense of the word "nice"; and it was being used, too.

The thing was, the papers of the five top stars on the ballteam were exactly like it. Except for the different kinds of handwriting, you couldn't see a difference. Even the spelling was correct, something you didn't always see in all cases.

Hell, they can't think I'm that stupid, he thought. They're smart kids; they must know I'd know. He pulled up short. They did know, of course. Only, they were so secure, so sure of themselves, that they didn't care.

He chucked the whole batch of papers into his wastebasket.

Go home, eat, rest, cope with it tomorrow, he thought. If I can cope with it; there doesn't seem to be much I can do.

As he came out on the steps of the building, he saw that the windows of the gym were lighted, some of them open; he could hear the crack of Alison's voice, grating a little hoarsely now, and the swish and thump of rubber-soled feet up and down the floor.

Wow, those kids have been at it since one o'clock, and it's now—

The clock on the steeple of the old Union Church, across the street from the high school, said twenty to seven. His own watch, he saw, was ten minutes slow, and he paused to reset it.

Surely, they must have had a break since one. Wonder if McIntosh's knee's holding up, or if he's had to have another shot of novocaine?

From the school entrance, Al could see down the length of Main Street, the black asphalt strip piled on either side with old plowed snow, and lighted by street lamps, neon signs, the glow from shop windows. Nobody was around, no parked cars, no people. Except for the illumination, it might have been a ghost town. One of the big Westerns was showing at this hour on the TV—the town loved Westerns. The West was too far away to amount to much, but it was also too far away to be real; a world of sweet illusion, in which the greathearted cowboy, bemused by humanity's ancient dream, rode forever into the sunset after doing good to his fellow-man.

Darkness, already fallen, was overcast, with fog; east wind from the harbor blew heavy with the smell of salt and frozen clamflats, raw to the throat, stinging in the lungs. To the west of town lay miles of field and forest, locked and silent in February night; to the east, the miles of sea. Two emptinesses, punctuated by the lighted strip where Main Street flashed its colored signs against the sky.

DRUGSTORE. HOT DOGS. EAT. CHAMBER OF COMMERCE. DORCAS SOCIETY. ESSO. TROY'S GROC.

Gaudy light and tinted shadow flecked the tired fronts of the business blocks, the many and varied types of architecture—imitation Dutch, phony English, bastard Renaissance, or plain peeling New England clapboard, like the Odd Fellows Hall, built by a local contractor after his own plan; all outmoded, all shabby, all outworn; as if, years ago, an insane and embittered architect had flung down at random a hodgepodge of such odds and tail-ends of what he could remember from the days when he had respected his art and before he had lost his wits.

Across from the high school, the old Union Church, its white Doric columns stark and impaled by the remorseless glare of twin floodlights, alone admitted the purity of thought and aspiration of another age. It had been built on this same slight rise of land, the "upper" end of Main Street, as had the school; so that people always spoke of going "up to the church" and "up to the school"; as if they felt that a hill was the place for what they valued most, a place for temples.

The two buildings, each the finest architectural product of its respective day, faced each other across carefully landscaped lawns. The school building, ten years old, had cost the town a cool half-million, and was not yet paid for. It had been more than the town could afford and had raised the bill for education to a whopping sixty percent of the tax dollar, about which the older inhabitants, like Martin Hoodless and Sidney Widgett, griped continually.

The school building had everything needful, in the way of equipment, in laboratory, shop, and classrooms, gymnasium and cafeteria; the structure itself was modern, clean-lined, and functional.

The old Union Church had cost a great deal less, having been built in the early days of the town by donations and volunteer labor. It had, in its day, been as great a center of local pride as the new school was now, and, in a way still was, though services had not been held in it for nearly a century. In the early 1850s, half of its congregation had got mad at the other half; and the blistering town row that followed had left the church standing high and dry on its hill, deserted because no one would use anything which anybody he was mad at had owned a piece of. So both factions moved out and started churches of their own, which, in time, divided again; so that now there were five churches in town, of various denominations.

In the twenties, when summer visitors to the town had begun oo-ing and ah-ing over the beautiful old building, and looking askance at its dilapidated ruin, the ladies of the Historical Society had started a fund to restore it, and now it was both restored and endowed, and could be visited as a monument and a museum. It was not used for services, because nobody knew now who owned the pews. Hundreds of heirs of the original squabblers had scattered through the years to all parts of the country, and the fact that they were still the legal owners made the townsfolk too uncomfortable.

Alfred had learned the story of the Union Church from Ellen Callander's landlady, Miss Eloise Marcy, the local historian, whose great ambition was to write a history of the town. For years she had collected information; she had a room in her house stacked with boxes of notes. Alfred, himself a lover of backgrounds, had seen enough of these notes to know that some of them were completely fascinating; he hoped, someday, to find time to study them more, with a view to putting them in order. Miss Marcy admitted that she might never do anything with them, herself. She had made so many notes, she said, that her head was all fogged up, which was a disadvantage, since in her head was where a good deal of her material was. The story of the Union Church was all in her head; she had always been too disgusted by it to write any of it down.

"Oh, there might be some account of it there, in my grandfather's papers," she told Alfred. "Me, I'd rather leave it right out of my his'try. People is cussid. They may look nice and seem nice, but in the long run, you'll find most of 'em cussid. If a town ever has a good old tomcat row, you can bet your boots it'll be over one of the two best things they've got, the church or the school. If only the Bible didn't say 'Love thy Neighbor,' it might help some. But there 'tis, down there in black and white, and if you don't abide by it, you can't be a Christian. Only, people is cussid, they ain't going to be told what to do. They'll have a fight and split up the church, and each take a pan of the coals and go start one of their own; and then for a year or so afterwards, both sides is some old religious to make up for it."

Miss Marcy, now in her late seventies, had the name around town of being slightly pixillated; by and large, she was a misanthrope, and Alfred did not agree with her. Himself, he believed that people might be cussid by fits and starts, but in the main their motives were good. So far as he could see, this town was not much different from any other. Summers, with the work-gang, he had covered a good deal of ground, seen many American towns, and last year, on his tour of the country, he had seen many more, along with large sections of the West, outside of his own home area.

Arizona, Montana, New Mexico, Cimarron, Tombstone—the magic names which now bemused an entire nation—for it had always tickled Alfred that in the West nearly all the TV programs were Western, too; that there, too, the Universal Cowboy rode, under the magnificent high sky. And the ghost towns, he thought. Tuzigoot . . . Jerome . . .

Tuzigoot, the prehistoric Indian ghost town, which faced across the Verde Valley of Arizona the modern American ghost town of Jerome, had very likely been destroyed by cussidness—archaeologists thought that the Tuzigoot men might have been massacred by their neighbors. The end of Jerome, which took place in 1947, came when the ore under Mingus Mountain ran out. Fifteen thousand people packed up and moved away, leaving hotels, bars, houses, the five-and-ten, and the A and P; so that when you walked down Main Street there, you might think that here was a town, a city, a going concern, until you smelled it, the air in the street spongy with must from deserted, closed, rotting buildings; and you realized with a cold curdle of blood behind your breastbone, that there was nobody in the houses; the people had gone away. The smell inside the Union Church was exactly the same; but what probably had reminded him was the deserted look of Main Street tonight.

I'm getting worse than old Miss Marcy herself, he thought. I'd better snap out of this and get along to dinner. I'm late.

It would be too bad to spoil Ellen's dinner; she usually went to a lot of trouble.

Behind him, the lights in the gym were at last going out. Fog and night had thickened around the church steeple, so that its clock seemed to hover without visible support over the town. He saw, as he ran down the steps to his car, the round, yellow face, lighted from within, blandly and a little foolishly recording the passage of time.

Side by side, on a quiet residential street, were the two houses which Miss Eloise Marcy had inherited at the death of her brother. One, in which she lived, was a mansion three stories and an attic high, crowned by a square captain's-walk. It had been built about 1820 by her great-grandfather, Captain Jethro Marcy, who had made a fortune in the China trade in the days of sailing-ships. The other was an aged salt-box, dating from Colonial times, old even in Captain Jethro's day. He had, however, taken a great deal of pride in it and, in his time, had spent money to keep it shingled and in repair, as a memento to his great-grandfather, the town's pioneer.

Miss Eloise was the last of the line; she lived upon the tag-end of Captain Jethro's fortune and eked it out by renting the salt-box, in summer to tourists, and in winter to schoolteachers, an ideal arrangement. Because summer rent was five times winter rent, Miss Eloise couldn't have someone in there permanently, and of course by the time the tourist season started, schoolteachers had folded tent and gone. The only disadvantage was, the teachers were likely to complain. The house was old and drafty, heated by wood-burning stoves. It had a fireplace, which, however, was plugged with a sheet of zinc. Miss Eloise wasn't willing to have the fireplace opened up, because she was afraid something would happen to the pink paper fan. She had spent one whole winter, off and on, making that fan. It was very elaborate, made especially for the fireplace, which, of course, was the only place where it could be kept safely as well as seen. Besides, a fireplace only made you colder in winter; and if you took out that zinc, the plumbing would freeze.

There was a tradition, about town, that single female schoolteachers ought not to live alone; they should, for their own protection, rent a nice room with some nice family, or live at the Y.W.C.A. Miss Eloise usually refused to rent her salt-box to one young single lady; she required two, she said, or a nice couple; because, in a house, with a living room available, if the single lady was pretty, there was always the problem of gentleman-friends.

Gently and delicately, not wishing to imply anything, Miss Marcy had told Ellen Callander this on the day, early in the fall, when Ellen asked to rent the house.

"Yes, indeed," Ellen had said. "I do see your point so well, Miss Marcy."

She had sat in Miss Marcy's parlor, listening with a blue-eyed, attentive gaze, looking respectable and innocent in her dark-gray tailored suit.

"But you see, I shall have problems, Miss Marcy. I'll be giving music lessons, or tutoring sometimes evenings at home. I'll have band and glee-club rehearsals, and kids banging out scales, and do, re, mi, on the saxophone. The Y.W. wouldn't put up with that—even a nice family with a nice room to rent might think twice. I really need the house, you see."

"Well, I don't know as I'd think much of having a passel of young ones traipsing around through that house," Miss Marcy said. "That's a real, old-fashioned, genuine antique, that house is."

Ellen smiled. "Anyone can see it is," she said. "I should, of course, take care of it, knowing how highly you value it."

Well, there, Miss Marcy thought. I do believe she would. She's nice. Not like them rackety young twippets that go thistle-downing around, all they think about is men, men, men.

She said, before she thought, "Well, I guess you can have it, then," not knowing that she was not the first to yield to the charm of that smile; not knowing that within two weeks the fireplace in her old house would be opened, the chimney cleaned, the pink paper fan packed away in the attic.

Ellen Callander's people were Irish, though she herself had been born at Weymouth, in Dorset, on the south coast of England. Her parents had been entertainers, heading up a troupe of pierrots, who traveled, during the summer season, from one coast resort to another. It had been only by chance that she had been born at Weymouth; the troupe had happened to be there at the time. Ellen had been an accident anyway; the players had engagements, the show had to go on. And so her father had made arrangements to board her with a Weymouth woman, and as soon as his wife was able to travel, the pierrots went on to Blackpool.

It had been a wild, gypsy-like childhood, at least until Ellen was eight. Beyond making sure that she got enough to eat and stayed reasonably clean, the Weymouth woman paid her very little attention. Ellen was free to roam at will, almost as soon as she had been old enough to walk, coming home when she liked, going to school only when the school officials came after her; and the ancient, maritime town of Weymouth was a fascinating place for a free child to roam about in. It was a place where a child, hitching a ride on a truck, could find ships to see, and lighthouses and fossil stones; where, perhaps, if the truck went that far, she could see the very southern tip and end of England, Portland Bill.

At some time, during every summer, the troupe of pierrots came to Weymouth, but during the early part of the War, they came no more. Her parents were dead, the Weymouth woman said, killed by one of the bombs on London; and what was she to do with Ellen now?

Then, one winter's morning, without explanation, she bundled Ellen up, packed her few belongings into a battered suitcase, and took her to Ireland; to Cobh; to a ship; and sent her across the ocean to her aunt in Michigan.

"This is where you're going," she told Ellen, handing her a slip of paper at the dock. "Don't give this up to anyone. Don't ask questions, and don't cry," and she stalked away, leaving the child alone.

Ellen did not mind too much. She was not leaving anyone behind; she had not grieved for her parents because she had not known them long enough to miss them. As for places, she would miss the lighthouses of Portland Bill, particularly the candy-striped one; but you could not go there anymore because of the War, nor to the Chesil Beach, blocked off now with barbed wire. As for Chesil Beach, she had three of its round pebbles in her pocket.

She turned an intrepid, blue-eyed gaze on the winter sea; this was the ocean, stretching away to America.

Her aunt, after the first shock—for she had not known of her sister and brother-in-law's deaths, nor even of Ellen's existence—was delighted to have her; she took the ragged, excited, travel-stained waif into a heart that was as big as a barrel. Her husband was in the wholesale plumbing business—there was plenty of money; and plenty of room, too, though she had five children of her own.

For the first time in her life, Ellen found herself valued; she grew up petted and loved in a household where people had a great deal of love for each other. If the bleak time with the woman at Weymouth showed at all now, it was in a certain reluctance Ellen had to love, to give more than good company and conversation to anyone until she was sure, of them and of herself. Alfred Berg, if he had known this, might have found it a comfort to him.

He sat, now, relaxed and full, on the divan in front of Ellen's fire. Dinner had been wonderful—steak and a green salad, exactly what he liked.

"The first meal like this I ever saw," Ellen had said, putting the steak on the table, "I thought my Aunt Edith was crazy. Expecting anyone to eat a great chunk of red meat, still bleeding it was, and chopped-up raw greens in oil! Ooh! Then I saw everyone else was eating like a cannibal, so I did, too. Only all my little cousins stared at me, fascinated, and my uncle said, 'Ede, for goshsake, cut the kid's meat up for her,' and I said, 'I don't like to cut my meat, I likes to tear it.' Oh, I was a little savage, let me tell you!"

Now, he sat watching her while she crumpled up the envelope from James Goss's note, tossed it into the fireplace.

"Well," she said. "You would be a teacher, you dope. By now, you might be well on your way to a nice medical degree, quiet and peaceful, with the sick and the dead. Don't you wish you were?"

"Sometimes," Alfred said.

"Are you bitter because someone's called you a kike?"

"Uh . . ." Alfred began. He glanced over at her, surprised, the wind a little taken out of his sails, and Ellen laughed.

"I should tactfully not speak the word?" she said. "You're a kike, so you're a kike. So what? I'm a limey. Or, if you like, a mick. A Black Irish mick. I wasn't even born in this country. Try that over on your harmonium, Old Buggsy."

Alfred grinned, wryly. "At least, I've got a nickname."

"I know. Buggsy. That's lovely. That's the top. Good nicknames are common, don't pride yourself. They are one of the pleasanter customs of St. Trinian's, and Mr.-Parker-the-School-Committee's stock in trade.

By the way, you should have seen us all down at his garage the other day, Miss Eloise, Mr. Parker, and me."

"Oh? What happened there?"

"Well, Mr. Parker, it seems, admires me. So he gives me to understand."

"He does, does he?" Alfred muttered. He glanced over at her, and Ellen, who was in the act of fixing the fire, looked at him and grinned.

"Mm-hm. All this business of tending to my car-servicing personally, himself? You know? And looking for the proper spot in the conversation to declare intentions? I mentioned it to Miss Eloise, and she said he does that with all the girls. Member of the Board or no, she says, Win Parker is a feeler, it is because he is a red-headed man, and never trust a man who has got red hair. So the last time I needed garage work done, I took Miss Eloise with me. You should have seen the three of us, Mr. Parker poking around in the car's innards and sneaking an ogle at me, and Miss Eloise standing there, putting the double whammy on him like a basilisk—"

Alfred roared. "Good for Miss Eloise!" he said. "I've been so busy at the ballgames that I haven't had an evening lately to help with the history. How is she?"

"As you see," Ellen said.

She gestured toward the living-room window, where, thirty feet away, beyond the passage that separated the two houses, Miss Eloise sat facing her own window, busily writing at a table.

"My life is an open book," Ellen murmured.

"Why don't we pull down the shades?"

Ellen gave him a sidelong glance. "You know perfectly well why," she said. "If she can't see everybody, every minute, she comes over. The other night when Chet was here—"

"Oh," Alfred said. "He was here again, was he?"

"Certainly. I'm sociable. I have lots of company. Well, Chet was down-cellar, fooling with the plumbing. It's terrible plumbing, a do-it-yourself job, Miss Marcy's brother put it in all by himself the year before he died, and I think he put his all into it; there's one pipe that goes 'Bring me two bottles of beer,' all night long. Maybe it's him;

the house is supposed to be haunted anyway. Well, Chet thought he might be able to fix it, he's practical about such things."

"I can imagine," Alfred said. He sat glowering at the fire, his hands thrust deep into his pockets. "So am I, practical," he muttered.

"Well, maybe you can fix it; Chet couldn't. Though he might have, if he'd had time. I was down there with him holding the flashlight, and Miss Eloise couldn't see a soul in the living room or the kitchen. She didn't think about the cellar, and of course the only other possibility's the bedroom. So over she came. Said she was sorry to barge in, but Mr. Alison ought to know that his car was parked too near the fire hydrant." Ellen giggled. "Chet said he appreciated her interest, but he'd taken care of that when he parked the car. You know how Chet can be when he knows he's right."

"Uh-huh," Alfred said, glumly. "Who better?"

"Well, Miss Eloise gently produced a fifty-foot steel tape from her apron pocket. Belonged to her brother, she said. It seems she'd measured. The car was two feet too close. So Chet had to go out and move it. He was huffy. And what's more"—Ellen's eyes began to dance—"Miss Eloise stayed to dinner."

"She did! Why, God bless her little pointed head! Did you invite her?"

"Oh, she wangled it. Anyone should know better than to tangle with Miss Eloise. Chet left before she did. And then she settled in for a nice visit. Told me about this house, how it was headquarters for Colonial troops the time the British attacked the town by sea, and they brought in the wounded and laid them out over the floor. Over this floor," Ellen went on, with a wave of her hand at the aged, white pine boards. "They even picked up one British marine who bled very badly and died in here. That was why, Miss Eloise said, she was still thinking twice about letting me use the fireplace—"

"Eh? The fireplace?"

"Oh, we have had a real go-round about the fireplace, Miss Eloise and I. All sorts of reasons. This last one was a dandy. Seems they built a big fire in here to keep the wounded warm, and it warmed the Yankees all right, but the British boy just got colder and colder. After that, no matter how many times her great-grandfather's great-grandfather planed the floor, the bloodstains always came back, every time he built a hot fire on."

"Oh, my!" Alfred said. "Have you seen them?"

"No, but Miss Eloise told me just where to put the scatter rug. I reminded her that I am British, too, or was, and that maybe British bloodstains wouldn't appear to friends but only to enemies, but she said not to count on it, a British marine of seventeen seventy-six would consider me the worst kind of a traitor. You know, getting naturalized. No, no bloodstains; but bats. Oh, yes, bats! She said there would be bats in the chimney, and there were. When we took out that zinc plug, four flew out. Three I have—ugh—met and disposed of, the other is still living in the house with me. We, ah, avoid each other. And then, of course, there was Elinor Glyn."

"Elinor Glyn? Three-Weeks Glyn? That one?"

"Mm-hm. I couldn't think why these books kept turning up on the living-room table. Three Weeks. One Day. High Noon. Finally, Miss Eloise dropped something that let me know why. It seems a fireplace abets immoral ladies. At least, it's an accessory. You lie on a leopardskin, she says, in your shape. In front of a fire, to entertain gentlemen."

Alfred shouted. "Well, remind me"—he choked, and pulled out his handkerchief to wipe the tears of laughter from his cheeks—"remind me to bring you a leopardskin."

"Thanks," Ellen said. "I'd love one."

"Well, she likes me," Alfred said. "At least, I've got that edge on the competition."

"She certainly does. You know, I haven't seen her writing before, she usually sits and watches. I think she's singing a siren song of research. She wants you to come over, boy. Hey, do I have competition!"

Alfred glanced over at her, thoughtfully.

Does she by any chance want me to clear out? he wondered. We seem to go up and down like a seesaw. I just get pleasantly cheered up, thinking I'm making some time, and bang! He said aloud, "You know, I might just do that, after a while. Those dusty boxes of hers—they really do sing a siren song. The historical records of a town from Colonial times on—what a story it would make. Makes me drool. Fingers itch, and such. If I only had more time . . ."

He was pleased to see that Ellen looked a little dashed.

"Go and leave me with all those dishes?" she asked.

"Let's do 'em," Alfred said. He got up, caught her hands, and pulled her to her feet. "And then maybe both go over for a while. You could help like crazy, sorting, if you wanted to."

"Mm," Ellen said.

In the kitchen, without further comment, she began washing the dishes. Standing a little behind her in the small work-area, industriously wiping, Alfred noticed again as he had before how her hair grew at the nape of her neck, neat, clipped and silky against the creamy skin. Ellen had black hair, naturally curly, the short, crisp ringlets covering her head like a cap; she had the Irish complexion, with blue eyes that could turn gray-green in moments of temper, and might, he told himself, be just a little gray-green right now, if only he could see.

"Limey," he said, under his breath. "Black Irish mick."

"Mm-hm," Ellen said. She flashed him a grin. "Kike. Old Buggsy, for heaven's sake! Oh, Al, darn those kids! You know you're really doing a terrific job up there."

Her eyes, he saw, were not gray-green at all, only blue, direct and friendly.

Try and keep up, he thought. It's a puzzler how to.

Aloud he said, "Oh, I don't make too much of it, Ellen. I admit, I felt glum for a while, it—But, after all, I'm a stranger here, with a name that sounds foreign, isn't locally familiar. In almost any town there are always some who feel sensitive about a Colonial heritage, if they have one; try to protect it against anything foreign settling down. It's a human failing; it isn't only here and now."

"I know," Ellen said. "It's a fine old historical precedent. It goes back. Away past the time when the Pilgrims left Boston Stump for the sake of freedom. To the time when naked savages threw rocks at anyone who didn't belong to their tribe."

"Oh, come. Nobody's thrown any rocks."

"No. Here, now, you're too civilized to throw rocks at a man with a 'funny' name. You just don't let him buy a house in your town; or if he somehow manages to 'get in,' you make fun of his name."

She wrung out her dishcloth with a sharp twist, snapped it in the air to shake out wrinkles, slapped it down on the rack to dry.

"You've been stewing over this?" Alfred asked. "Don't. It isn't worth it. I shouldn't have told you. It happens sometimes; let it roll off, is the thing to do. And look. The fact that nobody's thrown any rocks means that civilization's come at least a little way from the savages."

"Humph!" Ellen said. "We've also come some way from Boston Stump."

"Religious freedom? Oh, come. The Pilgrims weren't after religious freedom for everybody, only for them."

"I know. It hangs over, doesn't it? Sometimes I think, what a spectacle, if all the money spent on educating ignorance out of people were laid end to end. It would make a four-lane highway from here to Plymouth Rock. And so, what happens? We have to buck sports, as big business. Every school child a champion at the age of twelve."

"Yes, but, Ellen—there are some changes being made. For instance, did you read about the high school near the ski resort, the one that got written up in *Time?*"

Ellen shook her head, smiling a little, watching his absorbed face. After Chet, he was certainly restful to have around; not quite so flattering to a girl, perhaps, but, at least, you didn't have to watch his hands to know just when you had to duck. There was a singleness of purpose about Chet which was, at times, hard to handle, and, at times, a bore. You had to admit that the continual presentation of masculine charm in one form or another without anything, apparently, to pad it out, occasionally palled. You could not be long with Chet without finding out that to him a woman was an idea; the idea of man's relaxation.

Without doubt, the masculine charm was pleasant; Chet was an attractive man. If you fell in love with him, you would not, of course, miss other things. At least, temporarily. But except for sex, Chet was a closed book, and if a girl had a mind, any mind at all, not to speak of an intelligent, highly trained one, she could see very little future in him, and thank God for Miss Eloise at the window.

On the other hand, here was Al, who was, at least he gave that impression, mostly mind. He, too, was attractive, with slim, clean-cut looks; dark hair that waved hack from a high forehead; a positive, intellectual kind of face. He had ideas about making a pass, too; you could tell. But he was too easily put off, too easily checked. By a word, a gesture. And that was very considerate of him, but still . . .

Granted, she thought, listening, that there are times when a man's work is the most important thing in life to him—well, it seemed, with Alfred, you had conversation.

She was, she realized, still a little put out with him for suggesting a visit to Miss Marcy, thereby breaking up their evening; and then, suddenly, the whole situation tickled her sense of humor.

Somebody had better pretty soon strike a golden mean, she thought, with a small audible chuckle.

Alfred hadn't heard the chuckle. He was going on talking.

". . . this ski-resort town, all the kids wanted to do was ski. Well, here's all this New Look in education—what's the matter with us, we're way behind with satellites, if we don't look out, the Russians'll have a man on the moon first; hell, we've got to teach our kids something, haven't we? So the School Board, in this town, decreed that all athletes to be eligible for games had to get at least a C average; and the school's math instructor took this seriously—he handed out a whole batch of D's, E's, and F's to the ski team."

Alfred paused, a faraway look in his eyes. "Beautiful D's, E's, and F's," he murmured. "The kind I dream about."

"Go on," Ellen said. "What happened?"

"Oh, my," Alfred said. "The glue schussed into the slalom. The Chairman of the School Board's daughter was just about to enter the Nationals; and she got an F in math. So the day of the races, her father himself took her out of school, and sent her up to ski, with his blessing. She won. She got time on TV and headlines in the papers, thereby proving the school people to be a bunch of dopes. The next week, fifteen or so kids got their parents' consents to go up the mountain and ski on school time. The school dopes, this time, didn't take it lying down. I don't know what happened to the math instructor, he's probably long gone, but in the higher echelons, the Superintendent of Schools upped and resigned. So the townspeople took that in a holiday mood; they hired another one. And guess who? The new Superintendent of Schools is the instructor, the coach, of the ski team."

"Oh, great," Ellen said.

"Well, there was a gimmick," Alfred went on. "Thanks to, of all people, the Russians. A few years ago, nothing would have happened. Nothing, nix, nyet! But this year, Sputnik. So our story gets noised abroad through various media. It made, for instance, a national news magazine. And Papa has been made pretty ridiculous, nationwide, in the eyes of some people whom he probably respects."

"Wonderful!" Ellen said. "And so you think you'll keep on being one of the dopes."

"I expect to. I like the kids. I've got a few up there I've done something for, Debby Parker, for instance, and young Ralph McIntosh. I wish I could make some time with his brother; the ballplayer they call Shirttail McIntosh has probably got the best brain of anybody in the school. Trained, it would be better than mine, I expect. But I guess he's a lost cause. I can't get to first base with him."

"I think he's awful," Ellen said. "All that conceit—"

"Yes, poor little devil, he's been pumped up out of all reason. It's too bad. With some, it wouldn't make a difference—Mooney, for example. Mooney doesn't know A from B and can't learn; the only reason he's in school at all is to play ball. Incidentally, I learned today that I'm going to have to weasel along with James Goss, give everybody a passing grade."

Ellen nodded. "It seems to be the custom in this school," she said. "You're going to do it?"

"Well, I hadn't made up my mind, really. But, yes, I guess I am. I'm not solid enough yet to buck the combination. If I try, out I go on my ear, and I would like another year here, to see what I could do. I expect I sound like a prize heel," he finished reflectively, "and I know I sound dull. I sound very dull, even to me."

Ellen looked at him. She leaned over, suddenly, buried her face in the front of his shirt, and bit him, hard, on the breastbone.

"Ow!" Alfred said. He stared, astonished, rubbing the place with his fingers.

"All right," Ellen said. "Just don't talk bunk to me, that's all. I'm on your side, remember? I like to see brawn fought with brains. Or do you—" She faltered a little, noting the expression in his eyes.

"Good," he said briskly. He reached across and took her by the shoulders. "I know," he went on, holding her firmly as she twisted ineffectually in his hands, trying to get away. "You don't like to cut your meat, you like to tear it, you cannibal." He put his lips down over hers.

The silence in the room was not long. Sunk deep, his head spinning, Alfred did not hear a sound; he became aware, merely of a tenseness in Ellen, and lifted his face from hers. Then he heard the knock, the delicate tap-tapping at the door.

"Miss Callander? Miss Callander? Are you all right?" "Yes," Ellen said. Eyes suddenly brimming over with mirth, she touched her finger to his lips. "Ssh, it's Miss Eloise."

Alfred grinned. "With a leopardskin," he said. "Tell her to bring it right in."

Part Seven

On a night toward the end of February, a magnificent display of northern lights dazzled the town. It appeared first in the east, almost with the going down of the sun, a strange red glow against the sky, so that people thought somewhere there must be a big fire. In any other season, they would have said, a big forest fire off to the east, but in the dead of winter, in February, not likely, with everything locked in ice and snow. As the night deepened, the red glow faded; its place was taken by an arc of cold light across the north, from which great shafts of pale color began moving upward, widening until the northern sky was filled with flickering red, blue, green, violet, shifting and changing, sometimes buckling inward, torn at the edges to rags and tatters, like colored curtains at some celestial window behind which blew a mighty wind.

In the town, radios started to hiss and fry as if someone had dropped cold water into a pan of hot fat; on TV screens the cowboys blew up to enormous balloons, then slipped and began to flow like quicksilver.

"Damn northern lights!" people said. "Might as well turn it off, give up looking. Can't see a thing with those cussid things going on in the sky."

Down in her cabin at the motel, Bessie Maitland snapped off her TV set, took one fearful look out the window. The snow-covered clearing past her back yard was bright as day, light strong enough to cast an icy-tinted glow upon the snow. The spruces stood black-etched against it, and on the far side of the yard, at the edge of trees, her enemy, the wild deer, stood, a statue carved in dark stone, staring bemused toward the cabin.

Bessie plunged into bed, not stopping to undress; she pulled the covers tightly over her head. From her childhood on the island, where to the loneliness of sky and forest had always been added the vaster, colder loneliness of the sea, Bessie had been afraid of northern lights. Some queer, awful ghost might be flapping around the sky; or maybe God was going to strike the world dead.

Charles Kendall was in bed and asleep. Tired with outdoors work, which he had been doing that day, warily negotiating the slippery paths around the motel on his artificial leg, he slept and did not awaken.

George Whitney, with an irritated grunt, snapped off the quick-silver-sliding images on his TV and went to the pantry, where he ate half a layer cake and drank three glasses of milk. He then went to bed, taking Hazel with him. A man had to do something, nights when the TV didn't work.

Ellen Callander had settled down at her desk, when Alfred's knock sounded at the door. He seemed excited as he came in; not stopping to say hello, he strode to the desk, turning off the light.

"Look," he said. "Look out the window."

Bewildered at first, then seeing, as her eyes became adjusted to darkness, Ellen gasped. "Oh," she said. "Isn't that lovely!"

She stood beside him at the window.

"Northern lights," she said. "I've never seen them like that."

She realized suddenly, with amusement, that if Alfred had been conscious of her when he came in, he certainly wasn't now.

"I've just been on the phone to the Observatory at Boulder," he said.

Boulder? Ellen thought. Oh, yes, the University of Colorado, that was Alfred's college.

"Doc Wellman says they've been keeping an eye on the sunspots," Alfred said. "And there's been a terrific solar flare . . . "

He went on watching, absorbed.

"Sunspots? Did they cause this?" Ellen asked.

When he did not answer, she nudged him a little, her eyes dancing.

"Mm," he said, absently. "What? Oh. Yes. Something to do with it, of course. No one knows for sure the exact how or why. All kinds of invisible and fascinating forces . . . television sets are out, radios full of static. Means the ionosphere's all ripped up, absorbing impulses instead of bouncing them back; so radio silence, a lot of places, no communication with planes in certain areas; Atlantic cables out, probably, everything scrambled. There's been what they call a magnetic storm. Lord, what a field for research that would be! Look at it! Ellen, what I came in for, can I use your phone? I want to get in touch with some kids in my physics classes, make sure they get a good look at this."

"Be my guest," Ellen said.

She thought, wryly, I can always go back to getting my classbook up-to-date.

"Put on the light," Alfred said. He made a dive for the phone book. "And then get into something warm, so we can go out and catch this from the top of a hill somewhere."

When she came back from dressing, Alfred had, apparently, finished phoning. He was standing in the middle of the room, looking woebegone, talking with Miss Eloise Marcy.

"Oh, Miss Callander," she chirped. "I saw your light go out, quick, like that, and I thought the electricity had failed, but then I saw my lights were on, and I knew that couldn't be it. So I said to myself, She's blown a fuse, that's what she's done, and I knew you wouldn't want to entertain Mr. Berg in the dark, so I brought over a candle. And now Mr. Berg tells me you're just going out, and it's so fortunate for me, because there's a great sight going on outside that will go down in history, and I didn't know how I would get anywhere to watch it, not having an automobile, to jot down some notes about it, but here you are, going, and with a whole empty back seat!"

Oh, blast! Ellen thought. What's the matter with him? Well, I suppose I'm lucky his whole empty back seat isn't filled up with his physics class.

And then Alfred lied, as fulsome and smooth-faced a lie as she had ever heard.

"I'm so sorry, Miss Marcy, I didn't make myself clear. We are going out, but it's to a teachers' meeting. You know, your best bet would be your upstairs bedroom window. And warmer—it's fearfully cold tonight. Slippery, too. Let me just see you back to your door, that walk is a glare of ice."

Firmly, pleasantly, he ushered Miss Eloise through the door, offering his arm, calling back, "I'll meet you at the car, Miss Callander. And hurry—you know what a terror James Goss is, if somebody's late."

Down at the gym, Chet Alison was putting the finishing touches on his championship team; and he had neither the time nor the inclination to look out of the window. Tonight, the most rewarding, most beautiful sight he had ever seen in his life was no natural marvel, but the miracle of Jerry Mooney.

In the past week and a half, Chet had taken his team apart and put it together again. Embittered by his publicity—most sportswriters had been congratulatory on the surface, but hardly one of them hadn't taken a swipe at him if you read between the lines—Chet had got really tough.

Shock tactics, he told himself. It was too late for anything else. Under the circumstances, the team might blow sky-high, but it was a chance he had to take.

At times, his ruthlessness had shocked even himself, or would have, if he had stopped to think about it. This had to work, was all.

It had worked. The kids, at first dazed and bewildered—wasn't he, for cripesake, giving them any credit at all for what they'd done?—had taken a few days to swing into line. But from the beginning, last week, anyone who stuck up had got chopped off; clobbered, but good. Tonight, Chet knew he had them.

He had only to lift a hand, jerk his head—give them any one of the signals which they knew—to see the smooth, precision machine which he had built go into action, functioning according to diagram, not flapping loose around the floor just because some punk thought he knew better than the coach did.

Watching them Chet drew a long breath. He couldn't help but know it—he'd done a superb job.

They're back now where they were. They're better than they were. McIntosh is better—that reaming I gave him really did some good, he's back on the ground now; but Mooney is terrific, Chet thought, his eyes carefully on the racing, swiftly changing scene out across the floor. And the second team is a darned good team by itself now; and if I live long enough, I might even make something out of Ralph McIntosh. I either will, or I'll plow him back in.

During the past ten days, Chet had been doing plenty of thinking. If he had to stay here as coach for another year—and he might have to, anything could happen in Boston—he'd need material for another team. This one would be gone, of course, graduated. Well, he could build another. He'd done it before. His best chance was to develop the tall boys; Ralph was tall, and clumsy kids had been known to develop.

Chet had concentrated on Ralph, nervously, venomously, to see what effect that kind of treatment might have. Part of his strategy had been to keep Ralph's name off the list of subs, now posted, to be taken along with the team to Boston, intending, if the plan worked, to include the boy at the last moment in someone's place. The psychology of that, he thought, might be darned good. He'll work his head off, if he finds out, all of a sudden, that he's going to go.

And now, Chet had hopes, anyway. The kid showed signs—definite signs that he was coming on.

He watched, with a creator's eye, the working-out of a diagrammed play. Mooney had just received the passed ball, plucking it one-handed out of the air. He faked, pivoted, and threw, all in one sustained, effortless motion. The ball rose in a beautiful, clean curve, dropped through the basket without touching the rim.

That's a work of art, Chet told himself, under his breath. A goddamned work of—oh, Jesus!

Bearing down full tilt, arms flapping, feet skidding, unable to stop, Ralph had plowed down on Jerry. Jerry, seeing him coming, sidestepped, neatly, efficiently, as he had been taught; but one of his long legs remained stuck out behind just long enough to trip Ralph, who turned a couple of somersaults, slid along the floor on his stomach, and brought up against the wall, where he sat, flat, blinking his eyes very fast.

It was as neat a job of intentional dumping as Alison had ever seen, made of course to look completely accidental; a sweet job, and all a part of training. Alison grinned to himself, being careful to hide the grin.

Attaboy! he muttered. That Mooney! No one was going to charge down on him, accidentally or otherwise. Let 'em come now, by judas, let anybody come!

He hustled down the floor to where the other players were gathering around Ralph.

"You hurt?" he barked.

Ralph shook his head. He had stopped blinking and was beginning to pick himself up.

"What to heck were you doing—playing whirlybird?" Alison demanded.

Ralph said nothing. On his face appeared his usual apologetic grin.

"Holy smoke!" Alison went on. "Every player on the floor practically standing still, and here comes old Delayed-Reaction McIntosh, flapping like a windmill! Well, come on. Get on your feet! We haven't got all night to stand around and watch you put yourself together. And once you get up, try to stay there, will you? The rest of us can't hold up action every ten minutes while you come unshackled and fall down."

Ralph stared at Alison for a moment. His grin cracked uncertainly, left his face.

"Hey," he said, in a puzzled voice. "But I didn't fall down. He tripped me."

"Tripped you!" Alison said. "You caught your big flat feet over his heel."

Not a player on the floor, including Ralph, but knew what actually had happened. Everybody got tripped every once in a while. You learned how to handle it, was all.

The teams trotted back to their positions. All except Ralph. He stood staring around for a moment, a little wildly; then he spun on his heel and walked off the floor.

Alison bawled something after him, but he did not turn back. He went down to the locker room, got out of his gym suit, and dressed. He was lacing his leather-tops when Carlisle came tearing down after him.

"Hey, what do you think you're doing?" Carlisle said. 'This is a helluva time to quit. Get on back up there! We need you!"

Ralph said inarticulately, "I was doing it for fun. It isn't fun—"

"Well, it's about time you got that through your thick head, quit futzing around," Carlisle said. "Come on, hurry up, get your suit back on."

For answer, Ralph hauled back his foot and kicked the sweaty gym suit as hard as he could, out of sight under the lockers. He walked past Carlisle, leaving him standing, went upstairs and out of the building.

"Darn little sorehead's gone home," Carlisle reported to Alison, warily watching him; but Alison only grinned.

"That's a thing I've lived a long time to see," he said, "that kid get mad. We'll make a ballplayer out of him yet. He'll be back, don't worry."

He shifted the line-up, put another second-string man in as center against Jerry Mooney.

Dumb little cluck, he thought. Futzes along all year, and picks now, when I need him, as the time to quit.

Because Ralph was the only second-string center Alison had tall enough to make Jerry Mooney stretch.

Susie was putting bread to rise, working at the kitchen counter, when Ralph came in. She glanced up at him, surprised; both teams, she knew, were practicing tonight, as they had been for the past ten days. She had seen very little of either of her sons except at meals.

"Hi," she greeted him. "You're home early. Practice over?"

Ralph said nothing. He headed for a chair beside the stove, began taking off his leather-tops.

"You didn't get hurt or anything, did you?" Susie asked.

Ralph grunted, "Un-hnh."

He finished unlacing one boot, hauled it off, and threw it hard behind the stove.

Susie turned around, startled. Acts of violence were unlike him, but, she reflected, for the past week he had been glum, altogether unlike his usual sunny, gabby self. She supposed it was because he was tired out. Carlisle was even worse around the house; he was unapproachable. Susie sighed.

"I suppose it isn't any use to offer you cake and milk," she said, "seeing you're in training. But there's half a layer cake in the pantry."

"Yes, it is," Ralph said. "Darn right it is. I eat what I d-darn please, from now on out." He slammed the second boot after the first, got up, and headed for the pantry.

"You do?" Susie said, not much surprised by this declaration. In the past weeks, she had watched him struggle with his better nature, more often than not losing the battle over sweet stuff, particularly cake.

"Yes, I do!" Ralph shouted. He appeared from the pantry, carrying the cake plate and a full pan of milk which he had taken from the shelf. "You got any cold potatoes?" he demanded, glaring icily at his mother's back.

This was rebellion. The pans of milk on the shelves were always set there to raise cream for butter; the drinking milk was in the icebox. For years, Susie had fought this battle.

"Now, look here," she began. She turned, her mouth open to say again what there was to say about this, and encountered the full blast of Ralph's glazed, miserable stare.

"In the icebox," she said quietly, and turned back to the big lump of dough on the breadboard, thumping it vigorously a few more times before she put it into the pan.

Why, the poor little duffer, she thought. He's all in rags and tatters. What on earth can be the matter?

She heard him get the potato platter, set it down on the enameled tabletop with a metallic thump. There was a silence, punctuated by slurps and splashes, as Ralph violently dunked his potatoes.

"Well, I've quit the goldarn ballteam," he said, finally. His voice slid into an upper register, then, carefully steadied, dropped to baritone again. "They can all go fry."

Susie was putting a clean white towel over the bread, setting the pan on the warm shelf back of the stove.

"Have you?" she said, and was about to go on, when Dorothy appeared at the kitchen door from the living room, where she had been settled down to homework at the table. Dot's hair seemed to be standing right on end, with some emotion or other, Susie saw, and she was staring at Ralph with disgust.

"Ralph McIntosh!" Dot said. "You have not!"

Ralph, whose mouth was full, said nothing for the obvious reason, though he made an attempt which resulted in a muffled gurgle.

"Dot!" Susie said. "Now, that's all—"

But Dot was too shocked and horrified to stop.

"Why, you awful, nasty sorehead!" she said, in measured tones. "Why, Mama, Mr. Alison needs everybody! Nobody can quit now. Not on the Jay-Vees, nor anybody! Everybody knows Ralph's lousy, he can't even dribble without losing the ball, but he's the only tall one there is for center on the Jay-Vees, and Mr. Alison—"

Ralph, with a massive gulp, bolted his mouthful of potato, picked up another. "You shut up your big mouth," he said, thickly, clenching the potato in his hand. "Or I'll let you have it."

"Why, all you are is sore because you can't go to Boston," Dot said. "You're a quitter! With a capital K-W, is all you are. With a capital K—"

"Dot!" Susie said. "Ralph, don't you dare to throw that—"

She was too late, and she doubted if she could have stopped it anyhow. The potato, already well mashed from Ralph's hot clutch, flew across the room, took Dot fairly between the eyes with a succulent smack, and splattered.

Dot let out a shrill squawk and pawed the air blindly for a moment, before Susie got to her with a towel.

"Now, you kids cut this out!" she said grimly. "I never saw anything so disgraceful in my life!"

Mopping, she discovered to her relief, that though Dot had a goodly layer of potato plastered on either side of her nose, she had blinked in time—she hadn't got any of it in her eyes.

"Now, stop bawling," Susie commanded firmly. "You aren't hurt a bit, you're just surprised. And I don't know but what you got a little something that was coming to you, sticking your nose into Ralph's business. And," she went on, glancing irately over her shoulder, "I'm pretty mad at you, too! Throwing stuff like that at your sister! You could have put her eyes out, you know that, don't you?"

At that moment, the telephone rang, and she jerked her head at it. "Answer that, Ralph, my hands are all potato. Now, Dot, for heaven's sake, simmer down! Go back to your arithmetic or run up to bed, I don't care which!"

Ralph got up from the table with a slow scrabble of feet. She heard him speaking warily, then laconically, at the phone.

"Yeah, Mr. Berg . . . There is? . . . They do? . . . Yeah, sure . . . I will . . . Do it right now . . . Sunspots, geez . . . Yeah, sure . . . Thanks, Mr. Berg. G'bye."

She heard the phone click back into place, and silence. Then she was aware of Ralph's glooming presence behind her.

"I suppose you're in trouble with Mr. Berg, too," she snapped.

"Nope," Ralph said. He stared at her and she had the impression that his entire face was hanging down at least two inches longer than normal.

Oh, Lord, she thought. When he's miserable, he's miserable all over.

"Well, what did he want then?" she asked, more for something casual to say than because she wanted to know.

"Says to go out on the back step and look at the northern lights," Ralph said dolorously. "Says he wants to talk about them in class tomorrow."

Past his immobile shoulder, she saw the square of the kitchen window, with a section of sky, and on the fields, the icy, green mysterious light, not moonlight.

"Oh, my goodness!" she said. "Oh, look, Ralphie, isn't that pretty?"

Together they stood on the doorstep, watching the shimmering shifting reds and yellows without warmth, green colder than the depths of ice, creating pale light over the trees and the diminished black roofs of the town.

Beside her, Ralph said, "Buggsy says, been a terrible explosion on the sun." His voice sounded nasal, as if he had been crying. "Sunspots nudgeling each other or something."

"Oh," Susie said. "It was nice of Mr. Berg to call you. I hope you thanked him." She spoke stiffly, stressing the name. He needn't think, after the way he'd acted, that she was going to get over being mad for a while, either, even if he did come mumping around.

"Uh . . . I guess I did," Ralph said.

He continued to crane upward at the sky, his lanky presence towering beside her. She could see his Adam's apple move jerkily as he swallowed.

"Geez-Louise!" he said, mournfully. "Geez-Louise! I guess all hell's broke loose in the old ionosphere tonight."

Ralph had quit the team on a Thursday. He did not go back. On Friday, at school, he found himself unpopular; most of his friends thought he was a sorehead, and said so. The only person at the school, it seemed, who thought kindly of him at all, was Mr. Berg, who, after his lecture on northern lights and magnetic storms, went to some trouble to explain further to Ralph, who had asked a question.

"Now, that's intelligent," Alfred said. "See, what we know, which isn't a whole lot, goes like this." He went into detail about Ralph's question, and remarked, as he finished, "You've got a logical brain, McIntosh."

Ralph was embarrassed, particularly since, out in the corridor after class, a couple of classmates addressed him jocularly as "Old Brainsy."

Debby Parker, however, coming out behind him, stopped him, holding out a paper. "Is this what he meant by that, Ralph? Is this how you understood it?"

Ralph looked at the diagram. "Well, yes, uh, yeah, all but this, right here." He pointed. "I thought it went this way—" He sketched a light line on the paper.

"Oh, yes! Why, sure, of course," Debby said. "Thanks a lot, Ralphie."

She went on her way, with a friendly wave of the hand to him, and Ralph stood looking after her.

Well, there was maybe one more, besides Mr. Berg, who liked him. She was sure nice, Carl's girl.

Logical brain, uh? How about that?

He went loping along the corridor, and at the door to the locker room bumped into Carlisle and Jerry Mooney, who were coming out, dressed for gym. At home, this morning, Carl had been like a bear with a sore head, until Susie had cooled him off.

"You let Ralph alone," she'd said. "I'm not putting up with any more fights in the house."

So Carl had let up; but now he grabbed Ralph by the front of the shirt and twisted.

"Practice, this period," he said. "You be there, or I'll bust you in two."

"Hey," Ralph said. He was big enough to yank Carl's hand out of his shirtfront, but the shirt tore and two buttons popped off, clicking on the hard tile floor. Then Jerry, behind him, pulled his shirttail out. "You heard the man," Jerry said.

"You cut it out!" Ralph said, spinning around; but they were merely strolling away down the corridor.

Oh, dammit, Ralph thought, surveying the damage. That was his good shirt, the one he liked. He'd put it on this morning, thinking maybe wearing it might make him feel better.

Well, Ma could fix it, if he found the buttons.

He was down on all fours peering around after the buttons, when he crawled head-on into a pair of feet, which were not doing anything, just standing there. James Goss had come along, silently, on his rubber-soled shoes.

"Have you been roughhousing in the corridor, McIntosh?" he asked, in his precise, level voice.

"Well, gee, uh, no, Mr. Goss," Ralph said. He stood up, began hastily to tuck in his shirttail.

"Your mother's not going to believe that, when she sees that shirt," James said. "I don't know that I—har—do, either. An hour's detention for—har—roughhousing, and I expect—har—another hour for not saying so when—har—asked. That had better be in my room, on the first Monday night after the—har—holidays."

Silently, with his forward motion, not up and down, on the balls of his feet, he went on down the corridor.

Ralph glowered after him.

Har—the old—har—laundry cart, he thought. Not tonight—har. Oh, no! Not when old Alison might need to—har—use me. But after the ball season's good and over, the first Monday night after school begins, I got to remember I got two hours' detention.

He banged into the lavatory, banged shut one of the toilet doors, and piddled bitterly into the urinal.

What to do now? Couldn't go to class, have everyone hoot at his shirt gapped open down the front. Show his underwear. He could put on his windbreaker, zip it up; and die, sweating, in the warm classroom.

He could, he thought, go to ball practice, wear a gym suit for the rest of the afternoon.

And listen to all the yak. Well, here's old sorehead back. Changed your mind, hey? Thought better of it, did you? Yak, yak, yak!

Ralph's underjaw came out.

No, he said to himself, I don't think I will.

He pried up the lavatory window, squeezed through, and dropped; then slipped silently and expertly out of sight behind the barberry hedge. Crossing the highway, he got safely into the woods behind the Union Church. There was a path he knew which came out in Martin's upper pasture; better take it, not go in plain sight along the highway. Up there, he could find something to take up his time till he could go home; not get home early, get asked a mess of questions. Practice set shots, maybe; oh, no, by gum, that was all over. He'd forgotten.

Gee, the woods were nice. No yakking, no trouble. Only trees and bushes that couldn't yak back.

The first thing he saw when he came into the pasture was the wreck of the chestnut. He'd known about it, of course; he'd been up here a couple of times to mourn. The tree house gone, and all that Indian stuff . . .

He'd heard the silly talk around, too, about why Grampa had cut it down. Nuts, those two dopes, Carl and Jerry, they'd had a fight, everybody knew that, everybody around the school at least. Ralph guessed he knew why Grampa had cut down that nice old tree. The tree house, he thought, staring moodily at the ruin. Got a day when he felt too mean to live, so he whacked 'er down.

Carl was going to let all that Indian stuff go. He hadn't even made a move to save it; though, of course, nobody had had any time. But when Ralph had mentioned it, he'd said to heck with it, who wanted it, what was the good of it.

The collection had always fascinated Ralph. Carlisle kept it to himself, too; it was only since he'd stuck it up here in the tree house that Ralph had known what a lot of stuff he had. Of course, the only reason Carlisle had put it here was because he was afraid Grampa would find it and heave it out. Grampa didn't have much use for such things, though he did, at one time, seem kind of interested in Ralph's collection.

Ralph had started out collecting Indian things, too, but he'd had to give that up. Carl had made it good and clear to him that he wasn't going to have anybody glomming around the shell heaps with a clamhoe; he had emphasized this with a good licking one afternoon, when he had caught Ralph down on Tanner's Island. Of course, Tanner's Island was his prize dig; and Ralph had supposed that if you dug in clamshells you ought to have the right tool for it, so he had taken along a clamhoe.

It seemed you dug with a hand-trowel and your fingers, you little knothead, like it said in the book, so as not to break the things you found.

So, after that, Ralph had for a while started collecting something else—something of his own. Old-fashioned iron tools, rummaged out of the barns and cellars of deserted farmhouses, or dug up out of old foundations. He'd found quite a few—old jackplanes and saws and broadaxes, abandoned by people whose houses had burned down, or who'd died or gone away. Martin had been interested—those things were like the tools he'd used when he was a boy. No good now, he said. Wood handles rotted, blades eaten out by rust. Just a mess of old iron, now.

Carlisle had hooted his head off. He wouldn't allow any of it in the tree house; so after a while, Ralph had come to think that maybe it was all pretty silly, just old junk, and he'd lost interest in it.

He stood now, looking speculatively down. That Indian stuff was too good to lose. Maybe it could all be got out of there and stashed away. Maybe Carl would want it back sometime. If he did, then it wouldn't be lost.

You need tools, though, to pry apart the frame of that tree house.

Ralph went cautiously down the hill to Martin's tool shed, creeping, bent over, so as not to be spotted. He brought back his grandfather's ax and clawbar to work with, and some old bushel baskets to hold the stuff.

The tree house had been a solid job of construction, with lots of nails; he grunted and sweated, ripping it apart. One corner section lay under a big limb of the tree, and Ralph, after worrying at it awhile, thought he might shift the tree a little by prying. He got a rock for a fulcrum, thrust the clawbar under the trunk, and came down on it with his full weight. Since the tree weighed a few tons, it didn't budge, but something gave, and Ralph pulled the clawbar out, astonished to see that he had straightened it right out straight. He did his best to bend it back, but it didn't look right.

By dark, he had salvaged the collection, flints packed in one basket, bone tools laid carefully in the other so as not to break. Some of the latter were broken anyway; he scoured the ground for pieces, wrapping them in his handkerchief. If you found all the splinters, they could be glued together good as new.

It took him three trips to get the baskets and the tools down the hill. He hid the baskets in a safe place he knew about behind the grain bins, and was headed for the tool shed to return the ax and clawbar, when he came face-to-face with Martin.

Martin took one look.

"What in hell you been doing with them tools? Look at that ax, by tar, look at that clawbar!"

He followed on Ralph's heels into the house; all through supper, he gave loud and continuous tongue.

Who within the living time of man had ever been known to straighten out a clawbar? By tar, if it didn't take some blasted fool of a kid, doing something with it that nobody had ever done or ever in the god's world thought of! His ax, by tar; his clawbar! And look at that ax! Nicks in the blade it'd take three hours of solid grinding to get out. So you knew who was going to turn the grindstone for three solid hours on Saturday morning, didn't you, hanh?

Ralph knew. Wearily stowing away supper, he thought, Well, at least Carl isn't home to stick in his two cents.

Carl had phoned; the team was going right on practicing throughout the evening; so Alison was blowing them all to supper at Joe's Lunch. And Ma, send Ralph down, will you, the coach needs him.

On Saturday afternoon, after lunch, Ralph wandered about aimlessly downtown. The session at the grindstone hadn't taken three hours; it had taken half an hour. Martin had got out of that one by saying that half an hour was all the time he had, he had to go to Fairport, and anyway, what was the use, that ax would never be the same again, no matter how much you ground on it. Ralph couldn't see but what the ax looked as sharp as it ever had; he shrugged a little. The important thing was that Martin took off for Fairport in the truck.

Downtown, Ralph poked his nose into his habitual haunts, one after another, and he got, everywhere, the same reception. He had always liked to hang around on the outskirts of things, listening, interested in what other people had to say, in a quiet way enjoying himself. Now he found, to his horror, that wherever he went he was conspicuous, pointed out for criticism.

At the poolroom the gang was gathered. After all, it was Saturday, and on Monday the team took off for Boston Garden. Melly Hitchcock looked up, saw Ralph.

"Fine old bull-sorehead you are, quitting Alison at a time like this!"

And someone else: "A day and a half left to practice, and you quit! Boy, that's loyalty!"

At the drugstore, it was the same.

"The only second-string center Alison's got able to give the boys any competition, and you pick now to get sore!"

"What kind of a kid are you? No school spirit, no town spirit, no nothing!"

Ralph had planned to buy himself a banana split at the drugstore, but he got out fast without ordering one. His mouth still watering, he jogged along the street.

Heck, Joe Galt and Billy Kinney, the countermen down at Joe's Lunch, were his friends. He'd go down there and have a sandwich and a milkshake.

But as he sidled up to the counter, Joe wouldn't even look at him. Joe said to Billy, "Hey, look who's here. Old John Leprosy."

Ralph's half-apologetic grin of greeting froze on his face. "Hey!" he said. "Hey, what's the matter?"

"You know damn well what's the matter," Joe said sourly. "Gwan, haul-ass out of here. I don't want to look at you. I don't know as I even want your trade. Well, give your order. I ain't got all day."

Silently, he banged Ralph's sandwich down on the counter in front of him, leaned back against the shelves behind him, picking his teeth with a sharpened kitchen-match.

Up at the other end of the counter, Billy Kinney said, "What's the idea, anyway? You gone lame or something? Your kneecaps fly off?"

"Ah-h," Joe said. "He's lame all right. In the head. Sore, you could call it. Because he ain't on the list of subs going to Boston."

"Well, hey," Ralph said. Red to the ears, horribly embarrassed, he sat looking at the sandwich. Seems as if you could think of something to say to your friends; you'd always been able to talk before.

"Fell down in the gym, by judas priest!" Joe said. "I heard the fellas talking in here last night. So you quit! What are you, yeller? Can't you take it?"

"Yeah," Ralph said. "I hear you talking. Yeah." Desperately, he said the first thing that came into his head. Bitterly, he took a great bite of sandwich, spoke through it. "To play ball, I got to stay in school, don't I? To play ball, I got to pass."

"Well, how about that!" Joe put both hands flat on the counter, leaned down. "Hey, Billy, you hear what I hear?"

Billy came over. "I told you, Joe. I told you there was more to this than met the eye. Who's been working on you, kid? Who said you wouldn't pass?"

"Well, nobody," Ralph said, swallowing. "Only Mr. Berg said the other day—"

It was no lie; Mr. Berg had had a talk with him the other day. Hadn't said he wouldn't pass; just said he could do better, said to use his head, it was stupid to think there was nothing in the world but basketball.

Might as well say that; if you said Alison had been piling it on, telling you you were lousy till you were half-nuts, they'd just think you couldn't take it.

"Berg, by god!" Joe said. He slapped his fist into his palm. "I knew it! Damn him, he's been working against the ballteam ever since he come here!"

"Who does he think he is?" Billy said. "By god, Joe, the town hires these teachers, pays their wages. They better, by the god, do what the town says. Or the School Board'll have a word to say."

"Well, old Win's sure going to hear about this," Joe said. He turned to Billy; they moved to the other end of the counter and stood there, their heads close together.

Unnoticed, Ralph slid down from the high counter-stool and went out the door.

It was a fine, blue afternoon; the late February sun was pouring the length of Main Street, bright, cheerful, with a little warmth, today. Again wandering, Ralph finally came to light in the sunny corner between Haslam's Electric and the A and P; at the entrance to the narrow alley between the two buildings was a jog just wide enough to take his back. He leaned there, feeling the old rough boards warm against his spine, the sun's heat striking through his heavy winter clothing.

A lot of people were on Main Street, going from store to store, Saturday shopping; not many noticed him, tucked away in the jog between the buildings. Some of the high-school crowd were around;

not many. Most of them were up at the school where the team was, and where the cheerleaders were putting the finish on their routine. A couple of Ralph's classmates, Ginny Rugg and Pratt Peters, spotted him; Ginny raised her eyebrows and said something to Pratt. Pratt shrugged. They didn't say anything.

Yeah, Old John Leprosy. That was but good.

Maybe I ought to go back. It's only today and tomorrow. I've bucked it all year, I could take another day and a half. I guess.

But why all this touse, when everyone, Alison, even the little kids, keep yakking about how lousy I am? You'd think they'd never miss me. But I quit, and the roof falls in.

The thing was, everybody was thinking about next year's team, maybe. This year, they were losing all the first string—all those good ballplayers graduating. They thought if he kept at it, if he got the combination, he'd be as good as Carl. For two years, Carl hadn't been anything to write home about; now, all of a sudden, now, he was Shirttail McIntosh.

What I am, I'm tall. And that's all. They want another Shirttail. And what they'll get is the old Witless Wonder. Well, I don't think they're going to get him.

Old Sidney Widgett came walking down the street, a side-and-a-half to a step, leaning on his cane, which was a gnarled bough of applewood, whittled down, polished, shiny with age and use. He came slowly, enjoying the sun, turning his head from side to side, missing nothing. As he came abreast, he saw Ralph, did a double take, and stopped, his white wisp of goatee pointing straight out. Everything about him seemed to stand up in hackly prickles.

"What's this I hear about you quitting the ballteam?" he demanded.

Ralph shifted uneasily. He said nothing.

"Well, you ought to be ashamed of yourself!" Sidney's fruity roar, only a little cracked by his age, which was ninety-seven now, seemed to Ralph to shake the street. People began stopping and looking, and there wasn't any doubt who at, because the old man was pointing his cane.

"Why ain't you up to the gym?" Sidney said. "What's the matter with you—got growing pains?"

The red started to creep again along Ralph's face. He hoped it didn't show. He tried to keep his voice from showing anything. He said, "Yeah. My kneecaps flew off."

"Hanh? Why, you fresh young snots, don't nobody ever learn you no manners, nowadays? A man my age asks a civil question, he rates a civil answer. Well, speak up! Does he or don't he?"

Ralph made no reply. He thought, Well, ask it civil, I'll answer it that way.

"I have been loyal to this town for ninety-seven years," Sidney said. He had his audience now, people stopping, gathering around on the sidewalk; so he reached up with his free hand and took off his hat, holding it over his heart to show his respect for the town.

"Ninety-seven years, ladies and gentlemen, a great age, nearly a century. I have seen this town grow from shacks around the tannery to the respected and important place it now holds in the sun. I remind you of that past. Ladies and gentlemen, I remind you, too, of the future; I would like to ask you, one and all, what you think the future will amount to, if young squirts like this can come out, barefaced, and desert the town in the hour of its need? You may say, ladies and gentlemen, that what is involved is only a game; I put it to you that it is more. It is the town's good name that is at stake; its reputation in the eyes of its neighbors. And if some young smart-aleck like this—"

Sidney stabbed with the pointing cane, and was suddenly aware that he was losing his audience, that some people were laughing.

"—some young smart-aleck like this," he repeated and realized that he was stabbing the cane at empty air. The jog between the buildings was empty. Ralph had slipped back into the narrow alley and had gone, how long ago Sidney couldn't say. Enraged, he clapped his hat back onto his head. "Small potatoes and few in a hill," he bawled. "That's what they are, compared to what they was when I was a boy!"

He had been well into his speech, which was, he felt, about to develop into one of the best he had ever made, in Town Meeting or at a church picnic. The reaction was bewildering; because all his life he had been accustomed to add to his personal prestige by riding the crest of whatever wave of sentiment rolled in the town. And this basketball thing was a tidal wave, something that well and truly deserved a speech or two.

But it was too late, the crowd was moving on.

"Comes of letting our decent girls marry up with them foreigners," he muttered, to anyone near enough to hear him. "It follows as the night the day, and that kid is a second Brant McIntosh, if I ever see one!"

Ralph came out of the alley into the back yard of the A and P, which was stacked high with old empty cartons and slippery with mud temporarily thawing in the sun. He skidded against a pile of boxes, knocking it over, but he did not see it fall, only heard the empty rustle of the corrugated cardboard crushing as it went down.

To the hell with it, he thought bitterly. To the lowest, deep-down bottom of the lowest hell there is with it.

Allen's Lane, a back street, led down to the river. Successive coatings of hardtop laid on it to turn it from a dilapidated old gravel road into a street had cracked and come out in chunks, so that it was rapidly turning back into a road again. The steep slope was slippery, bulged with frost-boils; Ralph took it at a dead run. Part of the way he slid, once nearly taking a header when his toe caught. He came out on the riverbank at the rear of the tannery, and kept on down the path toward the harbor.

It felt good to run. The crisp wind flowed backward against his still-hot cheeks, his face a wedge with his nose the sharp edge of it splitting a mass of cold air. Cold, but not cold, half-warm from the sun, and smelling of salt from the harbor. It went deep into his lungs, stinging and clean, as if with each breath he pulled in a solid chunk of sunny February day. The big muscles in his legs grew limber, the rubber soles of his leather-tops clumped and pounded. He let go and gave it every ounce of strength he had.

The river path, made by duck-hunters and wanderers up and down the bank, was hard and beaten down. The sun had melted all the snow here in the open, but had not drawn out much frost; the path was only slippery in places easy enough to avoid. Whenever Ralph saw an icy patch coming, he jumped, letting his body fly wildly through the air, landing with a thump and racing on.

Some way below the tannery, the river divided, its main channel going on to the west of a small island, Tanner's Island; to the east was Tanner's Brook, which was not a brook at all, but a long arm of the sea. Long ago, when people had lived on Tanner's Island, there had been a footbridge across the brook, built on a rough causeway of rocks, with a short gap in the middle to let the river current out and the sea-tides flow in. The woodwork of the bridge was long gone now except for an occasional water-hardened timber. Barnacle-covered and eaten by sea-worms, the ancient wood thrust out of the rocks like yellowed bones. The causeway could still be crossed when the tide was down, though the gap in the middle was a good stiff jump, and Ralph crossed it, heading down a narrow, alder-grown field toward the woods.

If he had stopped to look, he would have seen that this was not the best time to go over to Tanner's Island, or, at least, to stay there long, because down at the far end of the brook the flood tide was beginning to come in over the ice. But he made a last flying leap toward a fringe of thick bushes and ducked out of sight.

Panting, he slowed to a walk.

Couldn't run here. It was too rough going. Under the trees the old snow hadn't melted, except where a knobbly root stuck out; and he was winded, anyway.

He went along, following an old wood road partially overgrown with alders. Presently, as he caught his breath, he began to cool down and feel better.

It was nice over here. Lonesome and cold in the woods, maybe; but no houses left, only old foundations; nobody to futz you up, just in case you came out with some kind of a fool idea that your life was your own.

Ralph knew Tanner's Island pretty well. When he was a kid, before he had stopped bothering about his junky collection of old iron tools, he had spent a lot of time here poking around in the foundations of the houses to see what he could find; and, of course, it was here on Tanner's Island that Carlisle had dug up most of his Indian stuff. The shell heap here was six feet deep and ran two hundred yards back from the shore. The tribes had lived here, once, for thousands of years, and they had left a lot of their things lying around.

Ralph had come, almost without thinking about it, the full length of the island, mooching along under the dark of the trees. Suddenly he pushed through a fringe of stubbly bushes into the old Welch field, and sunlight that was almost blinding.

In the bright light of early afternoon, the field lay, still, with beyond it the blue spread of ocean and over it, the sky. On the shore, he could see the gray-pink granite ledges and hear the whisper of the tide. He stepped out into the matted grass, feeling it here and there crunchy with old snow, but soft under his feet as a carpet.

This field was hayfield once; old Neighbor Welch's hayfield. Grampa had a lot of stories about him and the farm he had had here on Tanner's Island. Grampa could even remember the buildings, though they were pretty well rotted down when he was a boy. He and his pals used to camp out here, duck-hunting, though even then the windows were all broken and the parlor open to the sky, and it always rained in on the kitchen stove. When old Neighbor died, before Grampa was born, the two Welch boys, Hiram and Byram, took over the farm; lived over here like hermits and never married, and both died on the same day. At least, people found them dead and frozen stiff, one in one bunk and one in the other, on the same ice-cold winter afternoon. They were all sprawdled out, so that a terrible time was had, trying to get them thawed enough so they'd fit into caskets. After them, the farm went back to wild.

It was a shame, Grampa said, because for years afterwards this field kept on growing hay in some places as tall as a man, the turf on it ten inches thick. Something to do with the lime in the land, from the shells underneath it, because this whole field had been built of shells from the Indian camp.

Ralph paused in his march across the grass to glance down into the two stony depressions which were all that was left of the house and barn. Still some old rotted wood down there, and a mess of odds and ends of old iron. Old Neighbor saved iron, misered-up iron, Grampa said; he and his boys used to have a smithy. They made all their own tools—they could make a broadax or an adze or a horseshoe; even their own horseshoe nails.

Poking around down there in the days when he was making his collection, Ralph had found a broadax-blade under the remains of a rotted shelf where it must have dropped when the shelf fell down, along with an old horse collar and a couple of iron rings; and two handmade sickle-blades, one marked HI and one marked BY, crude letters incised on the iron. Before that, Ralph hadn't thought of Hiram and Byram as real boys, but only as people dead in a gone time, too long ago to amount to anything. Yet all of a sudden, there they were—two fellows each making his own sickle-blade, maybe, in the blacksmith shop, and signing his name to it, so anyone would know what was his. Maybe they'd taken pride in the work they'd done. Grampa said they ought to.

"By tar!" he'd said, turning the rust-eaten blades over in his hand. "Them Welch boys' tools, them that's laid buried since the time of man over there under Granite Hill!"

Oh, Grampa used to be plenty full of stories, times before he grew to be so cussid mean.

Wandering alone, Ralph came out on the bank at the top of the shell mound. The three old thorn trees that grew there had a cant backward, toward the north, blown that way by the prevailing wind that swept the field. In summer, their leaves had a soft and southward-growing green, stubborn-looking, as if they blew against the wind; and on the middle tree was a thorn on which a shrike had once pinned a sparrow.

Two years ago, when Ralph had first found this, the sparrow had been fairly new; at least you could tell that the bird had been a sparrow. He had felt that this was quite a find, something you didn't often see; and he had left it alone, thinking he might find out how it got there. Did the sparrow, maybe, fly too fast into the tree and get stuck on a thorn?

He'd mentioned it at home, and Grampa had said that a shrike, a kind of little hawk, did that to smaller birds; the dead sparrow was a stored food supply.

The shrike had never come back, maybe something had got it, and each time Ralph came down, he looked to see if the sparrow was still there. He had never told anyone where it was. Carlisle might think he knew everything about this place; that it belonged to him. There he would be, digging in the shells, and not letting Ralph dig; and this remarkable thing hanging in the thorn tree not three feet above his head.

Ralph looked now. There it was. Dried by the sea wind, bleached by summer suns, the delicate small bones hung loose, about to fall; it seemed almost as if they would fall down, let once the wind nudge out a little more. So far, they hadn't; and Ralph could see that the thorn itself was worn, sandpapered down to polish by the slight-swinging bones of the sparrow.

With a slight grunt of satisfaction because the secret was still there, he jumped down the bank, feeling the piled old shells crunch beneath his feet.

Here was Carlisle's dig, marked off with neat, white, whittled stakes. Carlisle was a careful digger, following the instructions in his book, the one the man had given him that time. He would stake off an area, scrape down the rubble from the face of the mound, and then grub slowly in, marking the different layers of stuff—"horizons," they were called in the book. Sometimes he would spend an hour moving the trash around a bone tool, brushing with a paintbrush, wiggling out shells with his fingers. The old bone was almost always soft, almost pasty, from the dampness in the mound; it was easily crumbled, but when it dried, it hardened to bone again.

At the bottom of the bank, the bluish glacial clay was covered with ice, wet with runnels, thawing in the sun; the red-brown sand on top of it had long, dagger-like crystals of frost. The ground was frozen now, too hard to dig. Of course, Ralph didn't mean to dig; it was Carlisle's place. But he could look, couldn't he?

There were layers of ashes, pearl-gray, mixed with charcoal; layers of shells; layers of beach-gravel. Ralph could count the edges of three fire pits, one built on top of the other. That told, one way, how old the place was. Another way to tell, there were bones in there of animals whose kind had died off the earth, wiped out like the passenger pigeons; the gray seal, the Indian dog. Gone for good, at least from around here. But where it said in the book, the best way to tell was the Carbon 14 test. Take a chunk of charcoal from a fire-pit, measure its radioactivity. Stuff like that had only so much radioactivity to begin with; it gave off through the years; what was left could be measured and told you somewhere near how old it was.

Six thousand years old, give or take eight hundred years, some of these shell heaps were said to be. Or was it a thousand? Ralph couldn't remember.

A lot of things he did remember, though. That about the layers of beach-gravel in the mound. Nobody really knew why they were there. But the book pointed out that a pile of fresh shells after a while would get so it stank; so maybe the chief had the Indian boys lug gravel up from the beach and dump it down to douse the smell.

Well, after all, any old pile of clamshells had a hocious stink, any time; wow, try living over one six feet deep! Even now, Ralph thought, as he leaned forward and his face came inquisitively closer to the bank; even now, there was—yes, sir, by golly, there was!—a kind of smell. If you shut your eyes and breathed in deep through your nose, you could get a faint whiff of dead clam. How about that? A smell of clam, six thousand years old!

Concentrating, Ralph leaned forward a little too far. His feet skidded on the slippery slope, throwing him off balance. Arms flailing wildly, he toppled face-first into the bank; his nose plowed into a layer of crumbly shells, sending a shower of feathery flakes floating down; and then a whole section of the bank, undermined by the thaw and frost and by Carlisle's digging, came clattering down on top of him.

A big stone from one of the fire-pits missed the top of his head, nudged him firmly on the shoulder, before it rolled to the bottom of the mound; chunks of frozen sand and gravel thudded down; but what mostly fell was shells, so that when the racket stopped, and he had decided that he was buried, but not dead, he found he could move and roll over. His arms and legs would wiggle, too; the stuff didn't seem too heavy. Presently, he had cleared enough of it away so that he could sit up, stick his head out into daylight.

For a moment, all he could do was sneeze. His nose was full of lime-dust and ashes. He sneezed for quite a long time before he could un-bury his pants pocket, which also was jammed full of shells, and get to his handkerchief. His shoulder ached a little and his nose was bleeding from a long scratch where it had scraped into the bank; otherwise he wasn't damaged.

Geez-Louise, he thought, impressed, looking at the handkerchief. I bet I sneezed forty times. I wish I'd counted.

Cautiously, in case any more of the bank should come down, he dug himself out. Quite a chunk had fallen, he saw, the entire face for a couple of feet in. Carlisle's careful dig was as if it had never been. There by Ralph's foot was one of the whittled markers, with the neatly cut number "2" rubbed over with black dirt.

Horrified, Ralph stood looking, mopping at the scratch on his nose, from which his now-blackened handkerchief spread out an area of dust and ashes, well pasted on with blood. For a while, he had forgotten that feeling of being to blame for everything—everything, that is, that people around him didn't like.

Ah, I can't touch anything without I clobber it up. What'd I come down here for, anyway? All I was doing was smelling of it. Maybe Carl, the way he feels now, won't care, says he is through with all this crap, going to learn to play pro ball. But geez, all that work . . .

Ralph's eyes narrowed suddenly and sharpened. He leaned forward, looking at the cave-in.

One of the fire-pit stones that had fallen had left a hole, the imprint of itself in black dirt; and pressed down into the place where it had lain was a triangular piece of flint.

Something, he thought; some kind of a tool.

He reached into the cavity, poking and prying into the icy ashes with slowly numbing fingers, until the thing loosened and came away in his hand.

It was a knife-blade, chipped from dark green stone flecked with white. It was beautifully made; there was nothing crude about it. You could see where the fellow had known just how to take off a little chip here and a little chip there to sharpen out the stone and make a knife. It must've taken a long time. With nothing to work with but a piece of bone or a beaver-tooth or a chisel cut from antler. Whatever they had to use.

Ralph turned the blade over in his hand.

On the back was a diamond mark, carefully chipped in relief and rubbed to a polish, so that it stood out smooth on the rough stone.

Hey, the guy marked it! Maybe so people would know it was his. Signed his work, just the way Hi and By Welch signed their sickle-blades.

Ralph stepped back a little, staring at the mound.

Shells and shells and shells. Some whole and hard, some so old they were soft as a handful of silk, so that when you touched them they fell to limy dust. Six thousand years, and over that the turf—ten inches, at a hundred years an inch, of slow-dying, slow-dropping grass roots. A thousand years of summers, southwest winds and hard northeasters, of stars and sunrises, spring green and snow, just marked by turf alone.

How long since that guy lost his knife-blade here? Or maybe had to die and leave his tools, like old Neighbor Welch and his boys, up there in the field? That circle of burned-black crumbling stones, that was old Neighbor Indian's kitchen stove, and six thousand years the rain's been dripping into it.

My old collection of iron tools, maybe, isn't so much to kid about, for Carl to hoot at. Maybe it ought to be hung up with his; it's the same thing, only different people and longer ago.

There might be something else in that hole. No reason why he couldn't dig now, he couldn't do Carl's place any more damage than he had. In there, behind the cave-in, the ground didn't look to be frozen, at least lower down, and the shells, anyway, were loose.

Three hours later, in a hole big enough to hold a good-sized bear, Ralph suddenly realized that he was cold, that he had hardly light enough to see. He hauled himself backwards into the world, astonished to find that the afternoon was gone. The sun had set, the tide had risen until light ripples were lapping the beach almost to the foot of the mound. The cove was like glass, with a few pink squiggles from the fading sunset, and, on the west side, some upside-down reflections of spruce trees, black and still. He looked around appreciatively at conditions in the world outside his hole, still too absorbed to realize what they might mean to him, personally.

He had a haul. Stuff that, by golly, would make Carlisle look up and take notice, say he ever took notice of anything outside of ball. He had a harpoon made out of the leg bone of some big animal, maybe a moose, pointed, notched, drilled on the shank for a thong; a needle, like a darning needle, only made of bone, not steel, and somebody had done a job, cutting that little tiny eye in it; he had four flint arrowheads, and a whole tin can full of pieces of a broken Indian pot.

That last was a real find. Nobody ever found a whole pot. The Indians, so the book said, thought a part of their soul was in anything that belonged to them; mustn't leave their soul lying around loose. Things they lost and couldn't find, of course, they had to leave those when they had to move; but stuff they couldn't carry easily, like a big clay pot, they busted up and scattered the pieces. This wouldn't be a whole pot; but some of the pieces went together like a jigsaw puzzle; and even a part of a pot was rare.

Brrr-r! It was cold. Thermometer must've dropped twenty degrees since this afternoon, cold coming up as the sun went down, the way it did, this time of year.

He'd been sweating some, inside that hole, too. Well, get cracking.

He stowed the small flints in his pockets. The needle, which was punky still, he laid against a little block of driftwood, wrapped it carefully in his handkerchief, and buttoned it inside the breast pocket of his windbreaker.

Is Ma going to flip when she sees me, he thought, regarding himself.

His hands and the sleeves of his windbreaker were coal-black from dirt and ashes; his pants were black, too, and one knee had shredded through from kneeling on the shells. Even his boots were full of that black stuff; he could feel the grit down in his socks.

Holding the tin can in one hand and the big bone harpoon in the other, he went up the bank like a squirrel. The shadows were long on the field, dark down inside old Neighbor Welch's cellar-hole.

"So, Hi, old Neighbor, so you too went By," Ralph said cheerfully, saluting the foundation stones with his harpoon, and his wit tickled him so that he went chuckling into the woods, loping where he could, along the darkening forest path.

I'll stick these things on my shelf, along with Hi's sickle and By's sickle and some stuff of mine that's there, and when the shelf rots all our things'll fall down together, for someone else to find in time to come. So by then no one'll know whose was whose—they'll think old Neighbor Indian had a bicycle padlock, and old Neighbor Welch drank rum out of a clay pot, and Hi and By and I all cut our hair with sickles . . .

The idea suddenly seemed very funny. On the edge of the wood, Ralph burst out roaring laughing. From somewhere, the echo of his laugh bounced back. He stopped, listening.

Hey, that was an echo!

He called, loudly and jubilantly, "Hi!"

There was a pause of a second or so; then the answer came back clearly through the cold air.

"Hi!"

How about that?

He called again, this time, louder. "Hey, By!"

And heard, after the same measured pause, the answer.

"—ey, By!"

Darn place is haunted. Got ghosts. Must be still around, told me their names.

"How are you?" he yelled, and listened.

"—ow are you?"

Geez, whatever was bouncing that echo back was pretty far off. Building-walls, those old farmstands on the other side of Tanner's Brook, or the woods, maybe; or something to do with the air, atmospheric conditions from old Buggsy's sunspots. Made it sound as though somebody stood off there plainly and deliberately answering him.

He yelled again, happily, "Fine!" and started to count, "One green cantaloupe, two green cantaloupes," timing the seconds till the answer came.

"Fine!"

About one and a half seconds. That was some echo.

I'll bet it does have something to do with old Buggsy's magnetic storm. All that stuff whanging down, ker boompityboomp-boomp, onto the air. He said it would affect the atmosphere, and if it's strong enough to throw out TVs and radio transmitters and clobber up the Atlantic cables, seems as though you ought to be able to feel it.

Ralph stuck up one hand, the one with the tin can in it, two fingers spread, like a rabbit-ears antenna. He rotated slowly on his heel. It seemed, for an instant, as if he felt a slight tingling; but then, nothing.

The air was peculiar, though, with a heavy stillness, almost like before a thunderstorm, though the only cloud in the sky was one small pink woolly job over in the west, fading fast. Overhead, the sky was a deep blue, ice-cold. Nothing moved. Not a sound.

Well, there's the old radio silence for you, Ralph said to himself.

He trotted across the narrow field toward the shore, and as he went, he burst into song.

"I'm dancing with tears in my eyes,
'Cause the girl in my arms isn't you,"

coming bellowing out of the underbrush onto the shore above Tanner's Brook.

"—isn't you," said the echo, thinly, distinctly, finally.

Ralph stood, his roar dying to a wheeze, looking, at first unbelieving, then wildly, at the flood-tide water, running smooth as glass, silent, over the causeway.

When Ralph didn't come home to supper, Susie didn't worry about him. She thought he'd given in and had gone back to the gym to practice ball. In a way, she wished he hadn't; but she knew Ralph—his desperate wish to be approved of, to be popular, for all he was so shy—and if the particular Cain Carlisle had been raising around the house here were any sample of the pressure that was being put on, anyone would find it hard to hold out. She sighed a little, setting the boys' supper into the warming-oven, just in case.

Then, at seven, the phone rang, and it was Alison.

"I wonder if I could get you to help me persuade Ralph to come down for these last practice sessions, Mrs. McIntosh. I really do need him."

"Why," Susie said, surprised. "Isn't he there? I thought he was. He isn't here, Mr. Alison, I haven't seen him all afternoon."

"Oh," Alison said. "Oh. I see. Well, thank you, Mrs. McIntosh." He hung up with a snap; and Susie thought, My, there's a young man who doesn't waste words.

Obviously, he hadn't believed her. He sounded as though he thought Ralph was sitting right there, making motions to her to say he wasn't home.

She shrugged a little. She had heard enough from Carlisle to know that it was Ralph's height that was valuable, though so far as she could make out, very little else.

"You let him alone," she had finally told Carlisle. "The way you talk to him, nobody's given him much credit down there for what he has done."

"Well, what does he want?" Carlisle stormed. "Somebody to pat him on the head every five minutes, tell him how great he is? We've all got enough on our minds without coddling along a damn sorehead."

"All right, that'll do. It's up to Ralph. You let him alone."

Carlisle had been furious; he had stamped out of the house, around noon, and she hadn't seen him since. Shortly after that, Ralph himself had vanished; and where on earth was he?

Martin didn't know. He, too, was mad. All he knew, he'd laid out chores to be done and they weren't done. And his ax all nicked up. His clawbar bent. He sat immovably behind his newspaper, answering Susie with an occasional grunt, and at eight o'clock, he went to bed.

Left alone, Susie tried to still her growing concern.

It's early. Why on earth should I start worrying at this time of night? Plenty of times he hasn't got home before this and I haven't turned a hair. He could be anywhere around town. Somewhere watching TV, maybe, like Dot, who was over to Mooneys' tonight. Mattie Mooney's niece from upstate was visiting over there. Hez and Mattie had invited her down, so that she could drive to Boston with them to watch the Tournament; and Dot had been cultivating the Mooneys, hoping to get an invitation to go along. So far, nothing had come of it, and Susie hoped nothing would. She didn't see how she could possibly let Dot go—eleven was a lot too young for any such jaunt. The Mooneys probably wouldn't ask her, anyway. They were put out about something. Susie didn't know what; but Hez had been stand-offish down at the A and P the other day, and Mattie quite stiff on the telephone.

Something; heaven only knew what, but they'd get over it if left alone. A lot of times, it seemed, people got mad for the sake of something to do, and life could get pretty dull along the end of February.

Well, she'd have to call Mattie. Maybe Dot would know where Ralph would be. She dialed the Mooneys' number.

"Dot?" Mattie said. "Why, she ain't here. Hez drove her and my niece Paula down to the gym to watch the ball-practice. He's gone to lodge meeting, said he'd pick them up on the way home."

"What time will that be?" Susie asked. She sensed the stiffness in Mattie's voice, and thought, Well, I could be put out, myself. I told Dot she couldn't go down to the gym tonight. She went on aloud, "Dot has to be home by nine o'clock, or didn't she tell you?"

"Oh, does she?" Mattie said. "I don't know as I'd count on it, if I was you. Them little scamps, they've just got stars in their eyes over that ballteam. That's what I told them, bless their hearts. Just stars in their eyes."

"I guess they're not the only ones," Susie said.

"No, I guess not. And with all the reason in the world, wouldn't you say? Most of us do value them boys pretty high, though there's some"—Mattie's voice began to drip ice—"there's some, I guess, who ain't particularly careful about their life and limb."

"What?" Susie asked. To herself she said, Oh, Lord, here it comes; now it begins.

"And I'll tell you right now, Susie McIntosh, it's about time you had that crazy old man looked into." Mattie's voice began to vibrate the diaphragm, so that Susie had to move the receiver a little away from her ear. "Hez is some old mad, I can tell you, and he's all ready to sue, and if Jerry'd been worse hurt one mite, Hez would've sued, and he may yet, and I guess that'd give old Mart something to think about."

"For heaven's sake, Mattie," Susie said. "I haven't a notion on earth what you're talking about."

"Well, if you don't know, you're the only one in town don't," Mattie said. "And people is some old tore out, too. And you can tell Mart that it ain't a mite of use his trying to sell aigs to Harry Troy's market, because Harry called up today and took every aig we had on the place, and what's more, he left a standing order. And that's a standing order," she repeated with triumph.

"That makes it nice for you and Hez," Susie said. "But I—"

Mattie had not stopped at all. "So the next time that old snapper-jaw drops trees with houses in 'em on a couple of defenseless young ones, maybe he'll think before he does it."

"Trees?" Susie said. "With houses in—Mattie, will you please make sense?"

But Mattie, having said her say, hung up with a resounding crash.

Susie also hung up.

Whatever that is, it's something new and lovely, she thought. I thought she said trees with houses in them, but maybe I didn't hear right. Pa's done something, the Lord knows what.

She hadn't got anywhere at all in the hunt for Ralph, she realized, not even a question stuck in sideways. She dialed the high school. There was a long pause while the phone rang and rang, then a man's voice answered. Mr. Berg.

"Oh, Mr. Berg, have you been in the gym? Could you tell me, is Ralph there?"

"Why, I don't think so," Alfred said. "But hold on, I'll check."

Maybe he's come in since Alison called me, Susie thought, holding the phone clasped to her ear while she waited.

It was apparently gala night at the high school—the Saturday night before the team left on Monday for Boston. She could hear the squeal of voices, the thump and bustle of the practice session, and somebody kept letting off a long, shrill whistle.

Presently Mr. Berg came back.

"Mrs. McIntosh? No, Ralph isn't here. There seems to be quite a patch of irritation because he isn't. What's the trouble—have you lost track of him?"

"Well, I'm probably being foolish. But he hasn't been home since noon," Susie said.

"Mm, yes, I see. He's having a bad time, too, with this ball thing. Can I do anything? Let's see, I'm stuck here at the moment chaperoning this gang, but maybe we ought to—Let me ask around some more. Maybe I can find someone who's seen him. I'll call you back."

The concern in Mr. Berg's voice hadn't helped any.

Susie spent the next half-hour telephoning. She called Hazel, but Ralph wasn't there. She called any of Ralph's friends she could think of—they weren't home, they were down at the gym. From the drugstore and the poolroom, she received comments about Ralph's quitting the team, and some advice—a kid hadn't ought to be allowed to be irresponsible, to get away with stuff like that, not at a time like this.

Susie said, "Well, I can't see that it makes such an awful difference, he's only on the second team. If it was the first team, I could understand, but—"

When she made it clear that she wasn't going to put her foot down, that the decision was up to Ralph, the comments took on an undertone of acid. Nobody knew where Ralph was, anyway, if he wasn't up at the gym practicing ball.

Getting more and more furious, as she dialed one place after another, Susie finally got Joe Galt, down at Joe's Lunch.

"Naw, he ain't here," Joe said. "He was, earlier on, but Billy and I tried to talk him into going back to playing ball, and he went out of here like a shot out of a gun. I know what's the matter with him—" Joe's voice took on a note of righteous indignation, as he slid into a routine, which, repeated hour after hour, all day long, from the lunchroom counter, was now nearly perfect. "That Jew, been working on him. He knows Ralph's the only second-string center tall enough to make old Dead-Eye stretch, so—"

"What time was Ralph in there?" Susie cut in crisply. "If you can unstick your nose from a basketball long enough to say?"

"What? Oh." She could almost hear the creak as Joe stiffened. "Around one o'clock, I guess. Hey, Billy, wasn't Ralph McIntosh in here around one? Yeah, one, it was. You tried the drugstore? Maybe he's up there, cuddled down with a raspb'ry soda."

Susie exploded. "What's the matter with you men? Have you all gone crazy?"

"Crazy?" Joe's voice took on a dignified note. "I don't guess I know just what you're talking about."

"I'd just like to know what it would take," Susie said. "If someone should blow up the Town Hall, or every third one of you grew a mushroom where his nose should be, would anyone so much as look around? No, sir, there you'd all be, still faced the same way, like a lot of cows waiting for the barn door to open. You make me sick, every last one of you!"

"Well, set fire!" Joe said. "I guess you're some relation to old Mart, ain't you? He cut down any trees lately?"

"I don't know what you mean," Susie said. "But I'm likely to cut down something, if you and that gang down there don't let my kids alone. If Ralph doesn't want to play ball, he doesn't have to. It's a free country. Or is it? Sometimes you mess of sheep-minded idiots make me wonder!"

She hung up with a snap, leaving Joe with his mouth open. He took the receiver away from his ear and stared at it, as if something had jumped out of it and bitten him. Then he hung it up, wagging his head.

"Them Hoodlesses," he said to Billy, "is all nutty as fruitcakes. You know what she was talking about? Blowing up the Town Hall!"

Susie stood by the phone, wondering what next to do. She was really worried now. From the phone calls, she now had heard a fair cross section of what Ralph had had to contend with.

He just went off by himself this afternoon to get away from it, and I don't blame him. But where? He's a great one for wandering around in wild places, anyway, and if he's fallen, or got hurt, and is lying out in the cold . . . it is cold tonight, too.

She opened the kitchen door and stepped out on the back porch to look at the thermometer.

Yes. It was cold. In the light from the kitchen window, she could see that the mercury was nearly down to zero.

As they had done last night and the night before, the northern lights still streamed in the sky—no such great display as the first one, but still enough to cast the strange glow over fields and trees, over the town.

Susie thought, I'll call Hazel again. Charles and George'll help me look for him.

But as she turned back indoors, the phone rang. She snatched it off the hook.

"Mrs. McIntosh? Al Berg. Any news of Ralph?"

"No . . . no there isn't. You didn't find out anything?"

"Not much. A couple of kids saw him on Main Street, around one-thirty. That's all. Look, I can see you're pretty worried. Would you like me to get up a search party, take a look around? Of course, it's early yet—"

It was only nine o'clock, Susie saw.

"Oh, dear, I don't mean to be foolish," she said. "Of course he'll probably turn up any minute now. Look, let me talk to Carlisle, Mr. Berg. Perhaps he'll have some idea where Ralph might be."

"Oh, my!" Alfred said. "They're right in the middle of—But, yes, of course, Mrs. McIntosh. Hold on."

Susie waited. It seemed to be taking quite a while to get Carlisle to the phone. She thought, I can't stand much more of this, feeling her hand grow clammy on the receiver, as she waited.

Carlisle's voice came on, so loudly and suddenly that she jumped.

"Ma, for petesake! What a heck of a time to call me on the phone! What is it? Make it snappy, will you?"

"Carlisle, where's Ralph?"

"How would I know? Off sulking, if you ask me. Look, Ma, I'm busy! I've had to clobber a whole play."

"Well, that's too bad," Susie said. "Ralph hasn't been home since noon. And the way you and that crowd down there have been at him, no knowing where he's gone or what's happened. I want you to come home and help me look for him."

Carlisle's bellow of anguish cut in over her words. "Oh, my god! Oh, that dope! Look, he's just sore, he's just doing this! He'll wait till everybody gets stirred up, and then he'll come home on his own. Look, let me alone, will you, Ma? I haven't got the time."

He hung up.

All right, she thought grimly. So much for that. Everybody thinks I'm foolish. Perhaps I am. All the same—

She sat down for a moment at the kitchen table.

Nobody's worried but me, she told herself. Pa's gone to bed the way he always does, and all Carlisle did was get mad.

It's like hollering at deaf people; no, not deaf, maybe, just people who don't hear a word you say.

Sometimes I feel as if I lived between two high walls, she thought. Pa's wall, and the one the kids build up around themselves. Times, when they need clean socks, or want cold boiled potatoes, or a bandage on a skinned knee, we meet, and what we say means something in an everyday kind of way. But mostly, here I am, in a no man's land between two kingdoms.

For a moment, Susie contemplated the self-containment of the barriers behind which she lived. The world of the old, uneasy in growing dark; around which long life had set stone upon stone, moss-grown with habit, crusted with prejudice and old secrecy; the world of the young withdrawn behind sun-glittering towers; equally impenetrable, equally sufficient, each to his own.

Well, I'm not like that, she thought; I'm at a different place on my travels. Times, I'm lonesome, and times, I need help. And this is one of them.

George and Hazel would help. Charles would know what to do.

She put on her things, her winter coat, dressing warmly against the cold night. It took a little while in the icy garage to get the engine of Martin's old Chevy to fire, and then she had to wait while it warmed up. When at last she found she could back up without stalling, she swung the car around the turnaround and headed down the hill.

Charles and George, at first, also were inclined not to take Susie's worry too seriously. It was early yet, they said comfortingly. Ralph might be home any time.

"He's probably there now," Charles said, getting up from his chair by the fire. "Come on, George. We'll drive up behind you, Susie, and see."

But he was not there. The kitchen was empty, the light burning, just as Susie had left it.

"All right, George," Charles said. "Let's take a look around. Susie, if he comes, you phone Hazel. We'll drop by there, every so often, if we don't find him."

"I'm going with you," Susie said. "Pa'll stay here by the phone."

For Martin, always a light sleeper, and roused by the sound of voices downstairs, had got dressed and come down. He was in the chair by the stove, now, pulling on his felts-and-rubbers.

"Now, don't be a fool," he grunted. "You stay in the house here, where you belong."

For answer, Susie turned, marched out the door, and climbed into the front seat of Charles's car. She was not, she told herself, going through another time in that kitchen, alone.

After a moment, Charles and George came out.

'That's that," Charles said, climbing into the driver's seat. "Wow!"

"Ain't he the old heller, though," George said. "All the same, he's better off home. Old man, cold night like this."

"Don't kid yourself," Charles said cheerfully. "He'd outlast me, anytime, and I'm not so sure but what he'd give you a run for your money, George boy. Now, Susie, think. You've pretty well checked the town. Where are Ralph's places? Where, outside the town, would he be likely to go?"

Susie tried to think. "Anywhere," she said. "And everywhere. He likes to wander around, poke into old houses."

"Beachcombing," Charles said. 'Let's try Avery's Beach."

But Avery's Beach was silent and deserted, its length gray and mysterious under the northern lights and the sky, curving away to the tumbled mass of granite ledges that marked its end. At its foot, the sea's lazy ripple was muffled by a tongue of ice making out from the shore, carrying an occasional spiky glitter from the cold stars.

The beach was easy to explore; the shore road led along, just back from the beach rocks, so that Charles was able to drive its full length. From the car, they could make out the bare, rounded top of the beach, swept clean of driftwood and debris by the winter storms; though one long black object, lying flat, gave Susie a clutching twist at the heart before she saw it was only a castaway log.

"Nothing here," Charles said, turning the car around. "You still with us, Susie?"

"Yes," Susie said. "I—I guess I am, Charles."

Unexpectedly, he reached across and patted her on the shoulder. "Take it easy," he said. "We'll find him. He's somewhere, that's for sure."

"Yes," she said. "I know. Of course. He must be."

But there's so much of it, she thought, so many places. Woods, ledges, water—something in her mind stumbled and shied away. No. Don't think about the ocean. Not unless you have to . . .

Under the thick material of her coat, she could feel a warm spot, where Charles's hand had tightened, briefly. The spot lingered, seemed to loosen a little the cold lump in her throat.

Charles—Charles would find him.

We always go to Charles, she thought. And he always knows what to do. Through the years, all of us, George and Hazel, the boys and me, we've always gone to Charles.

For a moment, she almost thought she had said this aloud, for Charles turned from the wheel and gave her a long look.

"You want me to run you home?" he asked. "It's pretty cold, all this tracking around."

"No," Susie said. "I'd rather stay with you, Charles."

Charles said something under his breath which ended with "goddammit," she wasn't sure just what, but it had sounded like, "It's about time."

But at that moment George spoke from the back seat, suggesting that while they were here, they might go up and check the old Avery place; a kid might easy have got hurt ransacking around them old buildings, if so be old buildings was what he liked to ransack around.

"The floorboards is all rotten," George said. "I see that when I was up there last fall, deer-hunting. I come up through the orchard and just for the hell of it I peeked in the window. They's an old punkin-pine chest in there, and I was nosy, I thought I'd just have a look into it, but the minute I stepped off the threshold one of my feet went through the floor clean to the hip. If I'd hadn't've give a good buck-jump, I'd have gone ker-whango right down into the suller. There's an old cistern full of water, must be six-seven feet deep, right under where I was standing. If I'd gone into that, I'd've stayed there forever, for all anyone would've ever found me."

Carried away by the idea of what might have happened, and not a tactful man, George became suddenly aware that Susie had turned around and was staring at him, stiff with horror. He stopped dead, and stared back at her, stiff with horror, himself.

Charles said, between his teeth, "Shut up, will you, George?" and George did, thinking, Well, god, I guess I better.

But no one was around the old Avery place, nor had been. They were saved the trouble of looking inside the tumbledown old house and barns, because under the spruces which had grown up close around, the snow was unmelted, and there were no tracks anywhere.

They had stopped by Charles's house a couple of times, while Susie phoned home. The first time, Martin answered, grunting that no, Ralph hadn't showed up. The second time, it was Dot.

"Grampa went somewhere in the car," she said. "Mama, is Ralph really lost?"

"Well, we just don't know where he is right now," Susie said. "Are you all right, Dottie? Can you stay awake, and phone Aunt Hazel if Ralph comes in?"

Dot could; she seemed quite excited by the prospect. No, she didn't know where Grampa'd gone. He'd just gone off ugly, without saying a word.

All that night, the entire town hunted for Ralph McIntosh. When, at eleven o'clock, there was still no sign of him, Charles roused the town.

Over the phone, he organized search parties, sent them out over the countryside by automobile and on foot.

"Whoever finds him make plenty of noise," Charles said. "Take your gun along, if you've got one, and fire three shots. Then get back to a phone and phone Folsom to blow the tannery whistle. God knows if you can wake him up, but if you can't, ring a church bell."

Folsom was the tannery night-watchman, who had been known to spend his uneventful nights sleeping.

"And stay with someone," Charles went on. "Don't anyone go wandering off by himself. It's a damn cold night, and we don't want to lose anybody else."

Charles got up from the phone, put on his coat. "All right," he said. "Let's go."

They ransacked other old buildings before the night was over, drove down byways where branches met overhead and the big car skidded and churned, while George shifted uneasily in the back seat, remarking what to hell would they do if they ever got stuck in here, and Charles said nothing, merely didn't get them stuck. Sometimes they came up with other search parties—no one had found a trace, anywhere; and once, on the outskirts of town, they passed Debby Parker's little car, traveling fast, with Carlisle at the wheel. Susie caught a glimpse of his face, as the car flashed by without stopping.

She was too miserable now to be furious with him any longer; or furious with anyone. It seemed to her that the car had gone on forever, the headlights along the black tunnels of the roads, patched with ice and spongy patches of old snow, boring into woods, the shafted trees mottled with shadow, the cold, inhuman undergrowth.

It was three o'clock before anyone thought of Tanner's Island. It was such an out-of-the-way place; no one, in his right mind, would ever think of going there in the winter, anyway.

They had stopped at Hank Tiverton's junkyard, where George had insisted on getting out to throw open the doors of three or four old refrigerators.

"Hell, George!" Charles exploded. "He's too big a kid even to get into one of those, let alone be such a fool as to shut the door on himself. Don't be so damn stupid!"

"Well, it says on the TV," George said stubbornly. "A progrum I saw the other day. Them iceboxes, kids get locked in and stifle. Them doors ought to be took off anyway, according to law; if I live, I'll tell Hank Tiverton so. You let me out, Charles, you hear me? Won't take but a minute to make sure."

But he came back disappointed. Ralph wasn't in the iceboxes.

"Well, that idea never paid off, did it?" he said disconsolately, climbing back into the car. "What now?"

"I don't know," Charles said. He sat, wearily, a little bent, over the wheel. "I don't know, George. I'm trying to think."

"We been everywhere," George said. "There ain't no place outside of the cemetery we ain't looked. Say, you don't suppose he's got shut into that old tomb up there, do you?"

"Oh, god!" Charles groaned. "That place is sealed shut and padlocked and you know it. George, you have the damnedest ideas. Look, everybody think. Warm day in February, first good day for weeks there hasn't been any school, when we were kids, George, where'd we go?"

"I'd have gone duck-hunting," George said. "Down round shore."

"He didn't take the gun," Susie said. "The gun's home on the rack. That was the first thing I checked."

"Tanner's Island," Charles said. "Would he have any reason to go there? You know, he could have gone over there and got caught by the tide."

"Well, he could have walked off there by half-past nine or so," George said. "When the tide went down. If he was able-bodied, that is, if he ain't broke a leg over there. Or if he didn't slip and fall in, trying to jump that goddam gut in the middle of the causeway in the dark."

Charles said, in measured tones, "George, if you don't shut up that kind of stuff, I'll take a poke at you. How about it, Susie? Any reason why Ralph would want to go over to Tanner's Island?"

"Well, Carlisle used to go there a lot," Susie said. "To dig in the Indian shell heap. Sometimes he'd let Ralph go, too. But it was Carlisle's place. They had some kind of an agreement, I think. He made Ralph promise he wouldn't—"

Charles started up the car with a jerk.

She watched numbly while he drove along Main Street, turned down Allen's Lane. It was not entirely what George had said that had made the twisting in her chest tighten, so that she could hardly breathe. It had been in the back of her mind all night, faceless at her shoulder. The ocean. Because if anybody along these treacherous edges of rock and cliff and beach could not be found on the land, then where must he be?

At the tannery, where the hardtop ended, Charles did not stop. He turned the car sharply, sent it scrabbling and skidding along the shore path, two wheels on the hard surface of the path, the other two finding what traction they might in the tough grass and underbrush.

"Holy god and musselbanks!" George said. "You ain't thinking of *driving* down here, Charles! You'll bust every spring you've got, not to say dump us all ass-over-apple into the river."

"Somebody has," Charles said.

Certainly, from the dim track in the crushed underbrush, it looked as if a car had been along here, sometime.

"Maybe someone had the sense to come down here and check this place first," George said. "Ought to have thought of it first-off, seeing it's a place where them kids would be likely to come. Course, I wouldn't know, Charles wouldn't—"

"Oh, I know," Susie burst out. "I should have! Why didn't I think! Only they never have come here in the winter and it didn't enter my head."

Her voice had started up and she stopped it, realizing that if she didn't, the voice, which didn't sound like her own at all, but like somebody else's altogether, would start to scream.

Charles said, sharply, "Cut it out, Susie. You've done all right. No one could have—George, why don't you chew tobacco, or something, for a while, stop up that—Hey, look!"

Over on the shore of Tanner's Island, a fire was burning; at least, it had been burning, though it was now only a big pile of embers and a thin trail of white smoke, standing straight up into the windless sky. No one seemed to be near it, at least, in the dim light, no one could be seen. It was just a fire.

Charles, who had been looking at it, swore suddenly and jammed on his brakes just in time to avoid hitting the back end of another car, parked ahead of them on the riverbank.

A familiar back end, Susie saw, as she opened the door and jumped out. It was Martin Hoodless's old Chevy.

"Pa, down here?" she said. "What's he doing down here?"

"I had an idea he thought he had more sense than we did, when we left him," Charles said. He put back his head and let out a bawl. "Hey, over on the island! Martin! Ralph!"

There was no answer.

"Martin must be over there," Charles said. "If that's Ralph's fire—but no, if Ralph had built it, they'd be around there. They must be back in the woods somewhere. Martin came back and built the fire, hoping somebody'd see. George, how about it? Can we make it across that causeway?"

It was going on for three-thirty in the morning; the tide was rising now, not yet over the causeway, but already beginning to flow in slick-looking coils across the rocks and old timbers here and there, running through the gap in a millrace.

George stood looking down, glumly; and in the silence Susie heard the louder-growing chuckle of the water.

"God, I dunno," George said. "I guess so."

"Come on then," Charles said.

He had fished his cane out of the front seat of the car and started for the causeway.

"And what to the humping old hills of hell do you think you'll do," George burst out, "out there on them slippery rocks on that cussid brass leg?"

"I've seen worse," Charles said cheerfully.

"You cussid fool!" George said. "Ain't no need of but one of us going. Go on, git back there, or I'll take that leg off you and bust it acrost my knee. And here, I'll take that cane along, help me poke out where the holes are."

He went past, grabbing the cane as he went, leaving Charles teetering precariously at the edge of the bank.

"And I'll have you all know," George said, his voice rising to a howl, as he contemplated the slippery, uncomfortable passage ahead of him, "that I can't swim one goddam stroke, neither!"

Gingerly, he lowered one foot into the icy water, yanked it out with a yell. Then he proceeded, muttering and stumbling. From the bank, Susie and Charles watched his dim figure, advancing slowly across the causeway, feeling out the way with Charles's cane. They could hear his thumps and scrabblings, and suddenly there came a loud splash, as George fell down.

"Oh, Charles," Susie said. "Will he be all right? What if he falls off of there?"

"Well, the ducking wouldn't do him any good," Charles said. "But I could pull him out, Susie. He doesn't think so, but I can swim with one leg better than he can with two. As soon as he gets across, we'll go for more help. But I expect we'd better stay here till he makes it." He glanced down at her. "You're shaking all over. Go and sit in the car. I'll put the heater on."

"I'm—I c-can't," Susie said. She had been clenching her teeth, but the moment she opened her mouth to answer him, they started to rattle. "I've got to see—"

"Well, come here, then." Methodically, Charles unbuttoned his overcoat, pulled her against him, and then, reaching around in front, buttoned it again. "If I have to get to George in a hurry," he said, holding her tightly. "I'll likely jump out of here right over your head. But it's a big coat."

His voice, just above the level of her ear, shook a little; she could feel, against her shoulder, the sudden, sharp hammering of his heart. His breath was warm against her cheek; it was warm, against him; and Susie felt her shaking stop, except for the deep-inside tremors somewhere in the pit of her stomach.

"Better?" Charles said. "Look, if you're going to tromp on my foot, tromp on the tin one."

His arms tightened around her. "Susie," he said, under his breath, and stopped. "Looks as if George has stalled out there," he went on, and called, "Hey, George?"

On the causeway, George's blurred figure was motionless, and his complaints were silent.

"Hey, George, what's with you?"

"Hey, yourself, and see how you like it!" George's irascible bawl boomed out across the water. "Go git a boat! Don't stand there, git help!"

"What's the matter? You stuck?"

"Yes, by god, I am! That damn gut's ten foot acrost, come up to. What you expect me to do—jump it? Wade it?"

"Come on back, then. You can make it back, can't you?"

"No, I can't! I had trouble enough gitting here through that damn Niagara Falls, without I turn around and go back through it. Go git a boat, you cussid fool! You want me to wash to hellangone to Europe?"

"Okay." Charles's fingers were neatly, nimbly unbuttoning the overcoat. "I'll find a boat. But you better start back, George, falls or no falls, in case it takes me some time to find one."

He freed both Susie and himself from the overcoat, draped it around her shoulders. "Ought to be some duck-hunters' punts down along," he said. "Blast you, George, for running off with my cane."

"Charles, you can't!" Susie said. "Not with only one—Not down those rough rocks—"

"Shut up and get in the car," Charles said, "before you freeze your button off."

He took a few careful steps along the top of the bank, moving warily, watching for ice-patches. He had not gone far, when suddenly, he came to a stop, stood looking out over the water toward the island, and then turned and came back to the car.

George, seeing this apparent inhuman disregard of his plight, began to swear. Long cadences boomed out over the water, rising and falling, as George called upon his repertory, and, clinging to his tide-washed rock, gave it everything he had.

"Holy smoke," Charles said. "Listen to that, you could scan that like poetry. Take it easy, Susie. Your old man's coming. He's got a boat. The smart old duffer, he had the sense to take one with him."

"Ralph—" Susie said, through dry lips.

"All I can see is someone moving and the white sides of the boat," Charles said. "But if Ralph was over there, he's probably found him, Susie."

Straining her eyes, Susie could make out the vague shimmer in the darkness, which was the white punt moving on the water. George, apparently, had seen it, too, for his oration suddenly cut off in the middle, and he let go with a hoarse bawl.

"Hey! Hey, you with the boat! Get me off of here!"

They saw the boat veer downstream, as it met the thrust of the current pouring through the causeway; then it turned and circled. They heard the thump and squelch of George's shoes as he jumped down into it, George's voice speaking to Martin, and Martin's unintelligible, grunted reply.

Unable to stand the suspense any longer, Susie pulled away from Charles and half-ran, half-slid, down the bank. She stood at the water's edge, trying to count the blur of figures in the boat; she could not tell how many, and for a moment, her voice would not come. Then she called, "Pa! Is Ralph with you? Did you find him?"

Martin did not answer. He kept on rowing, the rapid chunk-chunk of his oars coming nearer; and then George's lugubrious tones spoke out of the darkness.

"No, Susie, god, no. He ain't found him."

So sure had Susie been that there would be three people in the boat that for a blurred moment, she thought she had seen three. But there were only two.

Martin drove the boat head-on onto the narrow beach; it stopped with a jerking crunch, unsettling George who was crouched in the bow. He teetered precariously to get back his lost balance, then stepped stiffly out to haul up the boat for Martin; but Martin was having none of that. He stamped overboard into the shallow water, splashed ashore, and started up the bank.

"Where've all you blasted fools been all night?" he demanded. "What was you, cuddled up in a cow barn somewhere, you didn't spot that fire?" His familiar bawl was reedy, a little breathless, but he got to the top of the bank before Susie did, and far ahead of George, who came up ponderously, his wet clothes crackling with ice.

"Get into the car, George, start the engine," Charles said. "Get the heater going. Martin, didn't you find anything over there?"

He sounded suddenly tired to death, and he had put an arm around Susie, holding her.

"Well, I found where the crazy damfool was all day," Martin said. "He's rooted out a hole in them damned old Indian clamshells big enough to hold a walrus."

"Where is he then, Pa? Is he over there hurt somewhere?"

"No, he ain't over there hurt. And how do I know where to god he went? There was a cave-in over there, but he ain't under it, I moved it. He ain't over there."

"You're sure?" Charles said. "We'd better get back, get a crowd over there, hunting—"

"What to hell do you mean, am I sure?" Martin's voice, thin, breathy, played out on him. He came to a full stop, breathed deep, went on. "What d'you think I've been doing since twelve o'clock, when I see that fire over here? I built it up again when I got here, throwed on an old tar-barrel off the beach. You gang of half-wits hadn't been blind in both eyes, some of you'd seen it. Chasing sheep, around up-country somewhere, when if you'd stopped to listen, two words, to me up to the house tonight, I could've told you where that kid would head for. But no, the old man don't know nothing—"

"All right," Charles said. "You're all in, Martin, we'd better get you home."

"So'd you be, if you'd moved upward of two tons of clamshells," Martin rasped. "You can round up your sheepherders and hunt over there if you want to. But Ralph ain't there. I found every track he made. He crossed over to the other side of the island, and he went around in the field some, and he dug that damn great hole, and then he come back. He see he'd got caught by the tide, and he went round and round on the beach there, picking up wood for a fire. When I got there, that fire'd been going a long time. Lot of coals."

"Look, Martin," Charles said. "It was high tide around—let's see. Five-thirty? Six? He could have walked across there by nine, couldn't he?"

"All right, go on, tell me what I know. I figgered he'd got hurt, sprained his ankle, maybe. I figgered I'd find him somewheres near that fire. But there wasn't nothing near it, only—" Martin's voice thickened, with rage, or disgust, or grief, which, no one could have said. "Only a tin can full of some kind of a smashed up damned old Indian pot. Ralph, all right, couldn't be nobody else, I kicked it to hell off into the woods."

Martin made a frustrated, furious movement with both his hands. He started for his car, staggered, and would have fallen if Charles hadn't caught his arm.

Martin shook him off. He straightened up. "Leggo of me!" he said. "And for godsake move that mess of gadgets and watchwheels out of the way, so I can get my car turned around. I'm going home. Tomorrow, we'll get a crowd down here to drag that brook—that's all we can do now."

"Get in the car, Susie," Charles said. He helped her, unresisting, into the front seat, got in himself on the driver's side, and backed up, so that Martin could get by.

"But Pa found where he was," she said, wildly, clutching Charles's arm. "Charles, we can't stop now!"

"I've got to get to a phone, get a crowd down here," Charles said. "Your father can't be sure, he couldn't have found all those tracks in the dark."

"He had a flashlight," George said gloomily, from the back seat. "I see it in his pocket."

"He's all in," Charles said. "Worn out, half-frozen." His voice went on, steadily, quietly. "Look, he's driving all over the road. We've got to see he gets home all right, and George can't do any more till he gets some dry clothes, and we've got to get some help, Susie."

Numbly, Susie saw the lights of Martin's car go jigging erratically up Allen's Lane, ahead of them, turn the corner into Main Street. Yes, Charles was right. Martin had better be got home.

Then George, sitting chattering in the back seat, gave mournful tongue.

"Well, god," he said hollowly. "All in or no all in, you good and well know Mart wouldn't've give up till he was sure. You know, I betcha what he thinks, he thinks that kid fell off the causeway. Tried to get acrost there when the water was too high, same as I did. G-god, Charles, that damn waterhole, that's no joke! Another five minutes, I'd been into it myself, and I'd never got out!"

"All right, George," Charles said, wearily. "Don't listen to him, Susie, he's had the sense soaked right out of him. There must be places Martin didn't look, couldn't have—" His voice died out, came again, strongly. "Can you find George some dry clothes, up at your place, get some coffee into him?"

Martin had the kitchen fire roaring when they got there—from the smell, he must have poured kerosene onto live coals in the firebox. He had the coffeepot on; and he himself was sitting with both feet thrust into the oven. He did not look up or speak when they came in.

Charles made a beeline for the telephone.

"Pa," Susie said. "Did Dot stay awake? Was she—"

Martin grunted. "She kept the living-room fire going," he said. His voice was stronger; he was still blue around the mouth, but he had some color in his cheeks. "She let this one get down," he went on. "Never had the sense. Dang it, the kitchen fire's what we needed, and some coffee on. I sent her to hell to bed."

He wouldn't change, Susie thought, if—what would have to happen to change him?

Then, looking more closely, she saw that Martin's head was shaking, a steady, slight tremor, as if his neck were too weak to hold it still. No, he wouldn't change. But he's nearly killed himself, tonight, over there on Tanner's Island; and passing by him, she let her hand rest briefly on his shoulder.

Martin shook it off irritably. "Go get George something dry to put on, can't you?" he growled. "The boy's freezing to death."

Susie went about the house collecting dry clothes for George—some warm long-johns of her father's, wool pants and a flannel shirt of Carlisle's. On the way, she looked in on Dot in the small bedroom off the kitchen; but Dot, apparently, had been so done in that she had gone to sleep the moment she hit the bed. There were traces of tears on her cheeks, and Susie stood for a moment, steadying herself by a hand on the head of the bed.

I have got to pull myself together, she said. I have got to.

But it seemed to her that she was two people, one standing here quietly making sure that Dot was safely asleep, the other curled into a great numb knot, shaking deep down inside and screaming.

Oh, hurry, George needs these clothes, she told herself; but it took a minute or so before she could make herself move.

She handed the clothes to George, shut him in the living room to change behind the big, hot airtight stove. George was in a bad way; his lips were blue, his teeth rattling.

She said, "Hurry up, get dry, George. By the time you're dressed there'll be coffee in the kitchen."

As she closed the door to the living room, she heard the tannery whistle start to blow, calling in the search parties. Charles had got through to the night-watchman.

In the kitchen, he was still at the telephone. Martin was up, pouring coffee.

No cream, Susie thought, glancing mechanically at the table, to see what was needed. Well, she had a full pitcher in the icebox, put away to be ready for breakfast.

She headed for the pantry, snapping on the light as she went in.

There, on the white enamel of the icebox door, was a great, sprawly, soot-black handprint.

Pa, she thought wearily. Well, I suppose he was too tired to wash his hands.

She opened the door, reached for the cream pitcher. It was empty.

There were smudges on the inside of the door, also, and somebody had torn great chunks out of a cold chicken. More than half of it was gone, both drumsticks, both second joints. Beside it, was a dish in which lay, exposed and lonely, one cold boiled potato.

Automatically, Susie picked up the empty cream pitcher. She closed the icebox door. She was halfway across the kitchen, before what she had seen hit her squarely, like a blow at the heart.

That dish, when she had put it there, had been full of the leftover potatoes from supper.

She gave a gasp that was half-scream and dropped the pitcher. It smashed on the floor; and she tore out of the kitchen and through the living room, not seeing Charles and Martin spinning around staring after her, galvanized; not even aware of the white form of George, or of his strangled yelp, as he dove for privacy behind the living-room stove.

What she did see, upstairs, as she thrust open the discreetly closed door of Ralph's bedroom and turned on the light, was the tremendous bone on the bureau—some kind of great, sooty-black animal bone, notched into a spear; the pile of wet, filthy, blackened clothes on the floor—the pants legs two tunnels, just as they had been got out of; and on the white pillow, the innocent, sweetly sleeping face, with the scratched nose in the middle of it, black as a coal.

Ralph had arrived home at around nine-thirty, just before Susie had got into the car and driven down to Charles's house. He had seen her, apparently all serene, sitting at the table in the kitchen, as he had crossed the yard, and he had thought, first with relief and then with resentment, Geez, nobody's missed me at all.

It seemed to him that he'd been gone nearly all night; that he must have been. From just before dark until a little while ago, he'd been sitting over on Tanner's Island by the fire he'd built to keep from freezing, waiting for the tide to go down. He'd built an old dowser of a fire, hoping someone would see it and come over for him in a boat; he'd ransacked the beach for driftwood, throwing on everything he could find—logs, old lobster traps, and castaway buoys; down along the shore, quite a ways, too, he'd found a couple of old tar barrels which he'd rolled back, two trips, one after the other; but he'd only had time to burn one, because, all of a sudden, the top of the causeway had started to show out of the ebbing tide.

It would have horrified George to know how much water had been running down over the causeway when Ralph had crossed it; though to Ralph it hadn't seemed like much out of the ordinary—a longer jump than usual over the gut; and, of course, he'd landed in water and got soaked to the skin. He had run nearly all the way home; so that outside the window, peering in at Susie, he wasn't even cold. But there was Susie, not even worried, just sitting.

If she sees me, how I've racked out these clothes, she'll cream me for keeps, Ralph thought. And then, nobly, No sense my tracking up her nice clean kitchen carpet. I'll just go up the piazza post and clean off some of this crud in my room, and then I'll go downstairs and root out some supper.

At the idea of supper, it seemed to him that the whole bottom of his stomach had started to fall away.

So Ralph took his Indian harpoon in his teeth and shinnied up the piazza post. He silently tiptoed along the porch roof to his bedroom window; and he had just laid the harpoon down on the clean white scarf of his bureau, when he heard the front door slam. Peering warily out of his still-dark window, he saw Susie go along the walk to the garage. He heard the Chevy's starter whine and start to slap over, and he listened, critically, his head on one side.

Uh-huh. Flooded her, he said to himself. Just like a woman. Maybe I better go down and show her a thing or two about starting a car. They can't ever learn about a cold engine.

But at that moment the car started. Its back end appeared at the garage door; then it was out of the yard and rolling down the hill toward town.

Good, now he wouldn't have to wait to clean up, and it was a doggoned lucky thing, because his stomach thought his throat was cut. In another minute, he'd be dead, starved to death, flat on the floor.

He made a leap for the door, his boots thumping and still faintly squelching; then brought up short, his hand on the knob.

Geez, Grampa! He'd be in bed by now, and he slept light. No sense taking a chance on his coming nosing out with his Where-to-hell-you-beens, the way he did sometimes when somebody got home late.

Ralph paused long enough to take off his wet boots. Then he went, silent as a shadow, along the hall past Martin's open door, leaving a trail of wet, blackened stocking-prints on the hall floorboards, on the stair carpet and across the living-room rug; and, of course, the smudges on the icebox door.

He had a fine meal of chicken, cream, and cold potatoes, and he found a great wedge of chocolate cake in the cakebox. He drank a whole panful of milk, cream and all. The cream, nearly a quarter of an inch thick, plopped into his glass, tasted wonderful. Even then it didn't seem as if he'd had quite enough; so he went back and tore off another leg and second joint from the chicken.

Ma would tick over about that tomorrow. She probably had that chicken saved up for a meal. But tomorrow . . . was tomorrow . . .

His head suddenly bumped on the table, sending a slight twinge of pain through his sore nose, and he jerked himself back upright, surprised. Geez, he'd almost gone to sleep right here in the kitchen. He must be some old tired. Well, no wonder, up this late. Eleven, twelve o'clock, whatever it was.

The kitchen clock, actually, said nine-forty, but he didn't think to look at it.

His nose was sure sore. Hey, that was some scratch. Went the whole length of his nose, right up into his forehead.

He leaned over, trying to see the reflection of the scratch in the enameled top of the kitchen table, and recoiled at the sight of the blurred, bloody, blackened visage which stared up at him.

Wow! That was awful! Better wash. Couldn't go to bed like that.

Better wash out in the laundry tub, not get that stuff all over Ma's sink. Besides, Grampa'd be sure to hear water running in the kitchen or the bathroom.

Ralph washed in the laundry, letting the water run from the faucet in a trickle, because Grampa might just possibly hear it out here, too. He left the soap black, the set-tub black, and a black kitchen-towel—all of which traces Susie might have seen, if she had happened to go out to the laundry off the kitchen. He found he could not wash his nose, it was too sore; so he washed around it; then he stole back upstairs, undressed, and fell into bed. The bed felt wonderful; cold sheets, shivery at first, slowly warming; and he savored this for the space of three breaths before he fell so dead asleep that he heard nothing—not even the commotion downstairs; not even the tannery whistle blowing.

Part Eight

Shirttail McIntosh went to Boston. The team left by bus on Monday afternoon.

At breakfast, on that day, Martin had delivered a speech.

It was school vacation, he said. There was work to do. Among other things, he had that big horse chestnut to cut up. The boys could start in on that after they'd helped him to load the truck with the weekly orders of eggs and dressed broilers, for downtown. When he got back from delivering them, he'd come up and help on the tree.

When he had got this far with the speech, Martin stopped and looked around the table, waiting for somebody to give him an argument. Nobody said anything. Dot sat still as a mouse, with an air of waiting; Ralph looked scared and walleyed, the whites of his eyes showing as he glanced from one to another of his family seated around the table. But Carlisle didn't look up from his plate. He went on composedly stowing away oatmeal.

"All right!" Martin said. He sloshed a good dollop of heavily creamed coffee into his saucer, put a fat doughnut in it, and stared stonily around the table, while he waited for the doughnut to soak to a proper consistency. "You fellers can use my big cross-cut saw," he said, with the air of one who bestows a favor.

"Gee, thanks," Carlisle said.

He still did not look up and his voice was expressionless.

Martin stared at him.

"And I don't want any of your damfool carelessness with it," he said. "Just in case you think you can bust it on purpose and get out of working because there ain't no saw. You better get going, if you want to get through before dark. That job's going to take a couple of days."

"No, I don't think so," Carlisle said. His voice was now bored, with a suggestion of amusement. "I figure about two hours on it. You keep your good old cross-cut for when you want to use it. I know where I can borrow a power saw."

Susie tried to catch his eye so she could shake her head at him, but he wasn't looking at anyone.

Martin let out a strangled blat. A small mushy piece of doughnut, entangled in his mustache, blew off and shot across the table.

Dot stared at it, and then, with a face of disgust, at her mother. "Mama, I'm through," she said in a prissy voice. "May I be excused? I have to get ready."

Susie nodded, impatiently waving Dot away from the table. Dot was going to Fairport to visit a classmate for a few days, as a sop to her feelings, hurt because Susie had put her foot down hard on any hopes Dot had about going to Boston. Even if the Mooneys did invite her, Susie had said, Dot might as well make up her mind—she couldn't go. The classmate's family had a TV set; Dot would have to make do with watching the game on that. It had been a battle, but Dot was now resigned. Susie was planning to drive her over to Fairport right after breakfast.

"Thank you, Mama," Dot said. She got up slowly, still eyeing the piece of doughnut with such marked distaste that Martin paused in his tirade about power saws and transferred his attention to her.

"What's the matter with you, Miss Priss?" he wanted to know. "You'll be lucky in life if you don't get hit with nothing worse than a piece of flying doughnut. You know I won't let one of them damn things onto the place," he went on, to Carlisle. "No, sir, by tar, you get on up there and cut up that tree with a cross-cut, the way a man ought to cut up a tree. Get your back into it for a change. A little hefty work ain't going to hurt you one mite."

"Okay," Carlisle said. He shrugged. "If you don't want it done in a quarter of the time, it's all right with me."

"Trying to get through so's you can go traipsing off again with that damn ballteam, are you?" Martin said. "Well, you ain't. You ain't going to be through for a week."

Carlisle said nothing more, and a little later, Susie, peering concernedly from the back kitchen-window, saw him, with Ralph, helping Martin to load the truck.

Of course he's got to go, she thought. I'll have to do something. But where to begin?

She was still shaky from Saturday night; she still felt all torn loose inside and jumpy; and tired to death. While all three of the children slept a good deal on Sunday, she hadn't been able to. Martin, of course, was up and around as usual; even though he looked hollow-eyed and gray in the face, he wouldn't rest in the daytime, and Susie kept feeling she ought to be downstairs before he jumped too hard on poor Ralph. Because Ralph, when he found out the trouble he had caused, was going to feel horrible.

She'd been right, at least partly so. Dot had been too relieved to see Ralph safe to say much; at least, yet. And Martin, to Susie's relief, hadn't really scolded Ralph, though the way he was acting this morning was an indication of things to come, and Ralph knew it; Susie could tell by the way he'd acted at the breakfast table. But Carlisle had been all cocked back and ready. As a matter of fact, he had been the one who'd told Ralph what had happened—the whole family, the whole town turned upside-down, just because of his damfoolishness . . .

Poor old Ralph. He had come downstairs, happy as a lark, late Sunday morning, full to the brim with his finds—his arrowheads, his harpoon—to run head-on into that! The sounds of battle had waked Susie; she had hustled downstairs herself to find Ralph backed up against the kitchen counter, looking wall-eyed and wretched, and Carlisle yelling; she didn't doubt that what caused his rage was relief as much as anything, but being worn out and nervous herself, she'd spoken out more violently, perhaps, than she'd needed to. Carlisle was still furious at her this morning, she could see.

He's furious at us all. If he could just see, once in a while, how things are with other people, she thought. And yet, in some ways, you can't blame him. He always was a concentrated boy, one thing at a time, with him, and his mind on it. I suppose anything outside of ball right now seems unimportant to him.

Sometimes I wish I couldn't see both sides of things. To be like Pa and Carlisle, just see your own side and shut out everything else—what a relief! Why, you could make up your mind in five minutes, and not all the time be falling between fences.

The next time she looked out, the truck was loaded, and Martin was over unlocking the tool shed. He kept the tools locked up now—he'd put a big padlock on the tool shed, a day or so after the ax and clawbar incident. She watched him dole out axes and the big cross-cut saw to the boys, and then turn toward the house, while they trudged up the hill toward the pasture.

The trouble is, he's right. It's time somebody cracked down. But it's the wrong time to do it, and oh, lord, if it isn't just like him to pick now!

She started to say something as Martin came in, but he gave her no chance; he went past her with a face like a meat-ax; upstairs, into his bedroom. She could hear him banging around up there, apparently changing his clothes. Oh, yes, bank morning. He would be going into the bank to make his deposit today.

Ordinarily, Martin didn't get out of his work-frock and overalls when he went to make his deliveries; but on bank morning he always put on his neat, dark-blue Sunday suit and his overcoat. The trip to the bank was one of the few occasions, nowadays, that the old man dressed up for.

He came downstairs, went past Susie as if she weren't there, banged the kitchen door, banged the truck door, and sent the truck roaring out of the yard.

Oh, lord, Susie thought. Peace at last.

She sat down for a moment and covered her face with her hands.

In a little while, her mind jogged at her, you've got to drive Dot to Fairport. For just now, it's quiet here.

She didn't even hear Charles Kendall's car drive up. The first thing she realized, Charles was standing there in the door.

"Hey, Susie. Susie! Oh, come on, now, nothing can be that bad," and the next thing, she was crying, with her face buried in his coat.

Up in the pasture, Carlisle paused for a moment beside the tree house. He glanced at it, then at Ralph; one eyebrow crawled upward on his smooth forehead.

"Yeah, I was working on it," Ralph said wearily. "That's how I bent the damn clawbar."

Carlisle grinned. "Shove it," he said. "I don't care."

He whirled the ax he was carrying a few times around his head, and sent it flying high in the air in a mighty heave.

He said, "Tell Grampa love and kisses," and trotted away across the pasture, ducking out of sight into the alders above the highway that led to town.

On the way down the hill, Martin had been accosted by Hezzie Mooney, who had pulled his truck alongside on the road, and had started to have over some kind of chat about Martin's cutting down that tree. The sheer gall of it, the idea of anybody's daring to haul a man up for cutting down a tree in his own back pasture—Martin had driven off without listening, and had stewed all the way downtown. But now, standing in front of the teller's wicket, tucking his bankbook away in his wallet, he all at once felt better.

That, by tar, had been a pretty substantial deposit for any man to make. He'd shipped a couple of truckloads of broilers to the company last week; got a good price, too. Didn't want to haul that big check around in his wallet, either, making deliveries all over town. It was some different now from the times, years back, when he'd come in here to see Jed Wallace about borrowing money. Mortgaged the farm, paid off the mortgage, three times, in his lifetime; twice bringing Helga along to sign, though the third time was after Helga'd gone. Slinking, by tar, was what he'd always felt like whenever he'd had to borrow money; slinking around was what he'd done, too, till he'd paid back every cent of the loan. Never felt like looking another man in the eye till he was free and clear again; and it had always seemed like a poor kind of a thing to ask Helga to do, too. Time was, big family trailing out behind, pulling himself up by his bootstraps, when he'd never come into the bank at all except to ask for a loan, or pay interest on one.

These days, he enjoyed the bank. He respected money. By tar, he knew what it was like to be without it! He liked looking around at the busy desks behind the grille; he liked the typewriters, the adding machines; the neat stacks of silver and bills; the papers; the counters, glossy with use. As much as anything, he liked the smell. The slight rubbery smell from the composition tile floor, mingled with the smell of ink and old greenbacks, many kinds of overcoats and cigars, the breath of people continually passing through the bank, said to Martin, "order," "responsibility"; serious people taking care of money.

He was turning around to leave, when Jed Wallace inside his glass cubicle saw him, came to the door and held out his hand.

"How are you, Mart?" Jed said. "Come in for a minute, if you've got the time, I got something to ask you. Kind of a favor, I guess. How's the hens?" he went on, ushering the old man into his office. "You seem to be making out all right. I notice you get down here once a month, regular's a clock."

"I'm making out," Martin said.

"That's good. That's what we like. Well, you're busy making it, Mart, I'm busy keeping it for you. I won't hold you up. You got a photo of yourself?"

"Photo?" Martin asked, puzzled. He glanced down at himself, embarrassed, with a sheepish half-grin. "Hell, no, Jed. Why?"

"Well, for the paper," Jed said. "For the bank's ad, this week. Now, wait. Hear me out. Don't blow up yet. What we got in mind, we want to print pictures, along with our ads, of responsible fellers, Mart, oh, say, like yourself, that make a bank possible in a town. The boys dreamed this one up, and I go along, one hundred percent. We picked out half a dozen, but, by cracky, the one we all fell on first, was you. One of the best customers we ever had; word as good as your bond. How about it? Might help you out, too, in this little trouble you're having with your customers."

"Trouble?" Martin said. He was astonished, not knowing what to make of this. "Why, I've done business with the bank all right, Jed. Don't owe anything now, don't know as the bank owes me. How in hell do you figure a photo of me would help your business or mine?"

Jed laughed.

"It'd show the town the kind of a man the bank likes to do business with," he said. "The kind the bank respects. How's about if I send Higgins up to the farm with his camera? Okay?"

"Why, I guess so, Jed."

Martin was puzzled—Jed's heartiness puzzled him. Wasn't any reason to make such a splurge, other men in town must've done a lot more business with the bank than Martin ever had—but he was also flattered. By tar, nothing like this had ever happened before.

"Good," Jed said. "Thanks a lot, Mart. And, oh, yes. I knew there was something else. Are you folks planning on Carlisle's going to college?"

Martin glanced at him. "Susie's talking of it," he said.

"Well, the reason I ask, there'll be some athletic scholarships coming through for outstanding youngsters at the school. No reason why Carlisle shouldn't have one. It'll take care of his heavy expenses, lift a big load off you and Susie. Costs, to keep a boy in college, nowadays. Around twenty-five hundred a year."

"Huh," Martin grunted. "Who's giving away that much, free?"

"Well, I'm glad you asked that, Mart, because it seems to me, from what I hear around, that you don't understand about the set up with the colleges, nowadays. No reason why you should, really. But you know, when you and I was kids, we had to flivver along, best we could, most of us didn't get nowheres near where we wanted to go. Right?"

Martin nodded. He said nothing.

"Had to work so doggoned hard, never did get a chance at schooling. Why, no knowing where some of us might have landed. Might have been President. Only we had to use all we had, just to keep our heads above water."

"That's right," Martin said, laconically.

He sat, his big bony hands spread, palm down, on his thighs, listening. It would be interesting to know just what Jed was trying to get at; you could spot some kind of a negro in the woodpile a mile away. Because if you remembered back, you could hear Jed's old man now, griping about what it cost to keep Jed in college. If you remembered back a little further, you could see yourself, a long-gutted, gangly kid, leaving school to go to work at thirteen; wanting an education damn bad, longing after one; and never able to get one.

"It always said in my reader that a boy could be President, if he wanted to work hard enough," Jed said. "Somehow, though, I don't see how some of us could've worked any harder. You, for instance, Mart.

But no knowing where you'd gone, a man like you, if you'd got your schooling."

"And been willing to go into politics," Martin said.

Jed glanced at him quickly, a flick of the eyes; he went on, "Well, yeah, there is that. But nowadays, if a boy's going to want to be President, he can get help, Mart. Times have changed. Now, it's got back to me that you're kind of set-foot against the sports program up at the school. It's got me to wondering if you realize just what being an outstanding athlete can do for a boy."

"I know what it's done for Carlisle," Martin said. "It's made a goddam fool out of him."

"Oh, now, Mart, wait." Jed held up his hand. "Hear me out. I know you think ball's nothing but a game, and by cracky, you're right, it *is* nothing but a game. But there's a little more to it, if you stop to think. A good ballteam, now, that's a healthy thing for a town. Gives people an interest, all winter long. Man comes into town, goes to the game. Spends some money. Better for the town, better for him. It don't do the town no good, *nor* him, if he sets home all winter long, grows mold around a TV set. A businessman, he's got to think about these things, Mart. *You* can understand it."

Martin nodded again. He remained silent, however, and his face was stony.

Jed cleared his throat.

"Then you take the school. The towns around here, their school budget's more than half of their whole tax appropriation. They put out all they can, it still isn't enough. That dough from the ballgames, that's pumped right back through the school to help out with expenses. Without it, your taxes would go up and so would mine. Don't really see how any of us can handle any higher taxes, do you? And then there's the kids. They get their muscles trained, good healthy exercise; and the kicker is, the colleges are crazy to get good ballplayers, they'll go to any expense, even bid for 'em. What better way is there for a kid to get a crack at an education?"

"So what's the kid going to college for? To play ball?"

"Oh, now, Mart, of course he'll pay the college back, play ball in his spare time, but—"

"That ain't what I'd gone for, if I could have gone. That ain't what I got in mind for Carlisle, either. His mother's got the money to send him. If it ain't enough, he'll work his way."

"What's the sense of that? Why put a young kid that far behind the eight-ball? You work him too hard, you'll warp his whole future. Why, a young kid, he ain't ready for too much rugged stuff, Mart."

"Hell's pink-whiskered, blistered bells!" Martin said. "Carlisle's great-grandfather took a vessel around Cape Horn when he was seventeen."

"Different times, Mart, different times. Nowadays, thank God, a kid don't have to get out and hustle. I wouldn't want my boy to have to work the way I did, the way his grandfather did. It don't make sense. What I want for him is the best there is, and in this world, Mart, thanks to you and me, there's some pretty good things. By gum and by gosh, my kid wouldn't take a ship around Cape Horn. Be damned if I'd let him!"

"Well, another thing," Martin said. "Your kid couldn't."

A slight flush came into the pale skin over Jed's temples, but he went smoothly on.

"About ball, now, Mart, you're right. If you think your kid ain't learning anything but a game, you're absolutely right. But games, athletics, is good for a kid, Mart—limbers up his muscles; the way manual training, shop, up at the school, teaches him how to use tools—"

"Well, if it does teach him how to use tools," Martin said—this was another sore spot with him, had Jed but known it—"by tar, I ain't seen any great effect from that. What they make up there, them end-tables—a boy wants to learn to be a carpenter, build a house, build a fishboat. Ain't much market for end-tables."

Jed's flush deepened.

"The colleges know what they're doing, Mart. They like for a fella to be a good all-round guy. Fine student, fine athlete. That's why your boy Carlisle's going to go a long, long ways. Only us older folks, we've got to give a little, you know it?"

"I ain't done nothing but give," Martin said.

"You've give a good bucket of milk, that's what you've done. Ain't no use, now, to kick it over."

Martin grunted. If there was any reason, he thought, for an educated man to talk like a hick, it was just to show you that he was on your side, he was a hick, too. On jury duty, which Martin had had a good many times, he had run into the same thing, and it had always annoyed him. The lawyers, addressing the jury, at times would drop so far into countrified speech that the jury themselves had difficulty in understanding what they meant. Jed was an educated man, a college man. Why in hell didn't he talk like one?

"Now, Mart, the ball season's almost over. Carlisle's done one hell of a good job. Why not relax, let him finish it out? Couldn't do no harm, could it?"

"Let him go to Boston? Look here, Jed, is that what this is all about?"

"Now, go on, Mart, don't get me wrong. You and I, we're just kicking this thing around here for what it's worth, like a couple of sensible men. I've got other fish to fry than to worry whether a kid plays a game of ball, you know that. I'm not after one single, solitary thing. But, you know, Mart, just for your own good, there's a lot around town don't feel the same way I do. Quite a head of steam backs up behind these ballgames. Take, well, take Harry Troy. He's nuts about the team. His boy's on it. He takes eggs of you, doesn't he? For the supermarket?"

"Always has."

"Well, try and sell him some, this morning. You can't buck a whole town without coming out black-and-blue. If you bust up that ballteam, people won't buy any more eggs. You know that, good and darn well."

"What have they, gone crazy? For godsake, grown men!"

"That's right. And grown women—the women's worse'n the men. They will be till after the games in the Boston Garden, then it'll all die down till next year. But shoot, it happens every year, in whatever town has the Championship team. You can't do anything about it, neither can I. If you try, you only hurt your business. They've already got this story going about you, don't amount to anything, you know what gossip is, but you know how it snowballs. No man in his right mind would ever believe that you cut down a tree, let it fall on a couple of kids, on purpose—"

Martin stared at him, flabbergasted.

"What's that you say?"

"Ah-h, nobody really believes it. Or nobody would believe it, in ordinary times. But, honest to God, Mart, if I was you, I'd let that kid go to Boston. If you don't, and the team loses, the town'll have somebody to blame for it, and God help you, you'll lose every atom of town trade you've got."

"Why, I cut down a tree," Martin said, in a dazed way. "Wasn't no kids around, only Carlisle and the Mooney boy. They was over in the field having a fight. I watched 'em a while. Wondered at the time why they hadn't taken time off from playing ball to learn that when you take a punch at a feller, it helps to double up your fists. That tree never fell near enough to them to make a touse over. Never come nowheres near 'em."

"Well, you know gossip."

"By tar, somebody made that yarn up!"

Martin rose to his feet. His angular, rawboned height towered over the desk, and Jed recoiled.

"Sure, sure, they did, Mart," he said hastily. "The kids did. They didn't want the coach to know they'd been fighting. You know kids. Times a lie ain't a lie to them, if they want something bad enough."

"By tar, I'll take a hoe-handle to Carlisle, and to that Jerry, too. I'll take the hide off both of them—"

"Don't do it, Mart. Kids'll fib, it's their nature. Carlisle just wants to go to Boston."

"Well, let him go to hell to Boston, all I care. I don't care what he does, if that's the kind of—" Martin stopped. His shrewd eyes, slightly red around the irises, focused on Jed. He said, "How much have you got bet on that ballgame?"

"Shoot, Mart. Just friendly advice, that's all. Don't get all haired-up over a kid's touse."

"And, by tar, that's just what it is, too, the whole cussid works of it. A kid's touse. About what you might expect from eight-year-olds, trying to get their own way. Carlisle's seventeen, but kids don't grow up so fast, I guess, as they used to. And some of them, by tar," Martin said, glaring at Jed's red face, "some of them never do!"

He started for the door. "You send that goddam Higgins up to my place with a camera," he said, "I'll haul it down over his head."

Jed, leaning forward to look out of the bank's plateglass window, watched him go down the steps, get into his truck.

The truck started with a roar, backed sharply out of its parking-place, narrowly missed a Chevy sedan, which was meandering inoffensively along Main Street. The startled driver stamped on his brakes, leaned furiously on his horn; but Martin, looking neither to right nor left, trod on the gas, went shooting through traffic and a red light and out of sight up the hill.

"Wow!" Jed said, under his breath.

That old man was a heller and the salt of the earth. It was too bad there weren't more like him. Those old boys were ignorant as dirt, but they were nearly all gone now, and the world would never see their like again.

Clipper ships around the Horn, at seventeen; you could believe they had done that. If you didn't, there were their logbooks to prove it. In the Historical Society's museum, up in the old Union Church, were plenty of artifacts to show what men—kids, if you like—had done in the high old times when the country'd had a frontier. Prominent among the harpoons and the scrimshaw, the carved figureheads, and old marlinspikes and sextants, the cobbler's benches and millstones, was young Solomon Hoodless's logbook of his voyage around Cape Horn.

Well, the old man was right, of course. Modern methods didn't turn out the same breed.

Kids, Jed thought. The car-crazy young devils made the highways a terror. Spent spare time hanging around planning deviltry. Give 'em an inch, they'd commit murder. Like that Arthur Grindle, getting out of jail this spring, and if he came back to this town he was going to get one cold reception. Give 'em the least excuse, like Halloween, even, they'd tear the town apart, cause thousands of dollars' worth of damage. Even the little ones, if you didn't want 'em to wreck your property, you had to bribe 'em. Seventy-seven times his own doorbell had rung last Halloween, and his wife had had to ladle out the Trick or Treat, or else.

And that was something you had to grin and bear, along with the rest of the damn crap; because you were shrewd, jolly old Jed Wallace, who loved everybody, including everybody's kids.

Wonder what would happen, if he ever got up to make one of those speeches the town was always calling on him to make, and said how he really felt about their little ones?

Keep 'em in a barrel and feed 'em through the bunghole till they're eighteen. Then let the Army, or the Navy, or the Air Force take over and ram some sense into 'em. Because the way you've brought 'em up, the only one in the world who can do anything with 'em is a tough buck sergeant. Thank God for the military—that's where most of 'em would end up, anyway.

Damned if it wouldn't be worth it. Just once, to say.

Jed lit himself a cigar before he reached for the telephone, dialed Chet Alison's office.

"I've just had a little chew with old Martin Hoodless," he said, when Chet came on the line. "He says Carlisle can go."

"Swell," Chet said, briefly. "I know he can go. He's here now."

"Well, don't let him go home," Jed said. "The old man's on the warpath. He might change his mind."

So Shirttail went to Boston.

Up at the farm, Martin changed into overalls, went out to the hen houses to get through his work for the day. He left his truck standing in the barnyard; didn't even bother to unload. Nobody wanted his eggs, let the damned things sit there and rot.

Of all the gall! The blistered, pink-whiskered gall, by tar!

Here he was, a decent, respectable man, living up here minding his own business; paying his bills and taxes; supporting his family; and that palaverer buttering him up; and then when he didn't fall for it, letting on that either Carlisle was a liar or he himself was crazy. Because that was what it amounted to. Let fall a tree that size onto a couple of kids!

Some people, by tar, had little to do with their time!

Martin grabbed a sack of grain, heaved it furiously off the floor of the hen house, grunting, feeling sweat start along his forehead and in the small of his back. He carried the sack along and up-ended it over a feeder.

Dust from the grain rose in a cloud. He could feel it settle dryly on his hands and face, taste it as it ran down onto his lips with his sweat.

The hens, like the bored females they were, came edging closer to him, where he stood at the feeder letting the last of the grain run out of the bag. They formed a circle, cackling over this big event of their day. One of them, a brash young red pullet, came mincing out to the feeder to grab a mouthful, and Martin flapped his elbows at her to scare her out from underfoot. He was starting to fold the sack, when he noticed her again. Standing there, head cocked to one side, glassy eye fixed, she was looking at him in a you-go-to-hell kind of way.

By tar! One thing more was too much.

Martin should have known better, but he wobbed up the empty sack and let it fly; it unfolded in the air and came down over the pullet like a tent. She let out a shriek, scrabbled frantically, and then, with the inspired foolishness common to hens, somehow managed to thrust herself inside the mouth of the sack. Encompassed, she tried at once to fly.

The rest of the hens, seeing this animated, horrible, unfamiliar object, the sack bobbling upright as if by itself along the floor, exploded into panic. For a moment, Martin stood in a gale of feathers, legs, squawking, wide-open beaks. One terror-stricken bird struck him full in the face as he made for the sack, missed it by an inch; then he caught it up, slatted the pullet out of it, and ran for the door. Outside, he stood coughing and sneezing hen-dust, mopping at his scratched face, while he waited for the frantic racket inside to calm down.

Whatever had got into him?

The cussid things would kill each other—he could count on half-a-dozen dead hens for sure, ten or twelve dollars' worth, by the time they got settled. All these years he'd raised hens, didn't know any better than to pull a fool stunt like that in a jam-packed broiler house. And now, for the next three weeks, every time he went through the door they'd go up in the air, like as not kill two-three more, every time they did it.

He'd have to let Ralph tend this particular house for a while. Ralph had a good way with hens; they never seemed to blow up on him. Better go get him now. Someone would have to go in there, pick up dead hens; might be able to salvage some of them, if you got them before the live ones picked the dead and injured to pieces.

Martin went out a little past the barn and hollered, "Hey, Ralph!" but his voice seemed hoarse and rusty, couldn't make enough noise. Damn hen-dust had got into his lungs. Dammit, he'd have to walk all the way up there.

But there was nobody up in the pasture when he got there; not a boy in sight. The two axes were leaned against the trunk of the chestnut; one end of the big cross-cut blade was buried a little more than its width in the tree; it had been left dangling, so that its limber length hung down toward the ground in a half-twist.

Martin did not make a sound. He had stopped, dead-still. Then, moving, it almost seemed, casually, he went over and laid his hand on the saw. Jammed tight, it was. The cut had been started crooked. That didn't happen if you watched what you were doing; but, if it did, you started over, you didn't try to force the blade straight in the cut.

He picked up an ax, and with a few careful strokes hewed out chunks of wood on either side of the blade, freeing the saw. Then with the axes in one hand, the saw over his shoulder, he went back down the hill. He moved slowly, feeling the wind cold against the back of his neck, starting a mousy chill down inside his clothes.

Darned if he didn't feel kind of sick. Chest felt heavy, from that cussid hen-dust. Just like somebody had fired a blunderbuss loaded with feathers right under his craw-bone. Head felt thick, too. Well, it would pass off. It came from that freezing he'd taken, Saturday night, hunting for Ralph. Darn kid, half-kill everybody, never turn a hair. It's part from the way I felt when I thought he was a goner, as if I'd never be able to move hand or foot again. Felt stiff and heavy, ever since.

Well, he had better snap out of it. There was too much to do around here for a man to go on feeling morger. He hung the tools in the shed, got the handcart, and wheeled it slowly toward the barn. Have to finish feeding the hens. That wouldn't wait. Them dead ones, might as well let them go, nothing he could do about that, now. What he needed was some help around here he could depend on.

It was warm in the barn. Sunlight poured through the two southern windows, fell across the brown planks of the floor, worn glossy with time and use. The two heavy work-horses and the three cows stood peaceably in their stalls; Betsy, the barn cat, slept curled in a corner on a few wisps of hay. Betsy wasn't active these days, being close to her time for kittens.

"You get yourself loaded every eight weeks, don't you?" Martin told her. He spoke automatically; this was what he always said to Betsy. "Varmints around this barn clean out the grain bin, for all you care."

Nonetheless, he leaned down and patted her sleek head. Betsy, stretching, let out a faint "Prr-t," but at the moment she was too preoccupied with her feelings to respond much; a man could see why. She was old, and in her time she'd probably had a couple of hundred kittens to no purpose, since each batch was popped in a bag and dumped in the river as soon as they were born. It was a hell of a life-work, never anything to show for it; all she could do was go back to the beginning and start over. No wonder she got discouraged, let rats and mice multiply. Maybe, this time, he'd just keep a couple of them kittens. Needed some new blood around the barn. Young toms, they'd make the varmints fly.

Martin came to a full stop, realizing suddenly that the place where Betsy was sleeping was where the day's supply of hay for the stock should be, and there wasn't any. That damn Ralph. He was supposed to do that, fork down that hay out of the loft. He hadn't done it.

Well, the old man would have to. Better do it now, so as not to get held up tonight, when the heft of chores came on.

Stiffly, he climbed the ladder into the hayloft.

The loft, too, was full of sunlight. A great bar of it poured in through the peak window, shone on the hay, turning it green-gold. You could still see some summer flowers in that hay. Dried as they were, the daisies and blue-eyed grass had kept a little color.

That was good hay, that right there. That was from the south meadow. Always been a dandy, that meadow. Might have a few weeds in it now, you couldn't keep them out of grass, but it was still a hayfield, not like most of the fields around the town, growing nothing but alders and poverty birch, while their owners sat in the house listening to a TV. That hay looked good enough to eat. Piled up there, with the sun on it, it looked like a place for a man to lie down in, to rest.

Well, you couldn't wallow down on good hay. Spoilt it for fodder. That was one thing he'd learnt as a boy. One thing he'd pounded into Ralph and Carlisle. A haymow may be a fine place to play on a rainy day, but you keep out of it. Tramp it down, get it dirty, it gets moldy, stock won't eat it. And how'd you like to have a cow or a horse stomping around on your dinner plate, hanh?

He drove his fork into the fragrant stuff, pitched a huge mound over the edge of the loft. It dropped with a soft, swishing sound to the barn floor, startled Betsy out of her sleep; but she was used to this procedure—it only meant a softer, deeper bed for the rest of the day; so she merely moved over and waited patiently for hay to stop falling.

Martin pitched down a lot of hay. The idea was to show Ralph how much was enough, just in case he thought he could get away with a few wisps. So maybe it was more than for one day's feeding. You could always use it tomorrow.

And might as well pitch some to the front of the loft while he was at it. Wouldn't hurt the hay to stir it up some, get the sun on it. Besides, he liked to handle hay.

He climbed the towering mound toward the eaves. It was a pleasure to find here the forkfuls he had laid in last summer, just as he had stowed them away. If you knew how to pitch hay, find the forkfuls, not stand on them and try to lift yourself with your fork, it wasn't any job at all. Do it in no time. Not even start a good sweat.

His fork struck something hard and slippery in the hay.

Now, what in hell was that? Couldn't be anything, up in here.

He jabbed again and felt the thing slide away under the tines; so then he drove the fork down underneath and surged up with a great heave. A big, round leather ball shot into the air, struck a rafter, and fell to the barn floor, where it bounced high a couple of times before it landed in a grain bin, sending up a cloud of dust.

Betsy let out a spitting yowl, and Martin heard the flurry and scrabble as she took cover. With a strangled grunt of fury, he hurled his fork over the edge of the hayloft after the ball.

By tar! Even in your own barn, you couldn't get away from it. What was the use?

Martin sat down, suddenly, in the hay.

He came to, with a start, to hear Susie somewhere on the place, hollering dinner.

What was the matter with her? It wasn't near dinnertime yet, he'd just got back from downtown . . .

She needn't think she was going to make him eat before twelve o'clock, just because maybe she wanted to get through early, so she could go prancing around town for the afternoon . . .

Why, here he was, lying down in the hay . . . been so cussid tired he'd just slid down here and had a nap. Maybe it was dinnertime . . . he wasn't hungry. His mind took up suddenly where it had left off.

Well, let 'em . . . he was sick of it . . . Let 'em do what they wanted to, the whole kit and caboodle . . .

They weren't worth bothering with, even if they were related to him . . . It was what came of Susie's marrying that foreigner . . . Martin could have told that, and he had told that, way back when . . . when the damned white nigger first came nosing around . . . Mix up blood, no good would come of it . . . them kids wasn't worth the powder to blow them to hell . . .

He was through . . . he'd find some good man, put him on wages . . . Cut into profits . . . but it'd be worth it . . . to save the wear and tear. Melly Hitchcock, downtown, needed a job . . . Melly'd been hitting him up for one all winter . . .

Well, go do it . . . damned if he hadn't got stiff, going to sleep up here in the hay . . .

Susie, coming into the barn to find him, saw him backing slowly down the hayloft ladder.

She said, "For heaven's sake, Pa, is that where you've been? I've hunted the place over."

But Martin walked by her as if she hadn't been there.

She caught a glimpse of his face as he went by, pasty under its brown, his set, wooden mouth, with one corner pulled a little down, and she thought, Oh, lord, he's so mad he's made himself sick.

He was hobbling, too, as if one leg were a little stiff.

"Pa!" she called after him, hustling to catch up as he crossed the barnyard, "you come straight in and have some dinner. And after that, you're going to rest! This is all foolishness, after that awful time you had Saturday night—"

Martin, however, didn't stop at the kitchen door. He kept on across the yard to his truck. At the truck, he turned around and stared at her for a moment.

"That'll be the day," he said. "When I slow down in the daylight."

With some effort, he got into the truck, started the engine, and drove off down the road toward town.

Well, I guess he must be all right, she thought, doubtfully.

There had been plenty of other times when rage had made him white in the face; and today, he had reason.

His still-loaded truck had been standing all forenoon in the yard; so he hadn't made his deliveries. Seeing it, Susie had phoned Mattie Mooney.

"You might as well tell me the whole story about the trees with houses in them, Mattie," she said, grimly. "I've heard enough to know you weren't talking through your hat."

"That story's so foolish it makes me sick," she said, when Mattie, only too happy, obliged. "And it ought to you, Mattie Mooney!"

"Well, my boy Jerry ain't a liar," Mattie said.

"Well, somebody is; and I don't know who else it could be. You ought to be ashamed of yourself, peddling gossip like that. You could have stopped that mean story dead in its tracks, if you'd wanted to, but oh, no, it's too much fun to pass it along, maybe add a little to it."

"Don't you dast to talk to me like that!" Mattie began.

"I dast to talk to you or anybody else like that," Susie said. "Pa's old, but he isn't crazy; and when you and the rest of this town get back some of the sense you've hollered out of your heads at the ballgames, you'll realize it."

Roundly, she hung up on Mattie.

And a little while ago, I actually thought I was feeling calmed down, she thought.

Charles. Pleasant, normal, above all, serene, Charles had comforted her, kidded her a little; asked what there was around that he could do; and had, finally, driven off with Dot, taking her to Fairport, so that Susie wouldn't have to—a Dot charmed by Charles and delighted to have a ride in his big car. He had left Susie feeling, almost for the first time in years, that a male wasn't just somebody who had to be smoothed down, ironed out, taken care of, and fed. And it had been wonderful.

But now . . .

Where could Martin be going? He must be hungry, he hadn't eaten since breakfast, and he looked sick.

He must know that the boys aren't up in the pasture; maybe he found out downtown that Carlisle's gone to Boston. Perhaps he's worked himself up to going down and hauling him off the bus. Please God, let it be gone before he gets there, or there'll be one awful row.

She herself had known that Carlisle had gone. Up in his room, making his bed, she had seen the signs of his packing. His suitcase was gone, and his good clothes; he must have sneaked them out of the house, at some time or other.

I wish he'd told me, she'd thought. I wouldn't have stopped him. The time to have stopped it was months ago, if I'd been going to; and, then, I didn't see any reason. The only reason for stopping him now would be his knee; and Dr. Wickham said he could play, it wouldn't hurt him. Well, maybe Carlisle'll phone me before he leaves. But Carlisle hadn't phoned.

A few minutes after Charles had left, with Dot, Ralph had come in, wall-eyed with worry. Carl had gone off, he'd gone to Boston. Ralph had tried to use Grampa's big saw alone and got it stuck in the tree. It was up there stuck, he couldn't budge it, and . . . and . . . and . . .

Susie, seeing him, put her arms around him and let him cry against her. He was worn out, apparently getting some kind of a delayed reaction from Saturday night; he was starting a cold, too. Susie dosed the cold and sent him upstairs to bed.

In the kitchen, now, Susie drained the vegetables, put the pots and pans full of her good dinner into the warming-oven. If he hauls Carlisle home, there'll be hell to pay, she thought wearily. But at least there'll be something decent for people to eat.

Since there was no dinner to get or dishes to wash, she might as well go upstairs, tidy herself for the afternoon. She looked in on Ralph, who was still sleeping, dead to the world. Susie touched his forehead—it was nicely damp and cool, so he probably wasn't going to be sick. He was just tired. Overwrought. Lying there, his looks, so much like his father's, gave her an odd little twist at the heart. It was such a good face; gentle; and mixed-up.

Over her dressing table was the photograph of Brant, with his War Medal pinned to the wall above it. How he had ever got a medal passed understanding; but he had, although—Susie smiled a little—it had not been for fighting. A cutter from his unit had spotted a submarine off the Florida coast, had radioed for help, and had tried to trail it until patrolling destroyers got there. The sub, not wasting a torpedo on small fry, had surfaced long enough to let go a salvo of shells, disabling the cutter and setting it on fire, and knocking five men overboard. While the rest of the crew fought fire, Brant had gone overboard, swimming a rope out to the two disabled crewmen he could see.

Susie mused, her eyes on the picture.

From a place in the back of her mind, she heard like an echo, far-off, lost, Brant's slow voice.

Shucks, Susie, let them old men quar'l. I had enough, and this war's enough for any man's lifetime. I'm done with quar'ling. I don't like quar'lsome people. Folks got little to do, beating on each other so.

At two, Ralph got up, feeling fine. He ate hugely of the warmed-over dinner, and then went out to the barn. A little later, Susie saw him with the handcart loaded high with grain sacks, headed for the far chicken house to fill feeders. She drew a breath of relief. That would help to jiggle Martin down.

Around four, she heard Martin's truck come back. She saw from the window that he had somebody with him; not Carlisle. A big man of forty-five or so, carrying a suitcase.

Now, who could that be? The man was back-to, with a cap on; she couldn't tell whether it might be someone she knew. In a moment, Martin came through the back door, carrying the suitcase. The stranger, she saw, was going toward the barn. She leaned over to peer out the window at him.

"That's Melvin Hitchcock," Martin said, behind her.

He set the suitcase down by the door. His face was still pasty-looking, and Susie thought, My goodness, is the corner of his mouth crooked, or is it my imagination? Something didn't seem to be quite normal; but whatever it was, Martin wasn't aware of it. He had an air of satisfaction about him; as he went by Susie, he gave her a sidelong, triumphant glance.

It was a look she had seen many times; and it had always made her blaze. It meant that Martin thought he had got completely and forever ahead of everyone.

"What is it, now?" she asked. "What have you been up to now?"

"Up to nothing that's got a thing to do with you," Martin said. "I've hired Melly to help me out here on the farm, and I want you to move Carlisle's things out of the kitchen chamber."

"What?" Susie said. The thing was so unexpected that it took the wind right out of her sails. "Move Carlisle's things? Whatever for?"

"So's Melly'll have a warm place to sleep," Martin said.

He went to the sink, turned on the faucet and let it run, so that the water would be cold for a nice long drink.

"Oh, Pa!" Susie said. "What do you want to be this way for? You know this business hasn't been anything I could help. I don't blame you, in a way, but I've done the best I knew how. Couldn't you wait, just a little? You don't need to be this mean."

Martin tilted back his head and let a whole glass of water run down his throat. When the water was gone, he made an "Ah-h-h" sound of relish, put the tumbler down on the drainboard, and started for the door.

Susie stepped in front of him.

"If you've hired some help, it's a good thing," she said. "You ought to have done it months ago. I know you think the kids haven't tried. But when they did try, it was all the same thing—what they did was never enough. You never thought that they had their lives, too. I've tried to think what was right, and working our board, helping, is right; but not the way we have to—never making any allowance for anybody else. Their things. Their feelings—"

She stopped. Martin was going right on, out the door, not listening.

"Where do you suggest I move Carlisle's things to?" she asked.

"I don't care. Throw 'em out the window. Put him in the spare room. That's the place for a boarder."

Inside, Susie felt fury starting to boil. That kitchen chamber had been Carlisle's ever since he'd been a little boy. The accumulation of his things would take hours to move. And the spare room had been unheated, unaired, all winter.

"And you can keep your kids away from my barn and hen houses," Martin said. "With all their traps and trash and their damned basketballs. I won't have 'em frigging around out there. I don't need them, they don't need me."

He went off out, shutting the door behind him with a snap which was just short of a slam.

All right, Susie said to herself. That does it. I've had it.

She had the telephone receiver off the hook before she thought of the party line. No. If she talked to Hazel on the phone, Mattie Mooney would have it all over town inside a half an hour.

Better go down there. Right away.

But she found, when she had her hat and coat on, that Martin had foreseen that. The key to the car was gone.

Setting her jaw, Susie called a taxi from town.

Ralph, to do him credit, had got through a lot of chores in the course of the afternoon. He had an idea that if he cuffed into the work, it might cool Martin down some, make up for Carl's running out on him, pay for work that hadn't been done on the tree. He was cleaning nests in the far chicken house around four o'clock, when he remembered that he hadn't pitched down any fodder for the stock. Geez-Louise! That was one thing that always burned Grampa up!

Ralph took off for the barn on the run; he burst in through the side door, full in the face of Melly Hitchcock, who, to his horror, was standing in the middle of the barn floor, idly bouncing the basketball up and down with the flat of his hand.

"Hey!" Ralph said, his jaw sagging. "Hey!" My gosh, that ball had been hidden, dug deep down into the loft. "What—where'd you get—"

"This's a pretty good ball you fellas got," Melly said. "Who's it b'long to? Old Shirttail, hanh?"

Melly Hitchcock, that dope! How'd he get here? He must've been up in the loft. Pitching down hay—there was a lot pitched down. Geez, if Grampa ever once got his eye on that ball!

"Yeah," Ralph said. Nervously, he held out his hands for the ball. "Hey, let 'er come, Melly. Le' me have it, will ya?"

Melly paid no attention. He went on bouncing the ball, judiciously watching it; the eye of the expert. "Nice leather. Dribbles like a son-of-gun, don't she?" He clumped along, dribbling the ball to the end of the barn, where he tossed it over a rafter as if he were shooting a basket, caught it as it came down. "Well, I see the team take off for Boston Garden," he said. 'With my old fifteen bucks riding right on their tail." He pivoted suddenly, let go the ball at Ralph. "Whoops!"

Ralph hadn't been expecting the ball. It shot between his nerveless hands, smacked him hard in the stomach.

"Holy smoke!" Melly said. "No wonder you quit the team, took up with the Injuns. Hell, you ought ha' seen me play, when I was your age. Goddlemighty, that ball would've gone right through ya. Come on, whang it back here. I'll show you some passing."

But Ralph, once he had the ball, didn't linger. Carrying it, he ducked back through the barn door, cut in behind the hen houses, and took refuge in the woods, where he sat down under a tree, sweating and panting.

Darned old fool! Had to shoot off his big mouth about that Indian stuff, like everybody else in town. Late yesterday afternoon, Ralph had gone warily down to the drugstore, and afterward wished he hadn't. The whole town was still boiling over with Saturday night's excitement, when everybody'd thought he was dead; and everybody knew, of course, how he'd been solemnly asleep in bed when people were breaking their necks hunting for him. They knew where he'd been and what he'd been doing, too. "Old Indian relics, hanh?" they said. And "Ugh-uh, ugh-uh," and "How!" Stuff like that, to drive a guy nuts.

You couldn't win. Just go ahead and try, see where it got you.

From the direction of the house, a strange car started up—at least it wasn't Grampa's Chevy. Cautiously, Ralph peered out between two trees, just in time to see his mother come out of the door and climb into a taxi.

A taxi? That was unheard of! Yes, sir, by gum. Henry Goldthwaite's taxi! Ma was taking off for somewhere. If she didn't use the car, it meant she was too mad to, she and Grampa'd had a fight. Aunt Hazel, that was who she'd head for.

Well, he would, too. He sure wasn't going to stay here alone with Grampa, till she got back

Ralph took out after the taxi, running as fast as he could. He did not, of course, catch up with it, but he kept it in sight until it turned down the side road to the motel. He slacked off, then, winded; and someone said, "Now, what would you be doing, showing your face on Main Street carrying a basketball?"

It was old Sidney Widgett, pointing his cane; and Ralph discovered that yes, sure enough, he was; he was walking right along the middle of the IGA block, still holding the ball.

"All right, to hell with it," Ralph said. He stared at old Sidney. "To the lowest, deep-down bottom of the lowest, dirtiest hell, with it!"

Looking neither to right nor left, he marched along the rest of the way to school. Some kids on the steps, still hanging around after the bus had left, let go with an Indian war whoop at him, but he did not stop or speak. He carried the ball to the door of the gym, dropped it, and when it bounced, drove his foot into it as hard as he could, sending it sailing the length of the floor.

So much for that damn thing. It was back now, where it belonged. And let it stay there.

Down at the motel, Susie had been welcomed with open arms. To have her and the kids with them was what Hazel and George had always wanted; they loved Susie and they had no children of their own. Hazel had always contended that Martin would be better off if he hired a housekeeper; then he could dominate all he pleased. She listened to Susie's distraught story with a grim face.

"He's our own father, Susie," she said. "And I hate to admit it, but not one of us but was glad to get out of there when the time came. Us girls all had a crack at taking care of him, Pauline and Georgianna and Mary and me. No wonder they all took off when they could for the far ends of the country. And now you. And look at you. Thirty-five years old and a darn handsome woman, and you've been slaving up there ever since Brant died. And what have you got for it? There hasn't been a one of us that Pa wouldn't have seen buried and snowed on, just so he could have a woman around the house to cook and wash and make potato yeast. Oh, that damned old potato yeast!" Hazel said, laughing a little, mopping at the tears in her eyes. "Never mind, Susie, don't cry, honey, we all did the best we could."

"I feel so mean," Susie sobbed. "And I'm not sure, but I think he's sick. He looked so—so—"

Hazel glanced at her. "Plenty of times he's got mad at me, I've wondered if he was going to have a stroke. I don't doubt that someday he will, it follows as the night the day. And when he does and drops down dead from it, you mark my words, Susie, whoever is around at the time is going to be made to feel to blame. He's traded all his life on making people feel to blame, and when he goes out, it won't be different. There he is, a good man, a fine man, worked his fingers to the bone raising his family. But he's never let go; and he's never figured that his children were anything but a comet-tail to him. If you went up there now and told him we were people, that your kids were people who had to learn to live in the world, he'd holler you off the place."

"He's old, Hazel."

"I know he's old," Hazel said. "But able; don't you forget that, Susie. He's able, and he's got money enough to buy and sell us all. Let him hire what he's always talking about—a good strong woman who'll never go outside the kitchen, nor want to."

"He's done so much for the boys and me—he's got an awful lot on his side—"

"There always was a lot on his side." Hazel's voice was quiet, her expression grim. "There always will be, you're telling me? Not a one of us, when we left, but felt the same way you do now. We owe, we owe, we owe. But the best thing that ever happened to me in my whole life was George Whitney. It may sound foolish, George is no ball of fire, but I would lie down and let him walk on me from my ankles to my neck, if he asked me to. Only he doesn't ask me. I love the old son-of-a-gun. The thing is, he'd lie down and let me walk on him, if there was any reason to. And there's the difference, Susie. George, God love him, thinks I'm people. He thinks I'm a person in my own right, not just a piece of him."

Hazel mopped busily at her eyes; then she got up, put her arms around Susie, and hugged.

"George and I are going up there and make sure Pa's all right," she said. "If he wants a housekeeper, we'll hire him one. You are going to bed. And you and the kids are staying here with us from now on out."

"Oh, Hazel, I'd love to, and I was so mad when I came down that I thought I would. But I mustn't. I'd better get back. Right away. I'd just got Ralph simmered down, and if he runs a-foul of his grandfather—Oh, dear, he probably has already. Will you drive me?"

"No, I will not drive you. You're all to rags and tatters, and no wonder, after Saturday night, and as far as I can make out, everything else into the bargain. What's to be done, George and I will do, pack up what you need, and old Ralphie, we'll just scoop him up and bring him along. We'll take Bessie to help, and if Pa wants a fight, he can fight with her. Anybody wants to fight with Bessie has my blessing."

Firmly, she ushered Susie into a spare bedroom, turned down the bed. It looked wonderful, made up with fluffy blankets, cool, crisp sheets. Susie sank weakly down on the side of it.

"Oh," she said. "Isn't that lovely! I never thought I'd fall in love with a pair of pink blankets."

Hazel knelt down, brusquely yanked off Susie's shoes. "Hmf!" she sniffed. "It's time you good and well fell in love with something. There's a pink nightie to match the blankets. Go to sleep. I'll call you suppertime; and there's scallop stew for supper."

To Hazel's surprise, Susie gave a little, desolate howl, buried her face in her hands, and began to cry again.

"For the land's sake, I thought I had you all calmed down," she said. She came back and sat down on the edge of the bed. "What is it now?"

"S-scallops," Susie choked. "And tamarinds, he used to bring home. For a party. T-tamons, he called them, remember?"

"I know," Hazel said quietly. "I haven't seen any tamons for years, have you? Where do you suppose they all went to?"

"I don't know. Old Mr. Kendall used to carry them, down at The Emporium. They came in little b-barrels."

They were both silent, thinking of Martin's fine meal, brought home for a treat, sometimes; an unheard-of extravagance, sign that Martin had at last paid off the mortgage; so, family, rejoice. Scallops—expensive, so that there was never enough for anyone; tamarinds, expensive, too.

"I guess tonight wasn't the night for me to plan scallops, was it?" Hazel said. "But there they are, and they'll taste good, Susie. Those days seem worlds away, don't they? Heaven knows, Pa was cantankerous then, too, but we were all a family together. It's different, now. I know he loved us in spite of the way he acted. But he's just used it up, Susie, and what's more, he doesn't need or want our love back. Oranges," she went on thoughtfully. "Each one of us girls had one orange for Christmas, and that was all the oranges we ever saw. Weren't they beautiful, Susie? I used to lug mine around for days, till it started to get soft and I had to eat it. Remember those long chocolate-covered sticks of butter crunch? Texas Williams, they called them. How we'd make a hole in the top of the orange and suck the juice out through a Texas William? Oh, that was the way to eat an orange, wasn't it? I'll never forget that taste. And tamons, sweet and sour. Chewy, with tough skins . . . But, Susie. It was always his triumphs, what he'd done, that we had the party for. We were all smart in school and you and Pauline both got the valedictory, headed up the class in the years you graduated from high school. Did one of us ever get a graduation present? Or even a word from him? He never even went to the graduation exercises, except one year he was Chairman of the School Board and had to. No, Susie. What you've got to remember is that even when he could afford it, there was never enough. Of anything. I know I sound heartless; I know we owe him something—love, I guess, and I wish it could be. If the time comes when he needs to be taken care of, we'll do it. But nobody owes anybody her whole life, Susie, let's face it."

"I don't know what to do—I can't just plunk in here on you with my whole family. And Charles—"

"You good and well know you'll be a godsend. We're always desperate for help, here at the motel. And as for Charles—" Hazel gave her a straight look. "Charles'll be delighted, and you know it."

Charles was; at suppertime, he beamed around at them all.

"Well," he said. "George, take a look at my family. Set fire, I've done pretty well for a single man."

Part Nine

A few days after the ballteam had left for Boston, the School Board met unofficially in the back room at Win Parker's garage. They often did this, just before a formal meeting; it was better, when James Goss and the Superintendent of Schools were not present, to get things talked over for final decision; then, at the regular meeting, preserve a solid front. Besides being private, Win's back office was comfortable, with a fire in the stove, good chairs, places to put up feet. Win was generally there in the evening, anyway; whether they had school matters or not to discuss, Harry Troy and Doc Wickham liked to drop in.

Tonight, however, they had something really weighty on their minds. They had not gone down to Boston for the early games of the Tournament; Doc Wickham had a pregnancy and couldn't leave, and it was better, anyway, to wait and see what happened; if the team got eliminated on the first go-round, nobody would want to go to Boston anyway. But there had been good news. The Hawks had won two games; they were now in the finals. Last night, the Doc had delivered the baby; and they were all driving down to Boston tomorrow. The sense of pleasurable anticipation, however, had been considerably dampened, this afternoon, by a wire from Alison. Seems he had been approached at the Tournament by some big high school in Connecticut; they'd offered him their coach's spot at twice his present pay. Chet was sorry, but of course he couldn't afford to turn it down. So he would be leaving.

"Damn them big schools to the west'ard," Harry Troy said, glumly. "They got twice the dough we have and we can't compete."

He pulled a square of cut plug from his pocket, bit off a generous chew, settled it into the pouch of his cheek. One good thing about Win's office, Win didn't care if you spit on the floor—he just had one of the mechanics' helpers sprinkle some stuff around every so often and sweep. You couldn't be comfortable like that at the supermarket, people wouldn't stand for it.

"That's right," Doc Wickham said. "My god, Harry, you like that stuff?"

Harry grinned. The grin was already brown, the insides of his lips coated from a previous chew. He said, "Now, Doc, you know I don't chew unless I got to think, and I can't think without a good thick juice running."

Harry had two large teeth in front, over which his lips never entirely closed; he was a small man with thin arms and legs, which always seemed to be moving; Harry was never quite in repose. These attributes, together with a sharp craggy nose, a set-back chin, and one cheek lop-sided from his chew, gave Harry an uncanny resemblance to a squirrel with a mouthful of nuts. Doc Wickham had remarked this, before; he thought it likely that Harry, as a child, had had rickets. He said, "Okay, so think. You're the chairman."

Harry cast a sidelong glance at Win Parker's broad back. Win was at his desk, hunched over some kind of a literary composition, whatever it was; still writing, he hadn't looked up.

It was true that Harry was chairman; he was also Win's brother-in-law, which meant he didn't have to think.

"You got any ideas yourself about a new coach?" he wanted to know.

"Not offhand. It's too soon," Doc Wickham said.

"I understand Billy Walker's looking for a job. Ain't that so, Win?"

Win grunted.

Wickham looked puzzled. "Billy Walker? Who's he?"

Harry did not show that he was in any way amused, or that he thought the Doc had walked into one. Deadpan, he said, "Why, Doc! I'm surprised at you. I thought you was supposed to be an authority. Billy Walker was star forward on the Boone Academy team. How come you missed getting him down in your book?"

The doctor waved a hand impatiently. "Why not say 'Steamer' Walker, if that's who you mean?" he asked. "Who ever knew his name was Billy? He had an athletic scholarship. Last I knew, he was doing all right in college ball."

Doc Wickham really was an authority—he had published a book on basketball, with the names and records of players for years back. He was used to Harry's little game of trying to trip him, and well-acquainted with Harry's reasons for it. It was all right for a doctor to have a university education—he had to have one in his business; but a book, any book, even one on ball, was likely to get the treatment from Harry.

Doc Wickham had settled here in town thirty years ago. Young and full of beans, just out of medical school and his internship in a city hospital, he'd had all kinds of idealistic notions about a general practitioner and his relationship to a town. In the beginning he had worked his head off. Establishing a practice had taken some doing. People were wary of him—he was young, he was a stranger, from out of town. They preferred the good, old doctors, whose ways they knew; whose only drawback was that they could not live forever. One by one, they wore out and dropped down; leaving Wickham. People were used to Wickham now; now, they came to him.

After thirty years, Doc Wickham had no more notions about his job or anything else. Three-quarters of it was nasty mess that had to be bandaged, cut off, set, sewed up, or plastered. He did this, as well as could be expected. But it was his confirmed opinion that the rural areas of the country were strewn with the wreckage of young doctors, who out of boredom, loneliness, and lack of companionship, sooner or later took to liquor, dope, or women. Actually, what was there here? Jed Wallace, Win Parker. Pregnant women and Harry Troy. Himself, Wickham took to sports—trout-fishing and basketball. He was an authority on both.

Quietly relishing his score against the Doc, Harry was going on. "Steamer Walker quit college for some reason, maybe got fired. I don't know. Anyway, he's decided to take up coaching. He's been hanging around Boone for a couple years, playing on the town team. Might make a pretty good coach, he's one of the best players ever turned out in the state."

"That may be," Wickham said. "It doesn't signify he'd make a coach. What we need is somebody with experience. Right, Win?"

Win grunted again. He said, "Be with ya in a minute," and went on writing. One big freckled hand, the backs of its fingers thatched with reddish fuzz, was flattened hard on the paper, the other drove the pen with dry squeaks across the page. The pen, apparently, suddenly ceased to deliver ink, for Win hauled back his arm and slammed it into a corner of the desk.

"Blast them things!" he said. "Always some kind of a goddamned gadget to complicate your life."

He swung around, his swivel chair squawking loudly under his weight, pulled out a package of Luckies, which he proceeded to tear open. "Ballpoint pens. Cellophane around the cigarettes—the only reason I ever see for that was, it makes it harder for me to get the package open."

"Oh, I dunno, now, Win," Harry said. "Keeps 'em fresh, don't it? You take that polyethylene, now, that's a godsend down to the market. We do up everything in it, makes things look nice, keeps 'em nice and clean."

"Yeah" Win said. "I know them polyethylene packages of yours. All the rotten vegetables hid, down on the bottom of a package that nobody could blast open with a stick of dynamite. Hell, I was hoping to git one letter signed before that damn pen wore out."

"Looks like you already signed it," Harry said, grinning. He jerked his head at the white sheet of paper, on which Win's fingers had left sweaty, smudgy prints. "Now, who in town wouldn't know that was you, Win?"

If this quip—it was in direct riposte for Win's criticism of the quality of Harry's merchandise—registered, no one would have known it. Win did not flick an eye. He said merely, "You fellas ever hear about the time old Bess Maitland cussed the ballpoint pen?"

Both Harry and the Doc had; but it was a good story, and Win could mock anybody in town; they'd heard him mock Bessie Maitland before.

"Seems one of the Boston ladies, right down off the crest of Beacon Hill, was registering in down at the motel," Win began. "And Bess was getting down her car-license number all Bristol-fashion, so's Charlie'd know who to get the cops to chase in case she run off with the towels. So Bess's pen played out and she didn't have another one handy, and the summer lady dug down in her bag and handed over hers for Bess to eke out on. That turned out to be a ballpoint and it wasn't working either, so Bess hove it into the wastebasket and give it a mouthful. The goddam things wasn't no goddam good—"

By the time Win got through repeating Bessie's mouthful, he had the Doc and Harry roaring—he really could mock people.

"So this Boston lady, she ain't never heard cussing like that in her life. She lets out a squark"—Win could mock Boston ladies, too—"she lets out a squawk, and out comes Charlie. Like he always does, when old Bess tangles with the high-class trade, he ups and fires her. But that night, come suppertime, who should be in the dining room, big as life and twice as natural, but old Bess herself, waiting on the tables. The Boston lady takes one look, and swells up like a sculpin.

" 'What are you doing here?' she says. 'I thought you was discharged.'

"So old Bess rars back, fixes her with a fish-eye. 'Why, goddlemighty!' she says. 'If here ain't the old bat that got muh twin sister fired off her job!' "

Deadpan, Win sat back, paying no attention to the laughter. "Lend me your pen, will ya, Doc? I guess I'll have to sign this. Feathers Ryan don't live in town, likely he wouldn't recognize none of my dirty-handed ways."

"Feathers Ryan!" Harry said, galvanized. "Holy mud on the mountains, Win! We ain't got a chance to git him, have we?"

"We have if the town'll stand for the price we'll have to pay," Win said.

"Why, hell, the town don't need to know nothing about it," Harry said. "It can be spread around through the school budget, and then—"

"Won't have to be," Win said. "Not with Feathers Ryan, think?"

"Why, no. No, it won't." Harry leaned forward, let go a squirt of tobacco juice at the rose in full bloom which decorated the door of Win's office stove. He nailed it, dead-center, and the moisture vanished with a sizzle and a slight puff of steam. Harry looked jubilantly at the doctor. "Whaddya know!" he marveled. "Wouldn't that be a feather in the damned old cap!"

"Feathers, you mean?" Doc Wickham winced slightly at his own pun. "What makes you think you can get a man like him to come here, Win? We haven't got much to offer for next year, our whole team's graduating. Won't add much to his reputation, will it?"

"Hell, we already got him," Win said. "I been on the phone to him, this letter's just to confirm it. Superintendent's office is making out his contract."

He folded his letter, thrust it into an envelope. "Ryan don't have to worry about a reputation, he's already got one. Seems he likes to take a green team, lick it into shape, and in about two years, ker-whango!"

"Good enough," Wickham said, shortly. As usual, all talked over. Well, that was all right with him. "Any other business, Win? I've got to look in on Ruthie Jordan—she had a nice little ballplayer, last night."

"Well, I told Berg to haul-ass," Win said. "Any of you want to write out a recommendation for him?"

"Hell with him," Harry said. "Tell him to beat it, all we need to do, ain't it?"

"Well, not exactly." Win got up, reached for his hat. "I'm devilish tired, guess I'll go home, hit the sack. The State Board of Education wouldn't stand for it," he went on. "Turn off that light, as you come by, will you, Doc? Berg's got to have a reason why he's fired, and unless it's immoral, somebody's got to write him a reference."

"Well, let Goss do it," Harry said. He snapped off the light, plunging the office into darkness, out of which his judicious tones came, sepulchrally. "Goss knows him, maybe he can think of something nice to say about his futzing up the ballteam, or not being the kind of a type that's welcome in this town. That's all the reference I could think of, by god!"

"Okay," Win said. "We'll tell Goss to do it. He's used to handling nasty things in a nice way."

Part Ten

The bus bringing the team home from Boston pulled into town at four-thirty in the morning. It stopped at the embankment by Martin Hoodless's pasture to let off Carlisle and Jerry Mooney, and then went grinding on down the hill toward Town Hall Square.

Carlisle glanced after it, the twinkling red tail-lights, the fat, waddling back end, pulling away down the hill in the darkness, thinking, I'm some glad to see the last of that.

The bare hillside was freezing cold, after the warmth and stuffiness of the bus. The east was gray-black, a mass of dark, woolly clouds, with daybreak beginning somewhere behind them; below, he could see the silent town, spattered here and there with street lights, and the grayish-white expanse of the river, frozen hard again, now that the weather had turned cold.

He heard a scrunch on the embankment as Jerry went up, the click of bare alder branches as he pushed through and out of sight, not saying anything, not even so long.

All right. Alison hadn't so much as lifted a hand to him, either, when he'd got off the bus. Carlisle didn't know as he wanted to talk to them, either.

He looked wearily at the steep embankment before he began to climb. Heck, it looked a mile high. His knee ached; when he put his weight on that leg, something made a grinding sound; along in the night, the novocaine, which had got him through that last game, had worn off; the ache had kept him awake, tuning up like a toothache as the night wore on.

All around him the others had slept, slumped in the bus seats. Dick Wickham, in the seat next to him, kept falling over, leaning his head on Carlisle's shoulder. It did no good to push him away. Whenever the bus hit a bump, over Dick would come, flop, his head and his collapsed, heavy body trying to locate something more comfortable than the slippery leather seat-back, until finally, Carlisle just gave up and let him lean. He moved as close to the window as he could, in spite of the draft, bracing his good leg on the foot-rest to ease the jerking on his sore knee.

Up front, he could see the driver's head and shoulders, his straining arms, outlined black against the reflected light from the headlamps; the two white streaks of light flowing out into the dark; the asphalt sliding under like a river. The cities, the towns, they passed through looked black, deserted in the night. Street-light shadows streamed across the bus windows, falling on the white, sleeping, exhausted faces around him. The night seemed to go on forever.

Carrying his suitcase, he scrabbled up the bank, sideways like a crab, favoring his knee.

Gray light was beginning to filter over the pasture; over a dusting of new snow, through which old grass showed in patches, frozen stiff, crackling underfoot. The pasture looked done, deserted, like the last end of earth on the last morning. He realized that he could smell smoke, and then saw; by the brook, the big pile of white ashes and smoldering coals, with a small swirl of smoke slowly rising against the sky. Where the chestnut tree had been, was a big pile of chunked-up firewood. Grampa had got his tree cut up, and the brush from it burned. Now, how had he done that?

He had built his fire right on top of what had been left of the tree house. A couple of charred ends of two-by-four stuck out of the ashes.

Well, good-bye Indian collection. Ralph had been working on it, so he'd said, but who ever knew Ralph to save anything? There might be a few flints left under those ashes. The bone tools, of course, would be gone.

Six thousand years and what did it amount to? Burned up in a fire built by an old guy in a bad temper.

Maybe someday, in times to come, somebody would happen to dig around here, find a few flints and ashes, and think there'd been a hell of a big Indian encampment on the banks of this brook.

To hell with it. They'd be fooled, and let 'em be. What of it?

Over at the house he could see smoke from the chimney. Grampa's breakfast fire. And there was a light in the kitchen. Trust him to be up and ready, all cocked back. No sneaking in without being seen. That was what Carlisle had meant to do; he thought suddenly he should have known better. Grampa was always up and raring by four-thirty; and it must be going on for five.

He eased carefully down the hill, climbed through the fence by the barnyard. The hen houses were waking up, too. He could hear sleepy movement inside, an occasional "cutctt"; in the cockerel house a young rooster let go with the hoarse, adolescent "craw-aw-kk," which, to him, was crowing.

Carlisle opened the back-entry door, set his suitcase down with a moan of relief. Leave it there, pick it up later.

He stepped into the lighted kitchen.

Grampa and some man or other were sitting at the table over plates loaded with ham and eggs, baked beans, fried potatoes. There was the haggled half of an apple pie on the cloth between them. The sink was piled with dirty dishes; pots and pans loaded the stove, along with a greasy, smoky fry-pan. The room smelled like an old hen house in which the hens had been burning ham. Carlisle had been hungry—half-starved. The game had been in the afternoon, and he hadn't felt like eating supper, so soon after it. But suddenly, he wasn't hungry; his stomach turned over with a flop that he could hear.

For a moment, he could only stare around at the wreck of his mother's neat kitchen, before his eyes came back, dazed, to his grandfather.

Martin, who had been sitting back to him, turned around with a jerk. The kitchen light was behind him, so that Carlisle, with eyes not yet adjusted to the bright glare, could see only the fringe of wiry hair, the glint of glasses.

"What you want?" Martin said.

"What?" Carlisle said. "Why, I guess I want mostly to go to bed, Grampa."

"Not here, you don't go to bed," Martin said. "Go on. Take off. You ain't got any bed in my house. Not anymore."

He turned back to his breakfast, shoveled in a big forkful, and began chewing.

Carlisle could hear the sound of it, see the motion of his ears. Except for the chewing, and an occasional "plop" from the percolator on the stove, the room was silent. He stared at Martin's back—the shoulders, angular, set with the stubborn slope of age, the broad, flat planes of the shoulder blades showing through the blue work-shirt.

"Well?" Martin demanded. "What are you hanging around for? Take off, I said."

"But where? Where to?"

Carlisle felt as if he'd been hit on the head, and his tongue felt funny, too, so that the words came out in a slurred mumble.

"What do I care, where to? Melly, why don't you shove that coffeepot back a little, the coffee's done."

The other man got up, and Carlisle, now actually seeing him, realized that he was Melly Hitchcock, whom he knew as a kind of hanger-on at the poolroom, downtown.

So what on earth was he doing here?

Melly moved across to the stove, glancing sideways at Carlisle on the way. Carlisle saw from the gleam in his eye, the little half-grin, that Melly was having a fine time, enjoying this. Well, it would be a great story to hand on to the boys downtown.

"All right," Carlisle said, between his teeth. "I'll go up and tell Ma I'm back, then I'll shove."

He took a step. Martin pushed back his chair with a scrape. He didn't get up; he merely stared over his shoulder. "You want to talk to your mother, go where she is," he said. "She ain't here."

Carlisle's head cleared. He could almost hear the click.

The old devil. So he couldn't have his own way, he took it out on Ma. Made it so hot for her, she'd gone. Well, if she was gone, she'd be down with Aunt Hazel, she and Ralph and Dot.

"You can sure see she's gone somewhere," he said. Disgust and rage made his voice shake, and he paused, glancing around the kitchen. "Now you can bring your damned old hens right into the house, can't you? Well, have fun!"

"Don't you give me none of your lip," Martin said.

He scrabbled a little, starting to his feet.

"Or I'll learn you a little something about fighting," he went on. "I don't slap open-handed, I double up my fist. I know how, by tar!"

"Yeah," Carlisle said. "You know how, don't you? And you fight fair. Well, I've had a bellyful of the way you fight. Double up your fists? You don't even use your fists. What you use is what you've chucked in my teeth all my life—you support me, so you've got the say. Open-handed, hell! I've had an under-handed fight with you ever since I could walk. So take it and shove it, and, as I say, have fun!"

He went out, grabbing up his suitcase as he passed it, slammed the door, and started across the yard.

Behind him, he heard the door open and close, and he spun around, dropping the suitcase, expecting to see Martin erupt from the kitchen. However, it was only Melly, thudding along after him in his muddy leather-tops.

"By god, Shirttail!" he said, panting. "It's time someone told that old bastard off—he's crazy. Or sick, or something, is all I can say, he don't make sense, and half the time he don't act right, neither. Look, who beat the game? He ain't even got a radio in the house, and he ain't let up on me one minute so's I could phone or get out anywhere." He thrust his face into Carlisle's. "Well, come on, tell me! Who beat? What was the score?"

"They did," Carlisle said. "A hundred and two to fifty-four."

"Oh, Jesus!" Melly said.

The avid look in his eyes was replaced by one of deep mourning. His shoulders drooped, his jaw dropped, as his mind took in the depth of the disaster.

"I had fifteen dollars on that game," he said. "Why you cussid little bums! Carried it clean past the State Champeenship and into the finals, and then lost it, on a shellacking like that! Somebody ought to take you out and drownd you, all the good you are! Oh, for the luvvuv a just god! You damn useless little bums, you!!"

Carlisle stared at Melly—the little, bloodshot, raging eyes, the gobbling mouth, the pink, quivering nose, on which hung a crystal-clear drop of water, about to fall.

"Damn bunch of no-good tramps!" Melly said. "God, I guess the old man's right! They ain't a one of ya I'd hire for a dollar a week."

Rage came up into Carlisle's throat, so strong that he could taste it, like brass, like old cartridges. He hauled back his fist and let Melly have it on the nose, feeling the satisfying squelch and thud as his fist landed, the jolt all the way back to his shoulder.

Melly reeled, almost fell, recovered.

"Why, you little son-uv-a—" He put his fingers to his nose, feeling it, astonished. "Why, I'll fix you—"

Carlisle saw the punch coming. He jerked his head sideways. The big fist whipped past his chin, and he grabbed Melly's other wrist, feeling the flat, thick bones, the tough tendons, twist in his hand. He saw, just in time, the knee coming up and jumped back so that it missed his groin; and he got a hand under the knee and heaved. Melly went backward in a staggering run ten feet or so and sat down. He sat there, as if dazed, and Carlisle, dazed, too, glared at him, waiting; but Melly didn't get up. He remained, thoughtfully fingering his nose.

"So you lost a bundle on the game?" Carlisle choked. "Who asked you to bet, anyway?" He tried to go on, chewing hard on the clot of disgusted words like a hard lump in his throat. "We got to the finals," he said. "And then we ran into a team that was better than anything I ever saw. Oh, don't tell me, I can hear you now, you and that batch of drugstore bankers!"

He was about to turn away, when he saw his grandfather in the kitchen window, braced back, his hands in his pockets, watching.

Well, let him look. At least, he's seen that one thing I learned in gym is what to do when somebody tries to knee you.

He stood there, the fury still sour in his mouth, giving the old man glare for glare.

Martin took his hands out of his pockets. He clasped them in the air and shook them slowly up and down. But his expression did not change; and he turned and walked away from the window.

Part Eleven

Now that the ball season was over and there were no more tickets to take or bus rides to chaperone, Alfred Berg found himself with the luxury of some spare time. He was busy, because he was trying, against odds, to help the ballplayers make up lost work; but now he could spend an occasional evening with Ellen; and the two of them had been going, now and then, over to Miss Eloise's house to help her sort out the notes for her history.

Tonight, however, Ellen had a music lesson to give.

"If I get through early, I'll be over," she promised him. "But if I don't, before you leave, come in for a night-cap."

Tonight, Alfred especially wanted to see Ellen; because tonight, when he had got home, he had found in his mail a letter from his old professor at the University of Colorado, offering him a job. It was quite a terrific job, in the research lab, at a salary which made Alfred's eyes bug out—at least, it seemed a lot of money compared to what he was earning now; and the professor had advised him to take it.

"It isn't in my mind to influence you unduly," the letter said. "There's no doubt you're tremendously valuable as a teacher—God knows, we need to teach the young. But with the present emergency in science, I guess we've got to call it that, we all feel that you'd be more useful here, and we need you."

For a moment, the picture of the laboratory swam before Alfred's eyes. The absorbed heads, bent over microscopes. The peace. The quiet. The heavenly quiet for long hours of concentration. No jungle noise of kids; uninterested, bored, ill-mannered kids . . .

Untaught, ill-equipped, uneducated kids . . .

He drew a long breath as he put down the letter.

To be valued, he thought. To be needed.

Above all, the meeting of minds; the logical, learned minds.

Leave us not go off half-cocked, he told himself.

But the fact remained. The letter had thrust home, with finality, what he had been trying to ignore for months—how homesick, how desperately lonely for that meeting of minds he had been.

Sealed off from a normal, casual intercourse with other people, as if a sheet of plateglass stood irrevocably between him and the world, through which he could see, but not communicate.

Because a teacher, let's face it, because a teacher is filed with the oddities of a community; because most people respect the name, but not the reality, of learning.

Leave us not be sorry for ourselves, he thought. I can't decide this until I've talked with Ellen.

To Miss Eloise Marcy, the history of a town was a vital, living thing.

"People ought to know about the past," she told Alfred. "If it's something to be proud of, they ought to take example from it; if it ain't, then they ought to buckle down and see to it that the present times should be better."

This town had a distinguished past, she said. Its men had fought Indians and repelled a British attack by sea; under difficulty and hardship, they had settled the land. The town had sent a sizable contingent to Mr. Lincoln, when he asked for 75,000 volunteers; its Honor Roll in the modern wars was long. Before the end of sail, it had been famous for its clipper ships and for the men who built and skippered them to the far ends of the earth, and broke records doing it, too. Captain Solomon Hoodless. Abijah Troy. Abraham Wallace. Jethro Marcy. And others, who had left behind many relics of their piping times.

"The past is so easy lost," Miss Eloise told Alfred. "I do feel that the facts ought to be kept and printed. Otherwise, in times to come, nobody's going to remember anything about this town except that its young men played a good game of basketball."

"Don't you believe it," Alfred said. "The same boys who flew bombers over Germany—you'd be surprised how many of them were ballplayers—good ones, too."

"M-m," Miss Eloise said. "I suppose so. But I've watched the young men, the ballplayers, Mr. Berg. They go away, I guess to college, and then they can't stay in college, so they come back here and play ball on the town team. You see their names in the paper once in a while, where they've won some kind of local title playing ball. And that's all. It seems a waste. Some of them are smart boys."

"Yes," Alfred said.

"And that sad boy, that Grindle boy, Mr. Berg—he was a very bright young man."

It was always a little difficult to work with Miss Eloise helping. She dearly loved to talk.

She had a mountain of material—even as a young girl she had been a researcher. She had collected old letters, with their quaint stamps of another day; copied logbooks and saved old diaries from the burning; written down stories and songs from the lips of oldest inhabitants. All her life she had cherished the picture of herself as a busy, literary old lady, sitting among her notes, using up the fading years—those years which to so many old folks were a waste, forlorn and lonely—by writing her history. Now she was afraid she had waited too long.

"Sometimes my mind doesn't seem to be quite clear," she told Alfred. "I can't think where to begin."

Alfred and Ellen had found the material fascinating; the job endless. A roomful of boxes of many sizes; papers piled helter-skelter in them or overflowing in bundles and crumpled wads; crabbed handwriting, too faded to read without a hand-lens; old maps; old sailing directions; Bowditch's *Navigator;* everything tossed together, like the past itself, with no regard for date or time.

They tried at first sorting everything according to date; but their interest inspired Miss Eloise herself to sort papers. Between their visits, she would work like a Trojan, happily dumping old containers and whisking papers about to the four corners of the room, until the disturbed dust started up her hay fever, and she would retire to another room to sneeze. By the time she had finished sneezing, she would have forgotten where she had been among the papers; and then she would start her treasure hunt from another angle, with a fresh batch jumbled out on top of the first one. Alfred and Ellen would come back to find confusion worse confounded.

Nevertheless, the project was interesting, was fun. And it had been here, in this room of dusty boxes, hands grimy from the grubbings among old papers, occasionally touching Ellen's over faded, ribbon-wrapped bundles of ancient secrets, that Alfred had finally made up his mind; so that, tonight he was going to tell Ellen about his new job; discuss it; ask her to marry him.

Thus he was not too well able to concentrate, sitting at Miss Eloise's work-table, across from her, with the papers spread out between them.

She was going on talking, this time about the recurring theme of cussidness. It was all very well, she said, for him to arrange things according to date; but that wasn't her idea. What she'd planned to do, was to tell the truth about the town, arrange that stuff according to times of cussidness.

Alfred smiled at her. "History," he said, quoting, "is the memory of the people—"

"Hnf, so it is. And what do people remember? What sticks up most? War."

"You're really in a tough mood tonight, Miss Eloise."

"Not a mite more than I generally am. Now, Mr. Berg. You're a teacher. You're taking 'em young. Can you teach them?"

"Why, some of them. Yes, I can, Miss Eloise."

"Well, I don't think you can, Mr. Berg. Most of people, they go around destroying, just taking what they think they want or can get. The way the deer eat my perennials. Life to most people is like winter to the deer; they starve so long and stand in snow so long, that come a time they see something green, don't matter what it is, they grab it. Could be belladonna, or whatever; it's pretty, it's green, it's different from what they've had, and they know they need something, so they not only grab it, they mess on it. I go out every spring, there it is. My delphiniums gone—they grow again, of course, not so good, but they grow. The phlox gnawed down so's you can see their roots; the Canterbury bells with the middles et out, that's the heart, that's the vital principle of the flower, they never come back. And that lily! Every year I watch it come up, it looks like a little green hand with folded fingers, and every year the deer eats it off. I guess I'll never live long enough to see what its flower's like; it's never had a chance to bloom."

Miss Eloise paused to sneeze.

"I'm going to have to mix us some lemonade," she said. "This dust makes my throat dry. But I tell you, I stand in the middle of that garden every spring, and I look at that pile of deer manure, excuse me, Mr. Berg, but that's what it is; and I look at the woods, and I say, 'Damn you, damn you, you're just like people. You can't stand anything pretty to be.' "

She went stamping indignantly off to the kitchen to mix her lemonade. Alfred mused, turning over the papers.

There was no doubt that, here and there, the theme of "cussidness" recurred.

Here was Gamaliel Troy, Abijah's grandfather. He packed up, drove an ox-team five hundred miles into new territory, trailing his wife and seven children, a milch-cow, ten hens, a cat and a dog, preferring "the Croel Sauvages of the Wilderness to his congregation of Wilful Nabors."

Solomon Hoodless had a sailor flogged and strung up by the thumbs, because the sailor complained of "maggits in the duff."

Abraham Wallace was settled down, had his clearing made and a cabin built; and when two other families moved in, within a few miles of him, he abandoned his work, everything, and moved to an off-shore island—he place, he said, was getting too "damn crowded."

There was the old Union Church row—Miss Eloise did not know it, but the whole story was recorded in the diary of one of her ancestors. The row had started in a low key, apparently, and then boomeranged, as people realized what was behind the action of two of the church's deacons. These worthies had felt that they and they alone were competent to say who in town was respectable enough to own a pew in the new church, and had arbitrarily sorted out the sheep from the goats.

In modern times, there was the record of what Miss Eloise called the "Doctor War." Two doctors, Dr. Maynard and Dr. Gorham, had each wanted the entire town practice for himself; one had tried to drive the other out of town. People took sides; according to Miss Eloise, there had been fistfights, lobster traps cut off, brother against brother; even now, after nearly a generation, there were people who still referred to others as "Maynardites," or "Gorhamites"; who were still unfriendly, on account of the "Doctor War."

The deer have their reasons, Alfred thought. They do stand in cold and snow all winter; in spring, the does are pregnant, they must have green. It is not cussidness, but only a blind will to survive. Yet in the very blindness, lay the parallel.

For centuries people hàve had it pounded into them: the disaster inherent in selfish grabbings; the aimless wanderings around, poking into concerns not rightfully theirs. The nasty mess in other people's gardens; the senseless chewings of the flowers.

Cussidness, he thought. And then: Cussidness and courage.

You did not drive an ox-team five hundred miles into wilderness, nor sail a ship around Cape Horn, nor move your family and all your worldly goods to a wild off-shore island, unless you had courage.

By and large, it was a hellish combination; and one fairly common to most of mankind. Man's courage, as recorded by history, left you with a shaken heart and a full throat. Yet history wrote with both hands. While the one recorded last stands, forlorn hopes, solitary journeys into wilderness, and oncoming tanks met with showers of stones, the other crossed t's and dotted i's on a parallel column—gas chambers and thumb-stringings; negro kids not allowed to go to school; whole races hounded about the world because of differences in color, religion, or politics. Oh, people in their time had been brave; magnificent! But the fact remained that they were not now, nor ever had been, able to stand each other.

Miss Eloise knew, as Alfred did not know, yet, that the School Board had not renewed his contract. While Win Parker had said at the informal meeting that he had told him, he had, in fact, not yet bothered to do so; let Harry start talking at the supermarket; it would get back to Berg soon enough.

And it's just like that gang, Miss Eloise thought, to let it be talked around all over town, before he knows.

This was one reason for her tirade, tonight, on "cussidness," though it hadn't added materially, she felt, to the bulk of information on the subject, picked up here and there throughout her lifetime.

She herself was too embarrassed to tell him; she was embarrassed for the town, and for herself, because she could not bring herself to tell him; she plied him with lemonade and cake, and at ten o'clock, said good night to him.

Ellen's music lesson should be finished by now, Alfred thought, coming purposefully out into the street; but he saw that a car was parked in front of the salt-box.

Dammit, that's a long session.

Well, it's a nice night. I can take a stroll.

He walked out to the end of the street, but not strolling. His impatient steps sounded along the deserted sidewalk, his heels, coming down hard, rang hollow.

Slow down, he told himself. Look at the stars. Or something.

He looked at the stars.

It's a nice night to propose.

"It's a good day for flying kites," somebody had said at the bombing of Monte Cassino.

Now, whatever had made him think of that? It was one of Uncle Ed's stories; Uncle Ed had been there.

Miss Eloise, he thought, smiling a little wryly. She leaves a flavor, does she not!

He did not slow down; he was back in front of Ellen's house before he knew it; the car was still there. It was no music pupil's car, he realized, taking a closer look. It was Chet Alison's.

Oh, great! Alfred said, between his teeth. But after all, she does have a date with me.

He had not seen much of Alison since his return from Boston. The ballplayers were all decorously back in their classes, trying with more or less success to make up lost work; Chet was not much in evidence around the school; at least, not much, compared to what he had been before his team lost the All-New England.

"All seasons come to an end," Alfred said, punching Ellen's doorbell.

Nobody came, but the front door was seldom locked. He pushed it open and went in.

He called, "Hi, Ellen, are you here?" before he saw the tableau in the living room—Ellen backed against the wall, as if she had got as far away as she could; Chet, one hand braced on either side of her, holding her there.

"Oh, Al!" Ellen said. "Come in!"

At the sound of her voice, relieved, near-hysterical, Alfred felt his neck bristle. "What the hell—" he began, and Chet spun around.

"What's the idea busting in here?" he demanded.

Alfred moved forward into the room. "I bust in here quite often," he said, and stopped, staring in consternation and unbelief. Ellen's hair was rumpled, her dress torn; she was looking back at him with a kind of desperate humiliation. Responsiveness, quick-understanding humor, dignity, were gone; ripped away.

No—no bastard has a right to destroy dignity, he thought, feeling, for a moment, outrage; then, pure fury.

Chet had stepped back; hands thrust into his pockets, he was regarding them both with amusement.

"You've got no kick coming," he said to Ellen. "You've been stringing me along all winter."

"I have not!" Ellen said. "I've been treating you like a human being. And that's all! You've no right—you had no reason to think—"

"Uh-huh. So when I think a gal would like to stop playing footsie and have a little bit of the real, I try a little bit of the real," Chet said. "So you don't like it—is that my fault?"

"Beat it," Alfred said. "Get out of here!" And he hauled back his fist and let go; and knocked Chet flat.

Chet landed on his back; he seemed to bounce. He advanced on Alfred, fists cocked, poised on the balls of his feet, the trained boxer's stance.

Alfred cocked his own fists; and he saw Chet's punch coming, almost like a delayed-action shot when someone slows down the camera, the clenched fist growing from normal size to something that looked as big as a football. It smacked against his jaw with a solid, meaty thwack, and Alfred went over backward, an almost complete somersault. He landed in the corner, his legs up in a V; his head banged solidly against the wall.

My skull's exploded, he thought; it's in pieces lying around; I'd better not move till it goes back together. A slight ticking sound began, which he listened to, the sound of his head going back together like a jigsaw puzzle; then his vision cleared, and he saw Chet, still cocked back, still poised on the balls of his feet. Alfred saw him through a haze which was not red, as one is taught to believe the haze of rage should be, but blue. Then he realized that he was seeing neither blue nor red; only, his glasses, still on his nose, were steamed up from the sweat of fury.

"Come on," Chet said. "Get up, you bastard!" He spoke through clenched teeth; his voice sounded to Alfred like the low buzz of bees.

"Oh, come, now, bud, fair play according to the book of rules," Alfred said. "Wait till I get my glasses off." He scrambled to his feet, his glasses in his hand, walked across the room, and laid them on the table.

A long time ago, when I was a kid, Uncle Ed and I used to box, he thought, groggily. He said I had a pretty good right. Or was it left? Which hand? I ask myself. Anyway, smite the bastard.

But neither hand seemed particularly effective; Chet's second blow steamed past his guard, landed in the same place on his jaw, only this time Alfred's reflexes functioned. All by itself, with no help from him, his head jerked aside a little; the blow glanced, so that this time he was knocked down, but not out.

He shook his head to clear it, working his jaw painfully to right and left, aware of the ticking sound now intensified to a far-off, continuous rattle, like a Fourth of July noisemaker. The haze, he observed, with some surprise, was still in front of his eyes, and even without his glasses, it was still blue.

Oh, hell, he thought, us eggheads probably see blue anyway instead of red; and he got up; and was cleanly, promptly, professionally knocked down again.

This is, obviously, a shellacking, Alfred told himself, lying flat on his back on the floor. What they call slaughter, according to the rules of the Boxing Commission. You do not hit your opponent while he is down; you wait until he gets up.

His mind seemed clear; the ideas merely formed slowly. One. And then another.

What I need is a club, he thought; and he got up; but this time he could not even lift his fists.

He had been lying on the floor, he thought, for a long time, probably two weeks; because it would surely take two weeks for his head to swell to such an enormous size. A barrel; an elephant; the Empire State Building, because it was elongated, too, a long spire, stretching away to infinite distance; soft in the back, though, squashy, like a sofa cushion . . . it was a sofa cushion; his head was resting on it, and spread over him was a blanket.

Where? he thought.

His fingers encountered the edge of a rug, felt along it.

Scatter rug. The one laid over the spot where the British Marine bled, far away and long ago.

Someone slipped a hand under his head.

"Don't do that," Alfred said. "Don't touch it, it's—"

There was no word to say what his head was.

He opened his eyes.

"I didn't see red," he said. "I saw blue. Eggheads see blue."

"Yes," Ellen said. "Oh, darling. Are you all right?"

"It's just a matter," Alfred said, "of being an all-around guy. I don't know his specialty any more than he knows mine." His head, elongated, suddenly snapped back to round. "A man is to blame for that," he said. "To blame . . . to blame . . . "

"Don't talk nonsense," Ellen said. "Chet Alison's a trained boxer. What chance does anyone stand against brute force?"

"That is the problem," Alfred said. "That is the sixty-four-thousand-dollar question." He lifted his hand, which felt heavy, and felt gingerly along the edge of his jaw. "Oo! What a wallop!" he said. "From most things, I could probably protect you," he said. "From bears in the bears' woods, from the terror that flieth by night. From brute force, it doesn't look as if—No. But will you marry me?"

Miss Eloise Marcy, that afternoon, had dropped into the supermarket, to pick up a chop for her supper. Harry Troy, who had waited on her, watched with unconcealed amusement while she went carefully over the tray of lamb chops, choosing one.

"That one suit you, does it?" he asked.

"No," Miss Eloise said. "It don't suit me. It's not lamb, it's mutton. But it seems to be the best you have, so will you wrap it, please?"

"Oh, come. First, high-quality spring lamb," Harry said. He winked at his helper, who was wrapping hamburger nearby, an invitation to watch; this was going to be fun. "Guess you'll have to find a new boyfriend to help you write your book, won't you, Eloise?"

"How's that?" Miss Eloise was fumbling in her pocketbook; she didn't seem to have heard.

"I was just saying that next year Berg'll be long gone from here," Harry said. "The School Board's give him his walking papers."

Miss Eloise stiffened. "Why?" she asked. "He's a very good teacher."

"Now, you know, Eloise, the School Board can't be too careful about what the kids is learnt," Harry said easily. "He may be a good teacher, for all I know he is, but he's a Jewboy, and they's some of us don't care much for that kind of a type."

"My dear Harry," Miss Eloise said. "The Jews had universities when your ancestors and mine were creeping out of trees." She picked up the lamb chop, dropped it composedly into her bag, and walked away. She paused in her slightly aimless fashion to pinch an avocado which lay on the vegetable counter, left it where it was, and went on her way.

Harry stared after her. "That old gal gits crazier every year she lives," he said to his helper. "She keeps on, the Selectmen's going to have to commit her, you know it?"

In the days that followed, Miss Eloise walked about the town. There was very little time left before Town Meeting; but she went from door to door, sitting in kitchens. It seemed true, to most, that her mind was not now quite clear; without a doubt, her manner was flighty. She carried on a slightly pixillated conversation on many matters, but from it the ladies of the town gathered one golden nubbin of gossip. Charles Kendall had come out and was going to run for the School Board this year.

Unheard of? Why, yes, of course it was, she said. Charles had stayed inside a shell for years; he was sensitive about his leg. But he was a fine young man, wasn't he? And of course those men who ran the town from the back room of Parker's Garage, for years had had no opposition. School Board matters did stink to high heaven, didn't they? Miss Eloise wasn't up on the school laws, it wasn't her place to be, but she thought she remembered something—oh, yes. Yes. That it was illegal for a town official to do business with himself. And Win Parker sold all the gas and oil for the school buses, and fuel for the school furnace; and Harry Troy supplied the groceries needed for the school lunch. It did look, didn't it, as if those men might be in it for what they could get out of it, didn't it?

Well, of course, the town could do something about that, if it wanted to. The ladies of a town, alone—well, the ladies of a town were a power in themselves. They could elect someone to be a check on all that. If they wanted to. Some responsible person, with a feeling of civic responsibility.

Because those who ran a school should certainly have some, shouldn't they? An education was a pearl of great price and schooling a great tradition. When Miss Eloise was young, people sacrificed for schooling, children walked miles. But now that it came painless, everybody could have it for nothing, and children hauled to it by bus, perhaps it didn't seem so important? Or the teachers respected in the town, as teachers once were, and looked up to instead of being made fun of? You couldn't help thinking, could you, about Daniel Webster and his law books? Or Abraham Lincoln, studying by firelight?

Thus Miss Eloise, poking away at the conscience of the town, which did indeed value a championship ballteam; yet which also had behind it the weight of a two hundred years' tradition about book-learning, about children learning reading, writing, and arithmetic.

Charles Kendall, people said. For goodness sake!

Well, that beat all, they said. Who would have thought it?

Why, yes, of course everybody knew that old Win and old Harry were in it for what they could get out of it, had been for years. But somebody had to be on the School Board, and who wanted to? It was a lousy job, paid fifty dollars a year, took up a lot of time; you never could please anybody—anything you did, you were out on a limb. But old Win, he didn't care. He just said that as far as being out on a limb was concerned, the School Board lived out on one, and one more was just a place to hang his hat.

And, Charles Kendall, they said. Well, might not hurt to have a little new blood, if he was fool enough to want to do it. Quite a little wave of enthusiasm started in the town, for Charles Kendall. Might make Town Meeting kind of interesting this year, some opposition to Win; hadn't been any since God knew when.

But then, just before Town Meeting, Win came up with Feathers Ryan.

Feathers Ryan! they said, at the poolroom, at the drugstore, at Joe's Lunch. Have you heard the news? Feathers Ryan's going to be the new coach of the ballteam! How about that!

Well, we didn't win the All-New England this year; we only got to the finals.

Wow, give old Feathers a crack at them kids, next year, the year after, ker-whango!

Old Win. Look what he pulled out of the hat.

Well, that's old Win for you. Who else could have come up with Feathers Ryan? I tell you, that boy's got connections.

At Town Meeting, the moderator, as he always did, asked the citizens to come down and drop a few votes in the box for Win Parker for the School Board; which they did.

Charles Kendall's name was not mentioned.

Had Charles Kendall been aware of all this, no one would have been more astounded than he. But he was out of town, and had not heard about the campaign to draft him. A few days before it began, he had driven to Boston to take Carlisle McIntosh to a hospital, to see if something could be done about his lame knee.

Susie McIntosh had found it wonderful to live for the first time in her life in a relaxed, happy household. She couldn't get used to being paid for doing work she enjoyed, and which seemed like child's play to her; for Charles's house had modern appliances; the equipment in the motel was up-to-date.

She and Hazel had both been up to see Martin. They found him with his feet dug in, his face turned against them. They offered to spring-houseclean his house, to find him a housekeeper. Hazel forestalled Susie firmly, when Susie started to offer to come back.

Martin said they had buttered their bread. Go lie in it.

He refused to allow them in the house.

He looked old and sick, Susie thought. Her heart turned over; but outside of giving in completely, returning herself and the children to the life they'd led with Martin, she didn't see what she could do.

He and Melly, Martin said, were baching it. The last thing they needed in the house now was a damn woman and a parcel of kids.

Down at the motel, Susie duffed in and made the work fly. Some of the units had to be painted; Hazel and Bessie always started early to get things cleaned and shipshape for the June opening. Charles and George had a string of lobster traps ready to set; Ralph was in seventh heaven, helping them; even Dot had settled down quite a lot; she was less edgy and a good deal less prissy, and much more fun to have around the house. Susie was feeling wonderfully at home, settled in, when the real trouble began with Carlisle's knee.

It had, seemingly, got better; at least he had stopped limping, when, one night after she had gone to bed, she woke up to hear someone prowling around in the bathroom, clinking bottles in the medicine cabinet. She got up to see what the matter was.

"Ma, haven't we got any aspirin?" Carlisle asked. His hair was on end and his face was flushed. "My knee's giving me the devil."

Susie found the aspirin for him and it helped; at least, he went back to bed and, she supposed, to sleep; for she heard no more out of him that night. But the next morning, the knee was puffy and red; it hurt to bear his weight on it and Susie made him stay in bed.

"I think he ought to have the doctor," she said, with concern, at the breakfast table. "I expect I'd better call Wickham."

Ralph, who had been engaged in scooping a large puddle of marmalade off his plate, paused with spoon arrested. " 'Aye,' " he said. " 'So could I or so could any man. But will he come when you do call for him?' "

George lowered his newspaper and stared at Ralph. Never having had kids around the house much, George was finding himself these days vastly entertained, more often, puzzled.

"Huh?" he asked. "What kind of talk is that?"

"Shakespeare," Ralph said largely. "Play I'm reading for my book review. I ran across it in the library. It's pretty thick stuff, only once in a while the old boy had a word for it."

Charles said to Susie, "What do you think's the matter? Does his knee look infected?"

"Well, I don't know. I've put on some hot compresses, till I can get hold of Wickham."

Wickham turned out to be away. A medical conference, his wife said. He wouldn't be back for a week.

"Some conference," Charles said, briefly.

While Susie was putting on more compresses, Charles strolled in. He kidded Carlisle along, sat by the bed, cheerfully, and watched for a while; but later, when Susie came down to the kitchen, he said, "Look, Susie, I don't think we ought to fool around with that knee. I saw some bad knees when I was in the hospital, and a delayed infection, if that's what it is, can raise the devil with a knee joint. You pack a couple of grips for us, and Carlisle and I'll take a run down to the city to the Clinic."

Susie stared at him, horrified. "You think—" she began.

"I don't think or know. But we mustn't poop around waiting for Wickham. Carlisle can travel now; if he gets worse, he won't be able to."

Susie hesitated no longer. Reasonably, Charles could be expected to know something about bad legs; Carlisle had complained of a throbbing sensation in his knee, and anybody would know what throbbing was a sign of. She flew to pack suitcases; and after the two of them had driven off, she suddenly remembered that, half out of her mind with worry, she hadn't even thanked Charles for his kindness.

Charles wrote, to say they had arrived safely. A day later, he telephoned. Carlisle was in the Clinic hospital. The knee was infected; the doctors expected that antibiotics would arrest the infection, but they also said there'd been an injury to the knee, inside the joint. As soon as the infection was cleared up, they would have to operate. He would stay, Charles said; if Susie felt she wanted to come down, then she must come and not worry about expense.

The phone conversation was characteristic of Charles—terse, efficient, kind. She couldn't, of course, let him be put to expense. The money she had put by, Brant's insurance, had better be used for first things first. Susie took the first train to Boston.

Charles met her at the station. There was no question of his leaving her here alone, he said; he would stay. A week later, while she waited at the hospital for Carlisle's operation to be over, she was glad he had. She didn't know what she would have done without him; how she would have got through the time between hospital visiting-hours; how she would have bolstered herself during the waiting.

"Look," he had said on the first day, when she had come out of the hospital looking dazed and distraught. Carlisle hadn't seemed terribly sick, but he was silent; there was a sullenness about him that puzzled Susie. She found she couldn't talk to him; he seemed detached from everything that was going on around him, as if he felt he wasn't where he was at all.

"Look," Charles said. "You can go back to the hotel and go nuts moping around and worrying, or you can come on out on the town with me."

"But, Charles, I'm so worried—he isn't a bit like himself. Is he sicker than they've told us?"

"He's dopey," Charles said. "He's probably had a couple of shots. The way he is, that's nothing unusual. They take care of you in a hospital, it's wonderful the way they handle pain. And they don't let you go off your rocker worrying, when you're getting ready to have an operation. Now, come on. We don't often get to Boston, and we've never been here together. So come on."

Now, in the hospital waiting-room, she thought, Without Charles this week, I'd be crazy by now.

He hadn't let her be by herself, to worry—outside of visiting-hours at the hospital, he'd had plans for every day and evening; so that when she fell into bed, late, she was so tired she'd gone right to sleep. On the first day, Charles had asked her with a certain amount of reserve in his voice, if she'd come with him to help pick out a new suit.

"I need one," he said. "I've always been kind of a fool about such things. Left alone, I'm likely to pick me out a purple tweed."

Mildly surprised, because she herself had never seen much wrong with his quiet, conservative suits, Susie went; and, sure enough, his choice was unerring. He went straight to a tailor shop, where it was obvious he had been before, and concluded the whole business in twenty minutes.

"There," he said, emerging from a dressing room. "That's over. Let's go."

Susie glanced at him, amused.

"You didn't ask me if I liked it," she said.

Charles looked dashed. "So I didn't," he said. "Er—do you?"

"Yes. You looked very handsome."

"I did?" He flushed a little, as he turned to pick up his cane. He was carrying it today because walking on concrete sidewalks bothered him, he had been careful to explain. If he forgot and put that boughten heel down hard, he said, he felt it all the way to the top of his head. "Cut it out, you'll have me vain as a peacock, Susie. All right, come on. Now I'll do the same for you."

"For me?"

"Why not? You can't come to the city and not buy new clothes, can you?" He grinned. "I don't know much about ladies' wear, but I know what I like."

"Oh, Charles, I mustn't. I can't afford it, not at a time like this."

"You can't afford not to, at a time like this," he said. "A time like this is when. Come on. I know a good place."

It had been years since Susie had bought new clothes. Most of her dresses had been housedresses which she'd made herself; and occasionally Hazel had brought her home something new. As they left the men's shop, she stole a glance at herself in a plateglass window.

Oh, heavens! she thought. What man would want to do the town with me looking like this? Neat and clean, but dowdy. Dumpy.

Aloud she said, "Willy off the pickle boat."

Charles grinned at her. "Well, that wasn't quite what I meant. You look all right to me. As a matter of fact, you look damned nice."

"All right, Charles. Where's the store?"

"Atta girl," Charles said.

In a new dark-blue suit, white ruffled blouse, new shoes, and a foolish hat trimmed with what looked like a stuffed canary sitting in a dish of pansies, Susie did the town with Charles. She had hesitated over the hat. It was expensive—far too much, she thought, for such a silly thing; but Charles made up her mind for her. He took one look and let out a delighted bawl.

"That's great, Susie! That's wonderful! Buy it."

"But, it's so high—"

"High, nothing! You look like that in a hat, you've got to have it! Here, how much?" he said to the amused salesgirl; and he pulled out his wallet, paid for the hat, and hauled Susie out of the shop by the hand before she could protest.

She did protest, however, every step of the way down the block, until Charles came to a stop in the middle of the hurrying crowd, and looked at her.

"I used to bring you fancy chocolates," he said. "And valentines. Once I brought you a live frog."

Susie laughed. "You were ten years old," she said. "You handed over that frog as if it were a treasure."

"It was a treasure," Charles said. "To me, it was. Right now, I'm fresh out of frogs. All I can find is a stuffed canary." He reached over and flipped the canary lightly with his finger on its synthetic beak. "Cussid cute little duffer he is, too."

He sobered, suddenly. “I’ve got a gall,” he said, shortly, glancing away. “But keep it, Susie. Let’s go places.”

Oh, dear, Susie thought, as she walked along beside him. She hadn’t intended to hurt him. He must know that she couldn’t accept an expensive present from him; yet obviously something about her refusal had hurt him deeply. His eyes, for a moment, had looked bleak; his voice had carried an undertone that sounded to her, forlorn.

Well, I’m not going to have that, she thought.

She said aloud, “Thank you for the hat, Charles. I’ll make it up to you this summer, at the motel.”

“Be sure you do,” he said.

He was quieter than usual for a while; then he seemed to forget all about it, as they went here and there, seeing the sights in the old, brown town.

Susie thought that the sight of her new clothes might cheer Carlisle up; she tried to interest him with stories of what she and Charles had been doing and seeing. When he seemed not to care whether she talked or not, she remembered what Charles had said about shots—maybe the medicine they were giving him was making him feel fuzzy. The infection was clearing up; the doctors were pleased about that. It had been a strenuous treatment, they said.

“Would you rather I didn’t talk?” she asked, at last, one evening. “Shall I just go away and let you sleep?”

“Oh, sure,” Carlisle said. “Go on away, if you want to, Ma. Have fun.”

“Oh, hey,” Susie said. “What does that mean, honey?” She went over to the bed, leaned down and kissed him. “I’m just killing time, you know that. I’m not really having fun.”

“Uh-huh,” Carlisle said.

Now, sitting waiting for the operation to be over, she kept wondering about him; what was going on in his mind. Drugs, of course; they always affected people. But surely the poor lamb couldn’t have thought I was using the occasion just to have a good time, a happy holiday? Because that’s how he made me feel.

Causes and effects. She kept going over them.

I'm to blame. I should have put my foot down. I shouldn't have let him play ball. But Wickham said he was all right, I supposed he knew. Oh, dear, the first thing they asked here was whether Carlisle had had any X rays, and of course, he hadn't; and when Charles told them, they looked as if they thought we were all crazy. Of course I could have stopped him playing, but if I had, he'd never have forgiven me . . .

"Take it easy, Susie," Charles said. He smiled at her.

"Oh, Charles!" Susie burst out. "What will I ever do if he's lame? I don't think I could stand it, if—"

"You could stand it," Charles said. "And so could he. If you find you've got to. Don't worry till you have to, Susie. They may be able to fix him up good as new. They think they will."

Something in his voice—an abruptness not usual with him—made Susie glance at him, startled; and, suddenly, she realized what she had said, and to whom.

For years, she hadn't thought about Charles's injury. He kept it concealed too well, most of the time; if he mentioned it at all, it was with a kind of bluff casualness—I've got it, it's there, so what?

People, at times, not often now, would sometimes talk over how awful it must have been for him to lose a leg, to have got smashed up like that in the War—a big, nice-looking fellow like Charles Kendall. At times, with the indulgent condescension of the able-bodied, someone would remark that Charles Kendall did pretty well for a one-legged feller, didn't he?

Able-bodied, Susie thought, suddenly. That's just what they are, and, for most of them, that's all they are. While Charles . . .

He sat there smiling at her, a big, broad-shouldered man, lean-hipped, angular; his square muscular hands resting loosely on the arms of the overstuffed reception-room chair—the kind of chair he hated, she knew, because its softness went down forever, threw him off balance, so that when he got up he had to scrabble. She thought of Charles Kendall at twenty, dancing with her, the two of them, light on the floor; Charles, who had wanted to marry her, whom she would have married, if it hadn't been for Brant.

"Oh, Charles," she said. She felt her voice thicken a little, and paused until she could be sure it was steady. "I'm so buried up in my own troubles, Charles."

Charles grinned.

"It's all right, Susie," he said. "I've had this gimp a good long time. A gimp is something you learn to live with, as soon as it gets home to you that you've got to."

"People are so—I'm so—"

"No, you aren't. And, for most people, they're just embarrassed. Then they think, what if they had it? So they realize they haven't, it's not them, it's you; and they haven't got much, but here's somebody they've got the edge on. After all that, they remember to be sorry for you. They can't help thinking that way. Most people have got so goddam much to put up with, they grab at straws, like 'Well, at least, I've got two good legs.' You can't blame them, and I don't notice it any more. Damn and double-damn this blasted chair!"

He levered himself up with some difficulty, walked to the window, where he stood with his back to her, looking out. "At first, I won't say it was easy to take," he said. "Having people sorry for me—that expression they get, mostly around the eyes. The first few times I saw that, I wanted to take a punch at someone. But shoot, you handle that."

"Nobody even notices it now," Susie said. "The way you are, the way you—Look at me, there I was gabbling along, not even thinking."

"That's what I like. Half the time, I forget about it myself, unless I run a-foul of one of those damn chairs, or something. Maybe a cat could have kittens in it in comfort, but it makes a human being feel like a coil of rope."

He stopped, then went on, his voice deepening.

"I get by," he said. "I miss out on some things, like I've always felt it would be a damned imposition to ask a woman to marry me. Couldn't help wondering how she'd feel, seeing me take this contraption off every night before I could get into bed."

"Why, Charles!" Susie stared at him. "Any woman—any woman would be lucky."

"Would you?" Charles said. He did not turn around, but still stood, leaning his hands on the sill, looking out of the window. "Would you feel lucky, Susie?"

"Yes, I would," Susie said. "Why, Charles, I'd—I'd marry you tomorrow, if only you would ever ask me."

She stopped, flushing red, appalled at herself; but thinking, as he came toward her, that everything was all right, there was no doubt of that.

"Susie," he said huskily. "Susie, my dearest. After all this time." And, a little later, lifting his lips from hers, "Not tomorrow, honey. As soon as we know, as soon as we find out how the youngster is. This afternoon."

The operating surgeon, coming in after Carlisle's operation, explained carefully what he had done. His talk, interspersed with terms like "intra-auricular cartilage," "synovial membrane," "pyogenic infection," was mostly Greek to Susie; but she finally gathered, in plain English, that he had removed some tabs of dislodged cartilage and repaired as much of the damage as he could; that Carlisle would be in the hospital for a while, for healing and manipulative treatment. As to whether the knee joint would be permanently stiff, they would have to wait and see.

Part Twelve

The first of June was lilac time. Around the houses, in farmyards, above deserted cellars in overgrown fields, the perennial bushes bloomed, sending forth perfume on the crisp spring wind. Lilac smell; once known, not forgotten; so that people far from home, scattered in cities and towns across the nation, would see the first lilacs in a florist's window, and stand gazing, remembering with a sting of homesick tears the soft, Oriental sweetness.

Lilac time was graduation time. Up at the school, boys and girls brought in great armloads of bloom to decorate the gym for graduation exercises. Final exams were finished, anxiety over. Everyone, it seemed, was going to graduate—if not with flying colors, at least graduate. There had been no real worry about any of the teachers co-operating, except Mr. Berg; he, for a time, had been the conundrum. But at the last it turned out that he, too, had passed everybody.

"James," he had said, at his final conference with James Goss, "some of these kids can hardly read or write. What are they going to do in the world? Where are they headed?"

"They'll get along better with a high-school diploma than they can without one," James said.

"Even if it doesn't mean a damn thing," Alfred said.

James nodded.

"We've got to get the seniors out of the way to make room for the freshmen, next year," he said. "At that, we won't have—har—enough room. And parents don't like it if their children don't graduate." He shrugged wearily. "You won't be here, Alfred, to see what a hell my life would be. So will you, as a favor to me, write down passing grades? I would—har—appreciate it."

"So send them out," Alfred said. "Ill-prepared, poorly equipped. What in hell is a school for?"

"It's a warm place to spend the winter," James said. "I haven't congratulated you—har—Alfred, on your new job."

"I'm more in line for condolences on my failure here," Alfred said.

James shook his head. "Nonsense!" he said. "In this—har—racket, success is counted by what you have to show, not what you couldn't do. You have Debby Parker to show; you have young Ralph McIntosh, who, I think, is headed the way—har—in which he should go. So far as the wreckage is concerned, neither you nor I is responsible for that. You haven't failed; you have merely failed to straddle the—har—fence already worn smooth by me. I can accomplish more, I find, by doing this than by—har—not doing it. I am asking you to straddle it once, Alfred, and pass those senior boys in—har—science."

"Har—" Alfred said. "James, I will."

So everybody passed. Class parts were assigned, and Debby Parker was valedictorian.

Up in his study, the minister chosen to deliver the baccalaureate sermon put the final touches on his oration—he was going to bear down hard this year on atom bombs and the part that educated men and women must expect to play in a threatened world.

For days, everybody had known about the athletic scholarships which were to be handed out officially, with proper ceremony, on graduation night. To Jerry Mooney, of course; it went without saying; Joel Troy had one; and Dr. Wickham's boy, Dick. But not Carlisle McIntosh, who was back now from the Boston Clinic, and seen occasionally around town on crutches.

Lilac time up at the farm was the time to guard the hens out on the range, to keep guns oiled and handy. Martin thought he had never seen so many varmints—foxes, skunks, weasels, and hawks. Melly Hitchcock was a poor shot, couldn't hit a bull in the stern with a board; not like Ralph and Carlisle, whom Martin had taught to shoot and whose twenty-twos had always kept the dead varmint count high. Martin was losing some hens, but let them go; and let the damn kids go, too; he wouldn't speak to a member of his family if he met one on the street.

Carlisle had been up at the gym all day, not so much helping as waiting around for Debby to get through. He had started out with the others, but the work of putting up the decorations for graduation was mostly on stepladders; fellows with two sound legs kept going ahead, past him, and doing it. Not that they were mean at all. It was always, "Oh, hey, Carl, let me do that," or "Hi, fella, get down before you fall down"; all nice and helpful. By lunchtime he was sulky and sick of the whole thing.

If they'd just pass it over, shut up; let him do what he could; but no, they had to keep bearing down.

A crip; a gimp; they thought they had to take care of him. So he took to hanging around on the outskirts of things, and they all, even Debby, seemed to take it for granted that he was better off out of the way.

He went over and leaned against the doorjamb, watching the noisy crowd down by the stage, where they were fixing lilacs around the American flag. Nobody missed him. He had to go down to the lavatory, sometime; that took effort, going up and down stairs; he might as well start now, be back to take Debby to lunch.

Every time you went out of or into the gym, you passed by the glass-enclosed cases where the basketball trophies were kept. There were quite a lot of small ones—area and regional awards—but only two big silver basketballs, the awards for the State Championships, 1948 and this year. Carlisle paused by the case. He often did, nowadays, when no one was around to kid him for looking in at his own photographs, or whatever they thought he might be doing.

Quite a few photographs had been set along the shelves among the trophies—group pictures of teams from way back when, shots of individual players, shots of the high spots in various games. Taken mostly by newspaper photographers, they were fine, clear, dramatic pictures. There was one that was a honey, of the monumental pile-up of Boone players and himself, on the night when he'd first hurt his knee.

"Look at that!" people had said, peering in at this photo. "Look at that! Isn't that awful, the way they tried to cripple him!"

Yeah, Carlisle thought. They sure did. Did a better job than they knew.

Not at the time, though. Heck, at the time, he didn't know, himself, that he'd been hurt. Got rolling so fast that he didn't feel any pain.

If only he'd been able to get going like that in that last Boston game. If only he could have started to ramble.

If he'd just been able to reach out and lay hold of that light feeling he'd always had in a big game, as if his feet were off the floor and he was traveling on air, nothing could stop him; if he could have got back that terrific thing that happened to him in the Boone game. He'd been counting on that; and nothing.

Maybe the different kind of auditorium, the Boston Garden, so much bigger than he was used to, had something to do with it; or the cheering-section, which had been tremendous and all hostile, except for one pitiful little patch of hometown fans, a bug in a bottle, not making much noise.

He'd felt jerky from the beginning, feet heavy, wrists stiff. And his leg, from mid-calf to mid-thigh, where the novocaine had taken hold, had seemed to be not there at all. The others on the team felt just as wonky as he did; he could tell.

But mostly, the opposing team had been hotter than a pistol that night; maybe they were always hot; it seemed as if they might be. Their game was easy, slick, smooth, almost professional; and two of them, those colored fellows . . . wow!

When the newspaper pictures came out, there'd been a hooraw around the town at home here—real-gone speeches down at the pool-room, centered around the insult to "our nice, clean, white, American boys." So on. A lot of crap. But it was all long gone. Nobody thought about it now, or if anyone did, all he remembered when he saw you gimping around, was that you'd lost their game for them, lost their money.

At first, the team had heard plenty about that. Every time one of them went anywhere, some joker made a crack, until they were all ready to fight.

If I'd stayed around town, hadn't had to go away to the Clinic before it all died down, Melly Hitchcock wouldn't have been the only one got a sock on the nose.

So now they all saw you, gimping around.

Oh, yeah, got crippled up, playing ball.

The idea seemed to be that you'd been numb to let it happen.

Nobody cared what you thought now, or what you did, just so you stayed in the background, kept out of the way so people wouldn't have to look at you. Half the time, they just looked away when they saw you coming. So all right, so nobody gave a damn.

Ma, in Boston. When you'd think that the least she could do was worry some, what did she do? Tooted off all over town, bought new clothes. Made a fine use of the occasion to get herself married to Charles Kendall.

Oh, it was all right with him if she got married. Charles was a nice guy, had some dough. But it just went to show. A guy's whole life was shot to hell. What chance did he have now to be anything but a damn bum? So things went right along just the way they always had gone, nobody so much as turned his head.

Since he'd got back, he couldn't even get right with Debby. She seemed to think he could do different.

Do *something*, she said.

Didn't say much, but you could tell she was blaming you all the time.

Work, she said. Dig into the books, honey, we'll go to college together next fall, if only you'll try to catch up. College! Who wanted that egghead stuff, now?

So all right, let her stick up the damn lilacs around the picture of Abraham Lincoln, along with the guys who had two good legs and could climb a stepladder.

He stood leaning against the glass showcase, staring in.

No more ball. No more ball, forever. Because if his knee ever did heal so it wouldn't be stiff, what kind of condition could he keep himself in, how could he ever get back what he'd had? The only thing he'd had. So what else was there?

To hell with it. A bum. A goddam useless bum.

He heard a noise behind him, spun around.

What a cluck! Let someone catch him gawping in here at his own pictures!

He opened his mouth, getting ready to put in first, to let off a mouthful before whoever it was could start ribbing; but the fellow who had come into the building from the front door was nobody he'd ever seen before.

He was a tall, sloppy young man, in an old pair of khaki pants and a black leather windbreaker, slouching along, hands in his pockets, bareheaded, so that you could see how the hair had receded a little from his temples. A middle-aged guy. Thirty, anyway. He had a potbelly, and he wore a pair of old, beat-up, basketball shoes.

The fellow said nothing. He gave Carlisle a short, sidewise stare, and ranged alongside, looking in through the glass at the trophies in the case.

Carlisle turned and had started to move away, when the newcomer spoke.

"Well, well," he said softly. "Whaddya know!"

"What?" Carlisle said. "Did you say something?"

"Yeah. I had a bet on, with myself. I lost."

"A bet?" On ball—that was nothing new.

The fellow said no more for a moment. He stood looking into the case. Then he went on.

"That was some game, you know it? So-ome game! Jesus, it was ten years back, and them pictures make it like it was last night. Look, that Charlesville forward—in about three seconds, he's going to stick out his foot and I'm going arse-over-bucket. Wonder what ever happened to him—God, I'd like to know if he lived to grow up before someone clobbered him for good."

He came to a stop, and stood looking.

"I bet they'd yank my pictures out of here, flush 'em down the john," he said. "They didn't, they left 'em in. Whaddya know?"

Carlisle came back. He looked at the fellow curiously. "Pictures?" he asked.

"Sure. Them photos, there. Those. That one."

He laid a finger on the glass, pointing.

"And drill my name off of that silver ball, by God," he said. "And there it still is. How about that?"

Carlisle stared at the photograph.

The tall boy. Snub nose, black wavy hair, brash, cocky tilt to his head. You-go-to-hell written all over him. About like anyone you knew of his age, only more so. Somebody you'd look at twice if he came up against you in a game. Arthur Grindle.

Holy old smoke, who would have known?

"Okay, you can quit looking," Grindle said, coldly. "It's me. You can tell it around town, so the women can lock their doors and keep the kids off the streets. Art Grindle. I just got home."

Carlisle turned red, aware that he had been caught staring, mouth open, jaw dropped. He swallowed with embarrassment, wondering what to say. What did you say to a man just out of jail?

"Oh," he managed feebly. "Well. Hi."

Grindle looked at him.

"Don't bust a gusset, kid," he said. "I didn't come in here to talk to you or anyone else."

He turned back, silently, to his contemplation of the trophies in the case.

Why, gee. Seems the first place the guy headed for, after all those years in jail, he came up here to see the basketball trophies, to find out if his photos and his name were still there.

"Hey," Grindle said, suddenly, looking at him and then back at Carlisle's own photographs. "You're McIntosh. Old Shirttail."

"Yeah," Carlisle said. "Yeah, I am."

"What's with the crutches? How'd you get hurt?"

"Bad knee."

"In a game?"

"Uh-huh."

"Was that what ailed you that last game in Boston? The Boone game, you was hotter than a pistol."

Carlisle stared. "How did you get to—" He stopped. The words "see it" died in his mouth.

Grindle shrugged. "They got all kinds luxuries down in the pokey," he said. "TV, newspapers, books, even a copy of *Mein Kampf* in the library. We watched the games. That Boone game, I got pretty excited. You went on a whingding, made some of the handsomest shots I ever saw. And then, down in Boston—"

"Don't tell me, let me guess. You'd never know I was the same guy."

Here it was for probably the thousandth time. Though this guy at least remembered the good game.

Grindle nodded. "An off-night," he said. "I knew it! The same as us, the year we went down. We got so hyped up to win the state that we went right up over the top and down the other side. Never could get back up there again. Us, we never even made the semi-finals, got clobbered the first game we played in Boston. An off-night. That how it was?"

"Yup."

"So ever since all you've heard is how lousy you were," Grindle said. "You heard how the referees were all on the other team's side; and how the rules out there are different, so no wonder you lost; but mostly, you were lousy, it was your fault, you couldn't play ball. That's what you heard in this town, when you got back."

"You forgot the two 'jigs,' " Carlisle said. "The ones they had on their team, 'so what was the matter, couldn't they find enough white boys?' "

Grindle said nothing. He stood looking in at his own photographs, his own name on the big silver ball of 1948.

"Ah-h-h," he said suddenly. "This goddam town! I'd like to see it burnt down. I'd like to see it hit with a hydrogen bomb, blow the crap to hell out of it." He swallowed as if he had a lump in his throat, as if it tasted bad and wouldn't go down. "They got the idea a hundred years back that they're the top, they're the best there is—made them, threw away the model. Nothing could happen to make them feel different, or that anybody else in the world amounts to anything; they're the end. Which end? I ask myself."

"What did you come back for then?" Carlisle asked.

Gee, this guy. The way he talked! Made you hot under the collar.

"Don't think I'm here to stay," Grindle said. "I wouldn't die here, for fear somebody might find me dead in this place. I had to come, my old man's died, and there's some crap about his estate—the few cents he had left he didn't spend trying to keep me out of jail. Oh, I could stay. Crawl around, take guff. Watch people go into a huddle every time I went by on the street, having it over about the jailbird, putting a rock on the top of the cookie can. Because that's all they got, cookie cans. Maybe after another ten years, if I didn't get out of line anywhere, I'd be a citizen in the town again. But, say I was? Say I got it all back, tomorrow? What's it worth, what they think? It ain't worth my time; or any man's time."

He swung around, flinging out a hand, thrusting his face forward. Carlisle got a whiff of his breath, foul with old whiskey smell and something else like garlic or onions; the bared strong teeth were yellow and two of the front ones were missing.

Grindle jerked a thumb at his crutches. “So you’re lame,” he said. “Give your all. Like me.” He turned back to the showcase again. “When that picture was taken, my whole foot was numb. I still got a couple toes ain’t right. But did I care? I still never wanted to do a thing but play ball.”

“People always said you were good enough for the pros,” Carlisle said, and stopped; because this, when you knew why Grindle had never gone to play ball with the pros, was the wrong thing to say.

“Do they, now?” Grindle said. “Why, God bless their little pointed heads! If you want to know, I wasn’t, not in a million years. Geest, I beat myself out, the whole summer after I graduated. But the pros, they’re college grads mostly, and all about seven feet tall. I wasn’t tall enough, but if I could go to college, play on a college team for a while, I figured I might get good enough. I couldn’t pass exams for college on what I learnt in this joint, and they weren’t so free with their scholarships then. So Pop said he’d send me a year to prep school. Hell, I never even knew enough for prep school, I couldn’t read the damn textbooks. I got bounced out after half a term.

“So I come home,” Grindle went on. “I hung around and played on the town team, but Pop wouldn’t stand for me doing nothing, said I better enlist. Well, that was forty-nine and the War was over, some fun; but I figured the Army might have a ballteam I could get onto. So I was planning to leave the next day, and that night I had Pop’s car and a date in Fairport, the last chance I had to say good-bye to my girl. Only no gas. And no dough, because Pop was sore anyway over my using the car so much. Feller in the gas station wouldn’t trust me, hell, he knew Pop was good for it, that was only his night for being a bastard. A few months back, this guy at the gas station, he would’ve give me the gas and a slap on the back, I could have had the cupola off the damned old Town Hall. So we lost a ballgame, so now I was a bum, couldn’t even organize five gallons of gas. This guy, he give me the ripe old bull about what bums all us young kids was. So I blew. I got out of the car and let him have it, knocked him to hell down. I was so mad I never stopped. I thought, Blast him, I’ll get my tankful out of it, so I filled ’er up.”

He glanced around, saw that Carlisle was listening, big-eyed, open-mouthed.

"I can see you're kind of taken with my tale," Grindle said.

"Yeah. I socked a guy, too."

"Did you, now? Knock him down?"

"Uh-huh."

"Then the only difference between me and you is that your guy didn't kick off, ain't it the truth? I got into the car and drove over to Fairport, said good-bye to my girl. Hell, I never even knew I was into anything. I never slugged the guy with a club, the way they said I did. Only my fist. He must've hit his head when he fell, because I just socked him on the nose. Just once. But the next morning, in the jail, somebody hands me a newspaper. There I was in the headlines. 'Youthful Thug Robs Gas Station, Kills Attendant,' it says. You know, they tried to shove me as far as they could see me go, but they couldn't make first-degree stick, so I got manslaughter. I was a good boy in jail, settled down and learnt to be a first-class mechanic; for nine years."

"Oh," Carlisle said. "That's how it happened."

His mouth felt dry. He ran his tongue over his lips, trying to moisten them, thinking, What if Melly Hitchcock had banged his head? He could have, when he went down. . . .

"Well, that's my side of it," Grindle said. "I dunno why I bother to tell it to anybody here in this town. If you'll believe it, you're the first one ever did. About five hundred old bats come down on me like a ton of bricks, like they do on any kid steps out of line. Hell, when he's little, he's cute, he's a dear baby, nothing's too good. But let him get to be fourteen, he's an outlaw, a thug. All it is, he's trying to learn something, get the works of things through his head, but it makes a stranger out of him, even to his own folks. Everybody's scared to death of him, and the way they use him, well they may be."

Grindle shoved his hands into his pockets, shrugged himself deeper into his leather jacket. He stared into the glass case. "Old James Goss, he used to be the principal here; is he still around?—Part of the crap he dished, culture, he said, it's what a man can get to make him different from the animals."

"He's still here," Carlisle said. "He's around."

"Be darned! Darned if I wouldn't like to see the old coot. We fought a running battle, him and me, for four years. Well, down there I read in the newspapers and magazines, them all yakking about you kids and the hell you raise, rock 'n' roll, it's a dance, so they call out the cops. It was the same kind of warmed-over old crud. Made me wonder if anybody over thirty, except Adolf Hitler, ever liked kids."

"Arthur Grindle," said James Goss's voice, unexpectedly, cordially, behind them. "I wondered if that might not be you."

He had come out of his office, noiselessly along the corridor, on his rubber soles.

"How are you?" he said, holding out his hand.

Grindle shook the hand. "Old Wheels," he said.

James smiled. "That's right. I—har—believe they still call me that."

"Nosing in," Grindle said. "Just like old times. Turn around quick, who's behind you? Old Wheels."

James nodded. "One of the—har—unsavory aspects of my job," he said. "To be where not expected."

"How much did you hear this time? Enough to heave me out of the nice, new high-school building on my ear?"

"I never saw reason for that, Arthur. I might have been ready to, in the—har—old days. You were a problem. I haven't heard much—only your remark about Adolf Hitler. Which puzzled me."

"Why?" Grindle asked.

He grinned, not nicely, rocking back and forth on his heels, his chest out. "You was always crowding my tail to read," he went on. "Read, you said. Read, read, read."

"And you remember it."

"I remember it. I read, all right. Everything I could get my hands on. About the War. About Hitler. Some damned old do-gooder stuck a copy of his book in the jail library."

"And what did you make of *Mein Kampf?*" James asked.

"You can ask me. I never got through it, it was too tough. I still don't read good, I only read more. But I got enough to know. That guy, he had it made. Guys like me, kids, anybody didn't have any place, he give them all something to do, made them feel they was somebody. I wish I'd been there. I'd have been his topkick. I'd sure like to hit into this town some dark night, with a bunch of them Black Shirts. I'd make it fit to live in. It's the only way you could."

"Arthur," James Goss said. "I know you. I suspect you have lain awake nights getting that speech ready to deliver here in this town, to me, to anyone you could find to listen. I congratulate you on your delivery; I think you may have learned some of it from me. If you had ever made as careful a preparation of any assignment for Public Speaking, I should have been a happy man. But your ideas are nonsense. I am not going to argue them. You know quite well what Hitler was; what happened to him."

"Pep talk. Tie a can to it."

"No, I will not! Hitler is in the past, thank God, so the verb you used should be 'gave,' not 'give.' And the nominative pronoun 'they' takes the plural. 'They were somebody.' Second: A man does not wait for, nor does he wish, to be given anything by anyone, and surely not by a megalomaniac dictator, for the sole purpose of creating a black disgrace upon history. A free man and a fighter finds his own place, his own job. He cannot become somebody unless he does it for himself. You are now free and you are a fighter as I—har—have reason to know. Now you—har—tie a can to it. Do you need a job?"

"Big words you still got. A job—in this town?"

"In any town."

"Look, I'm going so far away from here—I'm walking just once more down the Main Street of this town. To the bus."

"Can I do anything? A letter of recommendation?"

"I'm a mechanic. At least, they learnt me that down there."

"Taught," James said. " 'They taught me that down there.' I'm sorry, Arthur. But culture is still—"

"—all a man has to make him different from the animals." Grindle lifted a hand. "I'll be going. So long, Mr. Goss."

"Good luck, Arthur," James said. "If you come back with your Black Shirts, I expect you won't find me hard to wipe out."

"Ah-h-h, no, Mr. Goss," Grindle said. He looked shocked. "Not you, Mr. Goss. Old poops like you don't do no harm."

He turned and went down the corridor, his feet making a slight shuffling sound on the hard tile floor. The revolving door swung behind him; the sloping shoulders in the battered jacket passed out of sight down the steps.

James stood in front of the glass case, looking in.

Carlisle had stepped back into the corner by the end of the case. Knowing that the sound of his crutches on the floor would call attention to him, he was embarrassed to go away. He waited, hoping Mr. Goss would just shut up and go back into his office.

But James stood there, looking in at the photograph of the snub-nosed, black-haired boy, with the basketball brashly poised on the palm of his hand.

" 'I am a part of all that I have met,' " he said, suddenly, softly, under his breath.

Horrified, Carlisle watched him fumble in his pocket, pull out a handkerchief, and wipe away tears which had begun to trickle down his cheeks.

Why, the old slob's crying! he thought, and one of his crutches slipped on the floor, with a rubbery sound.

James's gaze swept over him, blindly. "Har—" he said. "You see how the man of culture—har—produces in emergencies at least an apt quotation," and he turned away, walking with his forward motion on the balls of his feet, went into his office, and closed the door.

Left alone, Carlisle stood by the trophy case; after a moment, he stepped in front of it and stood looking in.

That guy, Grindle, he thought. So he's what happened to the basket-ball star.

In the case, the black-haired boy met his eye. You-go-to-hell. So how are you any different?

Carlisle lifted a hand to him. "You and me both, bud," he said, under his breath.

Used us. Squeezed us dry and dumped the pieces.

If he had never been convinced before, he was now.

It wasn't anything we did. It was what was done to us. So you got jail, I got crutches. And who gives a good goddam?

Part Thirteen

The motel units were cleaned and open, except for one which had to be re-done. Two couples, wandering in for Memorial Day weekend, had gone on a spree in a double unit; they had had fun with seltzer bottles, gaily squirting walls, ceiling, and each other; and with the remains of a lunch, which had contained tomatoes. Ralph had helped Bessie with the paint job; he had done the ceiling, while she had relentlessly attacked walls and woodwork. Loping around the place, looking for Bessie on this warm June morning, Ralph finally found her, standing transfixed in the door of the unit.

"Hi, Bessie," he said. "Is it dry? Can we move the stuff back in?"

Bessie said nothing. She stood, hands on hips, nose wrinkled, underlip stuck out.

"What's the matter?" Ralph asked. He looked over her head, craning his long neck, trying to see what she was looking at. "Oh, my lord, what happened?"

Something had gone terribly wrong with his paint job. The ceiling had blistered; in places, rubbery tails of paint hung down in crinkled ribbons.

"It's that Shred," Bessie said. "That paint we used, it can't be no good. I been watching that for ten minutes. Look!"

Over in a corner, a blister of paint let go with an audible snap, and a new ribbon came crinkling down.

"What did I do?" Ralph said, appalled. "What did I do that wasn't right?"

He had been proud of that ceiling; it had looked nice.

"What did you wash it with?" Bessie asked.

Wordlessly, Ralph pointed to his equipment—bucket, rags, bottle of cleaning fluid—which he had left, yesterday, just inside the door.

"Did you wrench it off?"

"Well, no."

"Used it full stren'th? Didn't dilute it?"

"I had to, to get those stains off. It says on the bottle to. It says you don't have to rinse it."

"Uh-huh." Bessie eyed the bottle inimically. "Don't you worry, Ralphie, it wasn't nothing you did. It's them cussid chemicals in the cleaning stuff don't mix with what's in the paint, that's all. Look at that! If that ain't the darnedest sight you ever see in your life!"

She began to giggle, and presently burst out into peals of laughter, so that she had to sit down on the doorstep, wiping her eyes.

"Whole ceiling wiggling all over like a can of worms," she said, gulping. "My god! If them manufacturers don't get together on the stuff they put in their things, we'll all go up with the atoms, is all I can say. Well, hell." She scrambled to her feet. "It'll have to be done over, Ralphie. Might as well get to it. I'll start to this end and you start to that, and we'll meet with a crash in the middle."

Ralph gave a long resigned moan, and Bessie grinned at him.

"Well, that's life for you," she said, picking up a scraper. "You know what this ceiling reminds me of, Ralphie? That time last summer when I put the two kinds of stuff under my armpits, so's the ladies wouldn't get scairt by the smell of sweat whilst I waited on table. I put on a lot of that green stuff, 'Chase It With Flowers,' they call it; and it didn't do one mite of good. When I begin to steam, I sweat strong. So then I put some of that lavender-colored, that 'Patty Cake,' right on top of it, another whole dose. I says to myself, if one is as good as they make out on the Tee-Vee, two ought to be twice as good; but I will be goddamned if my armpits didn't start to fizz like a bottle of Coke. Everywhere I went for two days, fizz, fizz, fizz, till I like to went crazy. Wouldn't wash off, either," she went on, waiting for Ralph's yelp of delight to subside. "Had to wear off."

Ralph liked working with Bessie. When things went wrong, she accepted it. Instead of taking it out on you, she was more interested in seeing how they could be put right. With Bessie, you had a feeling it was you who took first place, not the work.

He climbed on the stepladder and started making half-hearted swipes at the ceiling with a scraper.

Stayed here last night till dark, he thought. Felt as if I'd done something. And now, look at it!

"You know something, Ralphie?" Bessie said. She had dragged a chair to the opposite side of the room and was now standing on it, her own scraper in hand. "You know, work is good, within reason. But the damn stuff can kill you."

"Eeyah," Ralph said, mournfully.

"Well, then. To hell with it," Bessie said. "We done this, all day yesterday." She shied the scraper across the room, where it landed with a *plunk* in a bucket. Ralph jumped and almost fell off the stepladder.

"Whoops! Basket!" Bessie said.

With considerable dignity, she stepped down off the chair. "Come on, Ralphie, let's go fishing."

"Fishing?" Ralph peered down at her. "Gee, but—what about this? Hadn't we ought to—"

"Ought to's one thing, do's another. Tomorrow's another day, and it'll come."

Ralph came slowly down the ladder. Geez, fishing would be wonderful. Out in the sun, in the skiff, on the harbor. But—

Try as he would, Ralph couldn't get used to work's taking second place with anyone. He was more relaxed here at Charles's than he had ever been in his life; he still bumped into things, but not so hard; he still broke things, but not so many. It was great, having Ma married to Charles; they were so happy, they brimmed over; seemed as though other people caught it from them, so that everybody felt good. Except, of course, Carlisle.

Ralph wished Carlisle would snap out of it. Of course, at first, no one would expect him to do much, on crutches; at first, Ralph didn't blame him. He tried to imagine what it must be like for Carlisle—a stiff leg, maybe for life, nobody knew yet; no scholarship; if he got to college at all, he would have to do it on his own; and he was so far behind now with everything that he wasn't even trying to catch up. Mr. Berg was trying hard to help him; and Charles said maybe there were a lot of sit-down jobs around the motel that Carlisle could do, but to heck with them, let someone else shell peas, Charles would be satisfied just to see Carlisle dig into the homework, catch up at school. Charles said that paying college expenses for kids was the best way he could think of to invest money; nobody had to worry about that, just the books.

But at school, Carlisle just sat; he might have a book in front of him, but he wasn't ever reading it.

He was on the outs with everybody. Even Debby—times she brought him home after they'd been out riding around on a date; Ralph could tell. Once, at school, he'd passed her in the corridor; she was just standing there looking after Carlisle, who was stumping away on his crutches; and as Ralph went by, she'd said in a half-whisper, "Oh, Ralph, what on earth is the matter with him?"

Ralph didn't know.

He didn't know, now, what to say to him. Of course, the easiest thing would have been to hand back to him as good as he sent, the way you always had. But you'd get all cocked back to let go with a good mouthful, and *whango!* it would come over you what things must be like for him, and you'd just stand there with your face hanging down and anything you'd been going to say dried up in your mouth; and he'd look at you as if he'd like to kill you.

Oh, Ralph had tried. One day, he'd got Uncle George to drive him up to the farm to get the Indian collection. If it was still there, hidden behind the grain bins in the barn; if Grampa hadn't found it and thrown it out.

He hadn't; the baskets hadn't even been moved; and Grampa wasn't around. At least, he didn't seem to be, and Ralph was glad of it. He hadn't seen Grampa since the day they'd all left the farm. He hadn't wanted to; sometimes, before he went to sleep at night, he would think how awful it would be to have to go back to the farm again.

But just as he and Uncle George were lugging out the last basket from the barn, stowing it in the trunk of the car, Martin appeared around the corner of the barn.

"Where do you think you're going with my bushel baskets?" he said. "What's in there? What you lugging off of my place?"

George said, "Take it easy, Martin. Just some stuff of the kid's."

"Well, them's my baskets," Martin said.

George started up the car. "I'll see you get 'em back," he said.

Geez, Ralph thought, as they drove down the hill. He looks awful old and sick and squizzled-up. And he's lame now. Geez, he looks terrible. I guess we're to blame for leaving him like that. Geez, I guess maybe it's our fault . . .

He wished he hadn't seen Grampa at all; hadn't gone up there. It hadn't been any use anyway, for Carlisle didn't care whether he had the Indian collection or not.

"I thought you might like to stick some of it up around the room," Ralph told him.

They had a third-floor room together in Charles's house, a heck of a nice room, up high, away from everyone; they could do what they wanted to; it reminded Ralph, in a way, of the tree house.

"Like it was in the tree house?" Ralph said to Carlisle. "I thought you might like to."

"Yeah," Carlisle said. And that was all of that.

Ralph himself was busy, working harder than he had ever worked in his life, at school, or up at Grampa's. He dug into schoolwork, figuring that maybe he had clobbered next year's ballteam, but if he showed up good in class, at least he'd have something, and after a while people would get over being sore. He went out for spring baseball—baseball was fun, it was just a game, you didn't have to worry about the Championship crap, and he was pretty good at shortstop. Alison was still rough on him, but it didn't seem to matter now; next year, Alison would be long gone. People had mostly forgotten about kidding him; oh, sometimes somebody would think of it and say, "How?" or ask him how the tribes were getting along. Kidding, he was used to that. He thought maybe, now, that if he worked hard enough, tried hard enough, he could make up for things; for the way Carlisle was acting; for feeling to blame about Grampa—it would be better to finish this job before he went fishing. Maybe . . .

"We haven't got any bait," he said to Bessie, an uneasy frown creasing his forehead.

Bessie untied her apron, flung it into the bucket beside the scraper. "You hop it down cellar, dig a pint of clams out of the freezer," she said. "Frozen clams, they ain't fit for humans, make a chowder taste like steel wool, but flounders don't know the difference. Come on, hustle, we don't want to miss high-water slack. I'll pick up my heave-aways and meet you down to the float."

Gingerly carrying the zero-cold carton of clams in aching fingers, Ralph met Hazel in the kitchen.

"We thought we'd go fishing," he told her doubtfully.

"Oh, fine!" Hazel said. "It's about time somebody did. George was saying yesterday how good a mess of flounders would go."

Ralph blinked.

You sure had to get used to the changes.

Relieved, happy, he took off for the dock on a dead run.

Bessie was waiting in the skiff, having lugged the outboard motor down from the shed. "You run the engine," she said. "You know how, don't you? You unscrew that little spugment and push *that* one, and then yank on the string."

Ralph nodded blissfully. Motors were his dear love.

When they were a quarter of a mile or so from the float, Bessie reached languidly down into the boat, and from somewhere in the region of her feet, produced a small bottle of something, which she flung overboard. She had a whole bucketful of stuff, Ralph saw, craning his neck inquisitively. Looked mostly like packages and bottles, though there were one or two boxes, like cereal boxes. He could read on one of these WHOLE-GRAIN GLUTENIZED WHITE MOPSIES, ENRICHED WITH—whatever it was, he couldn't see the rest of the label.

As they went along, Bessie proceeded to toss these objects overboard, one by one. Behind them, the boat's wake began to trail a line of bobbing small boxes and packages, with a bottle or two which didn't sink. It all looked like valuable stuff to Ralph.

"What is all that?" he shouted at last, unable to contain himself any longer, but knowing he couldn't hear much above the sound of the motor.

"Oh, my heave-aways," Bessie shouted back. "Stop here, Ralphie, they's a good patch of sand down below."

Ralph stopped the motor, swung the boat around to head into the tide. "How'd you know there is?" he asked. "I never knew there was any sand around this place."

Bessie let go the anchor.

"Well, there is," she said. "I found it once totally by accident, as you might say. I was setting dreaming, miles away, just dreaming, and the boat drug anchor, I didn't have enough rode out; and all to once we fetched up with a yank, and the flounders started to bite. I could've loaded the boat, only I didn't want to clean that many. I took marks, so's I could find the place again. See, you line up the Congo steeple with the cupola on the Town Hall, and you get Tanner's Island so it just ticks out by the end of Trypot Head. Now, pay out a little. Little bit more. There." Bessie made the anchor-road fast. "Now she'll swing right on the noggin." She ripped open the cardboard carton of clams, began sawing away at the frozen lump with a jackknife.

"Them clams—is some—old stiff," she said, panting with the effort. She succeeded in hacking off a sizable corner, tossed the remainder to Ralph.

"I thought you said 'heave-aways,' " Ralph said, beginning to hack in his turn.

"I did say heave-aways. Sozzle that overboard, Ralphie, I think it'll cut easier."

She paused, meticulously engaged in baiting her hook. "There, that looks nice. I'd like to bite that myself."

Hook and sinker plopped overboard. Bessie settled herself on the thwart, stretching damp, sneakered feet out to dry in the warm sun.

"Heave-aways," she said. "They come from me being a sucker for them good-looking fellas that pass the miracles on the Tee-Vee. I set there, waiting for a program to come on, and here instead comes on a young fella, pretty as a pot of pansies, nice as he can be; and all in the world he's interested in is whether my sinuses is draining prop'ly. First off, I would think he has little to do; but then comes on them pictures with all queer little creatures like Supermouse, running up somebody's noseholes, and I'm transmogrified; I never in all my life suspected that people's got all them holes in their head. It's God's living wonder, I think, that I ain't ever got anything but a plugged-up nose. So, thinks I, he's that worried, the least I can do is try it out, so I either send for a free sample, or I stop by the drugstore. Whoops!"

She began to haul in, vigorously landed a flat flounder.

"What'd I tell you, Ralphie? They're here. You had a tickle yet?"

Ralph started to shake his head. Then, "Yes!" he shouted. "I got a big one!"

When they were settled down again, Bessie went on.

"Well, now, a plugged-up nose with me means a good, rousing old cold, always has and always will. I ought to know, but I never learn. Maybe they have got something this time, I think. But then I have to write them a letter, saying your stuff ain't cured my cold. By the time I get an answer back, and they do write nice answers, my cold has run its course. I keep swearing I won't do it again; but then comes on pills playing follow-me-catch-me up and down somebody's pipes, or all them things that guarantees you to be a poison dream of beauty, put curl in your hair by smelling of it, I fall. Well, I guess I owe them a little something—I come by it honest, I could even be marked. Me being the direct result, as you might say, of the time my Pa got hold of some patent spoon-medicine called Buck-You-Up-O and drank a whole bottle of it at one sitting. Anyways, Ma said that was what it must've been; and she was some old mad, wouldn't speak to him for over a year. Whoops!"

Guffawing, watching her haul in, Ralph said as soon as he could speak, "Don't you ever get anything you like?"

"Oh, sure, I got some lovely physic once. And, of course, there's several things I can't vouch for, not having tried. I don't like the idea of gland-medicine, for instance, my hormones is funny enough at my time of life without my frigging around with them. But, by and large, Ralphie, come spring, I have a bucketful or so of heave-aways."

They caught flounders for a while, filling the creel. Then the ebb tide set in, the fish stopped biting. Bessie regretfully hauled in her line. "I guess that's it for today. Ain't it been fun, though? I hate to go home. Ralphie, what's that thing floating around out there? I been watching that for ten minutes."

"Where?" Ralph heaved himself around. "Oh. That? I don't know."

Some distance away, a white object some three feet across was undulating with the movement of the tide.

"Looks like a dead sheep," he ventured.

"Well, if it is, it's awful dead," Bessie said. She stood up, rocking the boat precariously. "Let's go over there and see." She began to haul up the anchor.

Viewed more closely, the thing was not like anything either of them had ever seen before. Yellowish-white, spongy, tallowy-looking, it floated low in the water. Lazy spring ripples washed over it; and a vague stench came from it, crinkling Ralph's nose.

"If that was a dead sheep," Bessie said. "You could see something about it to show that it was once a sheep."

She picked up an oar and poked tentatively; a big bubble came bulging up out of the middle of the thing, and burst. Bessie recoiled. "My Lord!" she said. "I thought for a minute, there, it was alive. Ralphie!"

Ralph jumped. "What?" he said nervously.

He'd been wondering if it wasn't some kind of a dead body. It didn't look like one, but Bessie knew a lot about most things, maybe she could tell.

"Do you know what this is?" she demanded. "I will bet you a dollar! You remember that Tee-Vee show, where the Coast Guard boys found the amber grease? I will bet you a dollar this is amber grease!"

"Ambergris?" Ralph said, swallowing. "It—it stinks so, Bessie . . . "

"They found some," Bessie said. "Floating around just like this. White stuff that stunk, dead whales puke it up, and it's worth millions of dollars!"

"No whales around here," Ralph said.

"It could've come in with the tide. Why, look at it, it's been drifting an awful long time—for all we know, this has come thousands of miles, from wherever the whale was. Yes, sir, I will bet you a dollar! Ralphie, we're rich! We got to take this home with us." She picked up the baling-scoop.

"In the skiff?" Ralph asked. He found his voice had a tendency to shoot up into the higher register, and he had to stop and swallow it back down behind his Adam's apple. He had seen that show; this stuff did look kind of like—"But couldn't we tow it?"

"And lose half of it? Half of a million dollars? Paddle me up alongside of that."

The transfer of the find from the sea to the skiff was not easy. The stuff had stubbornness; it fought back when interfered with. The deeper Bessie dug, the more noisome it became. She gasped and sweated; when she paused, Ralph took over, and with bare hands and the baling-scoop managed to get aboard all but a few ragged lumps, which went whirling away with the tide.

"I guess that's all I can get," he said. He was purple in the face. "I'll settle for three-quarters of a million, Bessie."

Charles and Susie were on the float when the skiff, with cargo, pulled alongside. They were painting the gangway.

"Hi," Charles said, amiably lifting his paintbrush in welcome, peering down into the skiff. "Did you catch any floun—*Jee-hovah!*"

He bounced back a matter of three feet or so, before he could bring himself to a stop.

"What is *that?"* he asked, hollowly. "No, Susie, don't go near it! No, no, don't bring it any closer, you'll scare every tourist there is plumb out of the state—they'll all go to Florida."

"Oh, Ralph!" Susie said. "Oh, honey, what now?"

But Bessie had seen too many TV shows not to know how these things came out. "Ralphie and I have found ourselves a fortune of money," she said, stepping briskly out onto the float.

"You have?" Charles craned, looked, turned his face away. "Well, they do say money stinks," he said carefully.

"All right, make fun," Bessie said shortly. "You wouldn't be the first to make the terrible mistake. To your own loss, I might say."

"I wouldn't? What do you think you have got there, Bessie? What is it?"

"Only one of the miracles of modern times, that's all," Bessie said. "Acres of diamonds, right in your own back dooryard, if you've only got the sense to pick it up."

"Diamonds?" Charles said, bewildered.

"Amber grease."

"Ambergris?" A light dawned on Charles, as he, too, remembered the TV show. He glanced at Susie, then hastily away. Little lumps came out at the points of his jaws, as he clenched his teeth against his laughter. "Is that what you think you've found?"

"Yes, sir. We have. Well," Bessie said, staring at him with umbrage. "Leave it to float around, you wouldn't expect the flowers of spring."

"No. I guess you wouldn't."

"But, there. Take it and make some use of it, it turns out to be a world's treasure, a pearl of great price. Where would be the place for us to send it, Charles?"

"I don't know as I'd send it all to anyone," Charles said. "That is, not all at once. I'd just get a box with a nice tight cover," he amended hastily, seeing Bessie's face, "and send a sample. A small sample's all you'd need; to a lab, somewhere, for a test. Maybe the State University."

"Maybe Mr. Berg could test it," Ralph said. He stood on the float, looking dubiously at the stuff.

Geez, probably this was all crumby, anyway. Charles seemed to think it was pretty funny.

"All right," Bessie said. "Where'll we keep it till we get word what 'tis? It'll dry out in the sun, lose weight. It's worth thousands of dollars an ounce, Charles."

"H'm," Charles said. "There's an old tarp up in the boathouse." He went on, soberly, "Put that over it, there in the skiff, and let her lay out there on the haul-off. The full length of the haul-off. Because, you know, that does stink, Bessie."

Bessie grunted. She started off up the gangway, taking long steps to avoid Charles's paint.

"There's an old cheese tin up there, with a cover," Susie called after her. "I think I remember seeing it in the boathouse, on the shelf."

"Whew-we!" Charles breathed. He stood looking after Ralph and Bessie as the two, with sunburned faces intent, trudged off up the gangway and vanished inside the boathouse door. "God, I hope that cheese-tin cover's tight," he said. "If they send any of that through the mail and it leaks out, it'll kill Amy Haslam deader than a coot."

Amy Haslam, the postmistress, was a lady of delicate sensibilities; Susie giggled, looking at Charles, and he burst out in a guffaw, quickly smothered.

"What is that stuff, Charles?" she asked. "Could anybody say?"

"My guess'd be dead moose. But it's far too late to say." Charles shook his head. "I've been called on too many times in the past for advice about Bessie's projects not to know, now, that the best thing's to let matters take their course. Somebody's going to have to take the shine off that, but let it be Al Berg, or whoever opens up that cheese tin at the University lab; it isn't going to be me."

In the library, Ralph pored over Volume One of the *Encyclopedia Britannica,* A to ANNO, looking up words as he went along.

The stuff he and Bessie had found was the wrong color, that was all. He tried, hoping against hope, to match up in his mind the way the spongy white stuff looked with what the scientific description said:

> "AMBERGRIS, a solid, fatty, inflammable substance of a dull gray or blackish color, the shades being variegated like marble, possessing a peculiar sweet, earthy odour."

The smell was all wrong, too. Earthy. That would be like the ground; like a clod of turf; like a fresh-dug potato. And sweet? Well, sweet like what? A lot of things smelled sweet. Cologne. Face powder. Lilacs. All different. *What* sweet?

That was the trouble with darned books. Why couldn't they say, tell you enough, tell you definite, so you could know. The smell of ambergris is sweet like lilacs. Would it break the guy's back to say so, or say what it was sweet like? Or was that too much to ask?

Anyway. What we have got, it doesn't smell sweet like anything. Slowly losing his hope, he read on:

> ". . . It occurs as a biliary concretion of the intestines of the spermaceti whale (*Physeter catodon*), and is found floating upon the sea, on the sea-coast or in the sand near the sea-coast. . . . It is sometimes found also in the abdomen of whales, always in lumps of various shapes and sizes, weighing from one-half oz. to 100 or more pounds, having a disagreeable smell . . . "

Disagreeable, huh? That was more like it! How about that! Disagreeable, that's for us! Maybe we got something, after all!

But how could anything smell earthy, sweet, and disagreeable, all at the same time? Gosh, these guys—sounded as if they'd never smelt of ambergris themselves, were just going by what they'd heard two or three different people say.

> " . . . and hardening on exposure to air."

Hardening . . .Ralph's hope, raised briefly up, sagged low again. The stuff we got is soft. Spongy.

> "Its specific gravity ranges from 0.780 to 0.926."

Not even definite on the specific gravity. Oh, well, maybe it weighs different, different times. Specific gravity we can test in the lab; see if it comes anywheres near . . .

> " . . . It melts at about 62° C. to a fatty, yellow, resinous-like liquid; and at about 100° it is volatilized into a white vapour. It is soluble in ether . . . "

Hey, maybe we're coming to something we can get our teeth into . . .

> " . . . and in volatile and fixed oils; it is only feebly acted on by acids. By digesting in hot alcohol, a substance termed *ambrein,* closely resembling cholesterin, is obtained, which separates in brilliant white crystals as the solution cools . . . "

Floating in the sea. That we got. Fatty, yes. Inflammable, we don't know; we can try, see if it'll burn. Color, all wrong. Smell, heck, how would you know, what the guy said? You read all that, you still don't know. Only thing, take a sample to the lab, see if Mr. Berg could find out about it. All that stuff; ought to be able to test it somehow.

The last paragraph caught his eye:

> "The high price it commands makes it peculiarly liable to adulteration . . . "

Geez, wouldn't you know! Some jokers, pick up a thing that comes free, just floating around, a nice thing really worth something . . . like Bessie said, a treasure, a pearl of great price. And water it down, stick something with it so it won't be so good . . .

Geez, look out for them. The jokers. The darned adulterers . . .

Part Fourteen

For a warm, bright, Saturday afternoon, when one came along, Debby had planned a picnic. She and Carlisle had always had a lot of fun eating out—riding a long way in Katy, stopping when they were hungry by a lake or a river or halfway up a hill. They had secret picnic places all over the state. If, when Carlisle climbed in or out of Katy, she could make believe that she'd noticed for the first time that his knee was better, maybe she could mention it; be surprised and delighted. Maybe that would work; nothing else had, and she'd tried everything she could think of.

His knee was better, but he hadn't said so. The only way she knew was by watching him move. She knew by heart what the doctors had said—that signs of limbering meant, probably, that the joint was going to be all right someday. Maybe, she'd thought at first, maybe it isn't enough to make him think it's better at all; he doesn't want to build up false hope, or give me any.

But as time went on, there hadn't been any doubt—he was moving more easily. In Katy, you could tell. In Katy, there wasn't too much room for a long leg that wouldn't bend.

Debby had waited, feeling a little desperate. It was so easy nowadays to say or do the wrong thing. Of course you couldn't blame him for feeling awful. So did she. Not only for him, but for herself and him, because things weren't casual anymore, or fun; and if you tried to make them so, then—Let's face it, she told herself, with a feeling of disaster, something all at once reminds you that you can walk without limping and he can't.

It wasn't so much anything he said; but it was something. She found herself walking carefully when she was with him; at times, it almost seemed to her, to limp.

Well, she could; if only that would make him feel better; make him realize that she was with him, on his side, and not a part of the world of not-lame people, whom he now seemed to consider his enemies.

Debby really spread herself, planning the picnic. She made all the kinds of sandwiches he liked—tuna fish, chicken, and a funny combination of peanut butter and ketchup, which they'd discovered, fooling around, on a picnic long ago. She put in potato salad and a big frosted cake. And then they drove north, along the River Road, to the best place—the riverbank by the old lumber yard.

The riverbank was wonderful—the water high, all kinds of things—old leaves, sticks, pieces of grass—spinning down with the current in the sun. Little new alder leaves were out, bunchberries in bloom; and from somewhere among the damp moss, out of sight, where twinflowers were, a smell of them drifted over the clearing.

All at once, to Debby, things seemed nice and normal again. Perhaps it was the place—they'd had lovely times here. Carlisle seemed quite cheerful and like himself; he even laughed a little, and he stretched out on a tarp spread under a tree, with the portable phonograph at his elbow, while she buzzed around getting out the lunch.

And then, he wouldn't eat.

Something made him feel bad, maybe because the place was so beautiful; though it seemed almost as if he'd planned, ahead of time, to feel bad, because he'd brought along one record for the portable, which he kept playing over and over, lying there with his arms over his eyes listening. It was the kind of oily baritone he hated singing some smarmy song about a guy who lived in the shadows while his girl was out in the sun.

Debby listened to it three times before she said anything.

"Hey, why don't we play something else? There's a whole box of records in the back of Katy."

Carlisle glanced over at her without any kind of expression. He wound up the portable again.

"Don't be marbly-eyed," Debby said. "It's only that your friend here gets kind of fruity in large batches. Isn't it?"

She let go of an imitation of the fruity baritone, which was quite a good one, while she got the box of records out of Katy, pushed them across the tarp to him. "Well, isn't it? Or is he supposed to bring us some kind of a message? Play that top one—that's Mary Martin singing 'I'm in Love with a Wonderful Guy.' That's more my speed today."

She went on unpacking sandwiches, laying out the picnic.

I won't unwrap all the sandwiches, she thought, because we'll want to eat supper out, too.

She put two big packages of sandwiches back into the basket, thinking, I'll wait till he starts to get up, and then I'll notice, with sound effects, that he can bend his knee, let him know that that's the greatest . . . Aware of a pregnant silence, she looked up, startled. Oh, no! she thought. He did intend that darn song to mean something. Or what ails him?

"Come on and eat," she said. "What'll you have? Or should I say, what'll you have first? I'm starved. Aren't you?"

"You eat," Carlisle said. "Go ahead, if you're hungry."

The implication was plain enough—under the circumstances, nobody ought to be hungry.

Debby stared at him.

"Don't you feel well, Carl?"

"Yeah. I'm okay."

She was hungry, so she went ahead. Things were a little tasteless. When she had finished, he still didn't seem to want to be disturbed. He lay there, stretched out on the tarp, with the same old record going. So Debby slipped away by herself for a while, and went for a walk along the riverbank.

Was he really trying to say something to me with that darn baritone? she thought miserably. He isn't on the "shady" side of anything with me, he must know that. Why, it's almost as if he got a charge out of feeling bad, making me feel bad, too.

No. I mustn't think so. He wouldn't.

But as she went, along the riverbank, in and out among the new-leaved alders, inevitably a picture formed in her mind—a picture familiar and clear as light.

When Win Parker suffered, whether it was trouble at the garage or sickness, or whatever, the whole family suffered with him. For six weeks, once, when he had been laid up with sciatica, the house had been a hell; when, in March, there'd been a rumor that Charles Kendall might run against Win for the School Board, everybody had tried to get out of one door before Win could get in another.

Oh, I mustn't! It isn't. It never could be the same.

Yet her mind, direct, realistic, kept repeating the picture, detailed as a photograph.

Her mother, scurrying in and out of Win's room, with one offering of food after another, trying to find something he would eat; carrying everything away untouched. A man who, everybody ought to know—that is, if they cared—was too sick, too worried, to eat; and who, later, when he thought no one was looking, sneaked out to under-run the icebox.

It seemed lonely, suddenly, along the riverbank. The spring wind had turned cold; mud squelched underfoot; her feet were wet. It seemed suddenly important to get back to company, back to Carlisle; feeling lonely, miserable, too, under his tree.

You ought to be ashamed, she told herself loyally. It's just being brought up in the house with Pop, you suspect everybody, you lamebrain.

As she came to the edge of the clearing, she saw that Carlisle had changed his mind. He was eating.

She was about to step forward, saying, "Oh, good, you feel better," when she noticed that he wasn't eating the lunch she'd left spread out; he'd got one of the packages of sandwiches she'd kept as a reserve for supper.

Well, he was fussy about sandwiches; maybe he thought the wrapped ones in the basket were better; still, she'd covered up the ones she'd left for him.

But something watchful, almost furtive, about him, made her step back behind a small, thick-growing tree, where she could not be seen.

Why am I being such a fool? she asked herself. And then, Because I'm scared. I've got to know.

From behind the tree, she watched him eat, heartily, healthily, gobbling down sandwiches in big bites; then, when he was finished, he packed everything, including what she had left out, neatly into the baskets, put the thermos on top, and closed the lids.

"Oh, you've packed up," she said, coming quietly into the clearing. "Did you find anything at all you felt like eating?"

For a moment, she thought he was going to make everything all right. It would have been so easy to. But he said, a little remotely, "I guess I'm just off my feed today."

The moment passed and was, irrevocably, gone. A little cold knot, like a lump of ice, formed down inside Debby's breastbone and stayed there.

"We'd better go home, I guess," she said.

"How about going down on the turnpike, giving Katy a workout? Maybe riding'll help."

"Okay," Debby said. "Maybe it will."

The turnpike was sixty miles away, but Katy had never found it an effort to travel far for the sake of a four-lane freeway, with a seventy mile-per-hour limit. Pale tan, string-straight, it stretched along a slight rise of land into glimmering distance, and she rolled into it, purring.

The swing, on the turn, dislodged one of Carlisle's crutches, which he had propped over the back of the seat between him and the door. Impatiently, he slammed it back into place with his elbow, and its head cracked against Katy's shining paint, making a small dent.

"Look, watch it, will you?" Debby said.

Surprised, he glanced over at her.

"You ought to hit your old man up for a trailer to carry my crutches," he said. "Doesn't seem to be room for all four of us in Katy."

"There won't be, if one of us doesn't quit acting like a sorehead," Debby said.

"Yeah. I know. You'd rather I made a dent in you. Maybe we could lash them to the top. So everybody'd know what you're hauling around with you, these days."

"Everybody knows. There's never been anybody with me in Katy but you."

"You try, don't you?"

"Yes. Wouldn't you?"

"Wouldn't I what?"

"If I were sick, or something I couldn't help, I wouldn't make it so you'd have to try."

"Well, well. The brave little heroine from her hospital bed looked up and said, 'Don't cry. They cut off my head at the neck, but see, I don't need my head. So if you see me running around without it, pay no attention, look the other way.' " He shifted, impatiently. "Where are we going—a funeral? Make with the foot, why don't you? Katy's dying on the vine."

For answer, Katy slowed down. She turned off the freeway into a rest-stop, parked at its far end, near a guardrail. Debby turned off the motor.

"What now?" Carlisle's patience was obvious, he would bear it, his manner said; he was only asking.

"I can't drive," Debby said. "In a minute, I'd have been up a tree."

"Well, that would be a change."

She said nothing. She sat, resting her forearms on Katy's wheel, looking out through the windshield, past the guardrail with its flecked and blistered paint, toward the woods beyond. The trees were as if hung about with a pale mist of green; along the margin of the woods, shadbush was in bloom.

"Well, wouldn't it?" Carlisle said.

"It would be more of a change if you'd come back from the hospital."

"Why, I'm back. The big, beautiful hunk of ballplayer, plus crutches. You want more?"

"Carl, don't."

"Don't what?"

"Look, this is me. Debby. This isn't your enemy." The look she turned on him was not accusing; but it was direct. "Your knee's better. You can bend it now. Two weeks ago, you couldn't."

He was still sitting indifferently, with most of his weight on the back of his neck; and he had, without realizing it, drawn up his knees. He looked down as if he marveled at the sight.

"Well, get a load of old Shirttail," he said. "He bends at the knee."

"That means it's getting better. You must have known; why didn't you say? Oh, Carl. It isn't as if—it isn't everything. It's only your knee—"

Carlisle stared at her. "It so happens that I value my knee. If nobody else does. Oh, you're only a lame knee, sweetheart, but I lo-ove you just the same—"

"You shut up!" Debby flashed. "I've cared, too. I've been about broken in pieces over it, and you know it! And it's better, and you haven't said. Once you'd have known how much it meant to me—just to know. And you mump around, trying to make people feel sorry for you!"

"Keep beating on it."

"What would I do? Keep still? Let you yak about a trailer for your crutch, not room in Katy? As if you were just a knee, not you at all, the rest of you doesn't matter?"

"So I'm given to understand. So they tell me. If they ever bothered to tell me anything. The big, beautiful hunk of ballplayer, he can't win games anymore, he's got a gimp. So what is he? A big, beautiful hunk of bum."

A slight breeze moved among the branches of the wood. It pulled a handful of petals from a shadbush, twirled them, sent them flowing across the parking-space like a little river. Debby watched the river stop flowing before she spoke.

"It doesn't do any good to blame other people," she said.

"Who's blaming anybody?"

"You are. You even blame me. At least, you take it out on me. I feel horrible, too—or I did, until you made me so mad that all I want to do is shake you till all that big, beautiful stuff falls off—"

"Yeah?"

"—because I don't think there's anything big or beautiful about it."

"So you don't, so what?"

"People are to blame," Debby said. Her voice was no longer careful; it held a note of harshness. "They pumped you full of being a hero, Shirttail, old Shirttail, get a load of that ballplayer, knee full of novocaine, has he got what it takes. So there you were. Up there. With nothing to hold you up but a lot of people yelling."

"Nice while it lasted."

"Lovely. While it lasted. But all you needed to do to lose it was to get hurt. Or maybe just grow a little older. It wasn't anything to count on forever. Who would want to spend his whole life listening to high-school cheerleaders letting off the locomotive, just for him? Wouldn't it get tiresome? It has to me."

"Look, you don't have to go around Robin Hood's barn. I know what's eating you. Why don't you go ahead and say we're through, that you can't stand a guy with a gimp—"

"Because that wouldn't be the reason." Debby's fingers had tightened on Katy's wheel. The knuckles were white. "I wish you had had my father," she said tightly. "You would know how much you needed to depend on—how much you needed to trust. What you have to do if you want your life."

"Hard words," Carlisle said. He had not moved; he still sat slouched on the back of his neck; he even smiled a little, in an indifferent, superior way. "That's a hell of a way for a girl to talk about her father."

"Isn't it? Carl, please listen, I'm trying to tell you. To my father, I'm his smart, pretty girl, for what he can get out of me. And he gets plenty. Fun. Satisfaction. Something to brag about. So I've paid him back something. As for my being anyone apart from him, he can't see it. And that's the parting of the ways. Because, to me, I'm Deborah Parker. A person."

"So this has got something to do with me?"

"People made a spectacle out of you, for fun. For their fun. For something to brag about. It was fun for you, too, so you gave it all you had. Now you're left flat with the large sum of nothing, you think they ought to care. They don't. I suppose I don't blame you, in a way, Carl; but what's really happened to you, what's going to happen, isn't up to them."

"Well, well, after all it's up to me! How about that!"

"I think you ought to know—I'm going to register at Chicago. This fall, I'm going there."

"Well, that's a nice long ways away."

"Yes. If you worked this summer, you could catch up. I could help you. I know that stuff cold, we could work together."

"I don't really go for that egghead stuff anymore. It doesn't sound like fun. And you know what you're doing, too, putting it up to me. If you really cared anything about me, it wouldn't enter your head to go. But here you come, and spring it. You're all set."

"Yes. Yes, I am. I'm going. You don't see why."

"Well, why? What for? All you'll do is get married."

"Even for that," Debby said. It wasn't the time for sarcasm, she knew, but she couldn't keep it out of her voice. "Even for that, I need to know more than I know. So do you, now there are no more cheers."

"No. There aren't, are there? No more locomotives. So what's left, I'm just a bum, and you make sure I know by throwing it in my face. Come out with it, why don't you, and say that what you want is out?"

Debby sat, not moving, looking out through Katy's windshield. A second quiet little river from the shadbush flowed across the parking-space into the wind from a passing car, which shattered it, blew a cyclone of petals backwards, swirling across Katy's hood.

I can't bear it, she thought, that spring will come, and summer, and I won't have him.

But I can't make him hear me any more than I can make my father hear me; and I know what it is like when you can't make someone see up over himself, no matter how things are with you. A life is only one life, you don't have two; you can't spend it yelling into closed ears that don't hear you; even love isn't that much, you couldn't keep it long. My mother loved my father when she married him.

"I didn't mean to throw anything in your face," she said. "I tried to say as well as I could how I feel. I don't think you listened."

"Oh, I heard. I read you loud and clear. You don't like guys with gimps."

"Gimps in the knee I don't mind," Debby said. "I guess in the head they make a difference to me, Carl."

She reached for the key, started the motor, slid Katy into gear.

"Come on, doll," she said. "We need that workout."

Later, some sixty miles down the road, a state cop cruising tranquilly along on his patrol was nearly blown off the road by the wind of Katy's passing. He did a double take, cursed under his breath, and set off in pursuit, siren howling. He had trouble overtaking; but finally the small car pulled off onto the shoulder and stopped.

The cop got out of his patrol car, yanking out his book of tickets and breathing fire.

Hell, two kids, he thought. Wouldn't you know?

Part Fifteen

Up at the high-school gym, the graduation ball was in full swing. From the open windows, lights streamed out on the June night; the rock 'n' roll of The Five Electric Flips, the city band hired for the occasion, carried the length of Main Street. Light summer suits, bouffant dresses spun past the windows, skeins of color, kaleidoscopic. The floor shook with stomp and scuff of feet. Gay paper streamers decorating the gym vibrated and trembled on the warm air.

Alfred Berg, who had been dancing with Ellen, stopped by a window, between numbers, mopping his brow. "Wow!" he said. "That's hot stuff. Let's take a walk and get cool."

"Why, you're getting old," Ellen said. She slipped her arm through his. "Just a beat old schoolmarm with sore feet."

"I resent the implication," Alfred said. "Beat I am. Sore feet, perhaps. But female, no. Take that back."

"Okay," Ellen said. "You have got hair all over your chest, my love."

"No, I have not got that, either. I can be licked, remember."

Ellen smiled at him. "Oh, my, and how!" she said. "But Chet had a black eye. I cherish that."

"Before you go cherishing what he had," Alfred said, "kindly recall that I had two black eyes, and a jaw that turned, over a period of time, to a horrible shade of mauve. It still goes *pop* occasionally, when I chew. If I ever got that mad again and clashed my teeth together, it would probably drop off."

"That is what comes," Ellen said, "of knocking down professional boxers. Kindly remember next time to pick somebody your size."

"Don't think I won't," Alfred said, moodily. "But I got the girl," he went on, brightening. "Against all the rules . . . he who protects defenseless womanhood never gets slapped; nor does he who gets slapped, seldom, if ever, get the girl."

"I know, darling. You're unique. Let's walk."

Arm in arm, they strolled down the steps of the building and along the concrete walk that led to the street.

"What a lovely night," she said. "Why is it that it's always so beautiful the night of graduation ball? I remember mine—horse chestnuts in bloom, and a full moon, like now. And I had a lovely time—about twenty beaux, all wanting to dance with me."

"Don't tell me," Alfred said. "I can see it now."

"Mm-hm," Ellen said. "Oh, the competition was fierce, I can tell you! But competition was fun. Why isn't it now, I wonder? These kids are just like little old settled-down married couples. Go to a dance, dance with the same boy all evening, year in, year out. I'd have been bored out of my life."

"Monogamy," Alfred said. "It has its advantages. These kids just got it younger, that's all. Every new generation changes the rules of the tribe. By the time our kids are sixteen, the customs'll all be renovated again."

"Twice over, unless we start pretty soon."

"You keep your shirt on," Alfred said. "You know what my plans are for the summer. A cabin in Michigan. My beautiful wife. I can try and I can hope, but—"

"Your beautiful wife will also hope and try."

"—but I warn you, for three months I am not going to think about the young of the species. For three months I am going to remember my own maturity, that I am a man. I am going to be concerned with my own feelings, and not with the problems of youth."

"Oh, my," Ellen said. "In that case, it will be twins—"

"I am going to be Al Berg. Not Old Buggsy."

"I like Old Buggsy."

"Right now, I don't. Right now, he is a tired old codger of twenty-six. He is a long drink of water. A square. Look at these cars," he said, with a grin, jerking his head at the line of darkened, parked automobiles. "Everybody pulling in heads, like turtles, as I come by. Watch it, here comes Old Buggsy! Know what I'd like to do? I'd like to run along here banging on all the car doors, yelling, 'Boo, youse! I've got a girl-friend too!' "

Ellen giggled. "Go on. Do it. I dare you."

"They'd be more shocked than I would," Alfred said.

They walked along, their footsteps making quiet sounds on the concrete sidewalk, deserted except for themselves and one or two other strolling couples; though other couples sat in the cars, quietening abruptly as they passed.

From one of the cars up ahead, a girl in a pastel bouffant dress got abruptly out of the front seat, slamming the car door as she left. She went by them swiftly, almost running, her head high. A couple of whistles from other cars followed her passage, but she looked neither to right nor left. She went up the walk to the high-school building and vanished through the door.

"Debby," Alfred said under his breath. "That must be McIntosh in the car."

"I haven't seen him around tonight," Ellen said. "Or Debby, either, come to think of it." She paused, in mid-step. "Oh, Al! Of course he can't dance, but surely he'd come to the dance with her."

"I don't know," Alfred said thoughtfully.

They walked on, past the car. Alfred could see out of the corner of his eye the shadowy boy slouched in the driver's seat, but he was careful not to turn his head.

"It's her graduation ball," Ellen said. "She ought to be having a terrific time. And she can't be, because according to their vicious little custom, she can't dance with anybody but Carlisle, if he isn't around, anyway. Oh, dammit, Al! Could you do anything?"

"I don't know," Alfred said again.

He went on for a few steps and slowed. "I'd only be sticking my neck out. As a matter of fact, I have already, and it is like talking in two languages, one of which never heard of the other. The poor little devil, he's ready to murder the world. In a way, you can see why. Going from top hero down to nothing's a dangerous journey."

"People!" Ellen said. The word came out in a little burst of furious breath. "I could strangle someone! He put everything he had into their blasted ballteam, and now, nobody cares if he did. It's small-minded and mean!"

"Nobody's been particularly mean to him, at least, not since a couple of weeks after they lost the All-New England. Nobody's been anything, actually. I expect that's what it is. He can't stand the general unkind disregard dished out to a fallen idol. He just feels he isn't anything at all now. I don't know, I suppose he isn't. But it's a damned shame. He's a smart youngster, all the brains in the world, only he won't use them. I've tried. I've busted all my strings, and he still couldn't pass any College Board exam in the country."

"Is that unusual? Mooney couldn't either. I've heard you say so."

"Ah, but Mooney hasn't got a lame leg. He's got it made. Going to Shangri-La on an athletic scholarship; going to do just what he knows how to do, what he's fit for. He'll probably go right up to the top in the pros, have quite a distinguished career."

"You talk as if that might be a good thing."

"Certainly. Of course it's a good thing. What's wrong with a career in basketball, for a boy who's good at it, not able to do anything else? Basketball's Jerry's particular genius, he'll do fine. Square peg, square hole. There wouldn't be anything wrong with ball anyway, if it were only kept in proportion. But with parents gone nuts, nation-wide, and the sports boys making pros out of every high-school team—ah-h, I'm through with all that. Next year, I'll be in a laboratory. Let's go back and dance."

"Yes. I can hear the next number starting. Uh—do your feet still hurt?"

"Who says my feet hurt?" "Well, I sense a hanging-back."

"Yes," Alfred said. "Can you entertain yourself a while, if I go and stick my nose into McIntosh's business?"

"Of course. I promised James Goss a dance. I suppose I could get that over with now." She looked at him speculatively. "Al," she began. "Don't—"

"Don't what?"

"Oh, never mind, honey. You'll know what to do."

She went up the steps, into the gym. A few couples were already on the floor. She looked around for James, saw him, unattached, on the other side of the dance floor, and waved a hand at him. James signaled back. He began to make his way toward her, skirting the dancing couples.

Ellen waited, watching the floor fill up, the bright heads, dark or blond, the light summer suits, the softly colored dresses. Beside the door, not far away, Debby Parker leaned against the ticket table. She looked passive and pleasant—a pretty girl, resting, enjoying watching the others dance while she waited for her partner to come in. If she were not having a good time, she showed no sign.

But she isn't, Ellen thought. And at graduation ball, where a girl shouldn't have a care in the world.

She thought suddenly, again, of her own graduation dance; of the wonderful time she had had—everyone cutting in, every pretty girl with the boys schooling, shoulder-deep, around her.

Why, if I'd danced with one boy for more than two minutes, I'd have been a social failure, and he'd have been embarrassed to death for being stuck with me.

Oh, maybe it's better, maybe it's worse—it's what they want and it's none of my business.

On the floor, each boy danced with his own girl; each couple a close, tight little corporation, enclosed in an impenetrable circle of possessiveness. According to the laws of the young tribe, if a boy cut in, her partner would have the right to sock him on the nose.

James Goss, materializing with his usual unobtrusiveness at Ellen's elbow, said, "I take it this is my dance?"

"It is," Ellen said.

James was an old-fashioned dancer, belonging to the twirl and dip school. Whatever the beat of the music, James waltzed.

"A lovely sight, isn't it?" James said, as they slowly twirled and dipped, to the amusement, not too politely concealed, of some of the younger dancers.

"Yes, it is, rather," Ellen said. If you can steel your soul against the undercurrents, she added to herself.

But she had to concentrate on slowing down to match James's steps.

Thank God I did dance with Tom, Dick, and Harry when I was sixteen. I can follow anybody's lead. I could, she thought, with a slight stir of triumph, follow the lead of a bull buffalo with plaster casts on all four feet, if called upon; which is more, I will bet, than most of these smug little experts could do, dancing with one boy all of their natural lives.

As she slowly turned, she saw suddenly that Debby Parker had found a partner. Head high, smiling, if looks meant anything, having a whale of a time, Debby was spinning down the floor with Ralph McIntosh. And she wasn't the one who was making heavy weather of it.

Out in the street, leaning against the open window of Debby's car, Alfred, also, was making heavy weather of it. So far, he had succeeded only in passing the time of day.

"I like this car," he said, finally.

"Yeah. It's a nice little bug," Carlisle said.

"How is it in mud or snow?"

"Oh, cool."

"You see a lot of these small cars around. People who own them seem pretty sold on them."

"They sure do."

"Ellen and I have been talking about getting one," Alfred said.

"Is that so?"

"Ellen's afraid my old boat won't hold together to haul us to Michigan this summer," Alfred went on. "I guess she's right. She likes the looks of this, but I've got some doubts. My legs are pretty long. How is that driver's seat—does it double you up any?"

"Seems to be plenty of room."

"Think I could try it on for size?"

"Why, sure, Mr. Berg. Go ahead."

Carlisle moved for the first time, shoving over out of the driver's seat, as Alfred walked around the car. He was neat and handsome in his graduation suit, his rippled, corn-colored hair carefully combed, his profile clean-cut, his voice quiet, polite, indifferent. Yet as Alfred opened the car door and got in, settling himself in the driver's seat, he felt as if the whole suave and beautiful structure of young flesh, smooth and impenetrable as a globe of glass and as enigmatic, cried out—as if it wept with a sound inarticulate, silent, far below the range of human ability to hear.

Oh, God, Alfred thought, even while he found the pedals and went through the motions of testing the comfort of the car. All this kid wants is for me to get the hell out of here, leave him alone; aloud, he said, "Sa-ay! Surprising, isn't it? I didn't think there'd be this much room."

"Oh, sure, there's plenty, Mr. Berg."

"Easy on gas, too, they tell me."

"Uh-huh."

"Know, offhand, how many miles to the gallon?"

"About thirty-eight, Debby gets."

Alfred whistled.

"Something to think about, all right," he said. Desperately, he thought, I could go on talking cars all night, and no way I can think of to butt in on this boy's business; and for God's sake, Berg, shut up and go away, it's probably a good thing. "I've talked about it some to Ellen," he said. "So far, she's had reservations, but that nice, low gas bill might very well be the clincher."

"Yeah. Could be."

"Different transmission, though. That's what would really bother Ellen," Alfred said. "It would probably bother me."

"Yeah. Universal. Like the old universal trucks."

Alfred opened the car door, started to get out. "Well, thanks," he said. "I'm sure going to think some more about it." Halfway out, he paused. "How are you set for the summer?" he asked. "Got plans?"

"Oh, sure, Mr. Berg."

"A job?"

"Yeah."

Alfred hesitated. His impulse was to mop his forehead, but he resisted. "That's good," he said. "Something down at the motel?"

"Yeah. I'll probably gimp around down there. Awhile, anyway."

It was the first break in the armor, and Alfred pounced.

"I was hoping to get to you first," he said, and even as he spoke, he said in his mind, Oh, Ellen, darling, forgive me!

"Ellen and I are going to Coon Lake in the Michigan woods—a friend of ours has lent us his cabin for the summer. I've got a lot of studying to do, some research stuff for my new job, but there'll be time for canoeing and fishing and, oh, batting around the woods. I thought maybe I could get you to come with us, if it was all right with your folks."

The silence in the seat next to him deepened. Alfred set his teeth. I might as well go whole-hog while I'm about it. Dammit, he can take it or leave it.

The impassive voice said, "Why, thanks, Mr. Berg. What would I do there?"

"Why, a number of things. Teach us to drive the new car, for one thing. Team up with me on chores—wood, water—whatever wouldn't be too rough on your knee. We couldn't make you a cash proposition, but I'll tutor you in physics and chem, and Ellen'll brush you up on liberal arts. We'll guarantee you to pass any College Boards they can throw at you, come fall."

"Well, thanks. I don't think I'll bother with college."

"Oh. Well, of course that's up to you. Why don't you think it over, though?"

"I will, Mr. Berg."

"Talk it over with your folks and let me know?"

"Sure will."

Alfred got out of the car. "Good night, then," he said. "Ellen and I'll wait to hear from you."

"Good night, Mr. Berg."

Back in the gym, Alfred presented himself to Ellen.

The exercise with James Goss had just ended, and she was, a little dizzily, standing by the door. She looked at Al's harried, worried face, saw him fish out his handkerchief and mop it.

"Is he coming?" Ellen said.

Alfred stopped mopping and stared at her.

"Are you psychic, for godsake?" he asked.

Ellen smiled. "I have heard too many ideas hit you in the head with a plop," she said. "A plop I can hear across the room. Well, you can take along a tent for him—he can't sleep in the cabin with us."

"He won't come," Alfred said. "If he does—well, you can shoot me, Ellen. I've not only clobbered our vacation. I've committed us to buy a new car. With one of those British transmissions."

"Oh, good. I was hoping you would. I can drive a universal truck, you know. Which is more than you can do, Buggsy, old boy."

Alfred stared at her. "Blimey!" he said.

"Blimey, yourself! My uncle's trucks were all universals. I and my girl cousins used to hitch rides. When we were young and full of hope. One blond truck driver I loved with all my heart, but nothing came of it, except I learned to drive."

"Part of the idea was that you be taught to drive," Alfred said.

"That, too, could be arranged."

"Well, he won't come, anyway," Alfred said. "I try these things, I should know better. I'll be better off in a laboratory, where—I am not tough enough for kids, Ellen."

"Do me some rock 'n' roll," Ellen said, holding out her arms to him. "Or a nice, old-fashioned foxtrot, or something. James has got me twisted up like a corkscrew. Oh, you darned fool," she went on, softly, under her breath, as they moved out on the floor. "You nice, soft-hearted, idealistic nut!"

Ralph was doing his best. What he lacked in accomplishment, he made up for in energy and goodwill. A couple of times he stepped on Debby's toe; once he kicked her in the ankle. Aside from a wince or two, she didn't seem to mind; but Ralph, anxiously peering down at her face, somewhere in the region of his chest, began to feel very funny.

Gosh, the way he danced, how had he ever got the nerve to ask Debby Parker to dance with him!

He had mooched around the door, watching her, for quite a while. Seeing her there, at first he'd thought nothing of it; she was waiting for Carl. But Carl didn't come in. Ralph got more and more uneasy. There she was, just sitting, waiting. If Carl had been there with her, the fellows would have taken care of it, seen she had a chance to dance, had a good time; but nobody was going to ask her behind Carl's back. He, Ralph knew from some judicious snooping around the premises, was sitting in Debby's car, outside.

The big dope.

Well, Ralph reflected, he himself was on kind of a nice, easygoing, workaday basis with Debby, right now. She had helped him and Mr. Berg run some tests in the lab on Bessie's doggoned old ambergris. Together, they had taken a chunk of it apart and put it together again, analyzed it right down into the ground. It had turned out to be some kind of decayed organic matter, probably dead animal, so that was that, no fortune, no treasure. But he had got better acquainted with Debby, and the experiments had been a lot of fun.

So Ralph went over, gulped once, and managed to bring up, "Like to dance, Debby?"

Debby smiled up at him. "Love to, Ralphie," she said, and away they went.

It caused a stir. Ralph caught some knowing glances out of the corner of his eye, which he sturdily ignored. He was too busy, anyway, managing his feet.

He wasn't a good dancer; not having a girl of his own to practice with, his efforts had been limited to an occasional try with one of the unattached girls in his class, and they generally wouldn't be very good, either. Debby was good, though; she was like a feather. After a while, he began to enjoy himself, even though people were looking.

Debby's brother, Bill, dancing by, grinned, and said to his girl, "Hey, dig old Sitting Bull"; and Joel Troy, passing close, said, "How. What did you do with the ambergris?" Ralph felt his face getting red. He missed a step, stepped again on Debby's toe, and couldn't seem to get "Excuse me," up past his Adam's apple, which just made a clicking noise.

Debby said, "Don't pay any attention, Ralphie. I'm having fun."

"Everywhere I go," Ralph said. "Funny stuff about Indians. What did I do with the ambergris? They never let anything rest. It gets my darn goat."

"I know," Debby said. "But why show it?"

Out at the end of his long arm, she spun, light on her toes, came back to him.

"If you don't let anyone see, nobody'll know it gets your goat," Debby said. "No goat, no kidding. Give 'em as good as they send."

"Oh, sure, I do," Ralph said. He brightened. "Geez, I will!"

What a cool idea! Of course that was the way to handle it. Ought to have thought of it himself. If there wasn't anything they could see to rib, the ribbing would stop.

Jerry Mooney, dancing by, nudged Ralph with his elbow. "Hi," he said. "Where's your dead moose?"

Ralph said, loudly, "Sold it to the glue factory!"

But at that moment the orchestra stopped playing. In the silence, his booming baritone resounded clearly all over the gym. People glanced around, grinning.

"Oh, God," Ralph said, hollowly.

Debby stuck her arm through his.

"Come on," she said. "Let's get a Coke."

She waited while he got into line at the Coke machine, dropped in his coins.

"You must be dry," she said, smiling, as he came along lugging the bottles, two in each hand. "I can't possibly drink two. Can you drink three?"

"Oh, easy," Ralph said. "C-Carl and I drank six apiece once, on a bet."

Between the dance floor and the Coke machine, Ralph had conceived a plan—get enough Coke, and then suggest that he and Debby take one out to Carlisle. It might not work; but then, again, it might. The first step would be to introduce Carl's name into the conversation. But he might as well have mentioned the moon.

Debby said nothing; Ralph paced along by her side, feeling the ice-cold necks of the bottles between his fingers, dripping as moisture condensed on them in the warm air.

"Hot," he said. "Let's take it out on the steps."

Half the crowd was out on the steps, cooling off. The other half walked, two and two, up and down the sidewalk under the trees. Cigarettes glowed in the shadows; the smell of their smoke was sweet on the warm air.

At the foot of the steps, Ralph would have kept going, but Debby stopped and sat down, so he handed her a bottle. "You forgot to take the top off," Debby said, patiently, handing it back to him.

"Oh, geez," Ralph said.

If he could just ever manage anything without his face turning red. It wasn't too dark out here, either, with the street light and the moon. She probably could see.

"I figured you'd have an opener in your car," he said, carefully keeping his flaming face turned away. "M-most people do."

He himself had a scout knife in his pocket, but to produce it hadn't been a part of his plan.

"Why, gee," he went on, "everybody carries an opener in their car. I just thought—"

"I do," Debby said. "You go get it, Ralphie."

"Well, Carl's there. I thought—"

"Give him a Coke," Debby said, between her teeth.

"Ah-h, Debby! He'll only bounce it off my head, if I go alone. Come on. Let's walk down and have it in the car."

"Look, Ralph," Debby said. "Noses out? Please? I'll wait for you here. If he bounces it off your head, bounce one back; you've got four."

Ralph gave a small moan of despair. He set off, one foot after the other, down the sidewalk toward the car.

Good idea, at the time. Flopped like a mop. Like most of his good ideas. And now look what he'd got himself into.

"Brought you a Coke, Carl," he said to the silent figure in the car.

"Oh, go on to hell and play with your marbles," Carlisle said.

"Ah-h, cut it out, can't you?" Ralph said. He stood uncertainly, stooping down, peering in. "Got four Cokes here," he said, and drew a little closer, as there was no response, no stir inside the car. "Forgot to take the tops off. D-Debby said there was an opener—"

He ducked as the opener flew past his head, landed with a tinkle on the sidewalk, bounced into the bushes.

"Darn it," he said, at a safe distance from the car window, "couldn't you just—" He had been going to say "have handed it to me," but stopped in time, feeling the treacherous sliding of his Adam's apple.

He turned toward the bushes. They were thick and high—the barberry hedge around the school grounds, full of thorns. Reluctantly, he made a few pawing motions, wincing as the sharp growths clawed at his palms. Geez, he'd have to find that opener. He couldn't just haul out the one in his pocket, have Debby guess. . . .

She came swiftly along the sidewalk behind him, her pale dress shimmering in the dark, with the shadows moving across it from the light of the street lamp filtering down through the elms.

"Carl," she said. "Carl?"

There was no response from the car.

You'd almost think he wasn't there. Oh, the dope, Ralph thought. The big dope!

"I told you I'd tell you after the dance," Debby said. Her voice was tense, breathless. "I guess I can tell you now. Will you please get out of my car, so I can go home?"

She moved as if to walk around to the driver's seat.

Ralph heard the sudden whine of the starter, the roar as the engine kicked in. Katy pulled away from the curb, out around the car parked in front of her; Ralph, blinking with astonishment, saw the red tail-light shoot along the street, grow smaller up the highway. He heard a slight sound, as Debby's hands, twisting her handkerchief, tore the light fabric.

Debby said, in a whisper, "Oh, no," as if what was happening was something she couldn't bear; and then, her head came up; she turned to Ralph, standing there, agonized, holding in one big clammy hand the four Coke bottles, their necks jammed and clutched hard between his fingers.

"Where's he going?" Ralph said. "What does he think he's—"

"He's just used to Katy, is all," Debby said. "He'll ride around and be back. He isn't going anywhere."

In the late night, little old Katy, the living doll, headed away, going nowhere in particular; just away.

The highway was mostly deserted—not much traffic at this time of night. Katy passed a truck-trailer combination barreling along with a load of freight for Boston; she pulled out around the Maritimes bus and left its pyramided glitter of red-and-green Christmas-tree lights as if they had been standing still. For a long time, she turned aimlessly from one byway to another, sometimes speeding, sometimes slowing down where the road was bad.

Sixty miles beyond Fairport, Carlisle stopped long enough to push the button that controlled Katy's convertible top; even with the window open, it felt stuffy inside the car; warm metal smell, car smell was making him feel sick. Obediently, Katy folded her top back; but the dark privacy of her interior was gone. Around him, instead, was the world; vast sweep of starlit sky; dark countryside; to north, to south, empty highway. He jerked his hand back to the button, brought the top up again.

Better turn around while there was some gas left; old Katy would run on little, but not on nothing.

The dance was long over, the gym dark, everybody gone home. It must be late; not long to daylight; three-thirty, he saw, by the clock in the steeple of the old Union Church. He left the car at Parker's Garage, got out his crutches, started walking. It wasn't far, down to the motel. A while ago, he thought, striding along, I couldn't have made it. Damn knee's better. Won't be long before I can play again; heck, I can always play on the town team.

Main Street was empty; from curb to curb, no cars, no people. The drugstore dark, the poolroom dark; lights out in Joe's Lunch. Black shadows on the fronts of sleeping houses; by a corner lamp, a chestnut tree, brilliant electric green, with prim white candles. Shadows on the concrete of the sidewalks; shadow of himself, foreshortened, the crutches foreshortened, moving across the patches; at the intersection, the traffic light, turning from red to green and back again, busily directing nothing.

About the Author

Born and raised in the Maine fishing village of Gotts Island, Ruth Moore (1903–1989) emerged as one of the most important Maine authors of the twentieth century, best known for her authentic portrayals of Maine people and her evocative descriptions of the state. In her time, she was favorably compared to Faulkner, Steinbeck, Caldwell and O'Connor. She graduated from Albany State Teacher's College and worked at a variety of jobs in New York, Washington, D.C., and California, including as personal secretary to Mary White Ovington, a founder of the NAACP, and at *Reader's Digest*. Her debut novel in 1943, *The Weir* was hailed by critics and established Moore as novelist, but her second novel, *Spoonhandle* reached great success, spending fourteen weeks on *The New York Times* bestseller list and was made into the movie, *Deep Waters*. The success of *Spoonhandle* provided her with the financial security to build a house in Bass Harbor and spend the rest of her life writing novels in her home state. Ultimately, she wrote 14 novels. Moore and her partner, Eleanor Mayo, traveled extensively, but never again lived outside of Maine. Moore died in Bar Harbor in 1989.